A Son of Perdition
An Occult Romance

by

Fergus Hume

Double 9
BOOKS

A Son of Perdition
An Occult Romance
by Fergus Hume

ISBN: 978-93-67140-12-3

Published by

DOUBLE 9 BOOKS

2/13-B, Ansari Road
Daryaganj, New Delhi – 110002
info@double9books.com
www.double9books.com
Tel. 011-40042856

This book is under public domain

ABOUT THE AUTHOR

Ferguson Wright Hume, also known as Fergus Hume, was a prolific English novelist who wrote detective fiction, thrillers, and mysteries. Hume was born in Powick, Worcestershire, England, as the second son of James C. Hume, a Scot who worked as a clerk and steward at the county pauper and lunatic asylum. When he was three, his family moved to Dunedin, New Zealand, where he attended Otago Boys' High School and studied law at the University of Otago. He was admitted to the New Zealand Bar in 1885. Hume moved to Melbourne, Australia, shortly after graduating and began working as a barristers' clerk. He began writing plays, but, was unable to persuade Melbourne theatre managers to approve, let alone read them. Hume returned to England, first in London, then in Thundersley, Essex, at Church Cottage, most likely on the invitation of the Reverend Thomas Noon Talfourd Major. Hume resided in Thundersley for thirty years, producing over 130 novels and various collections, the most of which were mystery stories, although he never regained the fame of his debut novel. He also wrote lyrics for songs written by his brother-in-law, Charles Willeby, and book reviews for literary periodicals such as The Bookman. The 1911 census shows him as 'author', aged 51, and living at Church Cottage, Thundersley, which comprised of six rooms. He had a housekeeper, Ada Louise Peck, a widow aged 69. He made regular trips to Italy, France, Switzerland, and other European countries.

CONTENTS

NOTE

The Author is indebted for the description of the Star-Worship contained in Chapter XV to Mr. C. W. Leadbeater's articles on "Ancient Chaldea," which appeared in the February, March, and April numbers of "The Theosophical Review" during the year 1900.

CHAPTER I
LOVE IN IDLENESS

"How can any one hope to transfer that to canvas?" asked the artist, surveying the many-coloured earth and sky and sea with despairing eyes.

"Easily enough," replied the girl at his elbow, "those who see twice as vividly as others, can make others see once as vividly as they do. That is what we call genius."

"A large word for my small capabilities, Miss Enistor. Am I a genius?"

"Ask yourself, Mr. Hardwick, for none other than yourself can answer truly."

Outside his special gift the artist was not over clever, so he lounged on the yielding turf of the slope to turn the speech over in his mind and wait results. This tall solidly built Saxon only arrived at conclusions by slow degrees of laborious reflection. With his straight athletic figure, closely clipped fair hair and a bronzed complexion, against which his moustache looked almost white, he resembled a soldier rather than a painter. Yet a painter he was of some trifling fame, but being only moderately creative, he strove to supply what was wanting by toilsome work. He had not so much the steady fire of genius as the crackling combustion of talent. Thus the grim Cornish country and the far-stretching Atlantic waters, so magically beautiful under an opalescent sunset, baffled him for the moment.

"I have the beginnings of genius," he finally decided, "that is, I can see for myself, but I cannot pass the vision on to others by production."

"Half a loaf is better than none," said Miss Enistor soothingly.

"I am not so sure that your proverb is true, so I reply with another. If indeed appetite comes with eating, as the French say, it is useless to invite it with half a loaf, when, for complete satisfaction, one requires the whole."

"There is something in that," admitted the girl, smiling, "but try and secure your desired whole loaf by sitting mousey-quiet and letting what is before you sink into your innermost being. Then you may create."

Crossing his legs and gripping his ankles, Hardwick, seated in the approved attitude of a fakir, did his best to adopt this advice, although he might well despair of fixing on canvas the fleeting vision of that enchanted hour. From the cromlech, near which the couple were stationed, a purple carpet of heather rolled down to a winding road, white and dusty and broad. On the hither side of the loosely built wall which skirted this, stretched many smooth green fields, divided and subdivided by boundaries of piled stones, feathery with ferns and coarse grasses. Beyond the confines of this ordered world, a chaos of bracken and ling, of small shrubs and stunted trees, together with giant masses of silvery granite, islanded amidst a sea of gold-besprinkled gorse, tumbled pell-mell to the jagged edge of the cliffs. Finally, the bluish plain of ocean glittered spaciously to the far sharp horizon-line. Thence rose billowy clouds of glorious hues threaded with the fires of the sinking sun, heaping themselves in rainbow tints higher and higher towards the radiant azure of the zenith. No ship was on the water, no animals moved on the land, and even the grey huddle of houses, to which the smooth level road led, appeared to be without inhabitants. For all that could be seen of sentient life, the two on the hilltop were alone in this world of changeful beauty: the Adam and Eve of a new creation.

"Yet," murmured the girl, to whom this stillness suggested thoughts, "around us are nature-spirits, invisible and busy, both watchful and indifferent. Oh, Mr. Hardwick, how I should love to see the trolls, the pixies, the gnomes and the nixies."

"Rhyme, if not reason," laughed the artist lazily, "one must have the eye of faith to see such impossible things."

"Impossible?" Miss Enistor shrugged her shoulders and declined to combat his scepticism beyond the query of the one word. As that did not invite conversation, Hardwick gave himself up to the mere contentment of looking at her. Amidst the warm splendours of the hour, she somehow conveyed to him the sensation of a grey and pensive autumn day, haunting, yet elusive in its misty beauty. He was wholly unable to put this feeling into words, but he conceived it dimly as a subtle blurring of the picture she had bidden him create. His love for her was like a veil before his conception, and until that veil was removed by his surrender of the passion, the execution of the landscape on canvas was impossible. Yet so sweet was this drawback to his working powers that he could not wish it away.

Yet it was strange that the girl should be attractive to a man of his limitations, since her alluring qualities were not aggressively apparent. A delicate oval face, exquisitely moulded, with a transparent colourless skin, and mystical eyes of larkspur blue, were scarcely what his blunt perceptions approved of as absolute beauty. Slim and dainty and fragile in shape and stature, her unusual looks suggested a cloistered nun given to visions or some peaked elfin creature of moonlight and mist. She might have been akin to the fairies she spoke about, and even in the strong daylight she was a creature of dreams ethereal and evanescent. Hardwick was much too phlegmatic a man to analyse shadows. A Celt would have comprehended the hidden charm which drew him on; the Saxon could only wonder what there was in the girl to impress him.

"You are not my ideal of beauty, you know, Miss Enistor," he said in such a puzzled way as to rob the speech of premeditated rudeness; "yet there is something about you which makes me adore you!"

The girl flushed and shrugged her shoulders again. "What a flamboyant word is 'adored'!"

"It is the only word I can use," said Hardwick stoutly. "The Venus of Milo, Brynhild in the Volsung poem, Jael who slew Sisera, Rubens' robust nymphs: these were the types which appealed to me—until I met you."

"How complimentary to my small commonplace looks! What caused you to change your mind, Mr. Hardwick?"

"Something you possess, which is not apparent."

"You talk in riddles. What attracts any one must be apparent."

"Well, that is uncertain. I am not a deep thinker, you know. But there is such a thing as glamour."

"There is. But you are not the man to comprehend the meaning of the word."

"I admit that: all the same I feel its influence—in you!"

"I don't know what you mean," said the girl indifferently.

"Nor do I. Yet the feeling is here," and he touched his heart. "If I could only shape that feeling into words,"—he hesitated and blushed.

"Well?"

"I might be able to tell you much—Alice."

"Why do you use my Christian name?"

"Why not? We are man and woman on a hillside, and not over-civilised beings in a drawing-room. You are Alice: I am Julian. It is quite simple."

"But too intimate," she objected, "you have known me only six months."

"Do you reckon knowledge by Time?"

"You have no knowledge: you confessed as much lately."

Hardwick looked at her earnestly. "I have this much, that I know how deeply I love you, my dear!" and he took her hand gently between his palms.

Alice let it lie there undisturbed, but did not return his pressure. For a few moments she looked straightly at the sunset. "I am sorry to hear you say that," was her calm remark when she did decide to speak.

"Why?"

"Because I can never love you!"

"Love can create love," urged Julian, again pressing her hand and again receiving no answering caress.

"Not between you and me. You may be fire, but I am not tow to catch alight." The flush had disappeared from her face, leaving it pure and white and calm to such a degree that the man dropped her hand. It was like holding a piece of ice, and he felt chilled by the aloofness of touch and look. "But you are a woman," he said roughly in his vexation, "you must know what love means."

"I don't: really I don't." Alice hugged her knees and stared with the sublime quietness of an Egyptian statue at his perturbed countenance. As he did not answer, she continued to speak in a deliberate way, which showed that his proposal had not touched her heart in the least. "My mother died when I was born, and I had Dame Trevel in the village yonder as my foster-mother until I was ten years of age. Then my father sent me to a Hampstead boarding school for eleven years. I returned only twelve months ago to live at Tremore"—she nodded towards a long low grey house, which basked on a neighbouring hilltop like a sullen reptile in the sunshine.

"But your father——?"

"My father," interrupted the girl in a melancholy tone, "has no love for any one but himself. At times I think he hates me for causing the death of my mother by being born."

"Surely not."

"Well, you have seen my father. I leave you to judge."

Hardwick was puzzled how to reply. "He is not a man who shows his feelings, you know," he said delicately.

"I don't think he has any feelings to show," replied Alice indifferently. "I am used to his neglect, and so have schooled myself to be quietly agreeable without expecting any demonstrations of affection."

Hardwick nodded. "I have noticed, when dining at Tremore, that you are more like well-bred acquaintances than father and daughter. Perhaps," he added in a dreamy tone, "that is what first made me fall in love with you."

"I see," said Miss Enistor ironically, "you have come across the line of Shakespeare which says that pity is akin to love."

"I have never read Shakespeare's plays," admitted Mr. Hardwick simply. "I'm not a clever chap, you know. But you looked so forlorn in that dismal house, and seemed so starving for kind words and actions, that I wanted to take you away with me and make you happier. Yes," the artist quite brightened at his own perspicuity, "that is what drew me to you—a desire to give you a really good time."

Alice looked at him gravely, but with a suspicion of a smile on her pale lips. "Do you know, Julian, that I believe you to be a good man." The artist blushed again: he had the trick of blushing on occasions, which showed him to possess still the modesty of boyhood. "Oh, I say," he murmured almost inaudibly; then to cover his confusion added: "You call me Julian."

"Yes," Alice nodded her head in a stately way. "Henceforth let us be the greatest of friends."

"Lovers," he urged, "true honest lovers."

"No, Julian. We would be neither true nor honest as lovers. Our marriage would not be one of those made in heaven."

"Are any marriages made in heaven?" he asked somewhat cynically.

She looked at him in surprise. "Of course. When one soul meets another soul capable of blending with it, that is a heavenly marriage."

"Well then," he cried impetuously, "my soul and your soul?"

Alice shook her head. "We don't strike the same note: we are not in harmony, Julian. As friends we can esteem one another, but as lovers, as man and wife, you would end in boring me as I should finally bore you."

"One would think you were fifty to hear you talk so," said Hardwick crossly.

"Do you reckon knowledge by Time?" she asked, harking back to the phrase he had used earlier in the conversation.

He had no reply ready. "Still it is odd to hear a girl of twenty-one talk as you do, Alice."

"You are speaking of my new suit of clothes. I am as old as the world."

"Oh, that is the queer stuff your father talks. He believes in reincarnation, doesn't he?"

"He does, and so do I."

"I wonder that you can. A sensible girl like you——"

"My dear Julian, you speak without knowledge," she interrupted placidly.

"That can't be knowledge which can't be proved."

"I think you must be a reincarnation of Nicodemus," retorted Miss Enistor.

"That is no answer."

"Now how can I give you an answer, when you have not the capability of grasping the answer, Julian? If a peasant wanted a mathematical problem proved to him, he would have to learn mathematics to understand it."

"Yes, I suppose so. But you mean ——"

"I mean that you have to live the life to understand the doctrine. Christ said that two thousand years ago, and it is as true to-day as it was then."

With his slow habit of thinking Hardwick had to revolve this speech in his mind before replying. Alice, with an impish look of mischief on her face, laughed also to prevent his answering. "I am taking you into deep water and you will be drowned," she said lightly, "suppose you begin your picture."

"No," said the man soberly. "I don't feel like painting the picture. I don't believe I ever could," and he looked at the fading glories of sea and land regretfully.

"Next time you are born you will be a genius," said Miss Enistor cheerfully, "as you are building up in this life the brain required by a master-painter. Meantime I wish you to be my friend."

"Well, it is hard to decline from love to friendship, but——"

"No 'buts.' Friendship is love from another point of view."

"Not my point of view."

Alice raised an admonitory finger. "You mustn't be selfish," she said severely.

"Selfish? I? How can I be?"

"By wishing me to give for your gratification what I cannot give for my own. I cannot love you as you desire, because there is not that spiritual link between us which means true love. Therefore to make me happy, if you really love me, you should be prepared to sacrifice yourself to the lower feeling of friendship."

"That is too high for me," murmured Hardwick despondingly, "but I see that you won't have me as your husband."

"Certainly not. I want a man to love me, not to pity me."

"It isn't exactly pity."

"Yes it is," she insisted, "you are sorry for me because I live in a dull house with a neglectful father. It is very nice of you to think so, and it is still nicer to think that you are willing to help me by tying yourself to a woman you do not really love. But I can't accept that sacrifice. You must be my friend, Julian—my true honest friend."

Hardwick glanced into her deep blue eyes, and unintelligent as he was in such subtle matters read his answer therein. "I shall do my best," he said with a deep sigh; "but you must give me time to cool down from passion to friendship. I want you to be my wife, and like all women you offer to be a sister to me."

"Or I will be your cousin if the relation will suit you better," said the girl, laughing outright at his rueful looks.

Julian took offence. "You don't pity me?"

"Not at all, since your feeling is not one of genuine love," was the cool response. "I would if it were."

"One would think you were a hardened woman of the world to hear you speak in this way."

"Perhaps I was a woman of the world in my last incarnation, Julian. I seem to have brought over a great deal of common sense to this life. You are a dear, sweet, placid thing, but although you have seen more of human nature and worldly existence this time than I have, you don't know half so much."

"Alice, you are conceited."

"Ah, that speech shows you are yet heart-whole, Julian. If you were really in love you would never dare to speak so to your divinity."

"Well, I daresay I shall get over it. But it's hard on a fellow."

"Not at all. Hard on your vanity perhaps, but vanity isn't you. Come," Alice sprang to her feet and took up her smart silver-headed cane, "the sun will soon go down and I must get home. We are friends, are we not?" she held out her hand smiling.

"Of course we are." Hardwick bent to kiss her hand and she snatched it away swiftly.

"That isn't friendship."

"Oh, with you friendship means: 'You may look, but you mustn't touch.'"

"Exactly," said Miss Enistor lightly, "consider me if you please as a valuable Dresden china ornament under a glass shade."

Julian heaved another sigh and began to collect his painting materials. "I must if I must," he admitted grudgingly; "there isn't another man, I suppose?"

The face of the girl grew grave. "There isn't another man whom I love, if that is what you mean," she said, reluctantly. "I have not yet met with my Prince, who will wake me to love and beauty. But there is a man who wants, as you do, to be the Prince."

"Oh hang him, who is he?"

"Don Pablo Narvaez!"

"That old mummy. Impossible!"

"It is both possible and disagreeable. He hinted the other day that he——"

"Loved you? What impertinence!"

"No," said Alice dryly, "he did not commit himself so far. But he hinted that he would like me to be his wife. My father afterwards told me that it would be a good match for me, as Don Pablo is wealthy."

"Wealthy be blessed, Alice," rejoined Hardwick with great heat. "You don't want to take your husband from a museum."

"I don't and I won't," she replied with great determination, "and for that reason I wish you to be my friend."

"Why, what can I do?"

"Stand by me. If my father insists upon my marrying Don Pablo, you must say that I am engaged to you, and this will give you the right to interfere."

Hardwick packed his traps, and swung up the hill on the home-path alongside the girl. "How can you ask me to take up such a position when you know that I love you, Alice?"

"If I thought that you did I should not ask for your help, Julian. But in your own heart you know that you really do not love me. It is only what you call the glamour of my personality that has caught you for the moment. It is not improbable," she went on musingly, "that there may be some slight link between us dating from our meeting in former lives, but it is not a strong enough one to bring us together this time as man and wife!"

"Oh, this mystical talk makes me tired," cried the painter in quite an American way, "it's silly."

"So it is from your point of view," said Miss Enistor promptly, "let us get down to what you call common sense in your robust Anglo-Saxon style. I want you to stand between me and Don Pablo in the way I suggest. Will you?"

"Yes. That is—give me a day or two to think the matter over. I am flesh and blood, you know, Alice, and not stone."

"Oh, nonsense, you deceive yourself," she retorted impatiently. "Don't I tell you that if I thought your feeling for me was really genuine I should not be so wicked as to risk your unhappiness? But I know you better than you do yourself. If you loved me, would you have chatted about this, that and the other thing so lightly after I had rejected you?"

"There is something in that," admitted Hardwick, as Alice had done previously with regard to his whole-loaf argument. "Well, I daresay I shall appear as your official lover. Don Pablo shan't worry you if I can help it."

"Thanks, you dear good boy," rejoined the girl gratefully and squeezed the artist's arm. "Don't you feel fire running through your veins when I touch you, Julian?"

"No," said Hardwick stolidly.

"Doesn't your heart beat nineteen to the dozen: haven't you the feeling that this is heaven on earth?"

"Not a bit."

Alice dropped his arm with a merry laugh. "And you talk about being in love with me! Can't you see now how wise I was to refuse you?"

"Well," said Hardwick reluctantly, for he felt that she was perfectly right in her diagnosis; "there may be something in what you say."

"There is everything in what I say," she insisted; "however, I shall give you another chance. Catch me before I reach Tremore and I shall be your wife."

Before Hardwick could accept or refuse, she sprang up the narrow winding path as lightly as Atalanta. More out of pique than absolute desire the artist followed. Although he now began to see that he had taken a false Eros for the true one, he resolutely sped after the flying figure, if only to have the pleasure of refusing the prize when he won it. But he might as well have attempted to catch an air-bubble. Alice was swifter than he was, and ran in a flying way which reminded him of a darting swallow. Down the declivity she dropped, following the twists of the pathway amongst the purple heather, and sprang across the brawling stream at the bottom of the valley before he was half-way down. Then up she mounted, with an arch backward glance, to scale the hill whereon Tremore gloomed amidst its muffling trees. At the gate set in the mouldering brick wall he nearly caught her, for pride winged his feet. But she eluded his grasp with a laugh and disappeared amongst the foliage of the miniature forest. When next she came in sight, he beheld her standing at the sombre porch of the squat mansion binding up her tresses of black hair, which had become loose with her exertions.

"You don't love me," panted Alice, who had scarcely got her breath, "if you did I should have been in your arms by this time."

"Pouf!" puffed Hardwick, wiping his wet brow. "Pouf! pouf! pouf!"

"Is that all you have to say?"

"It is all I am able to say. Pouf! Pouf! Well, my dear girl, Saul went to look for his asses and found a kingdom. I went to look for a kingdom of love and find an ass—in myself."

"Oh no! no!" protested Alice, rather distressed.

"Oh yes! yes! The love-mood has come and gone in the space of an afternoon, Miss Enistor."

"Alice to you, Julian," and she held out her hand.

The artist did not attempt to kiss it this time. "Brother and sister," he said, giving the hand a hearty shake, "and official lover when necessary."

"It's a bargain," replied Miss Enistor beaming, and so it was arranged.

CHAPTER II
THE PROPHECY

From the hilltop where Alice and her rejected lover had conversed, the house called Tremore could be plainly seen in its grey nakedness. But on the other side, in front and at the back, it was screened from the salt Atlantic winds by a dismal wood of stone-pines, yews, cypress-trees and giant cedars, planted by various Enistors in the long-distant past, when they had first set up their tent on the waste moorland. The gloomy disposition of the race could be seen, not only in the funereal types of trees chosen for sheltering the mansion, but in the grim look of the mansion itself. Never was there so dreary a place.

Tremore means "great dwelling" in the Celtic tongue, but the name could only apply to this particular house from the unusual space of ground it covered, since it was only one storey high. Built of untrimmed granite blocks and roofed with dull hued slates, it stretched in a narrow line towards the rear of the hill on which it stood. Here it divided into two other narrow lines, forming on the whole the exact shape of the letter "Y." One of the forks contained the kitchen, the servants' sleeping apartments and the domestic offices: the other held the bedrooms of the gentry, while the main stem of the letter was made up of drawing-room, library, sitting-room and dining-room. It was an odd place quaintly planned and curiously built: but then the Enistors were odd people.

One markedly strange thing amongst others was the absence of vegetation about the house, since nothing would grow near it. Flowers were conspicuous by their absence, turf was wanting, and not even weeds would flourish. The very trees stood aloof in sulky darkness, leaving the building isolated in an arid space of beaten earth. There it stood on the bare ground with its heavy porch, its thick walls and many small windows, bleak in its nakedness for want of draping ivy. True enough there was a kitchen-garden and a small orchard at the back, beyond the screen of trees, which flourished tolerably, but round the house greenery was wanting, as if the place was cursed. Perhaps it was, as the Enistors had borne a sinister reputation for generations. But whatever the reason might be, Tremore might have been built in the desert from the way in which it lay like a sullen snake on the barren earth. And a two-headed snake at that, like some demon of a fairy tale.

The interior of this undesirable mansion was desperately gloomy, as all the rooms were small with low ceilings, and for the most part panelled with black oak dull and unpolished. The kitchen and servants' rooms were more agreeable, as here Mr. Enistor had conformed to modern ideas of cheerfulness so far as to paper and tile the walls brightly. But his own particular portion of the house he would not allow to be touched, and although it was comfortable enough, it was decidedly depressing, with its sombre tints and stuffy atmosphere. Often did Alice leave its dark chambers and its dismal surroundings to breathe freely on the vast spaces of the moors. East and West and North and South stretched the treeless lands, covered with heather and dangerous with the shafts of worked-out mines The village of Polwellin below belonged to the Enistors, and over it and its inhabitants the present head of the old family exercised a feudal sway. But beyond this particular collection of dwellings, containing one hundred people, more or less, there was no house or hamlet for some leagues. Perchton, a watering-place haunted by artists, was the nearest town, and that was ten miles distant. Tremore would have suited a misanthrope, but it was not a place wherein Alice cared to live. She was young and inclined to mix with her fellow creatures, but never did any chance come by which she could enter society. It was no wonder that the girl was peaked and pining, and could see things invisible to the ordinary person. Isolation was unhealthy for one of her temperament.

Seated at the heavy mahogany table, whence, in old-fashioned style, the cloth had been removed for dessert, Alice almost regretted that she had not accepted Hardwick's proposal to remove her from such sad surroundings. The dull carved panelling of the walls, the sombre family portraits, the cumbersome furniture, together with the lowness of the ceiling and the limited space of the room, stifled her and depressed her spirits to such a degree that she could scarcely eat. Mr. Enistor and Don Pablo—the latter dined at Tremore on this particular night—were in accurate evening dress, and the whole apartment bore an aspect of good-breeding and stately ceremonial. The host was attached to the customs of his ancestors, and his meals were always served with quite royal etiquette. And by the light of the many wax candles in silver holders which illuminated the room—Mr. Enistor would have nothing to do with lamps—Alice looked curiously at the two men, whose want of vitality, as she vaguely thought, drew the life-power from herself.

She was wrong as regarded her father, for Korah Enistor was a handsome, healthy man in the prime of life, and had plenty of vitality in his robust frame. He looked somewhat austere with his dark hair, scarcely touched with white, his dark eyes and powerful face, which lacked colour as much as her own did. Like Hardwick, the man resembled a soldier, as he was tall and lean, well-built and active. Also, he possessed the imperious manner of one accustomed to command men, and spoke in a slow deliberate manner with compelling glances of his dark eyes. The most casual observer would have noted that here was a strong personality given to dominate rather than to obey. All the same, Alice noticed that her strong-willed father pointedly deferred to Don Pablo Narvaez, in a way which argued that he rendered *him* obedience. It was strange that she should entertain this idea seeing that the Spaniard was as frail as Enistor was strong, and did not at all look like one who could, or would, rule so aggressive a personality. This odd deference had puzzled her on previous occasions, but to-night the feeling that her father was thrall to Don Pablo was particularly strong.

A breath, she thought, could have blown the guest away like thistledown, so frail and weak did he appear. What his age was she could not guess, but conceived that he was an octogenarian. His scanty white hair, his shrunken figure, his small wrinkled face, and the false teeth which showed when he smiled, all favoured this belief. Don Pablo was like an expiring flame, which the slightest breath might extinguish, and the only thing, hinting to the girl's mind at enduring life, were his eyes. These were of a brighter blue than her own, extraordinarily large and piercing, so that few could bear their direct gaze. The idea entered Alice's head at the moment that here was a bunch of blooming flowers in a cracked vase of great age, or to be less fanciful, she told herself that Narvaez had a weak body dominated by a powerful will which kept the life intact. She could imagine him stepping out of that fragile shape, and still be alive, more powerful and more vitalised in another. His brain was clear, his speech was incisive, and always he used his dominating eyes to compel all those he gazed at to surrender to the spell of his powerful mind. There was something sinister about his interior youthfulness and exterior senility.

The girl both hated and dreaded him. Being sensitive she was responsive to influences which a coarser nature—say that of Hardwick—would never feel. Don Pablo impressed her as something terrible in spite of his weak looks. His frail body was only the jungle, as it were, that concealed the tiger, and she could imagine him putting forth powers whose force would shatter the aging tenement. What such powers might be she did not know, as he revealed nothing of his dominating nature to her. But she vaguely felt that what force he possessed was deadly evil, and would be used for purely evil purposes. Therefore, warned instinctively by her pure soul, she kept out of his way as much as possible. The stealthy attempts of her father to bring youth and age together, Alice resisted as best she could. But it was difficult to fight against two such commanding natures, and all the time there was the insistent feeling of being drawn into darkness. Alice often blamed herself for thinking in this hostile way of her father, but could never get rid of her doubts. It was firmly rooted in her mind that Narvaez and Enistor were dwelling in an atmosphere of evil, which they wished to extend so as to include herself. At the moment the pressure was particularly strong, and she sighed with weariness as the invisible forces came up against her. Hardly had the sound left her lips when Don Pablo glanced swiftly at his host.

"You are tired, Alice," said Enistor, rising to open the door. "The heat is oppressive to-night. Take a turn in the garden and you will feel better. Is your head aching?"

"Yes, father," replied the girl almost inaudibly, and glided out of the room like an unquiet ghost to seek the life-giving moorland air.

Her father returned to the table in his stately fashion, and poured himself out a fresh glass of water. On the shining mahogany there were no decanters of wine: only dishes of fruit, crystal jugs of water, and the three empty coffee-cups. Neither Narvaez nor his host drank any alcoholic liquor: they did not indulge in smoking and were extremely temperate in eating. An ordinary man would have missed the smiling good-fellowship which is usually to be found at a dinner-table. Had these two even laughed outright they would have appeared more human. But they did not, and throughout their conversation maintained a sinister calmness disconcerting in its aloofness from the chatter and merriment of commonplace mortals. Yet somehow this profound quietness seemed to suit the room with its menacing atmosphere.

"It is difficult," murmured Don Pablo, with a glance at the door.

"But not impossible," returned Enistor, answering the thought rather than the words. These two were versed in mind-reading beyond the ordinary.

"That is as it may be, my friend!"

Enistor frowned. "You mean her innocence?"

"Is it necessary for you to put that into words?" demanded the older man in a mocking way; "of course I mean her innocence. That very purity which makes the girl so valuable to me is the wall which protects her from the influence I wish to exercise over her."

"Constant dropping of water wears away a stone, Master."

"That proverb does not apply in every case," retorted the other darkly. "I tell you that I am helpless before your daughter. I am too old for her to love me, therefore her heart is safe. She is not greedy for money, or admiration, or position, or dress, or for half a dozen things which would tempt an ordinary girl. There is no foothold to be obtained."

The host cast an uneasy glance round, and his eyes grew piercing, as if he would force the invisible to become apparent. "She is guarded, we know!"

Narvaez' wrinkled face grew even darker than before. "Yes, she is guarded. I am aware of the power that guards her."

"So you have said several times, Master. Why not explain more fully?"

"The time has not yet come to explain. If you were advanced enough to read the Akashic Records, then you might see much that would explain things."

Enistor nodded gloomily. "I understand. The present situation is the outcome of the past."

"Everything in life is an outcome of the past," said Narvaez, "even a neophyte such as you are should be certain of that. Cause and effect govern all things."

"But if you would explain the cause, I might see how to deal with the effect, Master."

"I daresay," returned the other dryly, "but in spite of my superior knowledge, I am not yet omnipotent, Enistor. I can read a trifle of the records, but not easily. There are veils before my eyes which prevent me from knowing the exact state of affairs which has brought things to this pass in this set of lives. All I can say is that you and I and your daughter, together with two other people, were in Chaldea over five thousand years ago, and the lives then are linked with the lives now. The Karma of that period has to be worked out while we are all in the flesh to-day."

"Do you know who the other two people are?" asked Enistor eagerly.

"I know one. He is powerful, and hostile to you and to me!"

"He does not follow the Left-hand Path then?"

"No. He is a White Magician. You will see him some day when the hour strikes. I am teaching you all I can so that you may be able to confront him."

"I am not afraid of any one," snapped Enistor sharply.

"Oh, you have courage enough," admitted Narvaez, "but knowledge must be added to that, if you are to be victorious. As to the other person who has to play a part in the working out of this Karma——"

"Well! Well! Well?"

"I don't know who or what he is," confessed the other.

"He is a man then?"

"Yes, I know that much!" Narvaez drank a glass of water, and rose with an effort as if his bones pained him. "We had better understand the situation." In spite of his mind-reading Enistor could not understand and said as much with a puzzled air. Narvaez laughed softly for a moment and then became his usual calm self. "I refer to the position on the physical plane of you and myself and those surrounding us—the flesh and blood puppets I mean with which we have to deal."

"Are they puppets?" demanded Enistor dubiously.

"One is not. You can guess that I mean our powerful adversary. But the others—bah!" he swept the air with one lean hand. "I think I can deal with them, if you give me your assistance."

"I have promised to give it—at a price," said Enistor tartly.

The guest stared at him with a sphinx-like expression. "I know your price and you shall have your price," he dropped into his chair again with an air of fatigue, and his eyes grew brighter than ever. "Listen, my friend. I came here from Spain three years ago in search of you, as I learned by my arts that you would be useful to me. You have the blood of my race in your veins, as you know, since that Spanish sailor, who was wrecked on these coasts in a galleon of the Great Armada, married your ancestress from whom you are descended."

"I know all this, Master."

"Quite so, but I wish to refresh your memory. I found you here a poor man——"

"Which I am still," interrupted Enistor gloomily.

"Of course. The time is not yet ripe for you to gain your wish!"

"My wish! my wish!" the host rose and raised his arms, with a fierce look on his powerful face. "When will it be gratified? I want money—a large amount—thousands of pounds, since money means power."

"And power is the real thing you desire. The money, as we know, is only the means to obtain that power. You wish to influence men at all costs; to rule the masses; to be famous as a leader!"

The sneer with which Narvaez made this speech irritated Enistor, although he was sufficiently educated in mystic lore to be aware how important absolute self-command is to those who deal with occultism. That is, he knew such was the case, more or less, but could never attain to the necessary calm. "It is not a contemptible ambition," he snarled savagely.

"Our adversary of the Right-hand Path would say so," rejoined Narvaez coolly, "since you desire power and rule and money in order to gratify Self."

"I never knew that you worked for other people, Narvaez," sneered Enistor.

The Spaniard smiled coldly. "I don't, I never shall. I strive, as you do, for power, and, thanks to my knowledge, I have more than you, although it is not enough to content me. It is because your aims are the same as mine that we can work together. But Alice does not desire anything and that is what baffles both of us."

"In that case, she is useless to you, Master, and therefore it is no good your marrying her."

"Once she is my wife, I can influence her more easily, Enistor. As you know, I have no feeling of love for either man or woman. That philanthropic sentiment of sacrifice for humanity is disagreeable to me. In black magic, as in white, one must live like what is called a saint to be powerful. To be absolutely free you should never have married."

"Yet you propose to make the same mistake."

"There is no mistake about the matter," said Narvaez calmly, "my marriage with your daughter will be no marriage in the accepted sense of the word. I simply wish to bind her to me, so that I can train the clairvoyance she possesses which is so valuable to me. I can give her plenty of money ——"

"You won't give it to me," interposed the other hastily.

"Of course not. Why should I? Nothing for nothing is the rule of the Left-hand Path. But that I require your services and cannot dispense with them I should not waste my time teaching you my knowledge. However, the situation stands thus. I am to marry your daughter, and when I train her clairvoyantly—waken her sleeping powers, that is—we may learn from her reading of the Akashic Records what danger threatens."

"There is a danger then?"

"Yes, and a very real one, which has to do with this adversary I told you about. A desire to defeat him brought me to you, and as he is your enemy as well as mine, you are wise to obey me in all things."

"Yet I know that when you have no further use for me, you will cast me aside as of no account," said Enistor bitterly.

"Why not?" rejoined the other coolly. "You would act in the same way."

"I am not so sure that I would."

"Ah. You have still some human weakness to get rid of before you can progress on the path along which you ask me to lead you. I have no use for weaklings, Enistor. Remember that."

The host drew himself up haughtily. "I am no weakling!"

"For your own sake, to-morrow, I hope you are not."

"Why to-morrow?"

"Because a blow will fall on you."

Enistor looked uneasy. "A blow! What kind of a blow?"

"Something to do with a loss of expected money. That is all I can tell you, my friend. You keep certain things from me, so if you are not entirely frank, how can you expect me to aid you?"

Enistor dropped into his chair again, and the perspiration beaded his dark face. "A loss of expected money," he muttered, "and Lucy is ill."

"Who is Lucy?"

"My sister who lives in London. A widow called Lady Staunton. She has five thousand a year which she promised years ago to leave to me, so that I might restore the fortunes of the Enistor family. I had news a week ago that she is very ill, and this week I was going up to see her in order to make sure she had not changed her mind."

"It is useless your going to see Lady Staunton," said Narvaez leisurely, "for she *has* changed her mind and has made a new will.

Enistor scowled and clenched his hands. "How do you know?"

"Well, I don't know details," said the Spaniard agreeably, "those have to be supplied by you. All I am certain of is that to-morrow you will receive a letter stating that you have lost some expected money. As the sole money you hope to receive is to come from Lady Staunton, it is logical to think that this is what will be lost. You should have told me about this and I could have worked on her mind to keep her true to you."

"But it is impossible," cried Enistor, rising to stride up and down in an agitated way. "Lucy is as proud of our family as I am, and always said she would leave her fortune to restore us to our old position in the country."

"Lady Staunton is a woman, and women are fickle," said Narvaez cruelly. "I fear you have lost your chance this time."

"You may be wrong."

"I may be, but I don't think so. I was looking over your horoscope last evening, Enistor, and from what I read therein I made further inquiries, which have to do with invisible powers I can control."

"Elementals?"

"And other things," said the magician carelessly; "however I learned positively that you will get bad news of the nature I explained to-morrow. It is too late to counteract what has been done."

"The will——?"

"Exactly, the will. From what you say I feel convinced that my knowledge applies to Lady Staunton and her fortune. See what comes of not being frank with me, Enistor. You are a fool."

"I don't believe what you say."

"As you please. It does not matter to me; except," he added with emphasis, "that it makes my hold over you more secure."

"What do you mean by that?"

"My poor friend!" Narvaez glanced back from the door towards which he had walked slowly. "You are losing what little powers you have obtained, since you cannot read my mind. Why, I mean that with five thousand a year you might not be inclined to give me your daughter in marriage. As a poor man you are forced to do so."

"It seems to me," said Enistor angrily, "that in any case I must do so, if I wish to learn the danger which threatens me as well as you."

"Why, that is true. You are clever in saying that."

"But perhaps this possible loss of money is the danger."

"No. The danger is a greater one than the loss of money. It has to do with your life and my life in Chaldea; with our adversary and with the unknown man, who is coming to take part in the drama of repayment. I have a feeling," said Narvaez, passing his hand across his brow, "that the curtain rises on our drama with this loss of money."

"I don't believe Lucy will cheat me," cried Enistor desperately.

"Wait until to-morrow's post," said Narvaez significantly, "you will find that I am a true prophet. Our bargain of my marriage with Alice must continue on its present basis, as the want of money will still prevent your becoming independent. I might suggest," he added, opening the door, "that you forbid your daughter to see too much of young Hardwick. She might fall in love with him and that would in a great measure destroy her clairvoyant powers. She will be of no use to either of us then. Good night! When you sleep we shall meet as usual on the other plane!"

Narvaez departed chuckling, for disagreeables befalling others always amused him. He was absolutely without a heart and without feelings, since for ages in various bodies he had worked hard to rid himself of his humanity. Enistor was on the same evil path, but as yet was human enough to worry over the inevitable. Until he slept he did his best to convince himself that Narvaez spoke falsely, but failed utterly in the attempt.

CHAPTER III
FULFILMENT

Next morning Enistor was gloomy and apprehensive, for he had slept very badly during the hours of darkness. He tried to persuade himself that the Spaniard prophesied falsely, but some inward feeling assured him that this was not the case. Before the sun set he was convinced, against his inclinations, that the sinister prediction would be fulfilled. Therefore he picked up his morning letters nervously, quite expecting to find a legal one stating that Lady Staunton was dead and had left her five thousand a year to some stranger. Fortunately for his peace of mind there was no letter of the kind, and he made a better breakfast than he might have done. All the same he was morose and sullen, so that Alice had anything but a pleasant time. Towards the end of the meal he relieved his feelings by scolding the girl.

"I forbid you to see much of that young Hardwick," he declared imperiously, "he is in love with you, and I don't wish you to marry a pauper painter!"

Aware that her father wished her to accept Narvaez, it would have been wise for the girl to have held her tongue, since a later confession of a feigned engagement to the artist was her sole chance of resisting the loveless marriage. But Enistor was one of those people who invariably drew what was worst in a person to the surface, and she answered prematurely. "Mr. Hardwick proposed yesterday and I refused him. Therefore I can see as much of him as I want to, without running any risk of becoming his wife."

Enistor ignored the latter part of her reply, proposing to deal with it later. "You refused him? And why, may I ask?"

"He is not the man I want for my husband. He does not complete me!"

"Are you then incomplete?" sneered Enistor scornfully.

"To my mind every woman and every man must be incomplete until a true marriage takes place!"

"What is a true marriage, you silly girl?"

"A marriage of souls!"

"Pooh! Pooh! That foolish affinity business."

"Is it foolish?" queried Alice sedately. "It appears to me to be a great truth."

"Appears to you!" scoffed her father. "What does a child such as you are know about such things? At your age you should be healthy enough not to think of your soul and even forget that you have one. Nevertheless I am glad that you have refused Hardwick, as I have other views for you."

"If they include marriage with Don Pablo, I decline to entertain them."

"Do you indeed? Rubbish! You are my daughter and shall do as I order."

"I am a human being also, and in this instance I shall not obey."

Enistor frowned like a thunderstorm. "You dare to set your will against my will?" he demanded, looking at her piercingly.

"In this instance I do," replied Alice, meeting his gaze firmly. "I am quite willing to be an obedient daughter to you in all else. But marriage concerns my whole future and therefore I have a right to choose for myself."

"You have no rights, save those I allow you to have! In refusing Hardwick you have shown more sense than I expected. But Don Pablo you must marry!"

"Must I, father? And why?"

"He is wealthy and he adores you."

Alice in spite of her nervousness laughed outright. "I am woman enough to see that Don Pablo only adores himself. He wants a hostess to sit at the foot of his table and entertain his friends: he has no use for a wife. As to his wealth, I would sooner be happy with a pauper than with a millionaire, provided I loved him."

"Silly romance: silly romance."

"Perhaps it is. But that is my view!"

Enistor frowned still more darkly, as he saw very plainly that, frail as she was, he could not hope to bend her to his will. In some way he could not explain the girl baffled his powerful personality. Yet it was necessary that she should become the wife of Narvaez, if the danger which the old man hinted at was to be known and conquered. "Alice, listen to me," said the man entreatingly, "we are very poor and Don Pablo is very rich. If you marry him, you will soon be his wealthy widow, as he cannot live long. Then with the money you will be able to restore the fortunes of our family and marry whomsoever you desire. Be sensible!"

"I refuse to sacrifice myself to a loveless marriage for your sake," said Alice doggedly, and standing up like a weak lily against the force of a tempest. "You don't love me, father: you have never loved me, so why— —"

"I am not going to argue the point with you any longer," stormed Enistor, rising hastily; "I shall force you to marry Don Pablo."

"In that case I shall marry Julian Hardwick and ask him to protect me," said the girl, rising in her turn, shaking and white, but sullenly determined.

"Protect you! Who can protect you against me? I can deal with Hardwick and with you in a way you little dream of."

"What you can do to Mr. Hardwick I do not know," said the girl steadily, "but me you cannot harm in any way, nor can you compel me, else you would long ago have used your boasted power."

"Are you aware that you are speaking to your father?" demanded Enistor, astonished at her daring.

"Perfectly! I wish to be a good daughter to you, father, but in a matter which concerns my whole life I must decline to yield either to your commands or prayers!"

Enistor could have struck her pale face in his wrath, but, sensitive to invisible things, he became aware that there was a barrier around her which kept him at arm's length. He knew instinctively that the powerful influence pervading the room had to do with the unknown individual whom Narvaez called "Our Adversary," and felt that he was not prepared to measure his strength against such a force. So uncomfortable and daunted did he feel, that his one desire was to leave the room, and he began to back towards the door. Alice was astonished to see the perspiration beading her father's forehead and watched his departure in dismay. Unaware of what was taking place, she looked upon the withdrawal as a declaration of war, and believed, with some truth, that she would have to suffer for opposing resistance to the marriage with Narvaez. Yet she still held out, as she felt a singular sense of security. The same power which weakened Enistor strengthened her, but not being a trained occultist, she wondered how she could dare to face her father so boldly.

"I shall talk to you later," breathed Enistor with an effort, so hostile was the atmosphere. "Meanwhile you may as well know that if you decline to become Don Pablo's wife, you will ruin me."

The Squire—that was his title as the owner of Polwellin village—left his obstinate daughter in the room, and went to the library, which was his own particular domain. Here the opposing influence did not follow him. Sitting down heavily, he began to breathe more freely, and wondered why he had been so craven as to fly from the field of battle. Although he had been anxious all his life to acquire forbidden lore, he had only learned something of the practical side of occultism since the arrival of Narvaez, some three years ago. That ancient sinner was accomplished in black arts, and for his own ends was willing to impart something of his knowledge to Enistor. A considerable amount of sinister teaching had been given to the Squire, but as yet he was but a neophyte, and ignorant of many things. Narvaez withheld much purposely, as he was keenly aware of Enistor's powerful will and unscrupulous greed for power. The Spaniard did not so much desire to instruct his host as to make use of him. Those servants of Christ, who walk on the Right-hand Path, are possessed entirely by the Spirit of Love, and are only too anxious to teach to the ignorant all that they may be capable of assimilating. But the Brothers of the Shadow are too inherently selfish to be generous, and merely give out sufficient knowledge to render their pupils useful servants and docile slaves. Narvaez had no intention of cultivating Enistor's latent powers to such a strength that they might be dangerous to himself. Consequently, although the man was on the threshold of power, he had not yet crossed it, and therefore was unable to deal with the force in the dining-room, the strength of which he could not calculate. To influence Alice to work for self in a way which would lure her from behind the barrier of the protecting power required more knowledge than Enistor possessed. Yet Narvaez likewise professed fear of the Adversary, and could only use cunning instead of command. The Squire smiled grimly to himself as he reflected that the Master himself would have been ignominiously driven from the dining-room in the same way, had he been present.

Of course Enistor did not wish to injure his daughter in any way at which the world would look askance. He merely desired her to make a loveless marriage so as to acquire the wealth of Narvaez, and so that she might be educated in clear-seeing for the purpose of averting a possible danger. What that danger might be Enistor did not know, and so far as he could guess Don Pablo was equally ignorant. Therefore it was absolutely necessary that the latent clairvoyant powers of the girl should be brought to the surface and trained, if the safety of the Black Magician and his pupil was to be assured. Enistor was aggressively selfish, and to save himself was ready to sacrifice his daughter and a dozen human beings if necessary to the Dark Powers. Her body, her fortune, her honour, would not be injured, but—as Enistor very well knew—her soul would be in danger. For this however he cared nothing. Better that the girl should perish than that he should be balked of his daring ambition. But he did not intend to surrender Alice to Don Pablo unless his price was paid, and that price included unlimited wealth together with unlimited power over weaker mortals. Narvaez alone could instruct him in the arts which could command such things.

Meanwhile, as Enistor needed money, it was necessary for him to attend to practical matters, which had to do with Lady Staunton! For many years Enistor had influenced his sister strongly to leave her entire fortune to him, and until Narvaez had spoken on the previous evening, he had every reason to believe that he would get what he wanted. But the prediction rendered him uneasy, even though the expected letter had not yet arrived. The Ides of March had truly come, but had not passed, and although the fatal epistle had failed to appear in the morning's batch of letters, it might be delivered by the evening post. All that day Enistor was naturally uncomfortable and apprehensive. Positive that his sister would leave him her fortune, he had rejoiced when the news of her illness arrived, and in his fancied security he had not even gone up to London to make sure that all was safe. Certainly he had never dreamed of taking so long a journey to console the old lady on her death-bed; but he deeply regretted for the sake of the inheritance that he had not sought her company during her sickness. Also it might have been advisable to enlist the evil services of Narvaez to clinch the matter, and this omission the Squire deeply lamented. However, it was now too late to do anything save wait for the post and hope for the best. He suffered as only a selfish nature can suffer, and the agonies of a truly selfish man are very great when he is thwarted.

It was close upon three o'clock when he was put out of his misery by the arrival of an unexpected stranger. Enistor, finding that Alice had betaken herself to the safer spaces of the moorlands, had no one to torment, so he busied himself with evil practices in his gloomy library. That is, he used the teaching of Narvaez to concentrate his will-power on Lady Staunton, so that she might still desire to leave him her money. With her visualised image in his mind's eye, he was sending powerful thoughts to her sick-bed insisting that he and he only should benefit by the will. An ignorant person would have laughed at the idea of any one being so controlled from a distance, but Enistor knew perfectly well what he was doing, and made ardent use of his unholy telepathy. Later when the footman announced that Lady Staunton's solicitor, Mr. Cane, desired an interview, Enistor granted it without delay. It was better, he wisely thought, to know the best or the worst at once, without suffering the agonies of suspense until the evening post.

The new-comer was a bustling, rosy-cheeked little man, well dressed, expansive and voluble. He had no nerves to speak of, and still less imagination, therefore he was not in the least impressed by the grey atmosphere of Tremore. In fact before he condescended to business, he complimented his host on the breezy altitude of the house and the beauty of the surroundings. His courtesy was not at all appreciated, as Enistor soon let him know.

"I don't suppose you came here to admire the view, Mr. Cane," said the Squire irritably. "Your unexpected presence argues that my sister is dead."

Mr. Cane's lively face assumed a solemn expression, and his airy manner became heavily professional. "You are right, Mr. Enistor," he said pompously, "my lamented client, Lady Staunton, passed away to the better land in a peaceful frame of mind at ten o'clock last night."

Enistor frowned and winced as he remembered his wasted telepathy. "I am sorry," he said conventionally, "and I regret greatly that I was not at hand to soothe her last moments. But unexpected business prevented my taking the journey. Still, had I guessed that she was likely to die, I should have managed to be with her."

"Pray do not grieve, Mr. Enistor," exclaimed the solicitor with unintentional irony. "My lamented client's last moments were tenderly soothed by her best friend."

"Her best friend?"

"So Lady Staunton termed Mr. Montrose!"

"I never heard of him," said Enistor abruptly. "Who is he?"

A most unexpected reply took away the Squire's breath. "He is the fortunate young gentleman who inherits Lady Staunton's property."

Enistor rose in a black fury, with clenched fists and incredulous looks. "I don't understand: you must be mistaken," he said hoarsely.

"I am not mistaken," replied Cane dryly. "I was never more in earnest in my life, sir. It is hard on you as my late lamented client's nearest relative, I admit. In fact Lady Staunton thought so too, and asked me to come down as soon as she died to explain her reasons for leaving the money to Mr. Montrose. Otherwise, since your sister, Mr. Enistor, did not encourage legal matters being attended to out of order, you would not have heard the news until the reading of the will after the funeral. As Lady Staunton died last night, the burial will take place in four days. I have no doubt as a sincere mourner you will be there."

"A sincere mourner!" cried Enistor, pacing the room hastily to work off his rage. "How can I be that when my sister has cheated me in this way?"

"Oh, not cheated, Mr. Enistor, not cheated," pleaded the rosy-cheeked little man more volubly than ever. "Lady Staunton's money was her own to dispose of as she desired. Besides, she did not forget you entirely: she has left you the sum of one thousand pounds."

"Really!" sneered the Squire savagely, "and this Montrose creature inherits five thousand a year! It is wicked: infamous, scandalous. I shall upset the will, Mr. Cane!"

The lawyer remonstrated mildly. "I fear that is impossible, Mr. Enistor. My lamented client was quite in her right senses when she signed the will, and as I drew it up in accordance with her instructions, you may be certain that all is in good order. I feel for you: upon my word I feel for you," added Mr. Cane plaintively, "and my errand cannot be called a pleasant one!"

"Oh, hang your feelings: what do I care for your feelings! It is my sister's iniquitous will that I am thinking about. She knew how poor I was: she was proud of being an Enistor, and she faithfully promised that I should have the money in order to mend our family fortunes. What devil made her change her intentions?"

"No devil that I am aware of," said Cane with puny dignity. "Lady Staunton did make a will in your favour. But a year ago she signed a new one leaving her income to Mr. Montrose, who is now my client. I decline on these grounds to hear him spoken of as a devil."

"Oh. Then it was this Montrose beast who made her change her mind?"

"No. Certainly he did not. He is not even aware that he has inherited, as Lady Staunton asked me to see you first. Only when the will is read, after the funeral in four days, will Mr. Montrose learn of his good fortune."

"Montrose does not know," said Enistor, striding forward to stand over the little lawyer in a threatening way. "Then why not destroy this last will and read the old one which is in my favour!"

Cane wriggled beneath Enistor's fiery gaze and slipped sideways out of his chair. "Are you in your right senses to——" he began, puffing indignantly.

Enistor cut him short. "Oh, the deuce take your heroics! You know perfectly well that I should benefit rather than a stranger. I want the money and I intend to get the money. By righting this wrong you will be doing a good act, since it seems you have a conscience of sorts. If it is a matter of money——"

This time it was Cane who interrupted. "You insult me," he vociferated shrilly. "I am an honest lawyer——"

"Rather an anomaly," interpolated Enistor scoffingly.

"An honest lawyer," continued the little man sturdily, "and as such I am bound to consider the wishes of my client. You are asking me to commit a felony, Mr. Enistor. How dare you! How dare you!" he mopped his perspiring brow. "What have you seen in me to lead you to make so infamous a proposition?"

"I thought I saw some vestiges of common sense," said Enistor dryly. "But it seems that you are a fool with a conscience!"

"I have a conscience, but I am no fool, Mr. Enistor! I have a great mind to tell the world at large how you endeavoured to tempt me!"

"If you do, I shall put forth a counter-slander saying that you came down here to tempt *me*."

"To tempt you? To tempt you, sir?"

"Why not? If I say that you offered to destroy the last will and substitute the first provided I gave you a large sum of money, who will refuse to believe the statement?"

"Any one who knows me."

"Ah. But the whole world does not know you, Mr. Cane. Your immediate friends may reject the calumny, but the majority of people won't. My word is as good as yours, you know!"

"You will not dare——"

"Oh yes, I shall dare if you dare!"

"Am I dealing with a gentleman or a scoundrel?" asked Cane, appealing to the carved ceiling.

"Pooh! Pooh!" said Enistor cynically. "What is the use of calling names? Why, a gentleman is only a scoundrel who is clever enough not to be found out."

"I disagree: I disagree entirely."

"I thought you would. You are not strong enough to be original. However, all this chatter will not alter circumstances. My sister has sold me in favour of this—what do you say his name is?"

"Mr. Montrose. Douglas Montrose!" said Cane sulkily. "He is——"

"Won't you sit down and explain? You will be more comfortable."

"No I won't," said Cane sharply and still fretted by the proposition which had been made to him. "I doubt if it would not be better for me to retire after what you have said."

"Oh," said Enistor ironically, "your duty to your late lamented client forbids."

"It does, and therefore I remain to explain. But I shall not sit down again in your presence, nor drink your wine, nor eat your food."

"Better wait until you are asked, Mr. Cane. Go on and tell me about Montrose."

Confounded by his host's disconcerting calm, the little lawyer came to the point, but delivered his explanation standing. "Mr. Montrose is a young Scotchman, poor and handsome and clever. He is a poet and a journalist, who lives in a Bloomsbury garret, ambitious of literary fame. Eighteen months ago he saved Lady Staunton's life when her horses bolted in Hyde Park. He stopped them at the risk of his limbs, and prevented a serious accident!"

"Silly ass," muttered Enistor, "if Lucy had died then, the money would have come to me. Go on."

Appalled by this crudely evil speech, Cane started back. "Are you a man or a demon, Mr. Enistor?"

"You can ask riddles when you have delivered your message. Though, to be sure," said Enistor, sitting down, "there is little need. This handsome young pauper paid court to my sister, who was always weak and silly. His sham heroism and his good looks and effusive compliments worked on her feeble mind, and she made him her heir. Am I right?"

"Lady Staunton made Mr. Montrose her heir certainly," said Cane, shutting up his little black bag and putting on his hat to leave. "But your description of my new client is wrong. He does not flatter any one, and his heroism was not a sham. Nor was your sister feeble-minded, but a very clever — —"

"Woman," ended Enistor sharply, "and being so became the prey of this adventurer. Well, Mr. Cane, now that you have delivered your message you can go, and I shall be obliged if you will send me the one thousand pounds as soon as possible."

"Oh, certainly," cried Cane eagerly.

Enistor saw why he spoke so agreeably. "You think that by taking the one thousand pounds I condone the testament of Lady Staunton. Perhaps you are right, but I have more strings to my bow than one. I have been infamously treated and I shall have my revenge."

"You cannot revenge yourself on your sister who is dead," said Cane rebukingly, "and to punish Mr. Montrose, who is perfectly innocent of harming you, would not be the act of a Christian."

"Ah, but you see I am nothing so feeble-minded as a Christian."

"What are you then?" Cane stared.

"A wronged man, who intends to be revenged."

"I shall protect my client," cried the lawyer vigorously.

"Naturally, your fees will be larger if you do. But don't protect him at the cost of my character, or it will be the worse for your own."

"I am not afraid!"

"Indeed you are! Horribly afraid. However, you needn't faint on my doorstep as that would be inconvenient. Good-day: your trap is waiting."

Cane got away at once, quite convinced that Enistor was not wholly in his right mind. His rosy cheeks were pale as he drove away, and his courage was dashed by Enistor's unscrupulous threat.

"He is dangerous," thought the lawyer. "I must hold my tongue!" and he did.

CHAPTER IV
PLOTTING

The prophecy of Narvaez should have softened the blow to Enistor in the moment of its fulfilment. But it did not, for the simple reason that he had tried his best to disbelieve the Spaniard, in spite of his knowledge of the man's powers. Don Pablo, as the result of prying beyond the boundaries of the visible, possessed in active working super-senses latent in the ordinary man, and so he could literally see through a brick wall. Certainly his vision was not invariably clear, and at times the details of his prognostications were incorrect. In the present instance he had foretold that Enistor should receive his bad news by letter, whereas Mr. Cane had come down personally to convey the disagreeable intelligence. But the actual fact that Enistor would lose the money had been proved beyond all doubt, and the Squire found the one undeniable truth so unpleasant that he was careless about minor mistakes.

As soon as Cane, without bite or sup, had driven away in the direction of Perchton, Enistor made his way across the moors to the back-country where Narvaez had his abode. It was impossible that he could keep the knowledge of his bad fortune to himself, and moreover he wanted advice with regard to his future actions. The Squire was clever as men go, and usually decided all matters for himself; but in this instance it was necessary to consult a mastermind. Don Pablo was not only a shrewd and highly educated man, versed in knowledge of the world, but also possessed super-physical information which was both dangerous and useful. That is, the lore was dangerous to any who did not possess the spirit of love, and useful to an unscrupulous and wholly selfish man. Both Enistor and his master thought only of themselves and were prepared to crush without remorse all that stood in their way. At the present moment the unknown Montrose was an obstacle in Enistor's path and he wished Narvaez to assist in his removal. The Spaniard would only give his services if he saw that their use would benefit himself. And as the Squire knew that the wily old man wished him to remain poor in order to retain mastery over him, it was not likely that he would help him to gain a fortune. Enistor therefore was not certain that he would be aided, and more for the sake of talking himself free of care than for any other reason sought the cottage of the magician.

And Don Pablo's abode was really and truly a four-roomed cottage, where he lived along with a simple-minded old Cornish woman of sixty, who attended to his few wants. Enistor knew that Narvaez was immensely rich, and wondered why he should live so penuriously and humbly. But the man was almost wholly devoid of desire for things which mankind covets. He ate and drank sparingly: he cared nothing for society: his dress was plain but neat, and he was too much taken up with study to entertain. Narvaez, as his neighbour soon found out, was consumed by a passion for power: not that kind of power which is displayed openly by royalty or politicians or merchant-princes, but the secret power which sways the destinies of individuals and nations without apparent sign. For this he studied day and night, and crossed constantly the boundaries between the worlds visible and invisible. He obtained no physical benefit from the exercise of such command, but the passion of hidden sovereignty satisfied his soul, and that was all he cared about. He had long since risen above the sphere wherein the virtues and vices of men dispute pre-eminence, and lived above the healthy necessary turmoil of ordinary life to reign in solitude as a cold, calm, intellectual and merciless tyrant, doing evil because it gratified Self. He disobeyed the law of love which is giving, and isolated himself in a kingdom of his own, which his desire for rule had cut off from the great empire of God. His sole connection with men and women was to destroy their protecting will and make them slaves to his whims. In this way he acted with regard to Enistor, else he would not have taught the man anything about dark magic. But Narvaez knew well that Enistor, possessed of as fierce and unscrupulous a nature as his own, and almost as powerful a will, would never be a slave. Consequently he was obliged to act cautiously in his association with him. Enistor, if he became too learned in forbidden lore, might well become Don Pablo's rival, to dispute the bad sovereignty which the Spaniard loved. As a matter of fact Narvaez would not have meddled with the Cornish squire at all but that he knew that a common danger menaced both, which Enistor, through his daughter, might avert. Narvaez was clever and powerful, and wholly given to self-worship, but he was by no means omnipotent, and at times it was necessary to defend his position. Thus by the offer to teach Enistor how to realise his ambitions, he managed to make the man more or less obedient: but there was always the danger of revolt should Enistor learn too thoroughly the laws of the invisible world, which interpenetrates the visible. Don Pablo, however, was content with the position of affairs, as his pupil was not yet strong enough to measure swords. And before he was, the Spaniard hoped to secure his ends and leave Enistor in the lurch.

The cottage was of grey stone, a clumsy rugged-looking habitation set on the side of a purple-clothed hill, beside a grass-grown lane, which meandered down the valley. On the slope of the hill were many disused mining shafts with huge mounds of earth and ruined buildings beside them. The hilltops had been a Roman camp, and the boundaries could still be defined. In the centre and amongst many gigantic stones was a sacrificial altar of the Druids, with grooves cut in its hardness so that the blood of the victims might stream to the ground. Alice never liked this unholy hill, as she was sensitive enough to feel the influence which clung round it. But Narvaez had established his home beside the miniature mountain, because on moonless nights he could perform uncanny ceremonies on the altar, which was given over to the Dark Powers he worshipped and propitiated. Enistor had likewise taken part in these sacrilegious doings and shivered at the memory of certain things, when he sighted the sinister grey monoliths which crowned the hill. Great as was his courage, it was not entirely proof against the deadly influences of the evil beings who haunted the place, although in a lesser degree than Narvaez he could compel them to service by performing certain rites.

Enistor was ushered into Don Pablo's study by the housekeeper, a brown-faced cheery old woman, too simple-minded to understand her master's weird powers. The apartment was of no great size, and the limited space was but sparsely furnished. There were only a table, which served as a desk, two chairs, a well-filled bookcase and a ponderous iron safe, wherein Narvaez stored what valuables he had by him. The walls were draped with dull red cloth, and the floor, oddly enough, was covered with a black carpet. The effect was menacing and impressive. When the visitor entered, a fireplace wherein large logs flamed faced him, while opposite the one window looking out on to the hilltop was a closed door leading to a sealed apartment, which Don Pablo allowed no one to enter into save himself and his pupil. Across the passage was a dining-room together with a tiny kitchen and a bedroom for the housekeeper at the back. The cottage itself was placed in a disorderly uncultivated garden surrounded by a loosely built stone wall. There was no upstairs, and the house being roofed with slate covered with moss presented a sombre appearance. In its greyness it resembled a huge toad squatting amongst the heather.

"How can you bear a fire on this hot day?" asked Enistor, throwing himself into the vacant chair and speaking irritably.

"You are in that kind of humour which seeks any outlet for its relief," was the Spaniard's irrelevant reply. "How often have I told you that it is necessary for you to get complete command of your temper. I have a fire because this body I occupy just now is nearly worn out and requires artificial heat to sustain it."

"Why don't you get a new one?" demanded the visitor still crossly.

"Some day I shall," rejoined Narvaez significantly, "at present this one serves me tolerably well. I control it thoroughly: you do not manage yours properly: it is your master, Enistor. Ah! you have much to learn."

"I have reason to be cross."

"No one has any reason to be cross. To lose one's temper simply shows that one is not yet free from ordinary human limitations. However, at your stage of learning I excuse you. It is hard to lose a large income, as you have done."

"What, you know — —?"

"Not by any super-physical means, Enistor," said Narvaez, coolly leaning back in his chair. "I walked to the top of the hill with a field-glass, and saw that you had a visitor. As so few people come here, it is only logical on my part to assume that the man was some messenger sent to tell you of Lady Staunton's death and your own loss."

"Well, the news did not come in a letter, as you prophesied," snapped Enistor.

"I am not the Pope to be infallible," said Don Pablo dryly, "and the matter is so trivial that I did not examine into things sufficiently to be entirely certain of details."

"Trivial to you: not to me!" said the Squire gloomily.

"Nonsense! Your possession of that income is only delayed. You have not lost it altogether!"

Enistor looked up sharply. "Did you make an invisible third at my interview with Cane?"

"I?" Don Pablo shrugged his aged shoulders. "Do you think that I have nothing to do but to waste my time in that way? No! I only say that you will regain the money, because I shall assist you to get it. You must have your price even though it is but a temporary one."

"What do you mean by temporary?" asked Enistor unpleasantly.

"Any one who works for money, or earthly fame, or earthly power has to surrender what he gains when death comes. But he who labours to acquire super-physical powers as I do—those powers which can dominate men without their knowing, gets what he can never lose, however many the deaths or lives!"

"I shall work for that later, Master. At present I require money so as to take my proper position in the world, and sway men at will."

"A limited ambition," scoffed Narvaez. "However, what you desire you shall acquire, as you won't let me have your daughter without a price."

"Would you do something for nothing yourself, Don Pablo?"

"No," said the magician honestly. "I take what I want if I am strong enough to do so. Otherwise I buy what I require. Nothing for nothing and something for something—if there is no other way of getting it. That is my rule."

"It is the rule of the majority of mankind."

"True, my friend," chuckled Narvaez, settling himself comfortably. "Mankind has a long way to travel before the law of love is learned."

"The law of love?"

"You give all and ask no return! Think of it: how dull life would be then, Enistor! However, we have argued enough, and my time is valuable. What about your interview with this lawyer? I must have details if I am to assist you."

Enistor looked at his master with a sneer. "I should have thought that a man with your powers would have known everything without requiring explanations."

"If it had been worth my while I would have made myself acquainted with all that took place," said the other man blandly; "but your affairs do not interest me save the necessity of paying your price. Well?"

The Squire looked again at Narvaez, and this time with gloomy distaste. It was often borne in upon him how entirely selfish Don Pablo was. But by this time he knew beyond question that those who take the Left-hand Path are forgetful of all save themselves. And Enistor could scarcely blame Narvaez for owning a quality which was almost as highly developed in his own nature. "Might is Right!" is the rule of black magic, and the survival of the fittest is the sole way to attain supremacy. Enistor had fully committed himself to the worship of his own being, yet there was sufficient good in him to struggle at times against the isolating power of selfishness. However it was worse than useless to argue away accepted facts, so he swallowed his anger and quietly detailed all that had taken place.

"Hum!" said Narvaez, smoothing his wrinkled face when the last word was spoken. "You have made my task more difficult than was necessary."

"In what way?" scowled the Squire, who disliked correction.

"In several ways," was the serene response. "Your idea of threatening Cane was a good one, and had you called me to your assistance I could have worked along those lines. The man—from what you say—is weak, and my power added to yours would have secured the destruction of the second will, and the substitution of the first. Then you would have got the money without trouble. By weakening in your attack, you have simply turned Cane into your enemy."

"He won't dare to say anything, if that is what you mean."

"It is not what I mean, Enistor. Of course, since a lawyer, like Cæsar's wife, should be above reproach, Cane will not speak lest you should accuse him of offering to suppress the second will. But that doesn't much matter. The point is that you had him at a disadvantage and did not press your point. A well-directed thought would have brought me to your house, and I could have compelled the man to yield."

"I am not so sure of that. He is honest."

"What does that matter?" asked Don Pablo, opening his eyes contemptuously. "Honest or not, I should have obsessed him to such a degree that he would have committed himself too far to retreat. Of course if he was guarded my control would have effected nothing. But our Adversary only protects Alice, and in this instance would not have interfered. And yet," Narvaez suddenly looked round, as though aware of some new influence, "he might have prevented my exercise of power. It is necessary for the money to go to Montrose so that the Chaldean Drama should be played out in this set of lives."

"Is Montrose the other man you spoke of at dinner last night?"

Don Pablo threw up his hand to compel silence, closed his eyes to shut out the world of sense and listened intently. As he did so, his face grew dark and angry. "I defy you: I defy you!" he said vehemently, addressing some invisible person, as it appeared to Enistor. "Plot as you will, I can counterplot!" then he was silent for a moment, and opening his eyes lowered his hand. "The Adversary," he said quietly to his guest, but still looked fierce. "He is aware of our schemes, and says they will not succeed, if he can prevent their success. Well, I shall pit my strength against his."

"The Adversary then is not absolutely certain of success?" asked Enistor.

"No. Because man has free-will. If Montrose and Alice are guided by the Adversary, our task will indeed be difficult. But if you and I can make either stumble, the game will end in our favour. As I said, Enistor, this loss of money is the beginning of the drama. You can see for yourself, because by its going to Montrose it brings him on to the stage. And yet," added Narvaez with a furious gesture, "had you called me in to deal with that lawyer, I might have suppressed the second will and have prevented Montrose coming into the matter. The Adversary told me just now that he would have intervened also, but Cane being weak and having free-will—as all men have—could not have stood out against my domination."

"Well," said Enistor gloomily; "it seems that owing to my ignorance——"

"Your folly," interrupted the other sharply.

"Folly if you will then. But owing to my ignorance or folly we have lost the first move in the game. What now?"

Narvaez shrugged. "We must take a roundabout way instead of going by the direct path. That is closed by your not pressing your advantage with Cane. Now Montrose will obtain the money! Very good. He can retain it until I get it back from him to give it to you."

"The money is rightfully mine," cried Enistor vehemently, "and come what may I intend to gain it!"

"You will never gain it if you bluster and fume in that way," said Don Pablo coldly; "keep your temper and self-control, and we shall soon be at grips with the Adversary. He is no mean antagonist, I assure you."

"Well, Master, what is to be done? I leave myself in your hands!"

"I wouldn't assist you otherwise." Narvaez considered for a few moments. "I think it will be best to send Alice to London for a few months. The time of her stay will depend upon her chances of falling in love with Montrose."

Enistor jumped up and stamped. "She doesn't know Montrose," he declared in an angry manner, "she will never know him if I can help it."

"You are unable to help it," said Narvaez frigidly. "The Karma of Chaldea is bound to bring Montrose and Alice together. This much I am sure of, although I am ignorant of the details. Well, let us carry the war into the enemy's camp, Enistor. With this thousand pounds which you inherit, give Alice a few months in London on the plea that she requires a gay life to cheer her up. She will meet Montrose and he will fall in love with her. I am certain of this as his fate and her fate are intermingled. Then you can give your consent to the marriage——"

"What about your desire to marry Alice?" interrupted the Squire, much puzzled.

"That can be gratified later," said Don Pablo coolly. "Don't you see what I mean, Enistor? When Alice desires to marry Montrose, you will naturally invite your proposed son-in-law here to acquaint yourself with his character. Once he is on the spot"—Narvaez smiled cruelly and drew a deep breath—"I think you can safely leave him to me."

"What will you do?"

"Never mind. I have a plan in my head which may or may not succeed. There is no need to tell you what it is. You shall see its results. Your work is to send Alice to London."

"I don't quite understand," said Enistor, trying to read his master's thoughts, but in vain. "But I shall obey your instructions. But if Alice is to meet Montrose in society I fear it will be difficult to induce her to go out for enjoyment so soon after her aunt's death."

"Oh, Montrose as the heir of Lady Staunton will feel the same way. But it is not necessary for the two to meet at public functions. A quiet evening here, a little dinner there, and the introduction is accomplished. You need not trouble about details, Enistor. The accumulated result of good and evil, which we call Karma, will bring them together."

"You are willing to surrender Alice, I see."

"Oh, dear me, no! Montrose can make love to her until he is in my net. Afterwards, when the money comes to you and Montrose comes to the gallows, Alice can be my wife."

"The gallows. You don't mean——"

"I mean nothing at present," interrupted Narvaez impatiently, "but you can't fight battles with squirts. Montrose is in your path and mine, so he has to be removed. The means may be unpleasant, but they will not harm you in any way. I assure you of that emphatically."

"Will they harm Alice?"

"Only through her affections; not otherwise. What a heap of scruples you have, Enistor," sneered the old man; "one would think you were a school-girl instead of a grown man. You don't care for Montrose, or for your daughter."

"Not at all," admitted Enistor selfishly. "All the same, murder——!"

"Oh, if the word frightens you, call it blood-atonement. And the restitution of the fortune may be managed without the sacrifice of Montrose's life, if you will insist upon this silly weakness. If you wish to tread the Left-hand Path, Enistor, you must get rid of scruples. Trample on every one, slay, ruin, devastate: as the stronger you have the right to do so."

The Squire winced at this abominable teaching, although in his innermost heart he subscribed to it. And after all, as he thought, in the world of to-day the weaker is still the prey of the stronger. He was only carrying out more thoroughly what every one did in a lesser degree. Without further pangs he gave in to the necessity of Montrose being removed by a legal death. "But his hanging will involve the commission of a murder by him," he said suddenly.

"Perhaps," said the other man ambiguously. "But you had better wait and see, Enistor. I can't waste time in arguing down your scruples. If you can't face these things, leave the matter alone and deal with the future danger yourself. But remember that only Alice can describe what that danger is, and she must become my wife to be trained as a clairvoyante."

"You didn't want her to love Hardwick because you said the passion would destroy her powers," said Enistor irrelevantly. "What about her love for this Montrose? Won't that do harm?"

"Unfortunately it will," sighed Narvaez vexedly, "but I can't prevent the blossoming of the love. The great law of Karma is stronger than I am. I can only deal with the free-will of both and warp their natures if possible. I think you had better go now. I have much to do!"

Enistor scowled at the imperious tone and tried—as he often did—to match his will against that of Narvaez. It suddenly came to him that he could find an easier way out of the difficulty and reduce Don Pablo's power over him by acting in the ordinary selfish way sanctioned by custom. "One moment," he said testily. "Montrose has the money, it is true, and legally there is no chance of getting it from him. But if he becomes my son-in-law, I shall be able to keep the income in the family."

"Quite so," assented Narvaez indifferently. "If you want the money for the family—to build up the Enistor fortunes as county people I suppose you mean—your suggestion is excellent. Montrose can take your name and along with his wife will be great in the land. Where you will be I leave you to say."

"I don't want Montrose to be great in the land, and I don't suppose that he has the brains to become so. But he and Alice will probably allow me to handle the income and——"

"And you will use it for your own advancement. Eh?"

"Why not? My advancement as head of the family will mean theirs."

"Probably, if you wish to waste time, energy and cash in building up your decayed race. But Montrose may have his own ideas to carry out, and those may not include consent to your possession of the family purse. Complete ownership of the money makes him stronger than you are."

"Stronger than I am? We shall see," and Enistor laughed at the idea.

"Very likely, when it is too late, you probably will see, and won't be pleased with what you do see. However, it is your business, not mine. I can return to Spain and learn what I wish to learn in other ways."

"But the teaching you are giving me?"

Narvaez sneered. "With an obedient son-in-law possessed of five thousand a year you will not want the teaching."

The Squire looked as alarmed as a self-confident man well could. He had scarcely counted upon this attitude being taken by his master. "I want the teaching more than I want the money," he confessed uneasily.

"You can have both if you will permit me to carry out my plans," said Don Pablo, acidly polite. "Otherwise you must be satisfied to sink back into the ordinary rank and file of humanity. My fee for teaching super-physical knowledge is possession of your daughter as my wife. Therefore your idea of securing the handling of this money by forwarding her marriage with Montrose does not meet with my approval. You can take your choice. I—as you will be pleased to observe—do not coerce you in any way."

"You can't," cried the Squire with sudden fury.

"Let us leave it at that," rejoined the Spaniard amiably.

Enistor stamped, swore under his breath and bit his nails angrily, while Narvaez smiled in a hatefully bland manner. Certainly the marriage of Montrose and Alice would bring back the money to the family; but it might not—and here the egotist saw danger—put it into his own particular pocket. Lady Staunton's heir might be self-willed, obstinate and foolish—there was no knowing what qualities he might possess likely to thwart his proposed father-in-law's schemes. And should he prove to be recalcitrant, Enistor recognised that the marriage would only make matters worse. He would gain by it neither the teaching nor the fortune, and would have bartered the substance for the shadow. To have the money would be good: to acquire the secret lore would be better: to have both would be best of all. And both he could have for certain if he agreed to allow Narvaez to take command. For the teaching would make him a minor god, while the five thousand a year—even if he got it, which was doubtful—would not even make him a millionaire.

"You remind me," said the tempter, smiling as hatefully as ever, "of an ass between two bundles of hay. With my help I repeat you can have both."

"The money and the teaching: the teaching and the money." Enistor opened and shut his hands, drawing deep breaths and thinking profoundly.

"Exactly! On condition that I marry Alice."

"I agree." Enistor came to the decision swiftly.

"Understand! I am to have a free hand and your obedience."

The other man nodded, not knowing how fatal to himself was that sign of acquiescence. At that moment he stood at the cross-roads, free to choose good or evil, and his fierce greed led him to take the Left-hand Path down which this dark guide beckoned him to destruction. With a little chuckling laugh Narvaez received his victim's allegiance, and turned to his work. Then in the same tone of voice he made exactly the same remark as he had made when Enistor first hesitated. "I think you had better go now; I have much to do."

Enistor thus abruptly dismissed returned home pondering deeply on the way. By this time he was sufficiently infected with the cynicism of Narvaez to accept the situation, and to do what was necessary to turn Alice into a decoy for Montrose. Whether the bird would be lured into Don Pablo's nest he could not be sure, as Cane might warn his client of danger. Enistor now saw how very foolish he had been to make the man his enemy. But he comforted himself with the idea that the little lawyer would not dare to speak in the face of a possible accusation of having offered to suppress the second will. Also, even if he did speak, Montrose being in love would never listen to him. On the whole therefore, Enistor felt confident on reflection that the fortunate young man would appear at Tremore. Then he could be left to the malignant devices of Don Pablo Narvaez.

That evening at dinner Enistor abruptly announced the death of his sister, the loss of the money, and the good fortune of Mr. Douglas Montrose. He listened quietly to Alice's regrets, then informed her that she could go to London for a month in a very short space of time. The girl demurred.

"I can't go out into society when Aunt Lucy is dead," she said.

"There's no need for you to go into society," said her father, who anticipated the objection. "You can stay quietly in town and enjoy yourself in a small way. This place is rather dull for so young a girl as you are. The question is who can chaperon you, seeing that your Aunt Lucy is dead."

"Mrs. Barrast can, father," said Alice eagerly and much flushed, for the prospect of escaping from that gloomy house was delightful.

"Who is she?"

"Julian's—I mean Mr. Hardwick's sister. I met her at Perchton last Christmas, and so did you."

"Oh, I remember; that frivolous little fool of a woman with no more brains than a sparrow. Yes! you can go to her, if she will have you."

"She will be very glad," said Alice eagerly. "She is fond of me."

"Very good." Enistor rose deliberately. "Then that is settled!"

CHAPTER V
THE MEETING

Having settled that Alice should go to London in that singularly short and abrupt conversation, Enistor refused to discuss the matter further. He ran up to town himself within the next four days, not so much to appear at his sister's funeral, which he duly attended, as to get the promised thousand pounds. He did not meet Montrose, since he purposely kept out of the young man's way, in spite of Cane's suggestion that there should be a meeting. Enistor, instructed by his master, decided that it would be best to let Montrose fall in love with Alice, and approach him in the character of a proposed son-in-law. Of course the Squire had no doubt but what the affections of the young people would be engaged as Narvaez predicted. The fulfilment of the prophecy concerning the loss of the money had considerably strengthened his faith in the Spaniard's powers.

With Cane the Squire got on much better, as he was anxious to obliterate, for obvious reasons, the bad impression he had made on the little man. Enistor pretended that he had only acted as he had done to see if Cane was honest, and professed himself quite willing to be content with his scanty inheritance. Whether the solicitor believed him or not it was impossible to say, but he feigned a belief and behaved with extraordinary civility to Enistor. Cane even went so far as to pay the thousand pounds out of his private account, so that the Squire should not have to wait for the winding up of Lady Staunton's estate. By the acceptance of this money, it was tacitly understood that Enistor would not contest the will, and Cane drew a long breath of relief when the receipt was given. There certainly was no chance that the second will could be upset, but the lawyer did not wish for any public action to be taken, lest mention should be made of the visit to Tremore. For even though that visit had been authorised by the dead woman, the vague threat of the Squire might come out in open court. Cane was quite innocent of wishing to destroy the will, and could deny the possible assertion on oath. But he knew well that however guiltless a man may be, there are always those who quote the "No smoke without fire" proverb. Therefore Cane was sincerely glad to have the matter settled without dispute, and for that very reason had given Enistor a cheque on his private account. When the Squire departed, the little man felt that all danger was at an end.

Enistor arrived back at Polwellin in very good spirits, as for many a long year he had not handled so large a sum of money. Being of a luxurious nature he bought many unnecessary things, and spent on himself a considerable sum which could have been used for better purposes. However, on the sprat-to-catch-a-mackerel theory, he set aside a certain ample amount for Alice's season in London. Acting the part of a fond father, he told her that she was to spare no expense, but to have all she wanted in the matter of clothes and jewellery and enjoyment. The girl was secretly amazed at this sudden kindness on the part of her usually neglectful parent, but being young, and being a woman, she gladly took advantage of the opportunity to purchase pretty things. In the selection of frocks and hats and feminine frippery she had the benefit of Mrs. Barrast's taste, and the little woman congratulated her on having so lavish a father.

"You will like Amy when you know her better," Hardwick had said to Alice, when the subject of chaperonage was broached; "but you will soon grow tired of her. Her sole idea in life is chiffons. She will be delighted to introduce you into her particular set of frivolous kill-time wastrels, but with your nature, Alice, you will never meet a man at her house likely to appeal to you as a husband!"

This was perfectly true, as in spite of her youth Miss Enistor was a thoughtful girl, who wanted more food for her mind than an endless round of bridge-parties and whist-drives and Cinderella dances and theatre visits, coupled with airy gossip about this person and that. Mrs. Barrast was only too pleased to chaperon a tolerably pretty girl of good family who was possessed of plenty of money, and she did her best to give her guest an amusing time. But what Julian prophesied soon came to pass. Alice grew weary of the dainty little woman's frivolity and shallow nature. It was like an industrious bee living with a butterfly.

"You are a darling," said Mrs. Barrast when Alice had been a week in the charming house in Hans Crescent; "quite the nicest thing I ever met. And your good looks don't clash with mine. That is so satisfactory, isn't it?"

"I am not good-looking," said Alice soberly.

"Of course not. Good-looking is a word which one applies to a man. But you are lovely in a moonlight, misty kind of vapoury way," babbled the other. "I think you look charming in that mourning, and Madame Coralie has such good taste. I wish you would marry Julian, dear: you are just the sort of romantic head-in-the-clouds darling he loves."

"Julian would not suit me, nor would I suit Julian," said Miss Enistor decidedly. "We have arranged to be brother and sister."

Mrs. Barrast sighed. "Such a dull relationship. Frederick and I live together something in the same way. Of course he's my husband and I'm his wife, although I don't know why I ever married him. But he goes his own way to Blue Books and politics and vestry-meetings and those horridly dull things, while I go mine, seeking for a heart that will understand me."

"That is a dangerous quest, Mrs. Barrast," said Alice seriously.

Mrs. Barrast pounced on her guest with many kisses. "You chilly darling, why don't you call me Amy, as I have asked you to again and again!"

"Well then, Amy, you should not let all these young men make love to you."

"But they will, my dear. There is something about me which draws them in spite of themselves, poor dears. And after all I don't mean anything wrong, you know, Alice. Platonic friendships are my delight."

"That is a dangerous word between a married woman and an unmarried man."

"Dangerous quest: dangerous word. My dear, you talk as if you were one hundred and forty years of age," cried Mrs. Barrast petulantly.

"I have lived much alone and have thought deeply, Amy."

"Oh, my dear, you shouldn't think. It always wrinkles one dreadfully to think, you know. Frederick thinks and just look at him. One would take him to be my grandfather."

"I like Mr. Barrast very much," said Alice quietly, and she did, for the master of the house was the only person to whom she could talk sensibly.

"Run away with him then. No," Mrs. Barrast reflected, "don't do that. After all Frederick is rich and my husband, though I don't know why I married him."

"Would you have married him had he been poor?"

Mrs. Barrast screamed in a pretty playful way. "Of course not, darling. What odd things you say. All Frederick's attraction lies in his money and his brains. He is clever, you know, and is too much taken up with politics to look at any other woman, which is so satisfactory. I was so poor when I met him that I was glad to marry him. And I'm sure I make him a very good wife, Alice," ended Mrs. Barrast in an injured tone, "so you needn't raise your eyebrows in that nasty sort of way."

"I only meant— —"

"I know what you mean. It's sure to be something to do with Dr. Watts's hymns, as you are that sort of girl. I wish you weren't so particular about mourning, dear, as then I could take you to heaps and heaps of places where one can have a really good time. We'll go to Hurlingham this afternoon. Now you can't refuse. I've set my heart on your going to Hurlingham."

It was little use Alice refusing, as Mrs. Barrast was one of those desperately persistent people who always get their own way. Miss Enistor, who had been fond of her Aunt Lucy, really wished to go out as little as possible, and but that she was anxious to escape from gloomy Tremore and the attentions of Don Pablo, would never have come to live with the butterfly. However, her hostess was so kind, and Alice was so young, and the contrast between London life and Cornish life was so great, that she really did enjoy herself immensely. Besides there was always Frederick to talk to, a tall grave man with iron-grey hair, who treated his pretty young wife in a most indulgent manner, and was as amused with her shallow frivolity as Richelieu must have been with the pranks of his kittens. There was really no harm in the dainty little woman and, in spite of her platonic philanderings, she never gave Frederick any serious cause for rebuke. One cannot be angry with a morsel of thistledown, and that is the best description of Mrs. Barrast. Always charmingly dressed and delightfully vivacious, she floated from house to house in a frolicsome fairy kind of way. Dullness fled when Mrs. Barrast entered a room.

It was strange that so airy and nimble-witted a woman should be the sister of a stolid giant like Julian, with his serious views of art and life. But he was very fond of Amy Barrast, although she flouted his advice and told him frequently that he was as dull as tombs, a witticism she had picked up from an American admirer. Hardwick came several times to London while Alice stayed in Hans Crescent, but always returned to his beloved west country, as the frivolity of his sister's circle was altogether too much for him. By this time he had accepted the rôle of Miss Enistor's brother, and the two were most confidential.

"Are you tired of all this, Alice?" asked Julian, after a particularly frivolous luncheon. "This rubbish must bore one of your thoughtful disposition."

Alice, who was looking unusually charming, laughed gaily. "I have left my thoughtful disposition at Tremore," she said in a light tone. "While I am in Rome I must do as the Romans do."

"Do?" said Hardwick; "they don't do anything!"

"But they do, Julian. They work harder than any labourer to kill time. I do not think that I should like to lead this life always, but it is a change from the dullness of Polwellin, you know. The month I have been here has improved my health and spirits. I am sure that I thought too much."

"Possibly! All work and no play is as bad as all play and no work. When do you return?"

"I have no settled time to return. Father says that I can stay as long as I like. Though of course I don't want to outstay my welcome."

"You won't, Alice. Never think that. Amy likes to have you here, and Frederick says that you are the most sensible girl he ever met. You should go with Amy to Cowes later on."

Alice shook her head. "I am not sure. I must go back some time or another, as father won't let me remain away for ever. Besides I really think that I shall grow weary of pleasure. Blue skies and constant sunshine bore one."

"Yes, I quite understand. But remember when you come back you will again be exposed to the attentions of that old mummy."

Alice shuddered. "Don Pablo? Is he as often at Tremore as ever?"

"More often. And when he isn't at Tremore, your father goes to his cottage on the moors. I can't understand why your father likes him so much. There seems to be something evil about Narvaez."

"Oh!" Alice laid a trembling hand on his arm; "have you felt that also?"

"Yes. I'm not a sensitive chap as a rule, but Narvaez makes me uncomfortable—just like Mr. Hyde in Stevenson's story, you know. Whatever you do, don't consent to be his wife, Alice."

"I certainly shall not, whatever my father may say. At the worst I can always marry you."

"That isn't a compliment," murmured Hardwick, mortified.

"Well, you know what I mean. I respect you and like you, even if I don't love you, Julian. And if I did marry you I should never give you cause to complain of coldness on my part."

"Oh, Alice"—his face lighted up.

"No! No! No! The compact still stands. Until I am driven into a corner we are only brother and sister."

"Of course. It's an odd arrangement."

"Well, I admit that, and only a really kind-hearted, sensible man such as you are would understand and keep to such an arrangement. Sometimes I think I am doing wrong in holding you to our compact, but on reflection

I don't think that I am doing wrong. If you loved me as a man should love a woman, it would be different and then I should be playing with fire. But you don't."

"No," said Julian honestly, "you are quite right. I like you: I have a deep affection for you, and at all costs would protect your happiness. But I am quite sure now that I don't love you in the way you would like to be loved."

Alice drew a deep breath of relief. "How nice to hear you talk so reasonably, Julian. We quite understand one another, don't we?"

"Quite," he hesitated, and then spoke softly. "Have you seen any one who——"

"Of course I haven't," interrupted the girl hastily; "you said that I should meet with no one to suit me here. Not that I am looking out for a husband, you know, Julian!"

"I do know. All the same you are sure to come across Prince Charming some day, and then I shall surrender my guardianship to him. You are certain to choose some nice fellow, who won't mind our continuing our brother and sister arrangement when you are Mrs. Somebody."

"H'm!" said the girl dubiously; "if Mr. Somebody loves me, he may object to a triangle of that sort. Besides, you may marry yourself, Julian."

"I may," said Hardwick in his stolid way, "but at present I am at your service as a stop-gap husband if Don Pablo and your father drive you into a corner, Alice."

"How dreadfully immoral a stop-gap husband sounds!" laughed Miss Enistor, but appreciated the offer all the same. It was impossible to combat alone two strong natures like those of her father and Narvaez; therefore to have Hardwick on her side was a great gain. Nothing would ever induce her to marry Don Pablo. Alice was certain of that.

But as speedy events proved it was not necessary for Julian to hold himself at Miss Enistor's disposal in this loyal way. Six weeks after Alice was in London, circumstances brought about the meeting with Montrose. The girl knew that this young man had inherited her aunt's money, but as Enistor, when informing her of the fact, had said nothing very bitter, she had no grudge against the fortunate legatee. Certainly she regretted the loss for her father's sake, but decided with instinctive fairness that Lady Staunton had a right to do what she would with her own. Alice had seen but little of her aunt in past years, although the old lady had sometimes invited her to pay a visit. Consequently she had heard nothing of Montrose, and wondered what he was like. When Mrs. Barrast mentioned the name,

Alice was curious to see the young man. And there was every chance that she would, as it appeared that Mrs. Barrast's doctor wished to bring him to dinner.

"And Dr. Eberstein is such a delightful man that any friend of his is certain to be a darling," babbled the little woman. "You haven't met my doctor, have you, dear. He attends me for nerves! I am a great sufferer from nerves, and I'm sure if those Christian martyrs they make such a fuss over suffered as much as I do, I quite understand them being praised. But I am sure they never did."

"Have you ever met Mr. Montrose?" asked Alice anxiously, for she wanted to have a sketch of the young man beforehand.

"No, my dear. Dr. Eberstein says he is very handsome and very nice, and has a lot of money!"

"That is quite true, Amy. Mr. Montrose inherited my aunt's money."

"Oh, my dear, what a disagreeable thing for you. I shall write to Dr. Eberstein and say that I can't ask him and his friend to dinner."

"Why not?" asked Alice bluntly.

"Well, you don't want to meet a man who has robbed you of——"

"He has not robbed me."

"Your father, I mean, Alice."

"Nor my father, Amy. Lady Staunton had a perfect right to do what she liked with her money. My father is not at all annoyed, nor am I."

"What a perfect, Christian feeling!" exclaimed Mrs. Barrast; "and how odd that you shouldn't be angry! How much money have you lost?"

"None at all," said Miss Enistor rather impatiently; "but my aunt left Mr. Montrose five thousand a year."

"Oh, how dreadful! My dear, if I were in your shoes I should scratch his eyes out. Of course your father is rich——"

"My father is very poor. I only had this season in town because my aunt did leave him a little money."

"Your father is poor! That makes his conduct and yours the odder, if there is such a word. I think it's very unjust, a sister not leaving her money to a brother and keeping it in the family. My dear," added Mrs. Barrast impressively, "this wrong must be put right. You shall marry this young man, if he is nice and agreeable. Then the money will come back to you."

"Don't make such plans, Amy. I don't want to marry any one."

"My dear, that's quite immoral."

"Oh, nonsense! If you begin to be a match-maker I shall refuse to meet Mr. Montrose."

"Then you don't want me to ask him to dinner?"

"Ask him if you like: only don't expect me to fall into his arms."

"As if I expected you to do anything so silly," said Mrs. Barrast, and withdrew to pen her invitation to the doctor and his friend. By this time, in her own mind, she was quite determined to arrange a match between Montrose and Alice, being one of those busybodies who will meddle with what does not concern them in the least. But Mrs. Barrast did not look at her proposed scheming in this light. She thought she was behaving very kindly to Alice.

The girl herself was really anxious to meet Montrose now that there was a chance of doing so. Never having felt the want of money, she had not given much thought to the loss of the inheritance, and did not know how vexed her father was to see Montrose get the income. Enistor had particularly refrained from expressing his vexation, since he did not wish Alice to be biased against the fortunate youth. Therefore Alice was quite prepared to be just towards Montrose, and to like him, if his personality appealed to her. A very unsophisticated maiden was Miss Enistor. In a similar position Mrs. Barrast would have schemed to recover the lost fortune by marriage, if the man had been as ugly as a Cyclops, and indeed, as can be seen, really did intend to right things in this way. But Alice was quite content to let Montrose remain a bachelor and enjoy the money after his own fashion.

Mr. Barrast had to attend to his political duties on the evening appointed for the dinner, which was perhaps the reason why his frivolous wife selected that special evening. Frederick was a kill-joy, she said, and moreover she did not wish to ask an extra woman to dinner. Mr. Montrose could attend to Alice and she, as the hostess, could attend to Dr. Eberstein. They would enjoy a pleasant meal, and afterwards could chat and have music in the drawing-room. Also Dr. Eberstein might be induced to tell their fortune, or prophesy events, or do wonderful things which, according to Mrs. Barrast, he was capable of doing when willing. As a matter of fact, Eberstein had the reputation of being a psychic doctor, and of knowing more about the unseen than most people. But in spite of Mrs. Barrast's babbling, he never by any chance performed the wonders which she spoke about. All the same, with the pertinacity of her nature Mrs. Barrast intended to ask him to give an exhibition of his powers, and as Frederick did not approve of such things, this was another reason why she chose an evening when he would be engaged. "Frederick is quite a heathen, you know, dear," said Mrs. Barrast, when the two ladies were in the drawing-room waiting for the two guests, "he says that to help poor people is better than being religious."

"To help the poor *is* to be religious, said Alice quietly.

Mrs. Barrast made a grimace and looked in a near mirror to see that her hair was in good order. "Oh, I know you are that sort of person also, dear. Julian tells me that you are hand in glove with your vicar."

"The vicar of Polwellin is a good man, Amy."

"How dull! I never did like good people, who are fond of the ragged poor and starving children and all that slum sort of thing. Though I'm sure I have helped dozens of times in bazaars and charity dances to get money for them. And I really needed the money more than they did," concluded Mrs. Barrast plaintively.

She flitted round the drawing-room in her usual restless manner, arranging the flowers, rearranging the many useless objects of luxury, and generally passing the time in meddling, chattering continuously. The drawing-room was suggestive of her brainless nature, as it was filled with costly things of no possible use; frivolous rubbish that had taken her fancy for the moment and then had been more or less forgotten. There was ample space, plenty of light and colour, and all the appliances of civilisation for an easy, luxurious existence. But repose was lacking, as the hostess had communicated to the room some of her abnormal restlessness. Mrs. Barrast was always screwed up to concert pitch and never gave herself, or any one in her vicinity, a single moment of peace. This incessant desire to say something or to do something, however silly, was gradually forcing Alice to consider seriously the necessity of cutting short her visit. There was an excess of oxygen in the atmosphere of Mrs. Barrast that disturbed the girl's serene nature.

"Oh, here they are at last," cried the hostess with another glance into the mirror, as her quick ear caught a sound outside the door. "I am so glad, as I am so hungry. Then you see, dear—oh, Dr. Eberstein, how are you? So very glad to see you. And Mr. Montrose! It *is* Mr. Montrose, isn't it? How do you do? So pleased to meet you. Dr. Eberstein, this is Miss Enistor, who is staying with me for a few weeks. Mr. Montrose, Miss Enistor. And now we can go to dinner. I am sure you are both dying for food!"

The doctor bowed gravely to Alice and remained somewhat in the background talking, or rather listening, to the voluble Mrs. Barrast. It seemed as if he had stepped back to be a spectator of the meeting between the younger people, for Alice felt, rather than saw, that his eyes were upon her. But she was too much taken up with Montrose to consider this for a moment. The young man advanced silently, a tall slim figure, graceful and virile. His dark eyes were fixed on Alice in a puzzled sort of way, as if something about her perplexed him greatly. On her part, the girl rose from the chair to meet his gaze more directly than was consistent with the first introduction of a youth and a maiden. She did not know why he appeared to be familiar to her. It was not his looks, for these were new to her. But in his eyes there was something which hinted that he was less a stranger than a very dear friend. Of course, what knowledge of reincarnation she had gained from her father told her that the body was nothing and the soul was everything. Certainly she had never seen Montrose before in the flesh, but through his eyes there looked a soul which she knew. All this flashed through her troubled mind in a second and the blood crimsoned her face as she impulsively held out her hand.

With a soft quick indrawn breath the young man took it. He was evidently as perplexed as she was. Only by an effort did he release the girl's slim hand and find his voice.

"I am glad to meet you, Miss Enistor!"

His voice broke the spell, and Alice became aware—at least she thought as much—that she had been acting foolishly. Of course he would be confused to meet the niece of the lady whose money he had inherited. That was the reason of his odd look and strange silence. But she would put him at his ease at once, since there was nothing to be gained by being stiff with a perfectly innocent person. And then—here came in the momentary memory again—she liked him at sight more than any one she had ever seen. She repeated his words.

"I am glad to meet you, Mr. Montrose!" and then the two smiled at one another in a somewhat embarrassed way.

"There's the gong," cried Mrs. Barrast gaily, "your arm, doctor. We shall have a pleasant dinner and a delightful evening!"

"I am sure of that, Mrs. Barrast," said the other positively. "The evening has commenced most auspiciously."

Alice asked herself what he meant and laid her hand on Montrose's arm. She did not get an answer to her mental question until much later.

CHAPTER VI
A CONVERSATION

Dinner was served, not in the large dining-room, used on high days and festivals, but in a small octagonal apartment, reserved for such minor occasions. Its walls were of polished white wood, gaily painted with wreaths of flowers bound with knots of blue ribbon and held by naked cupids, dimpled and rosy. There was a blue-tiled fire-place in which stood a brass cradle for the flaming coals, though at present, the weather being warm, this was filled with ferns and bulrushes. The ceiling was painted with sunset clouds, the carpet was moss-green sprinkled with bunches of daisies, and the furniture was of cream-coloured wood. In the centre stood a round table of no great size, at which the hostess and her guests took their seats. Two smart parlour-maids attended to their wants, as Mrs. Barrast preferred to dispense with footmen and butler, save when she gave a state dinner to people she did not care about.

"Frederick's friends, you know," she explained airily, when unfolding her napkin. "The people who like things-as-they-ought-to-be. I think things-as-they-ought-not-to-be are more amusing myself. More of a surprise, you know."

"If you pushed that theory to extremes, Mrs. Barrast," said Dr. Eberstein in a dry way, "you would find the world excessively disagreeable."

"Oh, I don't know, doctor. People in society all say the same things and do the same things and think the same things. I adore originality myself."

"If originality made you uncomfortable you would change your mind."

"I daresay. But that would be no novelty. I am always changing my mind!"

"Consequently your nervous system gets out of order and you have to come to me to have it set right."

"If I and others did not come to you where would your practice be?" asked Mrs. Barrast, accepting fish from the parlour-maid. "If one didn't change one's mind the world would stand still."

Dr. Eberstein laughed. "That is a deeper remark than you guess, Mrs. Barrast," he said quietly. "But there is one change of mind and another change of mind."

"Of course," the frivolous little woman opened her eyes widely, "if there were not another change of mind there would be no change at all."

"True, O Queen! You speak wiser than you know."

"Tell Frederick that, doctor. He says I have no ideas, and what I have aren't ideas at all. No! I don't mean that! But he says—well, I don't know exactly what Frederick says. Nobody ever does, especially when he gets up to make a speech in the House. But he's a dear fellow all the same, and do try that hock, doctor. It is particularly good!"

Eberstein smiled and refused, as he drank nothing but water. He looked on Mrs. Barrast as an irresponsible delightful child, who had everything to learn, yet who could not be taught, as it was impossible for her to concentrate her attention for one whole minute. A butterfly herself, she chased other butterflies and danced along a sunny path careless of whither she was going. The doctor knew that in the nature of things she would have to learn what life meant some day: but did not tell her so. Mrs. Barrast would not have understood him if he had.

While eating and listening to the remarks of Montrose, the youngest member of the party stole frequent looks at Eberstein. He was not very tall, rather stout, some years over fifty, and had a healthy clean-shaven face. Alice by no means considered him handsome, but when he smiled there was a kind and helpful look in his grey eyes which drew her to him. She felt that he was cool, wise, tolerant, and anxious to aid his fellow mortals. Mr. Montrose—so ran her thoughts—was very fortunate to have such a friend. In the hour of need Eberstein would prove staunch. Alice was positive of this although she had no experience of the man's nature. But added to the ordinary feminine intuition she possessed a subtle clairvoyant instinct, undeveloped though it was, and without any positive proof she would have staked her existence on Eberstein's being a really good and helpful man. One in a thousand.

But as a woman her feelings inclined to Montrose, since he was extremely handsome and likewise fascinating. The unusual combination of auburn hair and dark eyes was striking, and his clearly cut features of the Greek type impressed her with a sense of belonging to a thoroughbred stock. His shapely body, his slim hands and feet, his lithe active strength, suggested a racehorse perfection. A well-formed head showed that he had brains, and a resolute chin revealed courage and decision. Altogether Miss Enistor was favourably impressed with the looks of the young man who had inherited Lady Staunton's money, and thought that he would make good use of it. As to her other feeling, of his soul being familiar to her, she had not yet reasoned that out in a way to satisfy herself. At present all she knew was that she and Montrose seemed to be old acquaintances, and they chatted as if they were friends of many years' standing. Mrs. Barrast remarked this.

"You two get on very well together," she said shrewdly, when the dessert was placed on the table, and Eberstein smiled when she made the remark.

"We seem to suit one another," was Montrose's reply: then added, to avert personal remarks on the part of Mrs. Barrast: "I wonder how it is that one is repelled by some people and drawn to others at first sight."

"Ask Miss Enistor for the explanation," said Eberstein quietly.

Alice was startled by the directness of his speech. "How do you know that I can explain, doctor?"

"Oh, Dr. Eberstein knows all manner of things other people don't know," chimed in the hostess. "I am quite afraid of him sometimes. He is as wise as the sea and as deep!"

"And as useful, I hope," said the doctor, smiling genially. "However, Montrose has not yet asked Miss Enistor for a reply to his question."

The young man laughed and looked at the flower-like face of his neighbour with great admiration. "How is it some people repel while others attract?"

"The doctrine of reincarnation explains," replied the girl, forced to answer plainly while the doctor's calm, grey eyes were on her. "Those people who repel have done one an injury in some previous life: those who attract have done good, or at least have been friendly."

"Likewise in other lives?" questioned the doctor.

"Of course. Although I do not know if you believe in reincarnation?"

"Oh," Mrs. Barrast uttered a little shriek and dabbled her fingers in the bowl of rose-water at her elbow. "He believes in all manner of dreadful things, my dear. How he can do so I cannot understand, when he is so clever. I think reincarnation is rubbish myself."

"Oh, no! no!" protested Montrose.

"What! You believe in our having lived before also? Really it is very odd and queer of you. Alice too. My dear, where did you learn such awful nonsense?"

"From my father," said Miss Enistor dryly; "and if you met him, Amy, you would not think he was the man to teach nonsense!"

"Then he's got a bee in his bonnet."

"He doesn't wear a bonnet."

"Oh, Alice, you know perfectly well what I mean. He's crazy!"

Miss Enistor laughed. "I think my father is the sanest person I have ever met, Amy. Why shouldn't reincarnation be a great truth?"

"It isn't in the Bible," said Mrs. Barrast pettishly, for the conversation being beyond her was somewhat boring to her small intellect. "And what isn't in the Bible is wrong."

"You are of the Caliph Omar's opinion with regard to the Koran when he ordered the library of Alexandria to be burnt," observed Eberstein; "but if you will read St. Matthew, verse 14, chapter xi, you will find that reincarnation is plainly acknowledged. Also in St. John's Gospel, chapter ix, verses 2 and 3, it is plainly hinted at. Origen, the most learned of the Christian Fathers, believed in the law of rebirth and——"

"Oh, it's all nonsense," interrupted Mrs. Barrast, weary of the explanation.

"So be it," admitted the doctor quietly, "it is all nonsense. *Your* brain is the measure of the universe.

"I'm sure I don't know what you mean. Frederick says that I haven't any brain to speak of: as if I could live if I haven't," said Mrs. Barrast incoherently. "Let us have coffee here while you gentlemen smoke. Oh, I forgot: you don't smoke, doctor. Mr. Montrose?"

"Thank you," and the young man accepted a cigarette from Mrs. Barrast's own particular case. "You smoke yourself, I see."

"Oh, yes." Mrs. Barrast lighted her little roll of tobacco. "It soothes me. I am all nerves, you know. Alice, will you——?"

"No, thank you. I am not all nerves!"

"I'm sure I wonder you aren't, living in Cornwall with sea-gulls and moors and those sort of things. You will like this coffee, Dr. Eberstein. There is a vanilla bean in each cup, which makes it so nice."

"Very good coffee," said the other, sipping gravely, and wondering if Mrs. Barrast was aware of the rubbish she talked.

The little woman apparently was not, as she conversed volubly, darting from this subject to that after the manner of a swallow. She mentioned several novels which had attracted her frivolous attention, talked of some musical comedies she had seen, criticised the fashions, told one or two tales dealing with scandals concerning various people, and in every way monopolised the conversation, until it was time to return to the drawing-room. Alice, who wished to converse with Montrose, was pleased when this move was made, as it appeared to be the only chance of ending Mrs. Barrast's airy nothings. For a few moments she was alone with her hostess and seized the chance of asking if Dr. Eberstein was a German.

"I suppose he is," said Mrs. Barrast gravely, "his name sounds like it. But I can't say what he is. He talks all languages as well as he talks English, and never says anything about his father and mother. But he's very nice, isn't he, Alice? A kind of soul-doctor, you know, who tells his patients that mind is stronger than matter. Not exactly Christian Science, but something like it. He has never come to dinner before. I'm sure I don't know why, as I have asked him dozens of times."

Alice thought that she knew the reason, which had to do with Mrs. Barrast's frothy chatter, but was too polite to put her idea into words. "What do you think of Mr. Montrose?" she asked, anxious for a second opinion.

"Good-looking but stupid," was Mrs. Barrast's verdict; "not a second idea in his head. However, he has money — your money, dear, so you ought to marry him."

"He has not got my money," said Miss Enistor tartly, "and even if he had I certainly should not marry him for his wealth."

"I daresay: you are such a funny girl. Not at all like a human being. It's silly not to eat a pear that has fallen into your mouth."

"Mr. Montrose being the pear?"

"Of course. He is head over ears in love with you already. I'm not his style evidently. Not that I care," ended Mrs. Barrast, caring very much indeed. "Go in and win, Alice, and let me design the bridesmaids' dresses. Pink silk and white — —"

Mrs. Barrast's chatter about chiffons was put a stop to by the entrance of the gentlemen. As if it had been arranged, Dr. Eberstein walked over to Mrs. Barrast and engaged her in conversation. Montrose hesitated, then came to the corner wherein Alice was seated. He looked extremely handsome and attractive; she was more than ever taken with his appearance. Smiling amiably, she made room for him to sit down beside her on the ottoman, but waited for him to begin the conversation. He did so with an abruptness which startled her.

"I hope you are not my enemy," said the young man earnestly.

Alice raised her eyebrows. "Why should I be?"

"Well, you see Lady Staunton left me her money!"

"Why not, Mr. Montrose? It was her own money!"

"Yes. But do you think it was right that she should leave it away from her relations?"

"If she wished to. Why not?"

"You don't regret the loss?" He looked at her very directly.

"Not at all. I have never given the matter any consideration."

"And your father?"

"He is quite satisfied with the legacy left to him by Aunt Lucy," said Alice unhesitatingly, for she knew nothing of Enistor's wrath about the loss.

Montrose drew a long breath of relief. "I am glad to hear you say that," he said thankfully. "I don't mind telling you, Miss Enistor, that, when I heard of my good fortune, it was my first intention to surrender the money to your father. I was persuaded not to do so by Dr. Eberstein."

"He is a friend of yours?" she asked carelessly.

"The best friend a man ever had: the best friend a man could have. He cares for nothing save to do good. I see you raise your eyebrows, thinking of how he advised me to keep Lady Staunton's money. But he did so, because it was necessary."

"Why?" demanded Alice point-blank.

"I can't tell you. He said it was necessary, so I obeyed him."

"Would you have obeyed him if he had told you to give my father the money?"

"Yes," said Montrose truthfully and unhesitatingly. "And to put it plainly, Miss Enistor, it is harder for me to keep the money than to surrender it. I don't require so large an income."

"Yet my father heard from Mr. Cane that you were poor."

"Very poor. I was starving when I first made Lady Staunton's acquaintance, Miss Enistor. My parents died when I was a child, and I was brought up by an old aunt in Edinburgh. When I was eighteen years of age she passed away, leaving me what little she had. I came to London with the idea of writing poetry and plays. But my work would not sell, and when my money came to an end, I starved until I managed to drift into journalism. Even then I only managed to keep body and soul together in a Bloomsbury garret. When I saved your aunt's life, she gave me employment as her secretary to deal with her many charities. But I assure you that she never expressed any intention of leaving her money to me. If she had, I should have objected, since her brother was alive. However, she did leave me this large income, and I was ready to give it up, until Eberstein told me it was necessary to keep it."

"I wonder why?" said Alice thoughtfully, and greatly interested in the story he had told.

"Eberstein will not tell me. But he has a good reason for what he says and I always obey him, knowing his true friendship. A few years ago I was dying of starvation and pneumonia in my attic, and he saved my life. Since then I have been with him constantly. As you believe in reincarnation, Miss Enistor, I may as well tell you that there is some tie between you and me dating from former lives. What it is I cannot say, as Eberstein refuses to explain. He brought me here to-night to meet you."

"Oh!" Alice darted a swift piercing look at the young man's earnest face and wondered if he was as guileless as he appeared to be. "How did he know that I was here?"

"He is Mrs. Barrast's doctor, you know," said Montrose simply.

The girl did not reply immediately. She was considering if there was not some conspiracy on foot to entangle her in a marriage bond. Dr. Eberstein looked kindly and sympathetic, yet for his own ends he might have brought herself and Montrose together. Was he an honest man, or a schemer? Was Montrose his victim, or his accomplice? And what had she to do with either of the two men? As she thought thus, there came a wave of that same overpowering influence which she had felt in the Tremore dining-room. It seemed to sweep away the suggestion of evil with which she had almost unconsciously credited Eberstein and his young friend. "I don't understand," she said faintly and turned white.

"Are you ill?" asked Montrose, alarmed. It was plain that he did not feel the influence as she did.

"No! No! I shall be all right soon. The heat— —" here she broke off with a surprised look. "Why, I *am* all right. I never felt better in my life. Did you feel anything just now?

"Feel anything?" Montrose looked puzzled. "What do you mean, Miss Enistor?"

"Nothing at all," she replied quickly and evasively, for she decided that it would not do to be too frank with this young man until she knew more of him. "Only the heat, you know, and these dinners. I am a quiet country girl, Mr. Montrose, and am not accustomed to London life."

"I like the country myself, Miss Enistor," sighed the young man wistfully. "I have long since wanted to live in the country, as London in some ways worries me. I can't explain myself more fully.

"I know what you feel like," said Alice, nodding wisely. "You are sensitive as I am. To be in the country is like being in clean water, while London is like bathing in a dirty pool."

"Oh," Montrose's face flushed and brightened. "How did you guess?"

"Because I feel as you do. It is the evil thoughts that are in London which affect you. My father knows something about psychic matters and has taught me a little. That is why I believe in reincarnation."

Montrose nodded in his turn. "Eberstein first spoke to me on the subject and placed life in a new light before me. I used to wonder why I had such a bad time, and complained greatly about my lot. But he made all things plain to me. I can bear life's burdens now with a serene heart."

Alice was amused when she reflected on his position. "You have health and wealth, good looks and a good friend. It is easy to bear such burdens."

"Ah, but you forget that I went through many a long year of sorrow and bewildered pain, Miss Enistor. Besides, money does not bring happiness. I never can be enthusiastic over money."

"People with large incomes can afford to say that," said Alice cynically.

"Is that a hit at me?" retorted Montrose good-humouredly; "if so it misses its mark, I assure you. I am quite willing to give back the money to your father if Eberstein tells me to."

"Why should you obey him?"

"Because he knows more than I do. I look upon him as a guide."

Alice shook her head. "Every man should think for himself."

"So Eberstein says," replied Montrose unexpectedly; "and all he does is to give me hints, leaving me to take them or reject them as I choose. Fortunately I know how little I do know, and I am glad to have a more experienced man to help me."

"Experienced?"

"Yes. In the things of this world and the next."

"Is Dr. Eberstein religious then?"

"Not in the narrow sense in which the word religious is used. But he is a wonderful man, as you will learn when you see more of him. I don't want you to think me weak and without will-power, Miss Enistor, because

I constantly quote Eberstein. But the most accomplished general is glad to obey the guidance of a man who knows the lie of the land when marching through the enemy's country."

"The enemy's country?"

"You might call the world so."

Miss Enistor moved restlessly. "What an odd conversation we are having!" she said in a nervous way. "We have only met to-night for the first time, and yet we are quite confidential."

"It is better to talk as we are doing than to gossip," said Montrose sententiously. "And how do you know we have met for the first time to-night?"

"I have never seen you before," said the girl sharply.

"You have not seen Douglas Montrose, nor have I seen Alice Enistor," was the reply. "But in other bodies, in other lives, we have been friends: the very best of friends."

"How do you know that?" asked Alice, wilfully dense, although her heart endorsed every word the young man said.

"Need I explain?" He stared at her hard.

"No," she answered after a short pause. "I can guess your meaning. When we shook hands we were drawn together by—well, I can't say."

"By the friendship of the past!"

"Yes," she hesitated; "I suppose so! But other people would think we were talking sad nonsense, Mr. Montrose."

"What does it matter what other people think?" said the young man calmly.

"Not much. But one has to consider the world in which one lives."

"Mrs. Barrast?"

"No! No! No!" Alice laughed outright and rose, as she felt that he was getting on altogether too fast. "She is very tolerant."

"That is something in her favour, considering how narrow people are as a rule in this world." Montrose got on his feet also. "Before we join her and Eberstein, let me hear you assure me that you do not look upon me as a grasping enemy who has taken your father's money."

"I assure you of that certainly," said the girl frankly, and gave him her hand with a smile. "If you had not mentioned the subject I should never have referred to it. Keep the money, Mr. Montrose, and make what use you will of it. Both my father and myself are quite content," and she said this about Enistor once more, entirely unaware of its falsity.

"You are good," said Montrose impetuously. "Few people would take a loss so kindly."

"Well, like yourself I cannot get up any enthusiasm about money. Come, let us join Mrs. Barrast."

"One moment. Shall I see you again?"

"If you like. I am staying here for a few weeks!"

"If I like." The young man's face was eloquent and the look in his eyes betrayed his heart to Alice in a moment. With a laugh to hide her confusion she turned away to join her hostess, and came face to face with Dr. Eberstein.

"Well met, Miss Enistor," said the elder man in a genial manner and staring at her very directly. "I was just coming to take Montrose away."

"Yes," called out Mrs. Barrast, "he is going, and at eleven o'clock too. So very early. What can we do with the rest of the evening?"

"I advise bed," said Eberstein pointedly.

"Bed for me," endorsed Alice gaily. "I feel rather tired."

"I don't think you do," said the doctor calmly: and to Miss Enistor's surprise on consideration she did not. But as he spoke she again felt a wave of that strange uplifting influence and drew back, startled to find that it emanated from the doctor. Eberstein smiled quietly, "Good-night!"

"Good-night, Mr. Montrose," said Mrs. Barrast pointedly. "Next time you come, talk to me as well as to Miss Enistor!"

"I apologise for my bad manners," said Montrose quickly.

"What a compliment to me!" laughed Alice, shrugging her shoulders.

"Oh, you understand me, I think, Miss Enistor," he looked at her straightly.

She returned his look flushing. "I think I do," was her low reply.

"Such nonsense," said Mrs. Barrast irritably: for her the evening had not been a success.

CHAPTER VII
BEHIND THE SCENES

It was a delightfully warm summer night when Eberstein and his young friend left the house. For some little distance they walked on in silence, as Eberstein was never voluble and Montrose felt disinclined to speak at the moment. Oblivious of his surroundings, more or less, he moved mechanically by the doctor's side, dreaming of Alice and of the love which existed between them. Considering he had met her for the first time an hour or so previously, it seemed ridiculous, even in a dream, to think that she had any such tender feeling for him. But something in the deeps of his own nature was struggling to the surface to assure him that his dream was truth. Much as he valued Eberstein's company, he wished him away at the moment that he might puzzle out the meaning of this strange intuition.

"But that is impossible, just now," said the doctor quietly. "I wish you to come to my house, as I have much to say, and something to show."

Montrose was startled, as he often was at Eberstein's speeches. "You know what I am thinking about?"

"Is that so strange?"

"Well, it isn't, really. You have extraordinary penetration. Sometimes I am quite afraid of you."

"You are never afraid of me," replied Eberstein, shaking his head with a benevolent smile. "Think!"

"No!" Montrose reflected for a few moments. "It is true. I am not afraid!"

The doctor smiled approvingly. "That is right. Fear would prevent my aiding you in any way, and you need aid more than you guess. Remember what the Bible says, my friend: 'In quietness and confidence shall be your strength.'"

"Faith and peace of mind are so hard to get," complained the young man sadly.

"Very hard. The Blessed One said that the Path was difficult."

"The Blessed One!"

"Christ: your Master and mine," replied Eberstein solemnly. "Strait is the gate and narrow is the way which leadeth to life and few there be that find it."

"And those who do not find it are lost?"

"For the time being, not eternally. God is very gentle with His straying sheep, and we have many lives, many opportunities to find the way to the fold. You are coming to the strait gate, Montrose; therefore my aid is given to you lest you should faint on the hard uphill journey."

"I am not good enough even to approach the gate," sighed the young man.

"So you think! But the standard of goodness is not kept on earth, but in heaven, my friend. However"—Eberstein broke off to hail a taxi—"we can talk of these things when we reach my house. Get in, Montrose!"

The young man did so, and was followed by his master, who told the chauffeur to drive to Bloomsbury. Eberstein lived in that unfashionable district, not-withstanding the fact that his practice lay largely amongst wealthy and aristocratic people. Many of the doctor's patients wondered why he did not select a better-class neighbourhood, but Eberstein never gave them any information on this point. Yet his known character might have revealed the reason to an ordinarily shrewd person very easily. The man was greatly given to helping the poor and needy. Not so much the proverbial ragged paupers of the slums—although he helped those also when necessary—as poor curates, badly paid clerks, shabby governesses, struggling ladies, and such-like persons, who had to keep up some sort of appearance on nothing. His money, his sympathy, his medical skill, were all wholly at the service of those who could not pay, and the fees received from his rich patients went to ameliorate the sufferings of the self-respecting, who never complained and showed their pauperism as little as was possible. Eberstein made no boast of his philanthropy: he never even spoke of his many good works. It was perfectly natural for him to go silently attentive about the work of his Master Christ, as he knew he could act in no other way without going contrary to his whole being. To feed the hungry, to clothe the naked, to teach the ignorant, to comfort the desolate: for these purposes he was in the world.

In one of his exploring expeditions Eberstein had found Montrose dying in a garret and had set him on his legs again in a sympathetic brotherly way which had not offended the young man's pride. More than that, he had supplied food for the starving soul as well as for the starving body, and by explaining the riddles of Life in a perfectly reasonable way he had entirely changed Montrose's outlook. His protégé had been puzzled by this absolutely unselfish conduct, not understanding from inexperience that no return was demanded for these great gifts. But as his limitations began to expand through the teaching, he began to comprehend, and finally he accepted Eberstein as a kind of angel in the flesh, sent to help him in his hour of need. And the philanthropist was so unaffectedly sincere, so reasonable and sympathetic, that the rescued man grew to love him with a reverence rare in the younger generation. The doctor restored his faith in human existence.

"Here we are," said Eberstein, alighting from the taxi and dismissing it. "We can now have an undisturbed hour for conversation."

The doctor admitted himself into the quiet house with his latch-key, as the servants were all in bed. They were never kept up late by their considerate employer, since he recognised that they required their necessary sleep. So the two men entered the hall, ascended the stairs, and betook themselves to a large room at the very top of the mansion. Eberstein kept this entirely to himself, not even seeing his friends therein, much less his patients. Therefore it was with some surprise and more curiosity that Montrose stepped into the apartment and closed the door after him. Then he uttered an exclamation of pleasure—a soft exclamation, for the atmosphere of the place suggested a church.

"What a wonderful room," breathed Montrose, staring round him, "and how holy."

He scarcely knew what caused him to utter the last word, unless it was the unusual looks of the spacious room. Everything was white; the walls, the carpet, the ceiling, and even the light which radiated from two large lamps with opaque globes. The table, the few chairs, the bookcase, and the sofa were of white wood with silken cushions like mounds of snow, and the draperies which veiled the volumes and the windows were also the hue of milk. Yet there was no suggestion of winter in the colourless expanse, for the air was warm and the atmosphere so charged with perfect peace that Montrose felt quite at home. The room, he felt, expressed Eberstein himself. It might have been the chapel of The Holy Grail.

"You never brought me here before," said the young man, feeling that his dark garments were a blot on the purity of the surroundings, "although you have known me for three years, more or less."

"No," assented the doctor, seating himself before the table and indicating a chair for his guest, "it was not necessary."

"Is it necessary to-night?"

"I should not have brought you here, had it not been."

"But why this night of all nights?" persisted the other wonderingly.

"You have met Miss Enistor."

Montrose was more bewildered than ever. "What has she got to do with it, or with me, or with anything?"

"Ask yourself," said Eberstein, and looked steadily into the eyes of Montrose.

"I ask myself!" murmured the guest, mechanically compelled to the speech.

Those kind grey eyes on a level with his own a little distance away poured, as it seemed, such a flood of light towards him that Montrose voluntarily closed his own. Yet it was not a dazzling light which need have frightened him, but an all-enfolding steady radiance, which bathed his whole being in luminous splendour, until he felt that he was partaking of that peace of God which passeth understanding. The tide of glory lifted him up higher and higher beyond the gross envelope of the physical body until he felt himself soaring without wings into an all-embracing sphere of glorious music which expressed itself in colour. In this ocean of rainbow hues he floated, aware that he was using super-physical senses to view super-physical scenes. On him descended, with the swiftness of thought, a golden cloud more brilliant than the noonday sun, and this dissolved away to reveal the form of a young girl clothed in floating white draperies. The face was fair, the hair corn-coloured, the eyes deeply blue and the figure majestic and graceful. Anything more unlike the elfin beauty of Alice can scarcely be imagined. Yet he knew beyond all doubt that this was Alice in another shape which she had worn in another clime under alien stars. His soul flowed out to blend with her soul in one flame of unity. But there was a barrier between them which Montrose strove to break through. Try as he might he could not.

Even in that heaven-world, despair seized him, when he found that the invisible barrier withheld him from his beloved. On her side she seemed equally desirous to come to him, and held out her arms in vain longing. On his face and her face were looks of appealing love baffled by the impossibility of meeting heart to heart. Then a shadow grew up between them swiftly; the shadow menacing and dark of a yellow-skinned man, rather like a Chinese, from whose throat ran a stream of blood. Who this man was Montrose could not tell, even though he had recognised Alice in a different guise. And the enemy—Montrose felt that the wounded creature was an enemy—grew larger and larger until the blackness of which he was part blotted out the splendour of the girl. Blotted out also the atmosphere of colour and music and radiancy, until Montrose, sinking downward in the gloom, opened his physical eyes to find himself seated in the chair opposite Eberstein. Only a single moment had elapsed, for the journey had been as swift as that of Mahomet to the seventh heaven mounted on Al Borak, but he seemed to have been away for hours. The discrepancy was to Montrose impossible to reconcile, even though he grasped confusedly the fact that he had been—in the Fourth Dimension say—where there is no time.

"You now know what Alice Enistor has to do with you," said Eberstein in a quiet impressive tone.

"I don't in one way," faltered the still bewildered young man, "and yet I do in another. All I can be certain of is that she is mine."

"Undoubtedly. She is yours and you are hers."

"Then why could we not come together?"

"The shadow of your sin came between and parted you."

"My sin?"

"That which you committed five thousand years ago," explained the doctor patiently. "Then, self-willed, self-centred, you would not wait the striking of the hour which would have made you one, and therefore, seeking to obtain your desire by force, you broke the Great Law. The Great Law broke you, as it breaks all who disobey. For many ages your soul and her soul have been asunder, but now in the fullness of time you meet again on this physical plane in new vestments of flesh. But your sin has not yet been expiated, and you cannot yet be one with her you love. The shadow stands between you twain and will stand until the debt is paid."

"The shadow—the man?" stammered Montrose confusedly.

"You owe him a life!"

"But he is my enemy. I feel strongly that he is my enemy."

"He was and is: it depends greatly upon you if he continues to be. If one obeys truly the Law of Love, one must not be angered even with one's enemy. What says the Blessed Son of the Most High God?"

As if the words had been placed in his mouth, Montrose replied softly: "Love your enemies, bless them that curse you, do good to them that hate you, and pray for them which despitefully use you and persecute you!"

Eberstein bowed his stately head. "Such is the Law of Love."

Rubbing his eyes to make certain that he was entirely awake, Montrose sought for an interpretation. "I do not quite understand."

"There is no need for you to understand further, my friend. This much enlightenment has been vouchsafed you through the mercy of God. For the rest you must work and walk by faith, seeing as in a glass darkly, obeying the Great Law of your own free will, so that your unselfish love may cause hatred to cease."

"Whose hatred?"

"That of the man you sinned against. Only with the aid of the Blessed One!"—Eberstein made the sign of the cross—"can you prevent the Son of Perdition from descending into the Abyss."

"Who is the Son of Perdition?"

"Your enemy, whom Christ loves as He loves you. Your task is to make yourself a channel through which the grace of the Blessed One can freely pour for the salvation of this erring soul. Oh, think how glorious it is that you should be permitted to be the instrument of Christ in this mighty work."

"But I do not know how to go about the work!" exclaimed the bewildered man.

"Watch and pray, my son, for the time when you must act is near at hand. Only by making yourself receptive to the holy influence will you know how to act when the time is ripe."

"You will help me?"

"I am bound to help you since I am obedient to the Law. But much has to be done by yourself, Montrose. I cannot command, as each man has free-will with which even the Logos Himself does not interfere. Christ stands at the door of your heart, but will not enter unless you invite His entrance. Only by doing what you ought to do will the Spirit of Love enter and sup with you."

"But what am I to do?" demanded Montrose desperately.

"Ask your own heart."

"It says nothing."

"The time is not yet ripe for it to say anything. Watch and pray! Come," the doctor spoke in a more matter-of-fact tone, "it is growing late. Go home and sleep: you are becoming exhausted."

"But tell me, Eberstein, if I am right in what I think," pleaded Montrose earnestly. "I know intuitively that I met Miss Enistor in some previous life and that I loved her, as I love her now when we come together for the first time in this incarnation. I had all the feeling of being her friend. Oh what do I say! Friend is too weak a word—of being her lover. If I understand rightly, some sin committed by me has parted us, and that sin I have to expiate before we can come together again."

"That is the case. But ask me no more now. With the aid of the Blessed One you must work out your salvation in fear and trembling."

"Indicate my enemy and I shall forgive him for Alice's sake," cried the young man with impetuous generosity.

"You must forgive him for his own."

"How can I when I don't know why we are enemies?"

"You will know when it is necessary you should know."

Montrose passed his hands across his brow and stood up slowly. "It is all bewildering and difficult."

"Very bewildering and very difficult. I answered that question earlier in the evening. We talk in a circle. To do so is a waste of time. Good-night!"

Another question was trembling on Montrose's lips, but he refrained from putting it, and with a silent hand-shake departed slowly. Accustomed to come and go at will in this house, which was more a home to him than any habitation he had known, the young man descended the stairs and let himself out into the silent square. The balmy summer night was brilliant with stars, and charged with some mysterious healing influence, which soothed and relaxed his weary nerves. On all sides the great city was yet awake and alive with people, each one intent upon the realisation of his or her desire. But here, isolated from the roaring thoroughfares, the quadrangle was comparatively lonely and dark, as the passers-by were few and the lights widely scattered. The central gardens, with their trees and shrubs and turf and flowers, slept within the rusty iron railings, speaking every now and then as a wandering breeze woke the leaves to sigh and whisper. The hurrying steps of a wayfarer, the measured heavy tread of a policeman, the murmur of distant life: Montrose heard these things without hearing as it were, as without seeing he stared at the silent cats gliding through the shadows. He walked along, wrapped up in his own thoughts, seeking mechanically his rooms and bed.

Notwithstanding his accession to considerable wealth, the fortunate youth had but slightly changed his mode of living. He enjoyed better lodgings, better clothes, more nourishing food, and was free from the obligation of compulsory work to exist. But he still lived in unfashionable Bloomsbury, a quiet, inexpensive, and somewhat recluse life, not seeking to enter what is known as society. With his good looks and undeniable talents and newly acquired wealth, he would have been welcome to the gay throng who flutter in the sunshine of pleasure. But there was nothing in Montrose which responded to such aimless allurements. Once or twice friends had taken him to this house and that, where the butterflies gathered, and on this particular night Eberstein had induced him to dine at Mrs. Barrast's. But entertainments of all kinds bored Montrose immensely, and only the presence of Alice had aided him to endure the shallow chatter of his hostess and the artificiality of his surroundings. The after-events in Eberstein's room had both startled and awed him, so that he was still greatly moved by what had taken place when he reached his modest lodgings.

But, as common sense told him, thinking would not help him, as his thoughts spun in a circle and always brought him back to the same point. That point was the meeting with Alice and the weird feelings which contact with her personality had aroused in him. She belonged to his life in some way which he could not quite put into words, and he belonged to hers. They were together and yet apart, but what parted them it was impossible to say, as the vision had not indicated in detail the especial sin, or what had led to the commission of that sin. Soon he would know more—Eberstein had assured him of that. Therefore it would be best to wait for the knowledge. He had been given light enough in the darkness of the path to take the next step, and that light revealed Alice waiting for him to come to her. He was only too willing to do so, as the feeling that he loved her deeply grew with overwhelming swiftness. When she knew what was in his heart and he knew what was in hers, then the next step could be taken. What it might be and where it would lead to Montrose could not say.

However, the doctor had given him necessary instructions for the moment in the phrase "Watch and pray!" To watch for the dawning love in Alice and to pray that he might be worthy of such love seemed to be his task, and a very delightful task it would be. Therefore Montrose knelt down and prayed with all his clean heart that every possible blessing might befall the girl and that, if it was God's will, he might become her husband to cherish and protect her. Then he went to bed in a peaceful frame of mind. Sleep came to him almost immediately, but before his eyes closed he felt that Alice was near him, and knew that in some wordless manner Alice spoke to him.

"We have much to learn and there is pain in the learning," she whispered, "but we are together to suffer together."

"Suffering does not matter," said Montrose, as in a dream, "we are together!"

CHAPTER VIII
LOVE'S YOUNG DREAM

After the storm comes the calm, and when trouble has endured for a season peace descends to refresh the exhausted soul. Montrose had suffered a great deal during the five-and-twenty years of his present life, and it was time that he should enjoy a rest. Ever since he could remember, dark clouds had enshrouded him, and with a fainting heart he had groped his way through the gloom. The meeting with Eberstein had been the end of sorrow and the beginning of joy, for the doctor had bidden him raise his eyes to the hills made glorious by the rising sun. With the legacy of Lady Staunton the dawn had come, but only when he met Alice did Montrose feel that the sun was above the horizon. As by magic the darkness was swept away, and now he walked in golden sunshine, no longer alone. She was beside him, and he wondered how he could have endured life without her dear presence. For the next three weeks he was in heaven rather than on earth.

Of course the first desire of Montrose was to share with Alice the wonderful knowledge that he had acquired so strangely. But a note from Eberstein prevented this. The doctor wrote that he was going abroad for a few weeks, and that in the meanwhile Montrose was to tell the girl nothing of his late experiences. "Woo her as an ordinary youth woos an ordinary maid," said the letter. "She is yours and you are hers, so nothing can come between you for the time being. I say for the time being, since there is an ordeal which you must face before you stand before the altar. Whether you ever do stand there to take her as your wife depends upon your courage and forbearance and love. Meantime keep what you have seen and what you have heard to yourself. When I return I shall explain what is necessary for you to know!" This note was delivered the first thing in the morning after Montrose's weird experience, and when he called round to see Eberstein he found that the doctor had already departed for Paris. There was nothing left for him to do but to obey instructions.

Montrose did this very willingly. After all he was a man living in the world of men, and wished to make love like an ordinary person. Certainly Alice was an angel, and might not be satisfied with ordinary love-making, but she also was human, and appreciated the domesticity of life. Montrose remembered reading in some book Eberstein had lent him: "For every step you take in other planes, take two on the plane you know, since you are here to learn the lessons of this plane!" Thus the young man abandoned for the moment his search after super-physical knowledge and gave himself up to the joy of being an ordinary mortal. And in one way or another he hoped to elevate a commonplace wooing to a romantic passion, but all strictly within the limitations of the physical brain. When the gods descended from Olympus to follow after nymphs, they came as mere men. In a like way did Montrose set about his courting of Alice as the one woman in the world for him.

Mrs. Barrast quite approved of the romance. For a time she had been rather annoyed that so handsome and rich a young man had not laid himself at her feet. But being really good-natured, if extraordinarily vain, the little woman had ceased to play the part of dog in the manger, and forwarded the aim of Montrose by every means in her power. At heart she was a great match-maker like most women, and the fact that Montrose possessed Lady Staunton's wealth made her zealous to bring about the marriage. She looked upon herself as quite a *dea ex machinâ*, and, certain that all would turn out as she wished, had already arranged how the bridesmaids should be dressed, what people ought to be asked to the wedding, what present she would give, and where the young couple should spend their honeymoon. There was no doubt that Mrs. Barrast, like many another frivolous person, was a great hand at counting her chickens before they were hatched.

"But the dinky little things will come out of the eggs all right," she said to Alice, a week after that young lady had made the acquaintance of Montrose. "He's a nice boy and any one can see he's head over heels in love with you, my dear. But I wish you would dress in colours, Alice. It looks so silly for an engaged girl to go about in black."

"I am not engaged yet," replied Miss Enistor doubtfully, "and I never may be, Amy. My father has to be consulted."

"My dear," said Mrs. Barrast impressively, "he'll jump at the chance of getting the money back into the family."

"There is Don Pablo, who wants to marry me," ventured Alice anxiously.

"And there's Julian also," retorted the little woman. "What of that? Why, I had dozens of offers before I met Frederick, though why I took him I really don't know. Of course, as you told me this Don What's-his-name is rich and if Douglas—you don't mind my calling him Douglas, do you, dear?—was poor, I shouldn't advise you to throw the old thing over. But youth and good looks and money and all those nice things are better than an old man. And I am glad after all that you did not accept Julian," ended

Mrs. Barrast candidly. "He isn't rich either, and life's horrid without money. Besides, I wish Julian to marry a rich girl."

"If he loves her."

"Pooh, what has love to do with marriage? What old-fashioned ideas you have, Alice. I suppose you wouldn't marry Douglas if you didn't love him."

"Certainly not," said the girl firmly.

Mrs. Barrast made a grimace. "It's lucky you like him then, my dear. Of course it's not right to marry for money only," added the butterfly, contradicting herself boldly, "but when you meet a man with a banking account try and love him as hard as ever you can."

"I love Douglas for himself alone. If he was a pauper I should love him."

"I daresay you would. I'm sure there is madness in your family. It's a mercy Douglas is well off. Five thousand a year is very nice. Be sure you make him take a house near ours, dear, and get a smart motor-car with one of those nice chauffeurs who look like engineers but aren't. They're lots cleaner than engineers, aren't they? And do wear a blue dress, dear: blue suits you."

"No! no! I am still in mourning for my aunt."

"I'm sure you needn't be. I wouldn't mourn for a horrid, lean, old thing—she was lean, you know—who didn't leave me a penny."

"She left my father one thousand pounds, Amy."

"Just enough to make him hate her. I'm sure I would if I'd been treated in that nasty way. And do make Douglas take you out more. I'll come too as your chaperon, though perhaps I'm too young for the part."

"I go out quite enough, Amy. With my aunt in her grave——"

"Oh, don't talk about graves," cried Mrs. Barrast, rising in a hurry, "you set my nerves on edge, if nerves ever do have an edge, which I'm sure I don't know if they have. Not that it matters of course. Has Douglas proposed?"

"No. But we understand one another."

"Oh, my dear," said Mrs. Barrast in despair, "what is the use of that? I like everything to be signed, sealed, and delivered—I come of a legal family, you know, dear—to make certain. Don't lose your salmon after you've hooked him. Men do wriggle, you know, and if he sees another girl, he will——"

"He won't," interrupted Alice, with very red cheeks. "How can you talk so? I am the only girl Douglas has ever loved."

"Oh, he told you the usual lie then," sniggered the little woman provokingly. "How can men be so silly as to think we believe them! I wish you'd ask him to make love here, Alice, as I'd like to hear how he goes about it. It's absurd meeting in Kensington Gardens as you do. It isn't respectable."

"Then I am not going to be respectable this afternoon," said Alice, escaping from this wasp, "for we meet there in two hours."

"Make him give you an engagement ring," cried Mrs. Barrast, who always insisted upon having the last word, "diamonds, you know, dear. If the engagement is broken you won't want to keep the ring and can always get market value for the stones. I feel it is only right that you should have some of that money. Remember what I say, darling: remember what I say."

Alice, on her way to her own room, did not hear the end of this speech, although it was screamed out after her. She was rather offended that Mrs. Barrast should advise Montrose's capture like an unwilling fish, as if any marriage could possibly be happy with a reluctant bridegroom. But when putting on her hat, the girl laughed at her reflection in the mirror, and excused the little woman's well-meant speech. Amy really did mean well, although she had a rather brutal way of putting things. Miss Enistor wondered if Frederick had been bargained for in this mercantile way, and thought it was very probable. Mrs. Barrast was exceedingly modern, and modern women are very businesslike in dealing with what was formerly called romance. The Barrast marriage was a kind of mutual aid society. Frederick had secured a pretty woman to do the honours of his house, and Amy had captured a rich husband who supplied her with plenty of money and let her go her own frivolous way. Alice decided that the shrewd butterfly had made the best bargain, and was taking full advantage of her cleverness. Then she put Mrs. Barrast out of her head and started for the place of meeting in Kensington Gardens.

It was a warm afternoon, but not too dazzling, as a thin veil of clouds was drawn across the sky. Alice alighted from her taxi at the park gates and leisurely walked up the broad path towards the Round Pond. She preferred to meet Douglas here rather than in the Hans Crescent house, because Mrs. Barrast would always have been interrupting. And the girl was sufficiently in love to think that two was company and three a nuisance. As a matter of fact, she acknowledged to herself she was as deeply in love with Montrose as he obviously was with her, though neither of them had put the feeling into words. On this occasion, however, Alice decided that it would be just as well to come to some sort of understanding, since it was probable that she would not remain much longer in town. At least she fancied so, for her father had been grumbling about the money she was spending. Of course she had only known Douglas for seven days, and it was rather early to fall in love with him. But she felt convinced that in previous lives she had loved the young man, and that the present wooing was only the continuation of one interrupted in the distant past. What had interrupted it she could not say, but this time she was determined to bring it to a head, and learn for certain if Douglas felt towards her as she felt towards him. If glances and attentions went for anything, he assuredly did, but modesty or nervousness apparently prevented his plain speaking. Expecting at any minute to be summoned back to the gloom of Tremore, Alice felt that she could not go away without knowing what Montrose's feelings were. And if he really did love her to the extent of making her his wife, she gratefully recognised that she would have some one beside her to resist the pressure put upon her by Don Pablo and her father.

On arriving at the tree under which she usually met her lover, she was surprised not to find him waiting for her. His absence piqued her, especially as she was late, for he certainly should have been watching for her arrival with his heart in his eyes. With a pout she sat down on one of the two green chairs and stared unseeingly at the many children playing about the grass and sailing toy ships on the Round Pond. What would her father say if he knew that she was meeting Montrose, and now loved him to the extent of thwarting Enistor's darling project of uniting her to Narvaez. Poor ignorant girl! She little knew that Don Pablo by his black arts was keeping Enistor advised of all that was taking place, and that the two men were calmly watching her innocent luring of the fly into the web. Eberstein could have warned her of this infernal espionage, but he was absent, and neither Alice nor her lover had any knowledge how to guard themselves. They were even ignorant that protection was necessary, and it was only when the worst was at an end that they learned how the guardianship of the master had been withdrawn for the time being. The children had to learn to walk alone in their own strength and by their own will. Therefore, in the Garden of Eden represented by Kensington Gardens, did they lie open to the assault of the Serpent in the person of Don Pablo. But their ignorance and innocence and natural leanings towards the good baffled the black magic of the evil creature for the moment.

"A penny for your thoughts," said Montrose suddenly, and Alice raised her eyes to find that he had slipped silently into the chair placed a trifle behind that on which she was seated.

"They are only worth a halfpenny," she retorted rebukingly. "I was thinking how little you must care for my company when you are so late!"

"I have been hiding behind yonder tree ever since you arrived," explained Montrose, laughing, "and for quite an hour I have been waiting."

Alice laughed also. The boyishness of his action appealed to her. "But we are too old to play at Peep Boo like babies," she said, shaking her head with a would-be attempt at primness which was quite a failure.

"We are not old," denied Montrose, placing his chair in line with hers. "We are young: we shall always be young, for the gods love us. As to babies, look into my eyes and you will see yourself as a baby."

But Alice would not look, and the colour came to her cheeks. "There was a girl at school who talked of babies in the eyes. It was amusing to hear her talk, but rather silly."

"The silly things are the serious things of life at this moment."

"How do you explain that epigram, Mr. Montrose?"

"Do epigrams require explanations?"

"This one does, I fancy."

"Oh, no, it doesn't. You must guess that the explanation lies in the words I used. 'At this moment,' I said."

"Why this moment rather than others, Mr. Montrose?"

The young man drew back rather disappointed. "No. I see you don't understand, Miss Enistor, or you would not call me Mr. Montrose."

"You call me Miss Enistor!" replied Alice, wilfully dense.

For the sake of beating her with her own weapons, he answered in kind. "Naturally I do. I am a very polite person. But I daresay, in other lives, in other climes, and when we were clothed in other bodies, I called you Chloe, or Octavia, or Isabeau, or Edith."

"Greek, Roman, French, and Anglo-Saxon," commented Alice, amused; "you seem to have settled the countries we lived in. I suppose I called you Damon, or Marcus, or Jehan, or Harold—that is, supposing we were together in those days in those places."

"We have always been together," said Douglas decisively. "I am quite sure."

"Have you any proof?"

"Only the proof of my own feelings. I am not clairvoyant to the extent of remembering my former incarnations, nor can I—as some can—consciously leave my physical body at will and return to it with a recollection of what I have seen. Now you are more advanced."

"Indeed, I am not. I have learned much from my father, who knows a great deal about such psychic matters. But I have never been properly instructed and my knowledge is very limited."

"But you believe in the doctrine of reincarnation?" urged Montrose eagerly.

"Of course. It is a most sensible doctrine to believe, and explains nearly everything in a common-sense way. But I cannot prove my belief."

"There is no need to prove it to me," said Montrose, thinking of his vision, "for I know beyond all question that we have lived and loved before."

"Yes," assented the girl dreamily, "I knew you the moment you entered Mrs. Barrast's drawing-room."

The young man glanced round, and, seeing that they were more or less sheltered from observation, gently took her hand. She did not remove it, although her whole body thrilled to the touch. "You knew me as what?" asked Montrose.

"I can't say more than that I knew you as a familiar friend."

"So cold a word," pleaded the other softly.

"What other word can I use to you when we have only known each other for a single week?"

"That is in this life. In other existences we knew each other for years."

Alice looked down timidly. "It—is—probable," she breathed.

"Then why not take up the new life at the point where the old one left off?"

"We don't know how it left off, Mr. Montrose."

"No. But assuredly it did at a point where you called me by my then Christian name—Alice."

Her heart fluttered as he spoke thus intimately. "Perhaps we were not Christians," she said, rather embarrassed.

"Ah!" he dropped her hand, "you are fencing. I merely spoke in the style of to-day to illustrate my point."

"Now you are angry!"

"I never could be angry with you; only you will not understand."

"Perhaps I do," said Alice, with a whimsical smile.

"If so, why aren't you plain with me?" said Montrose, ruffled.

The mothering instinct, which makes every woman see in every man a child to be soothed and petted, rose within her. "Let us slap the bad, naughty table that has hurt baby," she said demurely, and Montrose looked up to see the laughter in her eyes.

"You little witch!" He caught her hand again and this time so roughly that she winced at the delicious pain. "You know quite well what I mean."

"I do—Douglas!"

"Oh!" He leaned towards her so violently that she swung aside in alarm.

"The eyes of Europe are on us," she said hastily, indicating the throng of children and nursemaids and grown-up people round the pond and on the paths and lying on the grass.

"Bother the eyes of Europe." But he saw that she was right and he did not dare proclaim his love by taking her in his arms. It was rather a poor thing to content himself with squeezing her hand. But he did, and so hard that she uttered an exclamation.

"Mr. Montrose, you are hurting me."

"Am I? Poor hand! I wish I could kiss it!" with a swift look round, he managed to do so. "There—Alice. Don't you dare to call me anything but Douglas."

"I believe you wish to take me by storm," she pouted, not ill-pleased.

"What! capture my own city?"

"Your own city? What do you mean?"

"I mean that I dwell in your heart. That city is mine."

"How conceited you are."

"Indeed, I am not. You know quite well that I am only speaking the truth. I loved you in the past and I love you now. All preliminaries of love were gone through ages ago. Why fence, as if we now meet for the first time? When I saw you in Mrs. Barrast's drawing-room I said, 'She is mine!' When you saw me you said, 'I am his'——"

"I'm sure I didn't," interrupted Alice hastily.

"You thought it, though."

"I shan't tell you."

"There is no need for you to do so. Oh, my dear," he went on entreatingly, "is there so much love in the world that you and I can afford to throw what we possess away? All my life I have been lonely: all my life I have wanted to meet you, to adore you, to——"

"How could you when you didn't know that I existed?"

"Fencing again. As if you didn't know that spirit is everything and form is nothing. We have been apart on earth until last week; but we have always been together in higher worlds, although neither you nor I can remember our companionship."

Alice laughed in a rather anxious manner. "Any one listening to us would be certain both of us were insane."

"I daresay. But as no one is listening, it doesn't matter. For the convenience of a world that doesn't understand such things, let us behave in a conventional manner. I shall visit at Mrs. Barrast's and court you in the approved style. In due time I shall write and ask your father if I may make you my wife. Meanwhile I want your assurance that you love me and have always loved me in the past."

"But a single week——"

"Time doesn't matter. You know it doesn't. You love me, Alice?"

"Yes!" She saw that the time for fencing was ended. "I love you, Douglas!"

He kissed her hand again, then, aware that the place was too public for him to take her in his arms, suppressed his feelings. Side by side they sat in a stiff kind of way, while each longed for demonstrations which the situation forbade. It was decidedly uncomfortable to be thus conventional. But it was just as well that they thus came to an understanding in the eye of the sun, as the self-control was quite an education.

"One would think we were a couple of old married people, sitting side by side in this stiff manner," said Montrose with a vexed laugh. "I should like to be a Sabine and carry you away by force."

"Perhaps you will have to do so," said Alice, thinking of Don Pablo. "My father will never consent to my becoming your wife."

Montrose looked amazed and anxious. "Why not? There is nothing against my character and position," he said rapidly, "and as I have inherited Lady Staunton's money, your father will be glad that I should bring it into the Enistor family again by making you my wife."

"I don't think my father cares anything about the money," said Alice, ignorant of her parent's true feelings. "He wants me to marry Don Pablo."

"A Spaniard. Who is he?"

"A Spaniard, as you have said. He is my father's greatest friend."

"Young and handsome and wealthy?"

"Wealthy, certainly. But very ugly, just like a mummy, and as old as the hills—older, I believe. He must be eighty."

"Then why does your father wish you to marry him?"

"Because Don Pablo is rich."

"Well, I am rich also. Five thousand a year is riches."

"Don Pablo has more, I fancy."

"I don't care what he has. He hasn't got you for a wife and he never will have. You will marry me and no one else."

"Yes, I promise you that, Douglas. But there will be trouble."

"Pooh!" Montrose laughed joyously. "I'd face a universe of trouble if you were the prize to be obtained by enduring it. Besides, Eberstein says that we belong to one another."

"How does he know?"

"He knows many things that are strange and true. When he comes back he will explain. He promised to do so. Meantime, all we have to do is to be true to one another. We are engaged. Say we are engaged, Alice."

"Yes. We are engaged. I shall marry no one but you."

"Hurrah! Then we shall be happy for ever and ever——"

"Amen," said the girl thankfully. "All the same, I fear Don Pablo."

Montrose tucked her arm within his own. "We are together," he said. "Unity is strength. You understand, dear!" And Alice did understand, smiling happily.

"It is the birthday of the soul," she said; "of your soul and mine, which are one."

CHAPTER IX
THE WARNING

Mindful that a premature engagement might lead to gossip, Montrose and his beloved acted with great discretion. They gave vent to their ardent feelings in private, and behaved prudently in public. Certainly the young man paid many visits to Mrs. Barrast's house, and was markedly attentive to her visitor. But it was natural that a bachelor should admire a pretty maid, so people merely remarked indulgently that evidently Montrose was falling in love with Miss Enistor. They little knew that the inevitable had already happened, and in a scandalously short space of time. Mrs. Barrast, with a shrewdness which did her credit, guessed that the couple understood one another better than they would admit; but even she did not guess how far matters had gone. She would have been annoyed had she really known the truth, not because of the private engagement, but for the simple reason that she had not been admitted into the confidence of the lovers. As it was, all she saw led her to believe that Montrose was conventionally approaching her guest with a view to marriage, and quite approved of his intentions. Therefore she welcomed him to the house, and made use of him and his money. It was only right, she thought, that he should pay for her kindness in forwarding his aims.

And the payment took the form of Mrs. Barrast plundering Montrose on all and every occasion. Frederick supplied her with ample funds for her frivolity, but Mrs. Barrast always wanted more than she could reasonably obtain, and cleverly got what she desired from Douglas. As both lovers were in deep mourning for Lady Staunton, the aunt of one and the benefactress of the other, they did not take much part in the gaieties of the waning season. All the same, Mrs. Barrast made Montrose give her concert tickets and boxes at theatres, which she used freely for herself and her friends. And as on these occasions she usually left Alice to entertain the donor in the Hans Crescent house, the young man was quite willing to be lavish in this direction. Indeed, he was in others also, for he supplied the butterfly with flowers and scent and gloves and similar trifles, which every woman likes to have and which no woman likes to pay for. Alice did not object at the outset to this generosity, as it was necessary to keep Mrs. Barrast in a good temper; but in the end she protested against such wholesale robbery.

"You will ruin Mr. Montrose if you take everything he gives you," she said to Amy, two weeks after that momentous agreement in Kensington Gardens.

"Oh, nonsense!" replied Mrs. Barrast airily. "The man has got more money than he knows what to do with. It's a man's duty to be agreeable. But of course, dear, if you are jealous——"

"I—jealous?"

Mrs. Barrast shrugged her elegant shoulders. "Well, my dear, it looks like it, you know. You needn't be if you are, I'm sure, for I can't marry him, and I have no intention of running away with the dear thing."

"He wouldn't run away with you if you wanted to," said Alice crossly, and could have bitten out her tongue for the speech.

"Really!" Mrs. Barrast tittered significantly. "Has it gone as far as that?"

"What do you mean?" Alice grew red.

"My dear! You are a woman talking to a woman, so there is no need for you to try and deceive me. You want to marry this charming young fellow!"

"I don't admit that, Amy."

"Whether you admit it or deny it, what I state is the case."

"You have no right to say so. I like Mr. Montrose. I admire him!"

"Words! Words! Words! You love him. Look at yourself in the glass, my dear. I think your colour tells the truth."

"What if it does?"

"Ah! Then you admit that I am right?"

Alice saw that it was useless to fence with Mrs. Barrast, who was much too clever to be deceived and far too dangerous to be tampered with. "Yes! I am in love with—Mr. Montrose."

"Why not say with Douglas?" tittered the little woman.

"Douglas, if it pleases you."

"My dear, the question is if it pleases *you* and—him. Am I blind? asked Mrs. Barrast dramatically. "Am I a fool? Do you think that during the past three weeks I have left you and that nice boy together without guessing the truth ages and ages ago? I never ask for tickets. He gives them to me to get me out of the way, which"—ended the butterfly justly—"is not complimentary to me."

"I don't mind Mr.—well then, Douglas, giving you boxes at the theatres," said Alice petulantly; "but why take flowers and gloves and——"

"Because I want such things," retorted Mrs. Barrast coolly. "If you are foolish enough not to take presents from him, I don't see why I should not. But I am glad that we have come to an understanding, dear, as I wish to know if you are in earnest, or if you are merely flirting."

"And if I am flirting?"

"Then I think it's very horrid of you. He has a heart and hearts can be broken. I don't flirt myself," said Mrs. Barrast, uttering the lie with the greatest composure, "but if you are making a fool of that nice boy I shall take him off your hands and be a—a—well, a mother to him."

Alice laughed outright. "You are much too young and pretty to be a mother to any one, Amy!"

"That's right. Taunt me because I haven't any children. Frederick is always complaining, as if it was my fault, which I'm sure it isn't. But as to this flirting——"

"It isn't flirting. Douglas and I understand one another."

"Really. How sly you are! Has he said anything?"

"All that I wished him to say."

"Then he has proposed?"

"Yes!" Alice contented herself with the affirmative and did not trouble to give the date of the proposal. Mrs. Barrast understood that it had taken place within the last day or so, and even that displeased her.

"It's quite immoral for him to be so hasty," she exclaimed, because the idea of Montrose adoring Alice and not herself was annoying and hurt her vanity.

The girl smiled, wondering what her hostess would say if she knew that the proposal had been made three weeks previously. "He's in love, you see!"

"There is sense in all things, my dear. He has only known you a month."

"Of course! But love at first sight——"

"I don't believe in such a thing."

"Oh, Amy, what about Romeo and Juliet?"

"They are only things in a play. I don't think Juliet was at all respectable, and if she had lived in London instead of Verona, I should never have allowed her to visit me. Mr. Montrose should have behaved himself properly."

"What do you call proper behaviour on his part?"

"Well, he should have spoken to me first!"

"Douglas's idea of propriety differs from yours, Amy. He thought it was best to tell my father that he wished to marry me, before speaking to you."

"He could do no less," snapped Mrs. Barrast, still ruffled. "Has he written to Mr. Enistor?"

"Yes. Two days ago; but he has not yet received an answer. Nor have I, for I wrote to my father at the same time, asking him to consent to our engagement."

"Oh, he'll consent quick enough—your father, that is," sniffed the little woman. "He owes me a great deal for bringing back that lost money to the family. If he is nice—I suppose he *is* nice, though Julian doesn't like him at all—I expect he'll give me a bracelet, or a muff-chain, or a——"

"Do you really mean that?" interrupted Alice, opening her eyes very wide.

"Of course! Why shouldn't I mean what I say?"

"How rapacious you are, Amy."

"What a nasty word when I'm only sensible. What is the use of men if they don't give us things?"

"Douglas will give you all you want, dear. After all, you brought us together."

This diplomatic remark cleared the air and banished the frown from Mrs. Barrast's small-featured face. "Of course I did. I saw that you two were meant for each other the moment you set eyes on one another. I advised you to get back your aunt's money by marriage, didn't I?"

"You certainly did," admitted Miss Enistor dryly, not thinking it necessary to explain that she loved Montrose for himself alone. "What you said has come true, Amy. Douglas desires to make me his wife, if my father consents."

"Oh, bother your father," cried Mrs. Barrast vigorously. "What does his consent matter when you have hooked a rich man?"

"Don't be vulgar, Amy!" said Alice, wincing.

"And don't be romantic. You can't deceive me. Mr. Montrose is rich."

"I would marry him without a sixpence."

"So you will," rejoined Mrs. Barrast caustically. "He has the sixpence, remember. I am glad, dear: you have played your cards well. Frederick will be pleased. He likes Mr. Montrose immensely, and you a great deal."

"I am glad he does," said Alice soberly, "but don't say anything until we hear from my father, Amy!"

It was with some difficulty that Miss Enistor induced the little woman to be silent, for Mrs. Barrast was so immensely pleased with what she took to be her own cleverness in bringing the matter to a favourable issue that she wanted to trumpet the news all over the place. There was no word now of impropriety or hasty wooing, for Alice let the butterfly think that the match was quite of her own making, and the butterfly spread sheltering wings over the happy pair. She did not tell Frederick, and as Frederick was wholly occupied with politics he did not see what was going on under his very nose. But with many mysterious becks and smiles and significant looks, the little woman managed to intimate that she was the fairy godmother of these particular lovers, whose romance was rapidly progressing towards fulfilment. Thus she made everything safe in a respectable way for Montrose to be constantly invited to dinner, and to be left alone with Alice more frequently than would have met with public approval had he not been courting. The young man's gratitude showed itself substantially and took the form of several pieces of jewellery, which the guardian angel was pleased to accept. Everything went as merry as a marriage bell, pending the reply of Enistor to Montrose's letter. That came four days after Alice had remonstrated with Mrs. Barrast for her shameless looting.

Mr. Enistor had written not only to Montrose but to his daughter with regard to the proposal, and when the two came together on this particular evening, they let one another know immediately that the fatal missives had been received. Luckily Mrs. Barrast, with a merry party, had gone to the Empire Music Hall and would not return until late. Montrose, as usual, had provided the box, purposely having done so to rid himself of an inconvenient third. Frederick was at the House, so he could not interfere, and Douglas had Alice all to himself in the large drawing-room. Mrs. Barrast, for the sake of propriety, had made him promise to await her return and have supper. Therefore everything was nicely arranged, and when quite alone, the lovers sat together on the sofa and looked into one another's eyes.

"Now," said Alice breathlessly, "the letters!"

"Not just yet," replied Montrose, taking her in his arms, "remember I have not seen you for forty-eight hours!"

"Oh, you foolish boy!"

Alice had some excuse for calling him so, although she liked the foolishness he displayed immensely. He dropped on his knees, holding her waist in his arms, and said all manner of delightful things, only interrupting his speeches to kiss her again and again and again. What he babbled need not be reported, as the talk of lovers, however pleasing to themselves, is extraordinarily silly when repeated to others. But the splendid glamour of love was over this pair, and what Douglas said sounded sublimely sensible to the girl, while the looks of Alice were those of a goddess to her adorer. Yet Montrose was a common-sense young man, and Miss Enistor only a tolerably pretty girl. The misleading passion of love excused each regarding the other as a divinity. They certainly did so and were as foolishly happy as Antony and Cleopatra were in their day of power. And like those famous lovers they would have regarded the world as well lost for love.

"But really!" cried Alice at last, recovering her reason first, which was natural since she was a woman, "we must be sensible."

"I think we are very sensible indeed."

"Other people would not think so."

"Why trouble about other people?" replied Montrose, reluctantly getting on his feet. "There are no other people. You and I are alone in the world."

"Indeed, I think we shall be unless my father consents," sighed Miss Enistor. "Not that there will be any loneliness with you beside me," she added.

"Darling!" Then another kiss and embrace before settling down to more prosaic conversation. "Tell me, dear, what does he say to you?"

"Much the same as he writes to you, Douglas, I expect." Alice took the letter from her pocket. "He is not angry as I expected he would be, and says nothing about Don Pablo. All he desires—so he says—is my happiness, and if he approves of you he is quite willing that we should marry."

"If he approves of me," echoed Montrose, reading the paternal letter over Alice's shoulder, "quite so. But suppose he doesn't approve?"

"Don't try to cross the bridge until you come to it, Douglas. Why shouldn't my father approve, now that he evidently has given up his idea of my marrying Don Pablo? Has my father asked you down to Tremore?"

"Yes!" said Montrose, producing his letter in turn, "how clever of you to guess that, dearest."

"I did not guess it, as you might have seen if you read my father's letter properly," said Alice quickly. "He says that he has asked you down, or intends to ask you down. I don't know which."

"Oh, here is the invitation," remarked the young man, waving his letter. "Mr. Enistor says that before he can consent to place your future in my hands he must become well acquainted with me. He invites me to Tremore for a visit of one month. In four weeks he hopes to give his decision."

Alice disconsolately replaced her epistle in her pocket and watched her lover put away his communication. "That doesn't sound very promising."

"Oh, but I think it does," said Montrose hopefully. "I don't see what else he could say if he entertains at all the idea of my marrying you. It is only natural that he should wish to know what kind of a husband I am likely to be to his adored daughter."

"Oh!" said Alice ironically, "does my father call me that?"

"Twice he calls you that in his letter."

"He doesn't mean it," the girl assured Montrose in a troubled way; "my father and I endure one another's society, but little love exists between us. The fault isn't mine, Douglas, as I was willing enough to love him when I came from school. But father has always kept me at arm's length, and hitherto my life has been loveless—save for Julian."

"Julian!" There was a jealous note in the young man's voice. "That is the name of Mrs. Barrast's brother, is it not?"

"Yes. I call him Julian and he calls me Alice."

"Confound his impudence!" fumed Montrose angrily.

"No impudence at all, Douglas. Julian is my very good friend: nothing more, I assure you. But if I had not met you, and if my father had insisted upon my becoming Don Pablo's wife, I should have married Julian."

"Oh, Alice," in a tone of deep reproach, "do you love him and not me?"

"No. I respect him. If I loved him you would not now be sitting beside me."

Still Montrose was not satisfied. "Is he good-looking?"

"Very; in a large stolid Anglo-Saxon way. He's an artist, but I don't think one would call him clever except as a painter of pictures."

"I see that you don't love him," said Douglas, his brow clearing; "but does Hardwick—that is his name, isn't it?—love you?"

"No," rejoined Alice promptly, "he thought that he did, but he really does not in the way a woman wants to be loved. He proposed and I rejected him on those grounds. Now he understands that I am right, and we have settled to be great friends."

"All the same you said you would have married him if— —"

"If my father had insisted on my becoming the wife of Don Pablo," interrupted Alice swiftly. "Can't you understand, Douglas? I detest this Spaniard, who is such a friend of my father, and of two evils I was prepared to choose the lesser. I did not want to marry Julian any more than I wanted to marry Don Pablo. But Julian is at least human, so— —"

"Isn't Don Pablo human?" asked Montrose, interrupting in his turn.

"I don't believe he is," said Alice thoughtfully, "there is something dreadfully wicked about him. I can't explain, but when you meet him you will in some way guess my meaning."

"Humph! I shall certainly accept your father's invitation both to see this Spaniard and Hardwick also."

"And you understand my position?" urged Alice anxiously.

"Yes. I think I do. All the same I want you to assure me positively that you love no one else but me."

"There is no need to tell you what you already know," returned the girl in a calm positive way. "We are made for one another!"

"Darling!" he caught her in his arms, "I know. But I hope your father will think as we do."

"He means well," said Miss Enistor with a sigh of relief, "or he would not ask you down to Tremore."

It was at this interesting point in their interview that the lovers were interrupted. The footman opened the door to announce Dr. Eberstein, and when that gentleman entered the room the servant promptly retired. Montrose came forward with a look of amazed inquiry, which was reflected on the face of Alice. Both the young people were astonished by the unexpected appearance of the doctor.

"I thought you were still in Paris, Eberstein," cried Douglas, as his friend shook hands with both.

"I arrived in London to-day!"

"Why didn't you let me know?"

"There was no need to. It was necessary that you should quite understand one another before I came on the scene." Eberstein looked from one flushed face to the other with a smile. "You do understand, I see."

"We are engaged," blurted out Montrose awkwardly.

"Then that means an understanding," said the doctor cheerfully, with a benevolent look in his grey eyes. "I hope it means also mutual trust."

"I am quite sure it does," cried Alice vehemently, "nothing Douglas could say or do would ever make me doubt him."

"And I would believe in Alice if all the world were against her," said the young man decisively.

"That is good hearing," observed the doctor pleasantly, "union is strength."

"Every one knows that, don't they, doctor?" said Miss Enistor rather pertly.

"Perhaps," he replied, "but few practise it. You wonder why I have come here to-night. It is because you both need me. All seems to be sunshine at the present moment. You love one another devotedly: you think that Mr. Enistor is well disposed towards your engagement——"

"Oh!" interrupted Alice, with a frightened look in her eyes. "How do you know that my father is aware of our engagement?"

"The letters you received to-day——"

This time Montrose interrupted, and there was a note of awe in his voice. "I believe you know everything, Eberstein."

"I know that you are invited down to Cornwall, so that Mr. Enistor may judge if you are the man he would choose to be his son-in-law."

"But how do you know?" said Alice, startled. "You make me afraid!"

Eberstein took her hand and gazed directly into her eyes. "Are you sure that I make you afraid?" he asked gently.

"Why, no!" Alice felt the momentary fear vanish in an unaccountable way.

"And you trust me even though you have known me such a short time? Remember, you have only met me once, Miss Enistor." He loosened his soft, reassuring grasp and leaned back in his chair.

"I do trust you," said the girl promptly, "you have been kind to Douglas."

"Is that the sole reason?"

Alice stared at him doubtfully. "It is the only reason I can give. No one but a good man and a kind friend would have saved Douglas's life as you did."

"Perhaps no, perhaps yes," said the doctor enigmatically, "but I advised our friend here to keep Lady Staunton's money. My interest in him may not be so philanthropic as you imagine it to be."

"Doctor!" said Montrose indignantly, "how can you talk so?"

"Hush!" Eberstein threw up his hand. "I want Miss Enistor to speak."

"What can I say but that I trust you? I am sure there is some good reason why Douglas should keep my aunt's money. You would not have advised him to keep it otherwise."

"But if your father pointed out that he should have enjoyed the fortune and that I wish Montrose to keep it so that I can make use of the money through him? What then?"

"Still I must believe in you and trust you," persisted Alice steadily. "My father does not want the fortune." Eberstein smiled slightly. "Oh, I assure you he does not. He has said nothing about it. As to doubting you, doctor, he does not know you."

"He will some day and then he may doubt me. Remember when he does and tries to turn you against me that I have foretold the possibility of such a warning. You say you will trust me. Good! I accept the assurance. Montrose?"

"I believe in you now as I always have done," said the young man eagerly. "I don't understand why you are talking in this way, though."

"You don't understand many things at present," said Eberstein dryly; "when you do, pain will come with the knowledge. Necessary pain. Go to Cornwall and meet Mr. Enistor. While the sun still shines you will not see me. But when dark clouds obscure the light, then I shall be at your side."

"You will come to Cornwall?" asked Alice quickly.

"When the need arises."

"Will it arise?"

Eberstein looked from one to the other quietly. "Yes! The need will arise."

"What need?" demanded Montrose, bewildered.

"Enough for the day is the evil thereof," said Eberstein serenely, "and that also applies to the good. All is well with you as yet, so enjoy the passing moment and draw from peace the necessary strength for conflict. Gold must be refined in the fire, and you must both be cast into the furnace. Yet be not afraid. The same God who saved Shadrach, Meshach and Abednego will save you. You are neither of you afraid," he ended positively.

Arm in arm the lovers stood and they glanced at one another as the doctor spoke. "We are not afraid," they declared simultaneously, and spoke the truth.

"Behold then," said Eberstein solemnly, "how great is Love which can cast out fear!" and over them he made the holy sign.

CHAPTER X
IN CORNWALL

It was August when Alice returned home. As soon as her father learned that she had become engaged to Montrose, he sent for her. Now that the mouse had entered the trap there was no need for the girl to remain in London and spend money. Mrs. Barrast was sorry to lose the companionship of Miss Enistor, not only because she liked her as much as one of her shallow nature could like any one, but for a more selfish reason. With Alice departed Montrose, and although he did not go immediately down to Cornwall, he scarcely came near the house in Hans Crescent. Thus Mrs. Barrast was deprived of the many presents which she loved to receive. However, she had done very well, and made the best of her loss, since the girl's visit, because of Montrose's love-making, had not been unprofitable to her. Mrs. Barrast was very affectionate when Alice departed, and made her promise to return when she became Mrs. Douglas Montrose. Alice readily consented, for though Amy was vain and selfish, yet the fact that the love-romance had taken place beneath her roof made the girl regard her as a most excellent friend. All the same she was not sorry to return to Cornwall, as she was weary of the frivolous London life.

In the railway train Alice became quite depressed. She was coming back to dreary Tremore, to her father's uncongenial society, and perhaps to the unpleasant attentions of Don Pablo. But on this latter point she was reassured by her father's letter. Although he had not quite consented to the marriage with Montrose, and would not consent until he had seen the young man, yet, in the face of his half-approval, he certainly would not allow her to be troubled by Don Pablo. Certainly the Spaniard had great influence with the squire of Polwellin, and might not be inclined to surrender the girl whom he desired to make his wife. But Douglas, as Alice reflected, would soon be on the spot, and he would deal with Narvaez, if the old man became troublesome. On the whole, therefore, even though matters were a trifle unsettled, Alice concluded that the new life would be better than the old. At all events she would not be quite so lonely, and that was something. Of course Dr. Eberstein had predicted trouble, but also he had agreed to come down when the trouble arrived. This comforted the girl not a little, as she had the greatest confidence in Montrose's friend. Why, she could scarcely say, as she knew next to nothing about him. But his mere look, let alone the touch of his hand, was enough to make her feel strangely brave and happy. If Don Pablo was all evil, Dr. Eberstein was all good. Yet why one should be this and the other that, Alice could not tell. Doubtless, as Douglas had suggested, Eberstein could have enlightened both on this point. But he had not done so, and beyond warning them that they could count upon his help in the trouble which was surely coming, he had said very little. Therefore, these two young people had to walk by faith, and very bravely did so.

At Perchton, which was the nearest station to Polwellin, Alice quite expected to find her father waiting for her, since, little as he loved her, he must surely be anxious to see how she looked after her long absence. But Mr. Enistor was not on the platform, and Alice with a rather forlorn feeling alighted from her compartment. In London she had grown accustomed to love and attention, so the neglect of the present moment brought on her depression again. But that vanished in a trice when a strong hand took the small bag she was carrying, and a strong voice sounded in her ears.

"Here you are at last," said Julian brightly. "I have been waiting for nearly an hour, Alice."

"Oh, Julian!" she took his hand, to press it warmly. "I am so glad you are here. I was feeling quite dismal because father has not come to meet me."

"I thought you would be. Yesterday I asked him if he intended to come to Perchton, but as he said that he had no time I came in his stead."

"And left your painting. How good of you."

"Not at all. We are brother and sister, are we not?"

"I don't think many brothers would take so much trouble to be kind to their sisters," said Alice brightly. "Did father send the carriage?"

"No. One of the horses is laid up. But a friend of mine has a motor, so I made him lend it to take you to Tremore. Where is your baggage?"

"Oh, I must look for it in the van and get a porter and——"

"You'll do nothing of the sort," interrupted Hardwick quickly, "go and sit in the motor; there it is. I can see to your boxes. How many?"

"Two large and one small," said Alice, and gladly settled herself in the very comfortable vehicle, while Julian went back into the station.

Shortly he returned with a porter and the boxes were duly placed on the motor. Julian stepped in beside the girl, and a word to the chauffeur sent the splendid machine humming down the narrow street like a giant bee. Then the two had time to look at one another, and Julian approved of the girl's appearance. Love had made her blossom like a rose. She was less ethereal than she had been, and the sad look on her delicate face had vanished. Also, as Mrs. Barrast had attended to her frocks, and had introduced her to Madame Coralie, the girl was singularly smart and attractive as regards clothes. A smile was on Julian's face as he looked at her.

"You went away a duckling and you return a swan," he said.

"Oh, what a doubtful compliment," said Alice gaily; "am I then, or rather was I, an ugly duckling?"

"No, my dear, you were never an *ugly* duckling, but what I mean is that you have turned from a fairy into a pretty nymph.

"That is better," said Miss Enistor graciously, as the motor whizzed out of the town and began to climb the long winding road to the moors. "You are improving, Julian. But you don't ask me how I have enjoyed myself."

"There is no need. Your appearance speaks for you."

Alice laughed. "Do you think that my looks are due simply to a short season of pleasure in London?"

"Well, not exactly," rejoined Hardwick in his stolid way; "in fact, seeing that you have been staying with Amy, I expected you to look more fagged than you do. Amy makes a toil of pleasure and is certainly a very wearing woman to live with."

"She is a dear," said Miss Enistor warmly, "and has been most kind. But you are right about her feverish pursuit of pleasure," she said, with an after-thought. "Amy never rests!"

"And never lets any one else rest, which is worse," said Julian grimly; he looked at her sideways. "Yes! Mere London pleasure cannot account for your happy looks. Well, let me know who he is!"

"Let you know who he is?" repeated Alice, blushing and looking prettier than ever, "do you mean— —"

"I think you know what I mean. You are in love at last."

Like a woman Alice did not reply directly to the remark. "Are you very angry, Julian?" she asked, laying a timid hand on his arm.

"My dear, I am not angry at all. We are brother and sister, you know. Long ago I discovered that you were right as to my proposal and I was wrong. All that I could do for you was to accept the situation of your future husband if Don Pablo insisted upon marrying you. But I presume I can now resign that position," ended Hardwick gravely.

"He is called Douglas Montrose," said Alice, still evasive.

"A very pretty name for Prince Charming. Yes, your father mentioned to me that the young man had written to him, and he also mentioned that Montrose is the fortunate person who has inherited Lady Staunton's money. So Amy got her own way, as I knew she would. An inveterate matchmaker is Amy."

Alice opened her eyes widely. "Did you guess then?"

"Not so much guess as know," replied Hardwick composedly. "Amy wrote about her desire that you should become Mrs. Montrose."

"And you?"

"I was pleased, of course. Amy told me how deeply you loved the man."

"She could not tell that for certain," pouted Alice doubtfully.

"I am not so sure of that. Women are proverbially clever and shrewd in anything that has to do with love-making. However, it seems she was right: your bright eyes and crimson cheeks tell me as much."

"I may as well confess that I love Douglas," admitted Alice boldly, "and he loves me. Already we have asked father's consent to our marriage."

"He will give it without doubt, Alice. It is a happy way of getting back the lost money."

"Oh the money! the money!" she cried petulantly; "you talk just as Amy talks, Julian. As if I cared for money. I love Douglas, and if he were a pauper I would marry him. And my father has not jumped at the chance of getting back the money, as you seem to think. He won't say yes and he won't say no."

"He must say something," remarked Julian, with a shrug.

"Nothing. He refuses to give his decision until he knows more about Douglas."

Hardwick nodded. "That is natural and sensible. So the young man is coming to Tremore to be put through his paces?"

"How clever of you to guess that. He is—in a few days. Oh, how anxious I feel, Julian. So much depends upon my father."

"He will consent, I am sure, Alice. With such a disposition as you have, you could choose no one but a really good man for your husband."

Alice laughed a trifle bitterly, which was strange considering her prospects and happy state of mind. "Goodness or badness matter very little when one is in love, Julian. And they do not matter at all to my father so long as I marry a rich man. It is a good thing for me that Douglas has plenty of money, for only in that way will things run smoothly for both of us. Otherwise I feel certain that my father would still insist upon my marrying Don Pablo."

"Humph!" said Hardwick meditatively. "The question is, 'Would Don Pablo marry you?' my dear girl."

"He is supposed to be in love with me," said Alice, puzzled. "You know how he has bothered me, Julian."

"Oh, yes, I know. But there is Rose Penwin, you know, that fisherman's pretty daughter."

Alice turned to look at him in astonishment. "What about her?"

"Señor Narvaez has taken an unaccountable admiration for her since you departed for London."

"Unaccountable!" Miss Enistor's lip curled. "There is nothing unaccountable in any man admiring a pretty girl, and Rose is more than pretty!"

"She is," said Hardwick calmly. "Pretty is not the word to apply to a beautiful and stately woman such as Rose Penwin is."

"Brunhild or Brynhild—what do you call that Norse goddess you said you so admired until you met me?"

"I never admired any Norse goddess," said Hardwick, laughing. "I simply quoted Brynhild as a type. Yes, Rose Penwin is of that type, but I am not in love with her."

"Don Pablo is?"

"So I am given to understand from village gossip. You know I chatter frequently to the fishermen and their wives. Well, Don Pablo has been paying great attention to Rose; giving her presents and— —"

"Does she accept his attentions?" interrupted Miss Enistor, astonished.

"Yes and no. She does in a way, as she wants to make Job Trevel jealous!"

"Job Trevel," said Alice thoughtfully; "to be sure! He is my foster-brother, Julian, as I told you how Dame Trevel brought me up. But I thought it was understood that Rose was to marry Job."

"Too thoroughly understood," said Julian dryly. "It seems that Job is so certain of Rose that he does not trouble to pay her those pretty attentions which a lover should. Thus, to make him jealous, Rose pretends to accept the attentions of Don Pablo."

"That old mummy. He can't even feel love."

"No! I agree with you there, and I am puzzled to know what his game is. Why should an old man of eighty run after a girl of nineteen?"

"He ran after me and bothered me enough, as you know," said Alice in a thoughtful manner. "He must be mad. Yet I do not think a madman would or could exercise such an influence over my father. However, Job can scarcely be jealous of Señor Narvaez, who might be Rose's great-grandfather."

"He is jealous, however. Don Pablo is wealthy and Rose likes pretty things, you know. She may not love the old reprobate: she could not. All the same the prospect of unlimited money — —"

"Oh, nonsense!" broke in Alice vigorously, "she would not be so wicked. If I see anything of her treating Job badly I shall speak to her. I am very fond of my foster-brother even though he has a bad temper."

"All the worse for Don Pablo if he has," said Hardwick significantly. "Rose is playing with fire. Love on one hand, wealth on the other: which will she choose, do you think? I assure you, Alice, that there are the elements of a tragedy in these things."

"It may be all imagination on your part," said the girl after a pause, "and in any case, if Don Pablo now admires Rose, he will leave me alone, and my father will have no excuse to forbid my marrying Douglas."

Julian wrinkled his brow disapprovingly. "Isn't that a selfish way of looking at the matter?"

"It is! It is!" acknowledged Alice with sudden compunction. "Love does make one selfish, Julian."

"Yet love should have the opposite effect, my dear girl. You usually have such a high standard that it seems strange you should fall short of it in this way. But you have been with Amy, and although she is my own sister, even a short time in her company does harm. She is not bad—I don't mean that, Alice: but Amy is excessively selfish and she seems to have contaminated you in some way."

Alice grew scarlet, as never before had Julian dared to speak to her in this reproving style. Yet she felt that he was right, and took no offence. "I am glad you have said what you have said, Julian. I should not have spoken as I did. It was narrow and selfish, as you say. I must think of others even if love for Douglas fills my heart. I shall see Dame Trevel and Job and in some way I shall learn the truth. You may be sure that I shall do what I can to put matters right between Rose and Job."

Hardwick patted her hand. "That is spoken like the trump you are, Alice, my dear. I knew that you were not thinking of what you were saying. As you are in love, there is some excuse——"

"No! No! Don't weaken your good advice, Julian. There is no excuse for one to fall short of one's standard. Your warning has done me good. You are a dear kind boy, and if I had not met Douglas——"

"You would have loved me," ended Hardwick, smiling. "No, dear, don't deceive yourself. If we had married we should have been comrades, but never man and wife in the true spiritual sense. The marriage made in heaven is the only true marriage. You said something of that sort when you refused me. How entirely right you were, Alice!"

The girl looked at him with a whimsical look in her eyes and wondered at his simplicity. "What a child you are, Julian. Nine women out of ten would take offence at such a cool assurance that your love for me has perished."

"Probably," returned Julian composedly, "nine women out of ten are dogs in the manger, but you, my dear Alice, are the tenth. I shall be glad to see Montrose. Tell me all about him."

"That is difficult," said Miss Enistor absently, "let me think for a moment."

Julian could not see why it should be difficult for a young girl in the first delicious phase of a perfect passion to talk to an intimate friend, such as he truly was, of her feelings. But he did not understand what was passing in Alice's mind. Her wooing was of so unusual a character, and had so much to do with psychic matters concerning which Hardwick knew nothing, that it was hard to explain the swift love which had drawn her and Douglas together. For one moment she hesitated, and the next decided not to speak. Julian would not understand, and she evaded a direct answer to his question by a truly feminine subterfuge. "I would rather you judged Douglas for yourself without looking at him through my eyes. He will be here in a few days and then you can give me your opinion."

"Well," said Julian in his usual stolid way, "perhaps you are right!" after which calm acceptance of the situation he became silent.

While the two young people had been talking, the car had pursued its way towards Tremore steadily and swiftly. Along the winding white roads it glided, with the spreading no-man's-land of purple heather on either side. How Alice loved it all; the vast moorlands sprinkled with grey blocks of granite; the tumbled steepness of black cliffs; the far-stretching spaces of the gleaming ocean and the life-giving winds that breathed across the limitless lands. For the moment she wondered how she had ever endured the narrow, muffling London streets, with their twice-breathed airs and garish lights. Like a thing of life the great car swung untiringly along, and the landscape widened out at every turn of the road. She felt as though she had come out of a stifling cavern into a spacious world, and flung out her hands in ecstatic greeting to the majesty of Nature. Reborn through love into a wider consciousness, the girl's seeing and hearing now embraced an appreciation of much to which she had been formerly deaf and blind. Sound seemed sweeter, colour more vivid and life dearer. There was a feeling of spring in the autumnal air, and Alice felt that she wished to dance and sing and generally rejoice out of sheer lightheartedness.

"I am made one with Nature," she exclaimed, thrilling to the beauty of land and sea. "Doesn't Shelley say something like that in 'Adonais'?"

"I never read poetry," replied Julian stolidly. "To my mind poets only say in many words what a journalist says in few."

"What a pagan sentiment," cried Miss Enistor gaily, "and how untrue. Oh, there is Tremore!"

Assuredly it was, and the grey house looked more sinister than ever in the pale sunshine. It placed its dark spell on Alice, for as the motor-car breasted the hill, her gay spirits left her and she became as pale as hitherto she had been rosy. With wonderment and regret Julian saw again the wan girl who had left for London weeks before, and anxiously inquired if she felt ill.

"No," said Alice, rousing herself with an effort from the lethargy which had fallen on her. "I feel quite well, but less full of vitality than when I arrived at Perchton. It is the idea of Tremore, I think," she shuddered. "You know what a gloomy house it is."

"Montrose will dispel the gloom when he arrives," suggested Hardwick.

Alice brightened. "Oh, I am sure he will. But how nice of you to say that. You are not a bit jealous."

"I believe you are annoyed because I am not, my dear girl," laughed the artist.

"Julian, how can you say such a thing?" she replied absently; then added in a markedly irrelevant manner, "I hope father will be glad to see me."

Mr. Enistor may have been glad, but he certainly did not appear at the door to show his gladness. Alice's boxes were taken into the house, and Julian departed in the car, declining to enter, on the plea that father and daughter would have much to say to one another. Alice did not seek to stay him. She felt chilled by the absence of welcome and the sombre atmosphere of the big house. The beaten space of ground upon which it stood seemed to isolate it from the warm laughing world of vivid life, and she entered with the feeling that she was descending into a vault. Nor did the greeting of her father tend to dissipate this impression of dismay. He received her in the library with a cold kiss and without rising from his chair.

"Well, Alice, how are you?" He looked at her keenly as she stood by the table, white and frozen into silence. "Your stay in town does not appear to have done you much good."

"Oh, I feel all right," said the girl, with an effort to be her true self.

"You don't look all right," snapped Enistor, rather disappointed. "After all the money you have spent you certainly should have a more healthy appearance. H'm! I think I understand," he paused a moment, then added bitingly, "your new lover has disappointed you. Is that it?"

"No!" Alice roused herself to offer a protest. "Douglas is all that I can wish, father."

"I hope for your sake that he is all *I* can wish. If he isn't I shall certainly not allow you to marry him. There is always Don Pablo to— —

At this speech Alice did wake up and a colour flushed her cheeks. "Don Pablo, if I am to believe Julian, has fallen in love with Rose Penwin."

"I didn't know that Hardwick was such a gossip," said Enistor coolly. "As to falling in love, Narvaez is much too sensible a man. He admires the girl for her beauty and has given her several presents of jewellery. At Don Pablo's age no one can object to that."

"Job Trevel can, and Job Trevel does."

"More gossip," sneered Enistor. "Your artist friend appears to have informed himself accurately of the situation. But it matters nothing to you or to me, since neither of us has any right to interfere with Don Pablo's likes or dislikes. You are the one he loves, Alice."

"I thought you said a moment ago that he was too sensible to fall in love!"

The Squire shrugged his shoulders. "I meant in the silly way of boys and girls. Narvaez' love is of a deeper and more spiritual kind. He admires Rose as a beautiful girl; he adores you as a soul."

"I don't want his adoration!" said Alice wearily, for it seemed hard that the usual wrangling should begin the moment she returned home.

"You prefer Montrose's adoration no doubt. Well, I have no objection so long as I approve of the young man and he does what I want."

"What is that?"

"He must restore the money which your aunt left him."

"I thought you did not care for the money, father?"

"I care very much indeed for the money, although I have never emphasised the fact. Only because he has it did I even consider the possibility of your marrying him. I should much prefer you to be Narvaez' wife. However, we shall see when the young man arrives. Meantime you had better lie down as you seem to be worn out by your journey. It's waste of money to send you away."

Alice bit her lips to keep back her tears and breathed a prayer that Eberstein should help her to throw off the deadly influence of the house. Even as she did so the relief came, and she felt a wave of vitality run through her body. The weary, languid sense of utter desolation left her; the colour returned to her cheeks, the brightness to her eyes and the strength to her whole being. Enistor saw the statue come to life, and in place of a wan, weak girl beheld a living, breathing woman, very much alive. He stared amazed.

"What has come to you?" he demanded, startled and puzzled.

"Love," said Alice quietly, "love and life instead of hate and death!"

Enistor quivered, since he knew that the first mentioned forces were at war with himself and his dark Master.

CHAPTER XI
THE SPIDER AND THE FLY

Alice returned to her home with the feeling that she was entering a hostile city. The atmosphere of the house was inimical, charged with disintegrating forces, which strove to break up and scatter her protective power. That the power came from Dr. Eberstein she was now perfectly certain in her own mind, as she had experienced his help so plainly when she arrived. Before her visit to London, Enistor had so dominated her with his cold cynicism and cruel insistence that he had almost entirely conquered her will. She had been like a bird in the coils of a serpent, and only absence had enabled her to regain her freedom. In surroundings less charged with deadly evil, the girl had recovered the youthful spirits which were her rightful heritage, and the unifying influence of Montrose's love had strengthened her considerably. Therefore, when fear again threatened to control her, she had been able to assert herself, but, on reflection, she felt positive that the attempt would have been vain had she not mentally appealed to Eberstein.

Why she had thus called upon him for help she scarcely knew, as she was ignorant of matters connected with the occult. All she did know was that the doctor had always soothed her with his serene strength when she was in his presence, and half unconsciously she had wished for him to be beside her when the insidious evil which overshadowed Tremore had surged round her to paralyse and control. Eberstein had not come himself, but his power had, and like an impassable wall it had fenced her in from danger. The hint that such help was obtainable in such a manner was enough for the girl. She persistently and particularly dwelt upon Eberstein's powerful personality, and whenever uncomfortable feelings assailed her, she swiftly imagined that he was close at hand to defend her. Also she constantly visualised the image of her lover, knowing that he was willing to lay down his life for her safety, and this in a lesser degree filled her with life and strength. If Enistor on his daughter's return doubted that the visit to London had done her good, he had no reason to doubt afterwards. Alice recovered, as by magic, the brightness of her eyes and the roses of her cheeks. She went about the dark house gaily and hopefully busy with domestic affairs, always cheerful and merry even to the extent of singing while at work. It might be thought that Enistor was glad to see how the girl had recovered her spirits and had benefited by the change. But in place of showing satisfaction, he gloomed and glowered in high displeasure.

"There is less chance than ever of our gaining authority over her," he complained to Narvaez, when on a visit to the magician's cottage. "We nearly controlled her before she left for London, but now her resisting strength has increased tremendously."

"It is not her own strength that defends her," replied Don Pablo quietly.

"Then it is the strength of love awakened by Montrose. You might have known, Master—you who have such means of obtaining knowledge—that there was that risk when I let her go to Mrs. Barrast's."

"I am not omnipotent and omniscient," answered the old man dryly. "Great as is my power, there are still many things beyond my control. I implied as much when I told you that the present situation is the outcome of the past. You know the Law of Karma—the Law of Cause and Effect—the Law of 'As ye sow so shall ye reap,' which governs the evolution of the present creation, and knowing so much, you should not be surprised that we are mastered by it as are all beings. Sooner or later Alice was bound to come into contact with our enemies."

"Who are they?"

"Dr. Eberstein and Douglas Montrose!"

"Alice told me how she had met Eberstein and how much she liked him. But she gave me no hint that he was an enemy."

"How could she, seeing she does not know," retorted Narvaez sharply. "Eberstein is the White Magician, against whom I warned you weeks ago. He is coming down here soon, as I prophesied he would. And Montrose also comes. We were all together in Chaldea five thousand years ago, and there engendered causes which have to be worked out in the flesh to-day. Why do you blame me for Alice going to London?"

"She has gained strength by going there and meeting these men. You should have warned me."

"I warned you as much as I could," snapped Narvaez, acridly sharp, "but I could not prevent the inevitable. Alice had to meet them, and the loss of that money under the will which left it to Montrose was the means used to bring them together. All I could do, being impotent under the Karmic Law, was to so arrange matters that Montrose might be brought down here along with Dr. Eberstein. That I have managed and now comes the tug of war. You are by no means a satisfactory pupil, Enistor, as I have again and again to explain matters which you already know."

"Then I take it that Eberstein has already declared war by bringing Montrose and Alice together?"

"The Great Law did that. Eberstein's declaration of war is the help that he is giving Alice to withstand the influence we strive to bring to bear upon her. For the moment, as you saw, she nearly relapsed into her former condition when she returned from her visit. But her intuition told her to call upon her guardian Eberstein and the help came. Her innocence protected her before: now she has the more powerful protection of love, both from Montrose in a personal sense, and in an impersonal way from Eberstein."

"Is he very powerful?"

"Yes," grinned Narvaez with a look of hate in his cold blue eyes. "He follows the Right-hand Path of Love, and has the universal power behind him. You and I on the Left-hand Path of Hate possess only a portion of that power."

"In that case it seems impossible to conquer," said Enistor irresolutely.

The Satanic pride of Don Pablo rose in arms against this insinuation. "Eberstein will find me no mean adversary," he snarled. "I shall fight and fight to the last. Already the fly in the person of Montrose has walked into my parlour."

"Oh! So you are the spider?"

"Yes! And I shall devour Montrose if I can. Already I have made my plans and started my work by paying attentions to that silly Rose Penwin, thus arousing the jealousy of Trevel."

"But I don't see— —"

"Never mind what you see," interrupted Narvaez impatiently. "Leave me to do what I intend to do, and then Eberstein will not find it easy to save Montrose, in spite of his power."

"But if he has more power than you— —?"

"Can't you understand?" cried Don Pablo, exasperated. "Montrose and Alice both have free-will. Eberstein can guide and coax; he cannot command. If the two yield to Self, then we triumph."

"And if they renounce Self?"

"Then we fail. But be of good cheer. Neither is yet so strong as to have entirely conquered the animal self, and that will fight in each for its existence. What you have to do is to play the courteous host, to permit the engagement of Alice and Montrose: then leave the rest to me."

This was only one of many conversations which Enistor had with his Master, while awaiting the arrival of his guest. He could not quite understand the situation, and Narvaez declined to explain further than was in his opinion necessary. All Enistor knew was that Montrose was to be trapped in some way, and that Don Pablo's courting of Rose Penwin with gifts had to do with the trapping. Contented with this knowledge, the man was markedly amiable to his daughter, and Alice felt nervously surprised by the unusual attention which her ordinarily indifferent father paid her. Formerly she had, with some reason, dreaded the sinister influence emanating from him, but now seeing in his demonstrations of affection a sign that he truly loved her, she regretted her possible misjudgment. In many ways she attempted to show her appreciation of the miraculous change from blame to praise, and on the whole found domestic life at Tremore unexpectedly pleasant. Nevertheless the natures of father and daughter clashed at odd moments, and it was only by constantly acting parts they did not truly feel that they could keep things smooth. More than ever did Alice long for the arrival of Montrose, so that she could display her true nature and exercise her true love.

Enistor's unnatural complaisance extended to Hardwick, as, now that he was aware of the artist's rejection, he did not forbid his visits. Julian guessed that the Squire merely tolerated him, and simply came to Tremore on all and every occasion to aid Alice, since he knew that she was something of an alien in her home. His host was always pointedly agreeable, and so— strange to say—was Don Pablo. The dark dour old man, for some hidden reason, appeared to take a great interest in the artist. As he had formerly neglected him in every way, Julian was puzzled to know why he should be thus honoured. Not liking Narvaez, he did not reciprocate this belated amiability, and always escaped with Alice on to the moors when it was possible. He trained her to observe the beauties of Nature, and opened her eyes to a more glorious world of form and colour. Alice accepted such behaviour with sisterly thankfulness, and looked upon him as a large comfortable Newfoundland dog, able to protect and please her. Therefore the young people found life very pleasant, and all was sunshine for the moment, as Eberstein had predicted. That more glorious sunshine would come with her lover's arrival Alice knew very well, but she never forgot that clouds would sooner or later overshadow the summer sky, although she could not see in which quarter they would arise. A vague feeling, however, intimated that disaster would come with Montrose, and that her belief in his love would be severely tested. Nevertheless, she looked forward to his arrival, knowing that Eberstein would follow him shortly. And in the doctor she had the most implicit confidence, assured that whatever sorrow descended upon her or her lover, Eberstein would guard them and help them in every way. Also there was Julian upon whom she could rely in the hour of her need. The suspense indeed was unpleasant, but Alice fought it with prayer and high thinking, girding herself as it were with armour of light against the time when the Dark Powers would assault the citadel of her being. But in her innocence she was ignorant, save from the hints of Eberstein, that an assault was intended.

At length came the golden day when Douglas was to arrive, and Alice rejoiced to receive a letter stating that the young man would leave London by the early morning train at five o'clock. At half-past three he would be at Perchton, and there Julian was to meet him in his friend's motor-car which he had again procured, so that Montrose might be with Alice as speedily as was possible. Enistor, indeed, mindful of Don Pablo's injunction to be courteous, had offered to send the carriage, but Alice, anxious that some swifter method should be found to bring her lover to her longing arms, had accepted the offer of Julian. She did not go to the Perchton station herself, but waited a mile beyond Polwellin village in a green nook beside the high road for the happy moment. Hardwick had purposely arranged to bring the lover to Tremore, as he was anxious for the sake of the girl's happiness to see what was the nature of the man she had chosen to be her husband, and deemed that he could discover the same more easily when Alice was not present. Apparently his reading of Montrose's character was satisfactory, for when the car came swirling round the corner, Alice saw that the two young men were chatting together as if they had known one another for years. Of course when Alice was espied waving her hand on the green hill above the nook, the car was stopped on the dusty white road, and equally of course Montrose jumped down to run like a deer up the ascent. In another moment she was in his fond arms, and heart was beating against heart. Neither could speak, so full of joyful emotion was the moment, and guessing this, Julian told the chauffeur to drive on. With some astonishment the couple saw the motor slipping round the bend of the road, through the village, and up towards Tremore, bearing the portmanteau of Montrose. They were alone in the purple world amongst the gorgeous coloured bracken, which was vivid with autumnal tints. The sun was just sinking and the glory of its rainbow hues bathed them in opal lights.

"That is one of the nicest fellows I ever met," said Montrose, when the first surprise at Julian's prompt action was over. "And he is so sensible. He knew I wanted to be alone with you at the first opportunity."

"Julian is always considerate," said Alice gaily.

"You call him Julian—Mrs. Barrast's brother?" said Montrose jealously.

"Dear," she took him by the lapels of his coat and looked into his dark eyes. "Of course I call him by his Christian name. I told you about Julian in London. How he proposed to me: how I refused him, and how we are now like brother and sister. There is no need to be— —"

Montrose stopped her mouth with a kiss. "Don't say the word. I am a fool," he said penitently. "I remember what you said in Town. And Hardwick is a brick; a really true, honest-hearted fellow. I like him immensely. And—and—oh, we have so much to talk about, Alice, that we need not waste the time in discussing Hardwick, even though he is so decent."

Alice quite agreed with this sentiment, so the two started to climb the hills on their way to Tremore, and talked all the way of near and dear matters so necessary and interesting to lovers, and so dull when a third person overhears. They went over their meeting in Hans Crescent, recalled what he had said and what she had replied; explained how each had been hungry for this precious moment of meeting and punctuated the enthralling conversation with frequent kisses. And as the magical light died out of the western sky, they conversed on graver subjects which had to do with some vague thought of evil coming to them both. Montrose explained how he had seen Eberstein shortly before leaving London.

"He sent for me yesterday," said the young man, fumbling at his breast, "and gave me this, which he said was necessary for my protection."

"Your protection," echoed Alice with a sudden qualm, and she stared at the small golden heart swung on a thin golden chain, which Montrose had produced unexpectedly. "Why should you want protection, Douglas?"

"Ah, that I cannot truly say. But I am so accustomed to obey the doctor implicitly that I did as he asked me and wear this amulet round my neck. He has always a reason for what he does, Alice. Remember, dear, he said plainly that our sunshine would not last for ever," ended Montrose gravely.

"There is to be a period of sorrow, I know," murmured Alice, nestling close to her lover's side. "But with Dr. Eberstein's help we shall come out of the darkness into the light once more. I don't know what he means," she added after a pause. "Why should sorrow come?"

"I have an idea that it has something to do with our meeting in former lives, Alice, and that we have enemies to encounter and conquer."

"Don Pablo very likely."

"I think so, although I am not sure." Montrose spoke dreamily, remembering his wonderful vision and the warning of Eberstein. "We must watch and pray, dear, for, more or less, we are moving in the darkness. This will aid us," and he held up the talisman, which glittered in the sunset rays.

"But how can that golden heart help?" asked Alice disbelievingly.

"You only see the exterior, dear. It holds," Montrose made the sign of the cross on his breast, "a portion of the Host, as Dr. Eberstein told me, and is therefore powerful against evil. I called it an amulet: rightly, I should have said a reliquary. Look, dearest!"

Then a most wonderful thing happened. The two had reached the shade of the wood surrounding Tremore, and had halted on its verge in a spot where the sunlight could not penetrate. But as Alice stared at the golden heart it blazed as a star with a far more brilliant light than any she had ever seen before. In a flash of thought she knew that her interior senses had been opened by the mightiest influence on earth. She was looking through the sheath of metal at the very Host itself in its supernal aspect, radiant, glorious, wonderful, holy. "Oh!" she breathed in a hushed voice and bowed her head reverently.

"What is it?" asked her lover in surprise, for her expression was angelic.

"Do you not see the light that is brighter than the sun?"

"No," he whispered nervously, and seized her hand, like a child seeking for the comfort of a mother's touch. "Where is the light?"

"It is gone now." Alice passed her disengaged hand across her brow. "It disappeared when you touched me. When you held up that heart it shone like a marvellous star of splendour."

Then Montrose understood. "You have seen the Power itself," he murmured, and with trembling hands restored the reliquary to his breast. For the moment what Alice had seen shook him to the core of his being. "How glorious to be able to see through the veil even for a single moment. But why should you not when it is said, 'Blessed are the pure in heart, for they shall see God'?"

Like children they clung to one another on the borders of that dark wood, and it was some time before they could proceed. The sacred light they felt was yet around them, and would act as a shield against all evil. That it did so far as Alice was concerned was certain, for while walking under the yews amidst the heavy darkness, her sense of protection was unusually strong. Not so Montrose, for even though he carried the reliquary, he was less sensitive to its helpful influence than the girl who was more attuned to spirituality. It might be that with him the preponderance of earthly desires placed him more in touch with the lower planes than with the higher, but undoubtedly he felt strongly the tremendous pressure of the evil around him. And when the two halted on the verge of the beaten ground, barren of herb and flower, the house of hate bulked largely, silent, black, brooding and menacing.

"Alice, how can you live here?" demanded Montrose, grasping her hand tightly.

"You feel it also?" she whispered, "that sense of doom and dread?"

"I feel the power that rends and tears and parts asunder: the disintegrating force of Chaos, which is necessary for creation before Cosmos—the Cosmos of Love can be formed!" and unconsciously he gripped her hand with crushing force, so great was the emotion which stirred him.

"Douglas, you hurt me," cried the girl, writhing.

"Oh, forgive me," he descended to the commonplace and tenderly kissed the pained finger. "But the feeling of dread was so strong that I forgot what I was doing. There," he kissed her hand twice, "is it better, darling?"

Alice laughed. "You are a child," she said, advancing towards the house.

Her lover sighed. "We are all children, I think. Afraid of the dark."

"There is no darkness where God is, dear. Think of God and the light comes."

"You are nearer to the Great Spirit of Love than I am," said Douglas, peering nervously into the gloom. Then he made an effort to throw off the still persistent influence of evil. "Let us get into the lamplight."

"Come then," said Alice, and stepping into the porch, she laid her hand on the handle of the door. Immediately, as by magic, it retreated from her fingers, and the portal swung wide to reveal Enistor on the threshold, dimly seen in what light still radiated from the fading sunset over the heavy tree-tops.

"I heard your voices," he explained genially, "and knew that our guest had arrived. Welcome to Tremore, Mr. Montrose."

"Thank you, sir, oh, thank you," replied the young man, reassured by this reception and warmly clasping the hand extended to him.

As he did so a strong feeling of repulsion possessed his mind with overwhelming force, and it was all he could do to prevent himself from wrenching his hand away. Not that there was any need for the action on his part, for Enistor actually translated the thought into swift doing, and loosened his grip, to stand back with a startled look. Without doubt the same repugnance at the same instant of time obsessed the older man, but, less self-controlled, he had been unable to prevent the unfriendly action. In the twilight each man strove to see the face of the other, but it was impossible to distinguish clearly. In shadows they met as shadows.

It was Alice who broke the spell of confused hatred, as, in spite of her clairvoyant faculty, she was apparently ignorant of the thunder in the air.

"I am sure you will be glad to have tea, Douglas. Is it in the library, father?"

"Yes!" muttered Enistor, regaining his self-control by a powerful effort, and with that one word he led the way into the lamplight. Douglas followed arm in arm with the girl, feeling that but for her and all she meant to him he would have escaped immediately from the grim house and its unseen owner.

In the mellow radiance which flooded the library Enistor beheld a slim and delicate man with the dreamy face of a poet. Scorning himself that such a stripling should cause him even momentary dread, and despising him as one of the enemies indicated by Narvaez, the Squire became good-naturedly tolerant. During tea-time he behaved courteously, and proved himself to be a genial and hospitable host. But Montrose was markedly silent, as his repulsion increased immediately he caught sight of that dark and powerful countenance. Also in his heart there lurked an uncomfortable fear that Enistor was in a position to injure him in some inexplicable way. It was not physical fear, for Montrose was a brave man, but a hateful influence which seemed in some way to paralyse him. Why this should be so he was naturally unable to guess, but the desire to fly the neighbourhood of an implacable foe was so strong that it took him all his strength to resist the desire for an ignominious retreat. But for Alice's sake he did so resist, as her gracious presence enabled him to bear the strain with some equanimity. Therefore, as he had been trained by Eberstein to control his feelings, he drank and ate in quite a conventional manner. Alice, still ignorant of the hatred with which her father and her lover regarded one another, presided over what was outwardly a merry little meal, chatting and laughing in a smiling and whole-hearted way, as though she had not a care in the world. As indeed she had not for the moment.

"I fear you will feel dull here, Mr. Montrose," said Enistor, formal and cold.

"Oh, father, what a compliment to me!"

"My dear, we are quiet folk at Tremore, you must admit."

"I like quietness," said Montrose, smiling, "and would much rather be here than in London. And of course with Alice— —"

"It is paradise," ended Enistor cynically. "You have the usual stock-in-trade of pretty phrases which lovers delight in. Well, we must see what we can do to amuse you. I am usually busy myself, but Alice can be your guide to the few sights of the neighbourhood. You can ride a horse, or a bicycle, and drive in the carriage or dog-cart. There is a tennis-lawn at the back of the house and golf-links in Perchton. Then you can go sketching on the moors with Mr. Hardwick and Alice; or Job Trevel will take you out fishing. Mr. Sparrow, the vicar of Polwellin, will show you the church and cromlechs and rocking-stones and other such things, as he is something of an archæologist. We can have music and bridge and conversation in the evenings, and— —"

"Stop! Stop!" interrupted Montrose, now more at his ease, as he saw that the Squire was endeavouring to make himself agreeable. "It would require six months to do all these things. I shall enjoy myself immensely, especially if you will introduce me to Señor Narvaez."

"What do you know about him?" asked Enistor sharply, and frowning.

"All that Alice and Hardwick could tell me. He seems to be a very interesting man, and an unusual character."

"He is original," assented Enistor quickly, "so much so that he does not choose to know every one. However, as he is my very good friend I daresay I shall be able to induce him to meet you here. You will find him very interesting indeed," ended the Squire significantly, and he stared hard at Montrose, wondering if he guessed how the Spaniard regarded him.

But the young man, having nothing to conceal, and quite innocent of Don Pablo's enmity towards him, met the Squire's gaze with a forced friendly smile. "I like interesting people, he said amiably. "And I hope you do also, Mr. Enistor, as my friend Dr. Eberstein is coming to Perchton shortly.

"I shall be pleased to welcome any friend of yours," replied the elder man in a formal way, and then rose to leave the room. He felt that he had done enough as host for the time being and wished to be alone, so that he might send mental messages to Narvaez about the new arrival. "You will excuse me until dinner-time, Mr. Montrose. Alice will entertain you."

When the Squire departed Alice did her best in the way of entertainment, but found it difficult to banish the thoughtful look from her lover's face. Pleading fatigue, the young man soon sought the room assigned to him, and pondered over the odd distaste which the sight of Enistor induced. He could not account for it, and wished that Eberstein would appear to elucidate the problem. Across his mind flashed insistently the question of Ahab, "Hast thou found me, O mine enemy?" and the deadly answer of Elijah the seer, "I *have* found thee! Much as he loved Alice, he felt that the situation was uncomfortable and perplexing and quite beyond human explanation.

CHAPTER XII
SMALL BEER CHRONICLES

"The emphasis of the soul is always right!" says Emerson, meaning thereby that the immediate feeling which individuals have for one another at first sight is a hint from the divine within them as to whether they should be friends or foes. This subtle impulse is never felt again, as self-interest and custom gradually blunt the spiritual perceptions, and those who cross each other's path behave as worldly circumstances bid them. And naturally so, for whenever the desires of the animal-self come into operation, the more latent powers of the Higher-Self are obscured. Therefore, he is the wise man who accepts the emphasis of the soul as guidance in the choice of friends and in the doing of deeds. Because men, influenced by selfishness, do not follow such a lead, their path in life becomes much more complicated than it need be. They hear the blatant trumpeting of desire: not the still small voice of conscience.

Not being particularly metaphysical, Montrose was ignorant of this safeguard, and did not heed the warning of danger given at his first meeting with Enistor. That schemer, better informed, accepted the knowledge that here was a foe to be wary of. It would have been surprising had he not done so, as apart from the hatred which sprang into lively being at the first touch of hands, Narvaez had spoken plainly, and moreover Montrose was the detestable person who had secured Lady Staunton's fortune. To regain it and allow the Spaniard to execute his dark designs, Enistor masked his hatred under a fine show of courtesy, behaving with such apparent sincerity that Douglas was entirely deceived. As the days slipped by and there was no change in the gracious attitude of his host, he grew to like him, to admire him and to enjoy his companionship. This was little to be wondered at, as Enistor, being well-read and well-bred, could make himself extremely agreeable when he chose to do so. For obvious reasons he did so choose, and so did away with the mysterious repulsion of the first meeting that it became only a dim memory to Montrose. At the end of seven days the visitor persuaded himself without any great difficulty that Enistor was a most excellent man, an agreeable friend, and one likely to prove an ideal father-in-law. Alice was relieved to see that the two men got on so well together, and more than ever decided that she had deceived herself with regard to her father's true character.

"You have, I think, bridged the gulf between us," she explained one Sunday morning, when with Montrose she was descending the hill to Polwellin church. "Father and I never got on well until you came."

"Dearest, your father's character takes time to realise," was the prompt reply. "He looks stern and is of a reserved nature. But when one comes to know him he has a sweet kernel for all his rugged rind. At first I did not think we should get on well together, but that was a mistake. He's a ripping fine chap, and as good as they make 'em."

"Do you like my father for his own sake or for mine?" asked Alice doubtfully.

"For both sakes," rejoined the young man positively. "And seeing that I am here to rob him of his dearest treasure, I think he is behaving wonderfully."

"H'm!" murmured Alice, not wholly agreeing with this valuation. "Are you so sure? Father looks at me in a different way from what you do."

"Naturally. It is a different kind of love. From what you said, I quite expected to find your father a bear and a tyrant. Instead of being either he is delightful in every way. I don't think you are quite fair to him."

"Perhaps," the girl was still undecided. "He has altered much since you came, Douglas. You have brought the best out of him. He is more human. All the same——" she stopped abruptly.

"Well then—all the same?"

"Nothing," said Alice abruptly, and passed swiftly into the church, where further speaking was out of the question, much to her relief.

What she had meant to say and did not say was concerned with an uncomfortable under-current of thought regarding her father's surprising attitude. Owing to the relationship between them it was difficult to judge him impartially; yet Alice wished to do so, if only to satisfy her own conscience. Remembering the man's lifelong indifference and coldness and utter want of consideration, the girl left that this aggressive amiability was assumed for some purpose. What that purpose might be she could not conjecture, unless it had to do with the recovery of the fortune which she now knew he had not lost with equanimity. But even if the marriage with Douglas took place, it was hard to see how her father hoped to benefit, and she knew from experience that he did not hold with altruism. Filial sentiment made her strive to please him on the forced assumption that in spite of appearance he really did love her. But somehow she could not convince herself that such was the case. He was acting the affectionate father as she was acting the affectionate daughter, yet she did not think that he believed in her any more than she believed in him. It was all very difficult and very disagreeable.

It was useless to discuss the matter with Montrose, and for this reason she had ended their conversation by entering the church. The young man and her father had become excellent friends, and he would never believe that Enistor was anything but what he presented himself to be. In fact, Douglas had told her very plainly that she had misjudged her father, and her own surface-thoughts implying that such was the case inflicted a pang. But intuition scouted the idea of misjudgment. As one human being adjusting herself to another human being she knew how to act, but as a child striving to understand her parent she was quite bewildered. Finally, she decided that the only thing to be done was to accept the situation as her father wished it to be accepted, if only for the sake of peace and quietness. The Squire was willing to permit the marriage, and was doing his best to be agreeable to his future son-in-law. Nothing else mattered for the moment. Having arrived at this sensible conclusion, Alice compelled herself to attend to the service.

It was by no means an interesting one, as there was a want of warmth and colour about it which reduced the whole to a monotonous repetition of fine phrases. The vicar was a thoroughly good man, earnest and self-sacrificing, but with so moral a temperament that he entirely failed to understand sinners. And not understanding them he was unable to give them that sympathetic help which a practical experience of temptation teaches. He would scold a wrong-doer with great anger—box his ears so to speak—not because he was a bad-tempered man, but for the simple reason that he could not see the sin from the wrong-doer's point of view. As Mr. Sparrow said again and again, he did not want to run away with his neighbour's wife; he did not desire to drink too much, or to cheat, or to swear, so why—he asked plaintively—should his parishioners desire to do such uninviting things? By this inborn obtuseness he missed his aim, as he invariably attempted to bully ignorant wrong into becoming enlightened right without necessary explanations. Naturally those he genuinely tried to help resented a process which robbed them of their self-respect, and which gave them no logical reason for doing other than their crude desires bade them. Therefore while some remained members of the church, and accepted ecclesiastical scoldings stolidly as part of the burdens of life which they were called upon to bear because they could not help the bearing, others took refuge in the beer-shops and rejected all authority. Also, there were a few who joined Nonconformist sects of the democratic type, where the congregation controlled the preacher, and turned him out if his views were unsatisfactory to their narrow understandings. The result of these things was chaos, and Mr. Sparrow lamented that he had to deal with such stiff-necked people. Yet had he been able to explain reasonably what he taught, and had he possessed the tact to coax instead of bullying, he would soon have reduced the whole parish to order.

As a matter of fact in one way the vicar was better than his religion: not that his religion was not true and helpful, but because he knew it only externally, and taught by the letter rather than by the spirit. In the first lesson he read about the angry and jealous God of the Jews, and in the second declared the everlasting Love of the Father, Who sent His beloved Son to suffer for His children. Naturally the congregation could not understand such a contradiction, and Mr. Sparrow did not explain, because he did not understand himself. Therefore on Sundays he was rather a failure, while on week-days he was highly successful. The fishermen and their wives could comprehend a parson who helped them in their small needs and talked kindly to them, and shared their joys as well as their sorrows. But what they could not comprehend was the priest who tried to bully them into seeking a vague state of existence, which to them appeared to be vapour and moonshine. They wanted proofs, or at least reason, and they got neither.

In his sermons Mr. Sparrow told those who listened drowsily that if they were black with sin, they would go to hell: if they kept innocently white, they would arrive in a dreamland heaven: but he made no provision for the grey people. And as the majority of the congregation, if not the whole, belonged to the third category, being neither particularly good nor particularly sinful, the alternatives did not interest them much. Those in church adopted various attitudes, said certain words, sang certain tunes, and went through a set ceremony, with a vague idea that it was all necessary somehow to arrange matters for a vague future. When Montrose came out he commented on their orderly behaviour, and utter ignorance of what it all meant.

"Though of course," he added truthfully, "there were some who understood more than the rest. Still, what a clockwork ceremony!"

"Oh, but, Douglas, the liturgy of the Church of England is very beautiful."

"The most beautiful the mind of man can conceive," he admitted readily. "What can be more glorious than the Litany, which includes all possible petitions that mortals can offer. Said understandingly nothing can be more helpful."

"Mr. Sparrow read it beautifully, and the responses were made correctly."

"Oh yes! But I missed the living spirit. It was all words, repeated parrot-fashion by the majority—I don't say all—of those present."

"But what can the vicar do, Douglas? You know how dull the people are?"

"They are children, more or less stupid," said Montrose with conviction, "and can grasp very little. Since Mr. Sparrow teaches them to love God and love their neighbour, he is doing all that he can do. But he could colour the greyness of his sermon: he could speak in parables as the Master did. Then he would arrest their attention, and some ideas, if put picturesquely, would stick in their minds. A man will forget a series of admonitions if stated baldly: he will certainly remember some if connected with a story."

"Perhaps," said Alice doubtfully. "But Mr. Sparrow is a really good man."

"Isn't that rather irrelevant?" observed the young man dryly. "I quite admit that he is a good man. It is not his fault that the Church has lost her esoteric knowledge, which was reserved for the intellectual, who wished to believe with the head as well as with the heart. But he is only a sample of many parsons. His intentions are of the best, but he does not speak with conviction to my mind."

"He is a true believer," urged the girl, rather distressed.

"I am sure he is everything that is genuine and kind," replied her lover, a trifle impatiently. "But he lacks that wisdom which comes from logical reasoning on the things he discourses about."

"But can religion be proved logically?"

"Certainly; but only when one knows the esoteric teaching which the Church had, but which the Church has lost. Eberstein has taught much of it to me during the last three years, and there are few questions connected with religion and the Bible which I cannot answer in at least a reasonable way. Go to Mr. Sparrow and he will assure you that half the questions you ask are a mystery into which you must not pry. What is the result, Alice?"

"I'm sure I can't say," she answered good-humouredly.

"The result is," continued Montrose, growing more vehement, "that whenever a man begins to think, he leaves the Church from sheer inability to gain the information which is needed to reconcile what is taught with common sense. Only the people who don't think, who are Christians because they happen to have been brought up Christians, remain in the Church, and accept emotionally and blindly whatever is told them on ecclesiastical authority. That, when examined, is no authority at all to the thinking man."

"And the inner teaching?"

"It gives a perfectly reasonable and logical explanation which proves that the exoteric teaching is true. I believe all that the Church sets forth save the one word 'eternal' before the one word 'hell.' But then I know why I believe and can defend my belief in a most positive manner, so that any man with common sense must admit the logic of my arguments. Think if the parsons knew of this teaching, and gave it out, how the churches would be thronged. People are not irreligious nowadays. There never was a time when men and women wished to know about the truth more anxiously than they do to-day. But they go to those in authority and are given a stone in place of bread."

"Why will not the parsons take this teaching?"

"I cannot say. It changes nothing they teach outwardly, save the horrible doctrine of eternal punishment, and gives back to all in a rational and convincing way the faith they are gradually losing. Yet the Church goes on blindly repeating the same things Sunday after Sunday, until they have lost their force. The inner teaching would revive that force, if accepted, and the Church would be able to fulfil her true mission, which is to lead civilisation. As it is, her children will not stay with her. Pain is forcing the most advanced souls to try and understand the problems of existence, and this understanding the esoteric teaching gives, as I have proved myself. But the Church should be the teacher: not pain, which comes from ignorance."

"But these fishermen and women would only be bewildered if they sought to understand the problems of life in the way you do."

"Of course: because I am at a higher point of evolution. But what they are I was, and only pain drove me to acquire further knowledge, as pain will drive them in future lives. What Mr. Sparrow teaches them is all right: they are satisfied with bread and do not desire cake. But what I maintain is that the vicar should know more, and then he could do more good with his simple instruction by luring them on to think D E F as well as A B C. However, he is a good man and does his best according to his lights, and that is well. I daresay he is an interesting man when he talks archæology, because that is his hobby and he is sincere."

"Oh, Douglas, I am sure Mr. Sparrow's religion is sincere."

"I am sure it is," assented Montrose quickly. "But his understanding is so limited that he is unable to make religion interesting. And believe me, Alice, that since I met Eberstein and learned what religion really is, I find it the most interesting thing in the world. I know little as yet, as I learn but slowly. Still I am beginning to grasp the great scheme of the present creation, and it is so glorious and beautiful that I shall never rest until I understand it sufficiently to take a conscious part in it, and do the work appointed to me as Douglas Montrose."

Alice was silent. What her lover said was beyond her understanding, as, save some discussions with the limited Mr. Sparrow, she had never talked about such great subjects. Her father never spoke of religion and never went to church, so she really only knew what the vicar could teach her. So far as that went all was well, but she sometimes yearned for a fuller comprehension of creation and for reasonable explanations of life's riddles. From what Montrose had said it seemed likely that he could teach her what she wished to know, and that Eberstein, to whom he had referred, could teach her more when the time came. Her face glowed at the idea and she felt anxious to be instructed at once. But by this time they had wandered down the path to the beach, below the black cliffs, and her lover was talking of other things. She therefore left theology alone for lighter conversation, and approved of Montrose's appreciation of the beauty which clothed sea and land.

"What a lovely place, Alice. I am sure the fairies dance on these yellow sands in the moonlight."

"Of course they do," said Alice, now talking on a subject about which she knew a great deal. "Fairies really exist, you know. Señor Narvaez calls them Nature-spirits. He showed me some one day."

Montrose turned on her in surprise. "Are you clairvoyant?"

"Yes! Señor Narvaez says so!"

"And does he know anything about clairvoyance?"

"A great deal. So does my father. They both take an interest in such things, you see, and study them."

"And you?"

"Oh, I know very little, save what information Don Pablo has given me. He says that my clairvoyant faculty must be trained before it can be of any use."

"True enough. Eberstein told me also that clairvoyance must be trained. But is Señor Narvaez the man to train it?"

"He knows much about the unseen, Douglas."

"I should not be surprised to learn that what he does know is of the worst, Alice," said Douglas dryly. "There is something evil about that man. I have only met him twice and each time I was uncomfortable in his presence.

He is like a snake, a toad—a—a—oh, any noxious animal. And to think that he wanted to marry you. I never heard of such insolence."

"He means well," said Alice soothingly.

"I doubt it. Anything he means is to his own advantage. I shouldn't be at all surprised to learn that he was a Brother of the Shadow, since he knows about unseen things."

"A Brother of the Shadow?"

"So Eberstein tells me Black Magicians are called."

"But are there really such men?"

"Yes. There are White Magicians and Black. They both have acquired super-physical powers the same in essence, acting differently when used differently. Good men use them to help: bad men use them to hurt. Just like dynamite, you know, dear. You can use it for a good purpose to blow up rocks blocking a harbour, or for a bad one to destroy life. But the thing itself and the action of the thing are the same. How did you see these fairies?"

"Nature-spirits," insisted Alice quickly. "Oh, one day when I was on the moor Don Pablo came along. He told me about them and I did not believe in such things. Then he took my hand, saying I was clairvoyant. In some way his touch or some power which he poured into me opened"—Alice was puzzled how the experience could be explained—"opened a third eye, as it might be. I don't know exactly how to put it, but in some way I saw——"

"Saw what?"

"Little men and women on the heather. Some were playing and others were at work. The ground I sat on was alive with them. Yet when Don Pablo took his hand away, the third eye closed and they vanished. But of course they were still around me, though I could not see them. I told Julian about pixies and nixies, and he laughingly said that it needed the eye of faith to see them. I daresay that was my third eye. Do you understand?"

"Perfectly. Eberstein has explained some of these things to me. And I had an experience——" Douglas broke off abruptly, remembering that the doctor had asked him to say nothing about his vision. "Well, it doesn't matter. But I quite believe that the veil can be lifted, or perhaps—a better way of putting it—the veil can be seen through."

It was lucky for Montrose that Alice's attention was distracted at the moment, as she might have pressed him overhard to relate his experience. And as she had her full share of feminine curiosity, she would not have been put off with evasive replies. But at the rude jetty a boat had arrived and in the boat was a tall girl, whom Miss Enistor recognised at once. She told Montrose to stay where he was and ran down the slope to speak with Rose Penwin. The reason why she did not want Douglas to accompany her was obvious.

"Oh, Rose, why have you not been up to see me?" asked Alice, when the girl moored her boat to the jetty and stepped ashore.

"I have been too busy, miss," replied Rose, smiling, and showing a set of very white teeth. "Did you want me?"

"It's about Job Trevel."

"Oh!" Rose flushed and drew herself up. "What's he been saying?"

"Nothing. I haven't seen him. But people are talking, Rose."

"Let them talk," retorted the girl sullenly. "If I'd a shilling for every bad word they say of me I should be rich."

Alice looked at her in pained silence. Rose was a magnificent-looking woman, tall and stately, highly coloured and beautiful. With her black hair and black eyes and perfectly moulded figure, she looked the embodiment of a sea-goddess. Also her dress was picturesque, with a touch of colour here and there pleasing to the eye. But what Alice looked at most was a snake bracelet of Indian workmanship in silver which clung round her right wrist. "Do you think it right to let Don Pablo give you such presents?"

Rose flushed still deeper and her eyes flashed with anger. "He might be my grandfather," she snapped in a savage manner.

"But he isn't," replied Alice earnestly. "Oh, Rose, you know how hot-blooded Job is. And if you give him cause to be jealous— —"

"I don't care if he's jealous or not, miss. The likes of me is a sight too good for the likes of him."

"But he's an honest man— —"

"So is Don Pablo, and what's more he's a richer man. If he was young I wouldn't let him give me things. But whatever they may say, an old gentleman like that don't mean no harm. Besides, I haven't said yes to Job."

"But you will say yes."

"That depends upon how Job behaves himself, miss. I'm not going to have him glowering and swearing as if I was doing something wrong, which I ain't. And begging your pardon, miss, I don't see what you've got to do with it."

"I don't want to see you get into trouble," said Alice indiscreetly.

Rose flashed round furiously. "Who said I was going to get into trouble? I like pretty things, and if an old gentleman gives them to me, where's the harm, I should like to know?"

"Job's jealousy — —"

"Let him keep it to himself," interrupted Rose, who was in a fine rage. "I ain't his wife yet to be at his beck and call. And perhaps I never shall be if it comes to that. Don Pablo says that a girl like me would make plenty of money in London as an artist's model: or I might go on the stage."

"I think Don Pablo should be ashamed of himself to poison your mind in this way," burst out Alice, angry in her turn. "Don't be a fool."

Inherited respect for the Squire's daughter kept Rose within bounds, but for the moment she looked as though she would strike Alice. With an effort she turned away, biting her lip and clenching her hands. "I'll forget myself if I stay, miss. You'd best keep away from me!" and before Miss Enistor could stop her she fairly ran up the path past Montrose on her hurried way to the village. Douglas turned to stare after the flying figure, and wondered what Alice had said to send the girl away with such wrath depicted on her face.

At the same moment as Rose disappeared Alice heard a deep male voice speaking to her, and turned to see Job clambering up on the hither side of the jetty. He was a tall, bulky, powerful man, with red hair and keen blue eyes, handsome and virile in a common way, and exhibited a strength which appealed to every woman for miles around. At one time it appealed to Rose, but since Don Pablo had poisoned her mind she had risked an unpleasant exhibition of that strength by her coquettish behaviour. Job looked dour and dangerous, and there was a spark in his blue eyes.

"I heard what you said, Miss Alice," he remarked, drawing a deep breath. "I was under the jetty waiting for her coming. But when you spoke to her I thought I'd just wait to hear if she'd listen to sense."

"It doesn't seem like it, Job," said Alice sadly, and looked with distress on the splendid figure of her foster-brother.

"No, it don't, miss," he responded gloomily. "She's got the bit between her teeth, she has. It's all that foreign devil, begging your pardon for the word, Miss Alice. I'd like to strangle him."

"Don't be silly, talking in that way, Job. It's dangerous."

"It will be for him, if he don't sheer off," muttered the man vengefully.

"Job, you know quite well that Don Pablo is an old man: he must be eighty if an hour. You can't be jealous of him."

"But I am, Miss Alice, and it ain't no good saying as I'm not. What right has he to give her presents and talk about taking her to London? I'll break his neck if he goes on with such talk."

Alice tried to defend the Spaniard, not because she thought he was acting rightly, but for the simple reason that she wished to talk Job into a calmer state of mind. At the moment the man was dangerous. "Don Pablo only admires Rose as a beautiful woman," she urged.

"Then he shan't. No one shall admire her but me. And if he wants to marry, Miss Alice— —"

"Oh, nonsense," she broke in. "Why, he's too old."

"Well, they did say as you were going to marry him," retorted Trevel coolly.

"I am going to do nothing of the sort," cried the girl, stamping her foot. "I think you should be more sensible than to suggest such a thing."

"I didn't suggest it," said Job stolidly. "But the Squire wants— —"

"I don't care what the Squire wants," interrupted Alice, with another stamp. "People say things they have no right to say. You are my foster-brother, Job, and I allow you more licence than most. But you must never speak to me in this way again."

"I didn't mean any harm, Miss Alice, and my heart is sore."

"Poor Job!" Alice became sorry for the big man. "You do suffer, and Rose ought to be ashamed of herself to cause you such pain. Get her to marry you at once and laugh at Don Pablo."

"She won't. He's got her fair under his thumb, Miss Alice," said Trevel gloomily. "I hate him, and so does everyone else. He's the only man as I ever heard the parson have a bad word for. There's something about that foreign chap," Job clenched a huge fist, "as makes you want to squash him like a toad."

Alice nodded comprehendingly. "All the same you must do him no harm, or you will get into trouble. And remember, Job, that I am your friend"—she gave him her hand—"and to prove it I shall tell you what will please you. I am engaged to that gentleman over there—Mr. Montrose."

Trevel shook the hand heartily and his face grew good-natured. "I'm fair glad of it, miss. I've seen the gentleman and like the gentleman. He's been down in the village with Mr. Hardwick, as we like also. As to that foreigner, miss—ugh!" Job scowled and turned away, while Alice went back to Douglas.

"I have been trying to reconcile two lovers, but I have failed," she told him.

"What is the cause of the quarrel?" asked the young man, amused.

"A dangerous one. Don Pablo," and she gave details.

"What an old beast!" said Montrose. "If I were that fisherman I'd screw his neck."

"Don't put such ideas into Job's head," cried Alice rebukingly. "He is angry enough as it is!"

"All the worse for Don Pablo, my dear!" and so they left the matter, which was of less importance then than it became afterwards.

CHAPTER XIII
FURTHER SMALL BEER CHRONICLES

When the young people went to church, Enistor took the opportunity of paying a visit to Narvaez. The effort to keep up an appearance of friendship for a man he hated was not easy, and the Squire wished to unbend in the society of one who knew his true sentiments. Also he greatly desired to learn what were Don Pablo's plans regarding the restoration of the fortune, for the Spaniard did not seem to be moving in the matter at all, and valuable time was being wasted. And since Enistor was anxious to get rid of Montrose as speedily as possible, he thought it was just as well to suggest that the scheme—whatever it might be—should be completed as soon as could be conveniently managed. The master of Tremore wanted to handle the coveted income; he wished to see his daughter married to Narvaez, and finally he desired to learn the nature of this danger at which Don Pablo hinted so frequently. Of course the marriage with the Spaniard, by making possible the training of Alice's clairvoyant powers, would soon disclose this last.

Enistor walked leisurely over the moor to where the evil mount with its crown of monoliths was indistinctly outlined against the grey sky. As it was now autumn, the heavens had lost their summer azure, and the earth had been stripped of its flowering splendour. He wandered through a ruined world, where the red and brown and yellow of the dying bracken were veiled in chilly mists. The ground was sodden, the herbage was dripping wet, and the cries of the birds sounded mournful, as though they were regretting the passing of warm weather. That Enistor should see the prostrate body of a man lying amidst the fantastic colours of the moorland seemed to be so much in keeping with the general air of decay and sadness that he did not even start when he bent over the still form. But he did utter an ejaculation when he looked at the white face and recognised Julian Hardwick.

Why the artist should be here in an unconscious condition Enistor did not pause to inquire. He was above all a man of action, and as it was necessary to revive Hardwick, he hastened to fill his cap with water at a convenient pool. The chill of the fluid on the white face flushed it with returning life, and when Enistor loosened the collar, and shook the body, Julian opened his eyes languidly. In a half-dazed way he murmured something about brandy, a hint which the Squire acted upon by searching the artist's pockets. He soon found what he looked for, and a drink of the generous liquor revived Hardwick so speedily that he was soon able to sit up and talk.

"My heart is weak," he said in a stronger voice, buttoning his collar.

Enistor was frankly amazed. "Why, you always look singularly healthy."

"Because I am big and well-covered with flesh it is natural you should think so, Mr. Enistor. But the heart doesn't do its work properly. That is why I live so much in the open air, and——"

"Don't talk so much. You are exhausting yourself."

Hardwick took a second drink of brandy, and as the heart quickened he began to look more like his old self. "I am all right now," he assured his helper, "I can manage to crawl to my lodgings and lie down for a time." He got on to his feet and stretched himself languidly. "I always carry brandy on the chance of these attacks!"

"You couldn't have used the brandy had I not been here to help you," said the Squire bluntly. "If you are liable to such seizures you should not venture to wander on these lonely moors by yourself."

"Perhaps not! But it is rarely I become so incapable. Thank you very much for being so kind. I shall go home now."

Then Enistor made an effort which rather amazed himself. "Let me take you home, Hardwick. You are not fit to go by yourself."

Hardwick was as amazed as the man who made this offer. "I didn't think you would bother about me in that way," he said weakly: then he straightened himself with an effort. "Thank you all the same, but I can manage!" And giving his preserver a friendly handshake, he moved along the path which meandered towards Polwellin.

The Squire stood looking after him, thinking that he might fall again and require further assistance. But the tall figure moved steadily through the mists, apparently possessed of sufficient vital power to reach the haven of home in safety. Then the Squire thoughtfully resumed his way to Don Pablo's cottage, wondering at the discovery he had made. Hardwick looked so strong and well, and was so massive and imposing in appearance, that no one could possibly have guessed that his heart was weak. But Enistor did not wonder at this alone: he wondered also at his own kind offer to go out of his way to help any one in distress. It was rather a weak thing to do, he reflected, and not at all an action of which Narvaez would approve. All the same Enistor resolved to tell the Spaniard if only for his own glorification.

Don Pablo was seated by a huge fire in his sinister study, with a paper in his hands covered with odd signs and hieroglyphics. With his usual serenity he murmured a welcome and pointed to a chair. But he did not speak further for the moment and Enistor employed the time in trying to read the inscrutable face, which was seamed with a thousand wrinkles and made quite inhuman by the passionless look of the cold, steady, blue eyes. Shortly the old man laid the paper aside with a sigh of satisfaction.

"What are you doing?" asked Enistor curiously.

"I have been casting Hardwick's horoscope," was the unexpected reply. "For the satisfaction of his own curiosity he gave me the day and hour of his birth," he smiled in a cruel way. "I don't think he will be pleased at what I have to tell him."

A telepathic message passed swiftly from one trained brain to the other and Enistor nodded in a surprised manner. "He may die at any moment," said the Squire, translating Don Pablo's thoughts. "Well, that is very likely. I found him unconscious on the moor a short time ago."

"He is not dead?" questioned Narvaez, with unusual interest.

"Oh no. I revived him with water and some brandy he had in his pocket. Also I offered to see him home."

"Why?" demanded the other coldly.

"Well, he seemed weak and——"

"How often have I told you that other people's troubles do not concern you, Enistor! If you choose to waste your powers on assisting weaker persons, you will lose much force better employed in your own gain."

"I am not quite so hard as you are," snapped the Squire, sharply.

"Not quite so wise, you mean," was the unmoved response. "However, I pardon your weakness on this occasion, as I don't want Hardwick to die— yet."

"Do you wish him to die at all?"

"My last word implied that I did. It is part of my plan to get the fortune you desire, which also means that I shall secure your daughter as my wife."

"But I don't see——"

"There is no need for you to see," said Narvaez tyrannically; "you do what I tell you and all will be well."

"Do you mean to kill Hardwick?"

"No! There is no need for me to move a finger. His horoscope shows an early death from natural causes. Having found him unconscious, I leave you to guess what those causes will be."

"I have no need to guess. Hardwick's heart is weak."

"Exactly. The organs of his body are healthy, but he has not a sufficiently strong heart. If he could get a fresh supply of vitality he would be a powerful and *long-lived* man.

"Do you intend to give him that vitality?" sneered the visitor.

Narvaez chuckled. "Yes! You will see that splendid body walking about filled with strenuous life some day soon."

"The body walking about." Enistor stared keenly at the mocking, cruel face. "I must say you speak very strangely."

"I speak as I speak, and what I mean to say I say," rejoined Don Pablo enigmatically. "Let us change the subject, as I am busy. Your errand?"

"I only came to get the taste of that young prig out of my mouth!"

"And waste my time. Why can't you rely on your own strength? I am not going to have you here draining mine, particularly when this body I have at present is so frail. Act the courteous host and give the young fool as much of your daughter's company as he desires. The rest can be left to me."

"But when are you going to move in the matter?"

"When the time is ripe and when I choose. How often am I to tell you that it is impossible to hurry things? Corn takes time to grow: a rose takes time to unfold, and everything in the visible and invisible world progresses inch by inch, step by step. Nature, as you should know by this time, is a tortoise and not a kangaroo."

"There is another reason why I came," said Enistor, accepting the rebuke with a meekness foreign to his nature; "that fisherman—Trevel!"

"Well? He is annoyed because I give the girl jewels, and waken her ambition to be something better than a domestic drudge."

"His annoyance extends to an intention to kill you," said Enistor dryly. "I advise you to be careful, Master. Trevel is dangerous."

"Dangerous!" Narvaez spoke with supreme contempt. "You know what I am and yet talk of danger to me from an ignorant boor. I could guard myself in a hundred ways if I so chose. But," ended Narvaez deliberately, "I do not choose."

"I wonder what you mean?"

"You may wonder. Threatened men live long. Content yourself with that proverb. And now go; I am busy!"

Without a word Enistor rose and walked to the door. There he paused to say a few words not complimentary to Narvaez, and he said them with a black look of suppressed rage. "You treat me like a dog," snarled the weaker man. "Be careful that I do not bite you like a dog."

"I trust you as little as any one else, and am always on my guard," said the magician mildly, and stared in a cold sinister way at his pupil. Enistor felt a wave of some cruel force surge against him—a force which struck him with the dull stunning blows of a hammer, and which twisted his nerves so sharply that but for dogged pride he would have shrieked with pain. As it was he writhed and grew deadly pale, the sweat beading his brow showing what agony he suffered. Hours seemed to be concentrated into that one long minute during which Narvaez held him in the vice of his will, and made him suffer the torments of the damned.

"I beat my dog when he bites," said an unemotional voice. "Go!" And Enistor, conquered by supreme pain, crept away in silence. As the door closed, he heard his master chuckle like a parrot over a piece of cake.

The Squire returned painfully to Tremore, cursing himself for having been such a fool as to defy a man possessed of super-physical powers. Twice before he had done so, and each time Don Pablo had inflicted torments. The man, more learned than an ordinary hypnotist, simply used in a greater degree the will and suggestion which such a one employs. A hypnotist can make his subject believe that he has toothache, or has taken poison, by insisting with superior force that he shall so believe. Narvaez, more learned in the laws which govern this creation, compelled Enistor in this way to feel the torments of a heretic on the rack, without resorting to the ordinary necessity of casting his subject into a hypnotic trance. If Enistor had concentrated his will, he could have repelled the suggestion, but he had not the terrific power of concentration which ages of exercise had given Don Pablo. He was in the presence of a powerful influence, directed by an equally powerful will, and therefore had no weapons with which to fight his dark master. In a fury Enistor wished that he could make Narvaez suffer in the same degree, but he knew that he could never hope to do so. Even if he became possessed of knowledge, of concentration, and of a more powerful will than was human, the Spaniard knew of ways which could baffle the attack. The sole consolation which Enistor had to pacify his wounded pride was that there was no disgrace in a mere mortal being beaten by a superman. Narvaez, in a minor degree, was a god, a very evil god, and those worshippers who did not obey him felt very speedily what their deity could do. Enistor had no wish to measure forces with so powerful a being again.

For the rest of that week he left the magician alone and devoted himself to entertaining his guest. It was impossible to induce Narvaez to act until he chose to act, and all that could be done was to obey his instructions and behave agreeably to Montrose, so that the visitor might be lulled into false security. Never was there so amiable a host as the Squire; never was there so genial a companion, and Douglas became quite fascinated with a personality which transcended his own. The young man was so much weaker than his host that the latter wondered why Narvaez did not compel him to surrender the fortune by putting forth resistless power. Had Enistor guessed that Montrose's desire to do good and to love every one nullified the evil spell, he would have wondered less. And at the same time Enistor would have understood how, not having unselfish love in his own breast, he lay open to the assaults of the magician. As he treated others so he was treated, and a realisation of this golden truth would have enabled him to defy Narvaez and his suggestions. But the mere fact that he wished to exercise the same might-over-right free-lance law prevented his understanding how to defend himself from a more accomplished devil. And Don Pablo was as much a devil as there is possible to be one, since he wholly obeyed the instincts, carefully fostered, of hate and selfishness. Enistor was a very minor devil indeed, as he had too much of the milk of human kindness in him as yet to equal or rival the superior fiend.

In his determination to act his comedy thoroughly, Enistor went to the great length of asking the vicar and his wife to dinner. As Mr. Sparrow had never before been invited to break bread under the Squire's roof, he was extremely surprised by the unexpected honour. At first he was minded to decline, since Enistor never came to church and never took the least interest in matters connected with the parish. But Mrs. Sparrow pointed out that this desire for their company might be a sign of grace, and that if they went, it might entail the reformation of their host. Also the dinner was sure to be good, and she could wear her new dress in decent society, which she very rarely had an opportunity of doing. Urged in this way and having a certain amount of curiosity of his own regarding the splendours of the big house, Mr. Sparrow sent an acceptance in his neat Oxford calligraphy. The Squire gave it to his daughter and told her to order the dinner.

"See that it is a good one," said Enistor genially. "Sparrow is as lean as a fasting friar and won't object to a decent meal for once. It isn't Lent or any of their confounded Church feasts, is it?"

"No!" answered Alice, very much puzzled by this unusual behaviour; "but why do you ask Mr. and Mrs. Sparrow to dinner? I thought you didn't like them."

"I don't! They are a couple of bores. But it is rather dull here for Montrose, and we must get what society we can to cheer him up."

"I think Douglas is very well satisfied with my company," retorted the girl, rather nettled by the implied slight, "and these two bores, as you call them, certainly will not amuse him."

"Very well; ask Hardwick also. He isn't a bore and Montrose likes him."

"Julian isn't very well, father. He hasn't been since you found him on the moor fainting. But I shall send the invitation. Shall you ask Señor Narvaez?"

"No!" said her father sharply and uneasily, for his body still tingled with the memory of Don Pablo's reproof. "I shan't submit him to the ordeal of enduring so dull a set of people."

"Complimentary to us all," said Alice dryly, then regretted the retort; "I am sure you wish to make things pleasant for Douglas."

"Of course! I wish him to stay here as long as he likes," said Enistor, with an emphasis which she could not quite understand. "See that everything is all right, my dear. I want the dinner-party to be a success."

Rather amazed at the way in which her usually selfish father sacrificed himself, Alice consulted the housekeeper, and made all preparations for this rare festivity. When the evening came, the parson and his wife duly arrived and at their heels followed Hardwick, who had willingly accepted the chance of an evening in the company of Alice, whom he loved as a sister, and Montrose, who appealed to him as an unusually agreeable and decent fellow. The Squire welcomed his guests cordially, and took Mrs. Sparrow in to dinner. She was a faded, colourless woman with a washed-out appearance, markedly accentuated by the gauzy grey dress she wore. Alice in a delicate pink frock, which set off her evasive beauty to great advantage, looked like a fresh sunrise beside a wet, misty autumn day. Douglas could not keep his eyes off her and Hardwick was equally pressing in his attentions.

"But you must not over-tax your strength, Julian," said Alice, when she found herself at the dinner-table between the artist and Mr. Sparrow, who had escorted her thereto.

"Oh, I am all right now," replied Hardwick, "no better and no worse than I ever was. You were surprised when your father told you?"

"I was greatly grieved, Julian. And it seems so strange that a big man such as you are should be so delicate. You should see a doctor."

"I have seen several, but they can do me no good," said the artist sadly. "In every way I am healthy, so there is nothing to cure. All I lack is what they cannot give me, and that is a new supply of life-force."

"If it is vitality you want, Hardwick," said Montrose, speaking across the table, "you should consult Dr. Eberstein, who is coming down shortly to Perchton. He is wonderful in many ways and I am certain he would do you good."

"He cannot breathe more breath of life into a man than what that man already has," said Mr. Sparrow, in a tone of sad rebuke. "God alone is able to do that."

"Therefore," murmured Mrs. Sparrow, in an equally sad tone, "you should pray for strength, Mr. Hardwick. We are told to do so."

"I thought that was spiritual strength?"

"And what more do you want?" replied the lady, forgetting the exact point under discussion. "Let us watch and pray lest we fall into temptation."

"My dear!" murmured the vicar in an undertone, for he felt that this conversation was too professional for the occasion.

"Quite so," said Mrs. Sparrow, taking the hint, and did not open her mouth for some time save to eat and drink. All the same she watched for an opportunity to lead the conversation towards such religious topics as she and her husband were interested in. This was to be done with a view of surprising the Squire with the extent of her husband's knowledge. Now she had managed to enter the big house, she did not intend to go out again in a hurry. Enistor was a valuable parishioner, and if he could be brought to defer to Mr. Sparrow much could be done with him and with his money.

The table looked charming with its snow-white napery, on which glittered crystal and silver, while the dinner-service was a thing of beauty. The scarlet and golden autumn leaves which decorated the board, the mellow light of the many wax candles, the well-cooked food and the delicious wines, all impressed the vicar's wife greatly. She even felt a little angry that such a heathen as the Squire surely was should possess these luxuries, while Mr. Sparrow—capable of being a bishop in her opinion—was content with unlovely surroundings and plain viands, prepared in anything but an inviting way by their one servant. No, not content—that was the wrong word to use. He put up with ascetic living, while the wicked—meaning Mr. Enistor—lived on the fat of the land. It was enough to shake the faith of a Christian lady in the fairness of things. And truth to tell, Mrs. Sparrow, in spite of her anxious faith, frequently doubted if the world was governed justly. She and her husband did all that the Bible told them to do in the way of living uprightly and unselfishly, therefore they should certainly long before this have sat under their own fig-tree, possessing beeves and lands according to the promise. As it was, they were as poor as rats, or rather as church mice, which seemed to be the more ecclesiastical comparison. Clearly there was something wrong somewhere in the way in which mundane matters were ordered.

Meantime, the Squire had started Mr. Sparrow on archæology, as the best way of keeping him off theology, and the parson was talking eagerly about a certain red granite heart, inscribed with weird signs, which he had dug up on the hill where the Roman camp was to be seen. "Near the cottage of that Spanish gentleman," he explained precisely.

"I know," said Enistor; and indeed he knew the hill very well in a way of which Mr. Sparrow would scarcely have approved.

"There is a Druidical altar there," went on the clergyman eagerly, "and I have no doubt many dreadful sacrifices took place there in the old days. This heart—which I shall be delighted to show you if you call at the vicarage, Mr. Enistor—no doubt had to do with the terrible rites."

"Earlier than that," put in Montrose unexpectedly, "the heart was the symbol of the Atlantean race, as the cross is the symbol of the Aryan. The hieroglyphics on it mean doubtless the sacred word 'Tau.' Aum is the sacred word of our present people."

"Tau! Aum! Atlantean!" echoed Sparrow, much perplexed. "What do you mean?"

"It would take too long to explain, sir. Dr. Eberstein, who told me about these things, is the best person to consult."

"I wish to consult no one," said the parson, drawing himself up. "I believe the heart to be a symbol of the Druids."

"A symbol of Atlantis rather," insisted Montrose; "this very land on which we are was part of the great continent of Atlantis."

"A mere fable, sir. You are thinking of the myth which Plato mentions."

"It is no myth, but an actual truth, Mr. Sparrow. Atlantis did exist and was overwhelmed by that flood you will find mentioned in the Bible."

"Absurd! The name of Atlantis is not mentioned in Holy Scripture. There is no proof that what Plato says is true."

"This much proof, that as far back as archæologists can go the civilisation of Egypt was in full swing. Where did that civilisation come from?"

"It grew up in the Valley of the Nile."

"Certainly, but the beginnings were brought to the Valley of the Nile by a highly civilised race. Remember it was the Egyptian priests who told Plato about Atlantis. They knew, because Egypt was a colony of that mighty continent. There was another colony in Central America, and you will find the vast ruins of its cities described in a book by Désiré Charnay. The civilisation of Mexico and Peru destroyed by the Spaniards was the last remains of the splendour of the Atlanteans."

"Where did you hear all this, Mr. Montrose?" asked the Squire quickly.

"From Dr. Eberstein. You can ask him for yourself when he comes down."

"I should like to meet him," said Mr. Sparrow primly, "but I do not think that I shall agree with a single word he says."

"Then why ask him?" asked Montrose, very naturally.

"To confute him, sir. What we know of the early world is all contained in Genesis. There is no mention of Atlantis there, although there is of Egypt."

"What about the chronology of the Bible? It has been proved, Mr. Sparrow—and you as an archæologist must admit this—that the civilisation of Egypt extends further back than the date given in Genesis as the beginning of the world. What do you say to that?"

"I could say a great deal," retorted the parson, whose archæological knowledge was always struggling with his religious beliefs; "but this is not the time or the place to say more. When Dr. Eberstein, who is your authority for these startling statements, arrives I shall be happy to thresh the matter out with him. It will be an intellectual pleasure. I get few opportunities of that sort down here."

"That is very probable," said Hardwick, nodding; "your parishioners are a good sort, but not very learned."

"They have no need to be learned, Mr. Hardwick. Let them fulfil their daily task, and be satisfied with the position in which they have been placed."

"If they take your advice," said the Squire dryly, "there will be no chance of their rising in the world."

"Why should they try to rise?" demanded Mrs. Sparrow, coming to her husband's aid.

"Well, my dear lady, it is said that the common or garden millionaire usually starts his pile with the proverbial halfpenny. If he accepted your husband's ruling, he would never attempt to rise."

"It is divinely ordained that some people must be high and some low."

"Rather hard on the low people. I think every one should be dissatisfied, myself: that is the only thing that makes for progress."

"Did you promulgate this extraordinary doctrine in the village, Mr. Enistor?"

"No!" replied the Squire, glancing at the parson, who spoke. "Why?"

"Because some of my parishioners are very dissatisfied indeed. Mrs. Trevel was hard up last winter, and prayed for money. She did not get it, and told me that she did not intend to pray any more, as it seemed useless."

"And what explanation did you give her?" asked Alice anxiously.

"I was horrified at her impiety, Miss Enistor, as any right-minded person would be."

"Of course," murmured Montrose ironically, "how dare she ask for money when she was hard up."

Mr. Sparrow took no notice of him. "I told her that God thought she required discipline and that she must not complain."

"Why should she require discipline rather than a millionaire?" asked Julian.

"She may have more original sin in her," said Mr. Sparrow, floundering in a bog and getting quite out of his depth.

"Well," said Montrose grimly, "if according to your teaching, Mr. Sparrow, we all start as brand-new souls, given a set of circumstances over which we have no control at the outset, and with the same goal of heaven or hell at the end, it seems to me that every one ought to start at scratch."

"Not at all," said the parson, doggedly illogical, "some are rich and some are poor; some are clever and some are stupid; some are ill and some are well. It is all divinely ordained."

"But so unfair," urged Julian, seeing the absurdity of the speech.

"What, sir, shall the clay say to the potter what it wants to be?"

"I really don't see why the clay shouldn't," put in Mr. Enistor, who liked to see the parson driven into a corner, "especially when the clay has nerves."

"All is divinely ordained," repeated Mr. Sparrow piously, "we must not murmur. I regard Mrs. Trevel as a most impious person for daring to rebel when her prayers are not answered."

"I told her that," said his wife, "and she only laughed."

"Bitterly, I expect," murmured Montrose; "poor soul, I shall give her some money in the morning."

"No, don't," said Mr. Sparrow. "It will only confirm her in disbelief."

"On the contrary it will restore her faith," remarked the Squire coolly, "as it will show that her prayers are answered after all."

Mr. Sparrow had nothing to say after this, although he greatly longed to preach a sermon to those present. But not being in the pulpit he feared lest his statements should be contradicted by these ribald people. Therefore he wisely held his tongue on religious subjects for the rest of the evening. On the way home, however, he made one scathing remark to his wife.

"They are all atheists, Jane. Just the kind I expected to find under the roof of a man who does not come to church."

CHAPTER XIV
PREPARATION

On the morning of the third day after the dinner, Montrose received a letter from Dr. Eberstein saying that he was arriving in Perchton that same evening. At once the young man decided to see his friend at the watering-place and stay there for the night. He was anxious to tell the doctor how Enistor's character had been misunderstood, and what an agreeable man he was to live with. Also he asked the Squire if he could bring back Eberstein for a few hours' visit, to which Enistor heartily agreed. The schemer was looking forward to meeting the man—if he was simply a man and not something greater—whom Narvaez called "The Adversary." Confident of receiving support from Don Pablo, the Squire was anxious to come to grips with the opposing power that wished to thwart his plans. The suspense of the delay in any decided action being taken chafed Enistor considerably, and he wished to arrive at the desired conclusion as swiftly as possible. Narvaez advised waiting and Enistor rejected the advice. He had not the inexhaustible patience of his master.

Alice suggested that as Hardwick was going on that day to Perchton to consult a doctor about his health, Douglas should accompany him. The artist as usual had borrowed his rich friend's motor-car, and when a message was sent to him, replied that he would be delighted to have Montrose with him. To avoid the necessity of the car climbing the hill to Tremore, Douglas went down to Polwellin with a medium-sized bag, containing what necessaries he required for his night's absence. Alice walked with him, and they left the bag at Hardwick's lodgings, where the car was to arrive some time during the afternoon. It was already long after midday, and having to get rid of an hour of waiting, the girl proposed that they should call on Dame Trevel.

"You said you would help her, Douglas," she reminded him.

"Of course. I should have seen her on the morning after the dinner, when I told Mr. Sparrow that I would give her money. It was wrong of me not to keep my promise. The vicar will think that I am like every one else, and say much but do little."

"I don't think the vicar will think anything about the matter," said Alice candidly. "Mrs. Trevel is a heretic in his eyes!"

"Simply because she won't believe blindly against her better reason. There is a great want of logic about priestly authority. With the teachers of exoteric knowledge it is 'Obey or be damned!' which is something like the reported motto of the French Revolution: 'Be my brother, or I'll kill you.'"

"But Mr. Sparrow is a good man, Douglas."

"I admitted long ago that he was a good man, my dear. But a good man with a limited understanding can do more harm than a bad man. There are other ways of teaching a child than by boxing his ears until he is stupid with pain."

"I don't think Dame Trevel would like to be called a child," said Alice, with an amused laugh.

"My dear, the majority of human beings *are* children. The longer I live, the more I see that. I am a child myself in many ways, although, as Eberstein is widening my limitations, I am beginning to grow up. Children," Montrose spoke half to himself and half to his companion, "what else? Instead of cake and toys, we want gold and lands, and power and pleasure. Whether we deserve them or not we clamour for them, just like a child. We become cross when things don't go as we wish them, and slap the bad naughty table that has hurt baby in the shape of anything which impedes our getting what we desire. Good Lord, how can any man be angry with another man, when he knows that his enemy is but a child? But to know that one must be more than a child oneself."

"Do you call me a child?" asked Alice, pouting.

At the very door of Dame Trevel's cottage Montrose bent to kiss her. "A very charming child, who shall never be put into the corner by me."

"You talk as though you were the only wise man in existence."

"Yes!" assented Montrose, laughing. "I speak as though I were the judge of the earth instead of being a denizen. La Rochefoucauld says that. Go in, Alice, and let us get our interview over. We haven't overmuch time."

Mrs. Trevel received her visitors in a clean little room, poorly furnished but fairly comfortable. She was a gaunt old creature, London born and London bred, so she did not speak in the Cornish way. But indeed, thanks to the authority of school-boards, the local dialects are fast disappearing, and the girl idly remembered at the moment how ordinary was the wording of Rose Penwin and her fisherman-lover. The sight of Dame Trevel seated in her big chair suggested the names, as the absence of the West Country shibboleth in her speech suggested the thought of the younger generation whose dialect had been, so to speak, wiped out. The old woman was glad, as usual, to see her nursling and highly approved of the handsome young man who was to marry her, as all Polwellin knew by this time.

"I hope it will be all sunshine with you two," said Mrs. Trevel, when her visitors were seated. "And that you'll live to see your children's children playing about your knees, my dears."

"With Alice beside me it is bound to be sunshine," replied Douglas heartily. "She is an angel."

"Ah, my young sir, men always call women so before marriage; but what do they call them afterwards?"

"That depends mainly on the woman, I fancy," said Montrose dryly. "A wife can make her husband whatever she chooses."

"A silk purse out of a sow's ear," retorted Miss Enistor saucily. "But Douglas and I understand one another, nurse, and there will be no cause for quarrels."

"I wish I could say the same about my lad and the girl he has set his heart on marrying," sighed Dame Trevel, laying down her knitting and removing her spectacles. "It's more her fault than his, though. Rose is a flighty piece."

"She won't listen to reason," said Alice, shaking her head wisely.

"Does any woman ever listen to reason?" inquired Montrose with a shrug.

"From a man she won't; but from a woman she will. Don't be cynical. But I have talked to Rose without success," ended Alice, turning to her nurse.

"So have I, my dearie, and then she told me to mind my own business; as if it wasn't my business to see that my lad got a decent wife."

"There's no real harm in Rose," cried Alice hastily.

"I'm not saying there is. But why she should take jewels from that foreign gentleman and make Job wild, I don't understand."

"Women are fond of jewels," suggested Douglas.

"And why not if they get them in the right way?" snapped Mrs. Trevel ungraciously. "But Rose is to marry my lad, and he don't want her visiting that old gentleman and taking presents."

"Old is the word, nurse," said Alice swiftly. "Job can't be jealous."

"But he is, and his jealousy is dangerous, just as his father's was before him, dearie. And the foreign gentleman puzzles me," added the old woman, taking up her knitting again. "They did say he was to marry you, my love—by your father's wish, I swear, and never by your own will. December and May. Ha! A pretty match that would be."

"I marry Douglas and no one else, nurse, whatever my father may say or do."

"He's a dour gentleman is the Squire," said Mrs. Trevel, shaking her head, "and not pleasant to cross. He never treated your mother well, and she faded like a delicate flower blown upon by cold winds. To me, dearie, he behaves cruel in the way of rent, for all my bringing you up."

"He doesn't mean to," said Alice, distressed, and driven to defending her father, although she knew only too well his high-handed methods with tenants who could not or would not pay.

"Out of the fullness of the heart the mouth speaketh," quoted Mrs. Trevel in a sour way. "If he doesn't mean it, why does he do it?"

"Do what?"

"Says he'll turn me out bag and baggage if I don't pay the rent," cried the old woman excitedly. "How can I when the fishing's been bad and Job can't earn enough to keep things going? I make a trifle by my knitting, but that won't boil the pot. And winter's approaching too. Oh, what's to be done?"

Montrose glanced at Alice and handed a piece of paper to the speaker. "Pay the rent with that, and use what is over to buy food and coal."

Mrs. Trevel grasped the banknote, with a vivid spot of colour on each faded cheek, and could scarcely speak in her excitement. "What is it: oh, what is it?"

"The answer to your prayer," said Alice, rising and looking solemn.

"My prayer! Why, it's a fifty-pound note. Oh, sir, I can't take such a large sum of money from you."

"It is not from me," said Montrose hastily. "I am merely the instrument. God sends the money because you asked Him to help you."

The tears fell down the worn old face. "And I told the passon as it wasn't no use praying," she moaned regretfully.

"Well, you see it is. He takes His own time and means, but in the end every petition receives the answer He deems best. Thank Him, Mrs. Trevel."

"I thank Him, and I thank you too, sir. Bless you, how the sight of this money do set my mind at rest. If it wasn't for Job and the contrary ways of that silly girl I'd be as happy as an angel."

"Pray for Job and Rose," advised Alice gently.

"Well, it do seem worth it, dearie. If He sends me this, He may turn Rose into a reasonable girl, which she isn't at present." Mrs. Trevel was about to put away her treasure-trove when she hesitated. "Should I take it, Miss Alice?"

"Yes. Of course you must take it. Mr. Montrose is rich and can well afford to give it to you."

"And the riches I have," said Douglas quietly, "are but given to me as a steward of Christ to dispense according to His will."

He did not say this priggishly, although to an ordinary man of the world such a way of regarding wealth would seem priggish. Nine people out of ten would have considered the speech as one made for effect, but Alice was the tenth and knew the absolutely impersonal way in which her lover looked at the money. With joyful tears Dame Trevel showered blessings on the young couple when they left her house, and was a happy woman for the rest of the day. Even the prospect of Rose's behaviour rousing Job's jealousy to the extent of leading to serious trouble ceased to cause her anxiety for the moment. Angels had come and left their gifts behind them. The old woman resolved to go to the vicarage and confess with penitent tears that she had been wrong to doubt the efficacy of prayer.

"Do you really regard yourself as Christ's steward?" asked Alice, when the two were on their way to Julian's lodgings, more from curiosity than because she doubted.

"Yes. I thought you knew me well enough to believe so, darling. Of course when you are my wife I shall use the money to make us both comfortable, and we shall have even the luxuries of life. But we must share our good fortune with less fortunate people."

"Why not sell all we have and give it to the poor?"

"I suppose there comes a stage when one does that," mused Montrose, more to himself than to the girl. "But I have not yet reached that point. I know what poverty is in its most sordid aspect, and I don't wish to undergo the experience again. The most I can do is to share——" he paused, then went on in a doubtful manner: "I expect the Blessed One knew that the young man who had great possessions, to whom He said that, was a miser. He was perfect in all ways, but he loved money."

"The Bible doesn't say so," insisted Alice quickly.

"I am reading between the lines, dear. And if Christ gives any one wealth to administer as a steward, what would be the use of the steward nullifying his office by getting rid at one sweep of what he has to administer? It's a hard saying in any case, Alice. I must ask Eberstein what he thinks about the matter. Besides, my dear— —" he hesitated and closed his lips.

"Well?" asked the girl, curiously.

"Nothing," answered Douglas, as Alice had answered on a previous occasion, but there was a puzzled and rather pained look in his eyes as he spoke the word.

The car was already standing at the door of Julian's lodgings and Julian himself was already in the vehicle. While Montrose bundled in beside him, Alice stared at the artist and laughed at his healthy looks, for he seemed to have entirely recovered from his experience on the moors.

"What a fraud you are, Julian, talking about your heart being weak," she said in a jesting manner. "You look big and strong and healthy. Your eyes are bright, your colour is ruddy and you are the picture of a Samson."

Julian nodded gaily. "I feel like a Samson to-day," he said, tucking the rug about his companion's legs and his own. "Sometimes, as at present, I could jump over the moon. At other times you could knock me down with a feather."

"How strange," said the girl thoughtfully.

"Man's a queer animal," cried Douglas lightly, and waved his hand as the big car got under way. "I'll be back to-morrow, dear. Think of me!" and he smiled at Miss Enistor's bright face, little guessing what it would look like when he next set eyes on its beauty.

Shortly they were clear of the village and spinning along the winding levels towards the watering-place. Julian, as Alice had noted, was full of life, and chatted a great deal about this thing and that. Also he asked Montrose questions about the teaching of Eberstein, since his curiosity had been aroused long since by some of the apparently odd things which the young man said so simply and serenely. It was not the first time that they had conversed on the subject of reincarnation and its kindred associations. Julian was not prepared to accept what he termed the theory of successive lives as gospel, and wanted physical proof for super-physical knowledge. This, as Montrose assured him, was absurd.

"When you are able to leave your body consciously and enter into the Unseen World, you will be given positive proof regarding the truth of Reincarnation and the Law of Cause and Effect, which is termed Karma by Eastern teachers. But until that time comes you must accept both laws on logical grounds, since they alone explain without a flaw the riddles of life."

"Can *you* leave your body consciously? asked the artist with scepticism.

"No! I shall some day, as Eberstein is training me. But you can't hurry the hour and you can't delay the hour. You have just to wait."

"It requires immense patience."

"Immense," assented Douglas, "but if you want a big thing you have to do big things to get it. Only by living the life of Christ can you attain to the Christ-like powers. Love, purity, unselfishness, serenity, kindness of thought and word and action: these things arouse the latent faculties which, inherent in every man, enable him to come into contact with other worlds. These are the laws of the Kingdom of Heaven by which one acquires the powers."

Julian thought for a few moments. "I had a talk with Narvaez the other day," he said after a pause, "and he offered to cast my horoscope. He seems, so far as I can judge in my limited way, to have powers beyond the reach of the ordinary man. Does he practise love and unselfishness and all the rest of the necessary requirements?"

"No!" said Montrose decidedly. "I don't think Narvaez is a good man, although I have no positive reason to say that he is a bad one. But an evil man—I am not speaking of Don Pablo, understand—can gain some of the power of the Kingdom by sheer force of will. Christ says: 'He that entereth not by the door into the sheepfold, but climbeth up some other way, the same is a thief and a robber!' So those who get in otherwise than through Christ the Door of the sheep—the door of love, that is—are the evil people who acquire super-physical powers by strength of will, and make use of them selfishly. It is black magic to do that. But those who follow the Master and enter through Him, as the Door, by living the prescribed life to which I have referred, get the powers. But these use them for the benefit of others and not to aggrandise themselves. That is white magic."

"It seems strange to use the word 'magic' in connection with Christ."

"The word has become polarised," said Montrose indifferently, "you can call anything that happens by working an unknown law of Nature 'a miracle,' or 'a wonder,' or 'a magical performance.' The one who performs such exceptional things, of course, can exercise the unknown law I speak of."

"Christ, being superhuman, could," argued Hardwick seriously, "because He had wisdom without measure. But the ordinary man——"

"If the ordinary man loves Christ and keeps His commandments and walks in His footsteps, he can gain knowledge of the power to work what are termed miracles. The Master said so Himself, when His disciples marvelled at His doings, and told them that if they followed Him they would do greater things. As you know, some of the apostles did work miracles in His name. They learned by living the life how to use the laws rightly, by means of the power of Love which came through the Blessed One."

"You appear to know a lot about these things, Montrose?"

"Indeed, I know very little. Eberstein can give much, but I cannot take all he is willing to give, because my understanding is yet limited. But everything will come in time. I must wait patiently."

This interesting conversation was necessarily ended when the car reached Perchton, and the young men parted for the time being. Douglas sought out the hotel where Eberstein was staying, while Hardwick went in search of his doctor. The artist arranged to meet Eberstein later, as Montrose was anxious he should do so, if only to gain an answer to certain questions. The young man being a neophyte could not explain much that Julian desired to know. But he was positive that Eberstein could and would answer all questions, as he never withheld any knowledge from a sincere inquirer.

In a quiet hotel, high up on the cliffs, the doctor occupied a light and airy sitting-room, delightfully peaceful and cheerful and bright. Through the expansive windows could be seen the calm waters of the bay, with little wavelets breaking on the crescent of yellow sand, and the tall white column of the lighthouse shooting up from the reddish-hued rocks of the promontory. Montrose, after early greetings had taken place, noted none of these things, but flung himself into the nearest chair, feeling unaccountably weary. Eberstein, who had welcomed his young friend in his usual sincere and kindly manner, looked at him keenly, as he observed the boy's wilted appearance.

"You seem to be tired," he remarked gently.

"Well, I am," admitted Montrose, with a perplexed expression. "I don't know why I should be, as I slept all right last night and came here in a comfortable motor-car."

"Whom did you come with?"

"A fellow called Hardwick, who is an artist. A really capital chap, who is a first-rate friend. He got the car from some one he knows and gave me a lift."

"Is he ill?" asked Eberstein, after a pause.

"Strange you should ask that. He isn't ill, and he isn't well; that is, he suffers from a weak heart—not enough vitality. He is seeing a doctor."

"I understand."

"You understand what?" Montrose stared.

"Why you look tired. In quite an unconscious way, this Hardwick has been drawing the vitality out of you."

"Can that be done?"

"Oh, yes! The weaker body frequently replenishes its life forces from any stronger body that is at hand. You have heard it said how old age eats up youth. That is a great truth."

"David and Abishag," murmured Montrose wearily. Then he opened his eyes with an astonished look. "I am growing stronger."

Eberstein smiled in an understanding manner. "I am giving you strength, and strength you will need very shortly, I assure you."

"You said in London that trouble was coming. But so far everything is all right. Enistor is an extremely pleasant man, who quite approves of my marriage with Alice. We get on capitally together."

"Was your first impression of him pleasant?"

"No! I disliked him no end when we first met. But as there was no reason for me to do so I grew to like him."

"Ah!" said the doctor with a world of meaning, "second thoughts are not always best. Have you met the man who wanted to marry Alice?"

"Narvaez? Yes! He's a beast. I shall never get over my dislike for him."

"You must not dislike him or any one," corrected Eberstein softly. "Pity Narvaez and pity Enistor, but be on your guard against both."

"What can they do?" asked Montrose, with the disdainful confidence of youth.

"Enistor can do nothing alone. Directed by Narvaez he can do much. And he will," concluded the doctor with emphasis.

"Does the trouble you predicted come from that quarter?"

"Yes!"

"Well, it is two against two. Alice and I can fight her father and Narvaez."

"Don't be over-confident, or you will invite disaster," said the doctor dryly. "There is much doing of which you know nothing. That is why I am here to aid you, my friend. I cannot do everything, as a great deal has to be done by you and Alice with what intuition and strength you possess. With Alice the ordeal has already commenced."

Montrose started to his feet. "Is she in danger?" he asked excitedly. "If so, I must go back to Tremore at once."

"There is no need. What she has to do must be done alone, and you would do her more harm than good by going to her assistance. Hitherto I have protected her with my strength, which has increased her own. Now for a certain time that strength has been withdrawn. Narvaez will know the moment I cease to guard her."

"What will he do?" demanded the young man, clenching his fists.

"Nothing that physical strength can deal with, so don't get ready to fight, my friend. Narvaez will not hurt the girl, but he will endeavour to learn from her something he has long wished to know. It is necessary that he should know and that his pupil should know also. Therefore, for a time he is permitted to work his will. There! There! He will only make use of her clairvoyant powers, so she will suffer little."

"I don't want her to suffer at all."

"Unless she does in some degree, she will not progress."

"Narvaez is such a beast."

"No. He is only a man blinded by pride in his intellectual knowledge. You must pity him for his blindness and do your best to help him. Hate only ceases when Love is used to vanquish it. Calm yourself, Montrose. What must be must be if the Will of God is to be done."

"I wish you hadn't told me," cried the young man, greatly agitated.

"That is a weak thing to say. I told you purposely, so that you may develop faith and patience. Can you not trust me?"

"Yes! Yes! Yes!"

"Then show it by waiting quietly here until I tell you to return to Tremore, my friend. This is the time of preparation to meet and baffle the trouble I warned you against. Stand in the strength of Christ and not in your own strength. He never fails those who trust in Him. To-morrow morning you must come with me to early celebration. By partaking of the Body and Blood of The Blessed One"—Eberstein made the sign of the cross—"you will gain the necessary strength to stand up bravely against the Powers of Darkness."

"Narvaez?"

Eberstein bowed his stately head. "God pity him and save him," he murmured, with infinite compassion.

CHAPTER XV
THE TRANCE

A man on a suburban road at noonday, with the sun shining brilliantly, walks along thinking of his private affairs and heedless of surroundings. But when the toils of day are ended, and he proceeds along that same road in a darkness scarcely illuminated by a few lamps, his feelings are less comfortable. Of course much depends upon the man being sensitive or stolid, but in any case this matters little in the present instance, as the illustration is merely used to symbolise the mental state of Alice during the evening of her lover's absence. One moment she was clothed in the radiance of perfect security and peace; the next, and a dreadful gloom descended upon her bringing anguish and distress. Naturally there was no physical change, but in some inexplicable way she felt that an inward light was quenched. Alice had never read St. Teresa's "Castles of the Soul," or the explanations of that terrible saint would have given her the key to her condition.

As it was she felt as though the sun had fallen from the sky, and quailed in the dense darkness pricked with feeble lights which now surrounded her. Little as she knew it, those same lights represented the sum of what experience she had gained with painful learning through many successive lives. The knowledge and attainments of Eberstein, who had reached an infinitely higher level than herself, beamed in that splendour which had been withdrawn. But what little light she possessed and what greater light he had gained were only what each could receive of The True Light "which lighteth every man that cometh into the world!" Hitherto, Eberstein had given for her use what glory he had earned; now—since the child must learn to walk alone if it ever hopes to come to maturity—he had stood aside for the moment, so that she could make the attempt with what strength she possessed. But Alice did not know all this, and could only feel supremely wretched and forsaken.

So listless did she feel that there was no energy in her to dress for dinner. For two hours she sat in the drawing-room, already darkened by the early gloom of the short autumnal day, longing to be in the haven of her lover's arms. Her lonely soul cried aloud for human sympathy, for human protection, since the higher love seemed to have withdrawn itself, and she put forth all the longing of her being to call back Douglas to her side. But no answer came. The gloom waxed denser, the silence became more oppressive, and all the girl could do was to concentrate her mind on Christ and His saving grace. There was some comfort to be got in murmuring that holy name over and over again. She felt as though she were drowning in a bitterly salt sea under a leaden sky, and that despairing trust in the Blessed One was the spar to which she clung in the hope of rescue. And unprotected as she was for the moment, save by her intuitive faith, she felt the evil forces of the house bear down upon her shuddering soul with terrific weight. She little knew how these destroying influences were being directed by a Brother of the Shadow, and as little did she guess that he would be permitted to go so far and no farther. Knowledge of this state being a necessary ordeal would have helped her to bear it; but the ignorance which made her sufferings more acute was part of the ordeal itself. And silent, unseen, motionless, the Powers of Good watched her endurance of the test.

In the library Narvaez, in an extraordinary state of excitement for one so trained to serenity, was conversing hurriedly with his pupil. He had come over a quarter of an hour previously and was informing Enistor of the girl's defenceless state. The Adversary had withdrawn his protection, as Don Pablo knew in some mysterious way which he declined to explain to the Squire, so now was the time to put forth the dark influence of evil and make use of the girl's clairvoyant powers.

"They are untrained, it is true," said Narvaez, striving to be calm, since he knew how much depended upon perfect self-control. "But she is so pure and so powerful in her purity that when I loosen her soul from the bonds of the flesh, she will be able to reach that exalted plane where she can read the past truthfully. Information will come through little coloured by her personality. I assure you, Enistor, as in so young and innocent a girl, it is not yet particularly strong. Where is she?"

"In the drawing-room! Moping in the dark."

"Ah, she feels the absence of her guardian, and is greatly bewildered. All the better for our purpose."

"How are you going to manage?" said the Squire anxiously. "Alice hates you, and will never submit to do anything for you."

Narvaez sneered. "But for The Adversary, I should have dominated her long ago without difficulty. Now that the protection has been withdrawn she is quite at the mercy of my superior knowledge and power. She can never oppose her will to mine, as she is ignorant and I am wise."

"You won't hurt her," said Enistor uneasily, and silently astonished with himself for giving way to such a kindly human feeling.

"No. Of course I won't," retorted the other impatiently. "I shall send her to find out what we want, and then recall her. Why she is unsupported now I cannot learn; but certainly for the moment she has been left to walk alone. This is our hour, Enistor, so let us make the best of it."

"How do you intend to act?" questioned the father tensely.

"Place that arm-chair in the middle of the room: put the lamp behind yonder screen. I shall sit here by the window where she cannot see me: you take up your position near the fire. Give me a saucer, a plate, a vase—anything."

The Squire obeyed these directions and sat down as instructed to watch the doings of Don Pablo. That gentleman, taking a red-hot coal from the fire, dropped it on a bronze saucer of Indian workmanship which Enistor had selected from amongst the ornaments on the mantelpiece. Placing this on a small table which stood near the central chair, Narvaez shook over the burning coal some special incense which he carried in a tiny golden box. At once a thick white smoke fumed upward, and the room was filled gradually with a stupefying fragrance. With the lamp behind the Chinese screen, the apartment was only faintly illuminated by the red glow of the fire, which smouldered without flames in the grate. The Spaniard moved about with an activity surprising in a man of his years, and when he had completed his preparations retreated into the darkness near the heavily curtained window. Thence his voice came low, clear and piercing to the Squire.

"I am putting out my power to draw her here. Tell her when she comes to sit in the arm-chair yonder. My influence and the scent of the incense will bring about the separation of the bodies, and she will go to the appointed place. You ask the questions, as my voice may move her to rebellion. Keep your brain passive and I will impress upon you what I wish to ask. You have been already trained to be receptive in this way, so you know what to do."

"Yes!" breathed Enistor, sitting well back in his chair and fixing his eyes on the library door, dimly seen in the reddish glow of the fire.

Narvaez did not waste time in replying, but the Squire felt that he was now radiating a tremendous influence, which seemed to extend beyond the walls of the library and throughout the entire house. Shortly, swift unhesitating footsteps were heard, and Alice simply raced into the room, so speedily did she respond to the call. She had all her waking senses about her, and was puzzled to understand the impulse which had sent her headlong in search of her father.

"Do you want me?" she asked, with quick laboured breathing, for the oppression of the room was terrible. "Why are you in the dark? What is the matter?"

"I want to talk to you about Montrose," said Enistor softly. "Sit down in that arm-chair over there."

"About Douglas!" Alice, with a weary sigh, dropped into the central chair, near the table where the incense curled upward in faint grey spirals, not discernible in the half-light. A whiff of the scent made the girl drowsy, and closing her eyes, she rested her head on the back of the chair. The action brought her face nearer to the bronze dish, and with the next breath she inhaled a lung-ful of the burning perfume. With a choking sensation she strove to open her eyes and lean forward, but her body would not obey her will, and she rested, inert and powerless, where she was. There was a momentary struggle between spirit and matter, a sick sensation of loosened bonds, and then she found herself standing upright gazing at her motionless body lying in the chair. It was alive and breathing, for she saw the rise and fall of the breast, but she, in a similar body, stood apart from her physical vehicle, distinct, and—so far as she knew—unattached. Before she had time to grasp the situation, the library vanished, and she was environed by a restless atmosphere of colour. It was as if she was clothed with the splendour of sunset, for there was no hard-and-fast outline; no visible form: all was cloud and colour, materials waiting to be shaped by the will into something which the soul desired. The silence was like a benediction of peace. "Higher! Higher!" said the far-away voice of her father. "Seek out the past where it is to be found. See yourself and those you know, in other times, in other climes, in other flesh." There was a pause, and then came the telephonic voice again, repeating the orders of Narvaez. "Use for the past the names by which you and those you know are called to-day. Higher! Higher!"

Alice again felt that struggle of spirit and matter, and—no longer afraid as she had been—passed out of her second body to become conscious in a third one. Now, as she knew intuitively, she moved in the sphere of Tone, and everywhere rainbow light spoke in music, though still she wandered in a cloudy atmosphere as in the heart of a many-hued opal. Wave after wave of murmuring light rolled over her, but there was no horizon, no boundaries, no up or down. She was in a dimension about which, as Alice Enistor, she knew nothing. But her eternal Self knew that the place was familiar, as she—having stepped behind two veils of matter—knew the Eternal Self.

"Seek out the Book of Time," commanded the thin voice which directed her doings, and ghost of a sound as it was, it penetrated to her through the choral harmonies of the glorious music.

In a moment everything as it were became solid, and she felt that she had dropped again to the earth. Clothed in a larger and more majestic body than that she wore as Alice Enistor, she moved amidst familiar surroundings, knowing the landscape she moved through and the people whom she found herself amongst. Then she was aware that she was still on a higher plane and had travelled in time through five thousand years to re-live for the moment an incarnation of the past. The Book of Time, as she dimly sensed it, was not a book, as the physical brain knows a book, but a state of consciousness. At this moment, when the rainbow had vanished and the music had ceased, and—as it might be—she was living amongst the living, her father's voice came for the third time.

"What do you see? What do you do? Who are you, and who are those you mingle with? Speak!"

So she was not entirely detached from her body of Alice Enistor after all, since a thin thread of light ran from where she was to where she had been when starting on the journey. Down that thread of light—so it seemed—she sent her voice: telegraphed, or telephoned, all that her father wished to know. The necessary goal had been reached, the necessary communication between the mental and physical planes had been established, and she proceeded to reply, compelled by some unknown influence which forced her to speak.

In the library Narvaez wiped the perspiration from his bald forehead, and sighed heavily with the efforts he had made to bring things to this point. But he did not speak with his own tongue, lest the sound of his voice should reach the girl in those far-off regions and make her rebellious. Silently he impressed his desires upon Enistor, and softly Enistor voiced those same desires, while he looked at the motionless figure of his daughter reclining in the deep arm-chair.

"What do you see?" asked Enistor, scarcely moving his lips, and in a thin silvery utterance, soft as a summer breeze, came the answer:

"I am looking on Chaldea, far back in the deeps of time. No—not looking: I am living in Chaldea, as the priestess of a great Star-Angel."

"The name of the Star-Angel?"

"You would call Him, Mars, although He has a different name in Chaldea. He is the Planetary Spirit of Mars, and I serve in His temple. The Chaldeans worship the Host of Heaven, as manifestations of the Logos, whose visible symbol is the Sun. The Star-Angels of the seven planets are the seven Spirits before the Throne, mentioned in the Book of Revelation. The Logos is not the Absolute God from Whom emanated the Universes, but the Being whose Body and Creation is the Solar System. He is the only God our consciousness can conceive. He is the One of this creation manifesting Himself in the many: we are the many ever striving to return to Him, by learning through experience how voluntarily to choose good instead of evil."

"Do the Chaldeans worship the Stars themselves?"

"No. They worship the Angels of the Stars: the power inherent in each planet which emanates from the mightier Power of the Sun-Logos. And His Power emanates from the Absolute God."

"Has each Angel a temple?"

"Yes! And the Logos has a Temple also. These are all placed on a wide plain in a fashion symbolising the Solar System: like an orrery. One collection of temples stands on one plain, another on another plain, and so on throughout Chaldea. On this plain where I live there is the great Temple of the Sun and near it the Temple of Vulcan; next that of Mercury, then that of Venus, until the last temple far away in the distance is dedicated to Neptune. The situations of the temples are reckoned to scale, and represent our System."

"Is there a Temple to the Earth-Angel?"

"No! There is one to the Moon-Angel, and near it a small dome of black marble typifying the Earth. But it is not a shrine."

"You are a priestess in the Temple of Mars?"

"Yes! I wear a brilliant scarlet dress. The priestesses of Venus are in sky blue, and those of the Moon are clothed in silver, while the priests of the Sun wear cloth of gold. Each Star-Angel has His particular colour, and each is worshipped in His own shrine. On great festivals all meet in the great Sun-Temple to worship the Logos."

There was a restless movement in Don Pablo's corner. Enistor, overwhelmed with curiosity, was asking questions on his own account, thereby irritating his master, who wished for more intimate information. A twist of pain brought Enistor to his senses, and he hastily submitted his will to that of Narvaez.

"Do you see me?" was the next question asked, as instructed.

"Yes! You are the High Priest of Mars: a big fat man like a Chinaman, with a rather cruel face. All the Chaldeans are like Chinese with yellow skins and oblong eyes."

"Perhaps they are Chinese."

"No! No. They are Turanians, the ancestors of the Mongolians. I am of the Aryan race, and I don't like the Turanians, who are brutal and lawless. Perhaps that is why you are so cruel."

"Am I cruel? Why am I cruel?"

"You like power, and desire to see every one at your feet. I am a vestal of the temple gifted with clairvoyance, and you use me to foresee the future and learn about other spheres. All this knowledge you turn to your own advantage. Oh, you are wicked. You really don't worship the Star-Angel."

"Whom or What do I worship then?" asked Enistor, again breaking away from Don Pablo's guidance, as the picture drawn by the clairvoyante did not please him.

"The Powers of Darkness: the Elemental Powers. Sometimes you steal away from the Temple after dark to see a very evil man, who is teaching you how to get power in a wrong way, through offering blood sacrifices."

"Who is the man?" questioned Enistor, still using his own will, in spite of signals from Narvaez.

"He is Don Pablo now. Then he was an Atlantean magician: one of the Lords of the Dark Face. You are his pupil, or rather his slave. He uses your intellect to make himself more powerful. There is some good in you, however, and you try to break away every now and then, but the chains that bind you are too strong."

For the first time Don Pablo spoke in a quietly enraged tone. "Stop asking questions on your own account, or I shall hurt you, Enistor."

A shiver passed through the body in the chair, as if that hated voice had penetrated even to where Alice was, and had recalled the detestation in which she held the speaker. Enistor was minded to rebel, but he swiftly considered that if he did so at the moment, he might break the spell, and then would not learn about the threatened danger. Therefore, he was obedient and set himself to obey his evil master. Narvaez became quiet again, and through his instrument asked another question.

"Do you live in the Temple of Mars?"

"Yes, along with other vestals. But none of them possess such great clairvoyant powers as I do, and that is why I am valuable to you. But you use my powers for bad purposes and I hate you. Behind you there is Don Pablo, with his dark designs, but I am supported," her voice took on a note of triumph, "I am supported by a good man, who is a priest of the Sun. He works for good, and is trying to take me away from your influence."

"That is The Adversary."

"I don't know whom you mean by The Adversary. But he is now Dr. Eberstein. Oh, and I see Douglas. He is a Chaldean noble and he loves me. He wants to carry me away from the Temple and from you, as you are killing me with the demands you are making on my powers of clairvoyance. I love Douglas: I want to run away with him. But he is hot-headed and foolish and will not take me away quietly. Dr. Eberstein tells him, when he goes to the Sun-Temple, that if he waits everything will come out right. But Douglas will not wait."

"Do you see Hardwick?" asked Narvaez, through Enistor's tongue.

"He is an old beggar-man who sits outside the Temple. I give him alms every day and speak kindly to him. That is why he is so willing to help me now."

"Does Douglas carry you away?"

There was a pause, and then the voice of the girl came sweet and clear: "I am in the Sun-Temple. It is a great festival. All the worshippers of the various Star-Angels are there in the dress and colour appointed to each. The Temple is built in the form of a cross with a hemispherical dome where the arms of the cross meet. It is something like St. Paul's Cathedral. But between the arms of the cross are passages leading to vast halls, so the plan is different. In the east arm of the cross there is an altar to the Sun, and the west arm contains an altar to the Moon. The great northern altar is for the whole Solar System, I think. The worship now is at this altar."

"What is the worship?" asked Enistor, to Narvaez' unspeakable annoyance.

"It is night, and along the roof of the northern arm of the cross there is a slit through which the stars shine. Mars is being worshipped, and his ruddy light shines through the slit on to a large silver mirror — I think it is silver, but I am not sure. It is concave. Beneath it is a brazier on which I am throwing incense. The priests and priestesses are singing and the worshippers are bowing their heads, as the Star gleams from the mirror through the grey smoke of the incense. And then — — "

"Have done with all this nonsense," said Narvaez angrily, in his own voice. "Tell me about the carrying away."

The body in the chair shivered again, but the soul was obedient to the powerful influence. "Douglas is there with many of his slaves. Towards the end of the service, he breaks through the crowd of priests and takes me up in his arms. The priests try to stop him, but many are struck down. There is a great tumult. You, father, as the High Priest of Mars, thrust at Douglas with a spear snatched from one of the slaves. Douglas lets me down for a moment, as I have fainted, and stabs at you with a knife. Oh," the voice shook with horror, "he has stabbed you in the throat. You fall and die, cursing him. I see Douglas carrying me away. Don Pablo is running beside him. He is drawing the life from me, and Dr. Eberstein is looking on sadly. He can do nothing: he can do nothing."

"Why not?" demanded Narvaez harshly, and now careless of using Enistor as his instrument.

"I owe you a life. I fell into your power when you were a magician in Atlantis—in the City of the Golden Gates. You have a right to take my life, or to forgive me, as I killed you centuries before."

"But I did not forgive you. I never intend to forgive you," said Narvaez grimly. "You were mine then and suffered: you shall be mine again and pay."

"Never! Never! By taking my life in Chaldea you lost your power. I was reborn free from your influence of the past, and you have tried again and again to get me once more under your spell. But Dr. Eberstein guards me. He will save me from you this time, as he has saved me before."

"He won't," declared the Spaniard savagely. "You shall marry me and again become my slave to use your powers for my benefit."

"I shall not marry you. I paid my debt of the past in Chaldea when you killed me. Douglas carried me safely away and then found that I was dead: you drew the life out of me in revenge for what I did to you in Atlantis. Douglas would have been killed for his sacrilege, but Dr. Eberstein as his friend, the Priest of the Sun, helped him to escape from Chaldea. Douglas became a hermit and died very penitent. Dr. Eberstein told him that he had lost me for thousands of years through his hot-headed haste, but that we would come together again when the past was expiated."

"But it is not," cried Don Pablo triumphantly. "Montrose owes Enistor a life. To pay that he must give his own life: he is at your father's mercy."

"Douglas will pay the debt, but not in the way you wish him to pay it."

"Enistor will enforce payment."

"Yes," said the Squire, his eyes glittering. "Now I know why I hated him the moment we met. He killed me in Chaldea: he has robbed me in England; I shall demand the payment of both debts."

"I feel the evil forces that are working in you both," said Alice wearily, "and they hurt me. The book is closed: do let me come back."

"Stay where you are and search out the future," commanded Narvaez, with a snarl of fierce command. "Search."

"I cannot see the future. It is on a higher plane where past and present are one," came the thin, tired voice, for the girl was becoming exhausted physically with the long-continued strain.

"Go to the higher plane: you can do so."

"Something stops me. There is a barrier I cannot pass. You are not permitted to know. Father and I and Douglas have to work out by our knowledge in the flesh the drama begun in Chaldea. This much is allowed: no more."

"But the danger which threatens me?"

"There are black clouds: red clouds: wicked clouds. You are cutting yourself off from the Life of God: you are isolating yourself from creation. You want to drag my father with you, out of space, out of Time, out of the arms of God. Oh, it is too terrible: it is too terrible. Let me return."

"See the future," shouted Narvaez, defiant as Satan in his isolating pride.

"I cannot: I dare not: I will not. I call upon Christ for help. Save me from this wicked being, O Power of Love. Deliver me from evil, Our Father who art in Heaven."

What happened at the moment Enistor never quite knew. He saw Narvaez advance to the middle of the room, looking powerful and making defiant gestures of insane pride. Then all the strength seemed to leave him, and he dropped on the floor like a stone, becoming motionless and powerless, a mere mass of evil matter uncontrolled by his wicked will. At the same time Alice stirred, sighed, opened her eyes and looked through the dim lights to where her father gripped the mantelpiece appalled at the conquest of his dark master by some invisible power he could neither hear, nor see, nor feel.

"You wish to speak to me about Douglas, father?" asked Alice languidly, and taking up her life at the point it had ceased when Narvaez laid his wicked spell upon her. "Oh!" she rose with a gesture of repulsion as she saw the prostrate form. "Don Pablo. I would not have come if I had known he was here."

"That is all right, Alice," said Enistor, recovering his will-power and speech. "He only came a short time ago, and withdrew into the shadow while I spoke to you about Douglas."

"But I didn't see him fall. I didn't hear him fall!" stammered the girl.

"The perfume made you faint for the moment," said the Squire, taking the lamp from behind the screen. "We must postpone our talk, Alice, as the heat of the room has made Narvaez faint. Go to bed. I shall attend to him."

"Good-night," said the girl, without arguing, and touching her father's lips with her own she went away. The hour of darkness had passed, and though she felt languid—with the strain she supposed that she had endured in the drawing-room—yet the light had returned and she felt safe.

Enistor, left alone, touched the old man, wondering how he would be able to revive him, as this was no ordinary faint. But the moment Alice left the room Narvaez sat up, apparently his usual self.

"Did The Adversary strike you down?" asked the Squire, still pale and unstrung.

"No! It was One I do not choose to name. But I defy Him! I defy Him!" He shook his fists in the air with impotent anger. "I shall win yet! I shall win yet!"

CHAPTER XVI
THE DISCIPLE OF LOVE

Next day at noon, Montrose returned to Tremore accompanied by the doctor, to be received by the housekeeper, as Mr. Enistor had gone to see Señor Narvaez, and Alice was still in bed. Knowing from Eberstein that the girl had been submitted to an ordeal, Douglas anxiously demanded if she was ill. But, much to his relief, the answer immediately reassured him.

"Ill, sir? No, sir," responded the housekeeper, who was a voluble talker, "though she did go to bed early last night with no dinner and only a glass of milk to keep her up, which isn't enough nourishment for a young thing like Miss Alice. But she was sleeping so lovely that the master said she had better sleep on. But I think she is getting up now, sir, and when she knows that you are here, sir — —" the housekeeper looked significantly at the young man and departed smiling, with her sentence uncompleted. She was an old and valued servant, who quite approved of the match.

"You are sure Alice hasn't suffered?" demanded Montrose for the twentieth time, and prowling restlessly about the drawing-room.

"Nothing to speak of," answered the doctor serenely, explaining himself as he would have done to a child. "Narvaez and his pupil were permitted to go so far and no farther. They have learned what they wished to know, and I hope the knowledge will do them both good."

"What is the knowledge?"

"There is no need for you to know at present, my friend. You saw what you did see in my London house, and with that you must be content to work out your present Destiny."

"If it is a case of Destiny I am helpless, doctor."

"I think not. Certain things must happen because you put certain forces into action five thousand years ago. But such events will work out for good or bad, as you apply the Law of Love or the Law of Hate. Man makes his own Karma, but he can modify the same to a certain extent by using his will-power."

Montrose sighed. "I am so much in the dark, I don't know how to act."

"You will know how to act when the time comes, if you are true to the teaching of Christ," said Eberstein gently.

"But if you would only advise me what to do?"

"In that case you would only gain the Karma of obedience: good in itself, but less than is demanded. Your future has to do at the moment with Alice and her father and Narvaez, but if I told you the precise reasons why you have come together, you would be hampered in your actions. Watch and pray, my friend, and abide by the Law of Love. Then you will receive the guidance of the Blessed One, who is building up Himself within you."

"I shall do my best."

"That is all that is asked of you and of any one. If a man acts up to the highest ideal he can conceive, nothing more is demanded. And one word of warning, Montrose. Alice is quite ignorant of the use made of her clairvoyant powers last night. Therefore do not ask indiscreet questions."

"Do you mean to say that she does not know what she told Narvaez and her father?"

"No, she does not. Ignorance is as necessary for her as for you at present."

Montrose objected. "If you would only point out the pitfalls to both of us, doctor, we might avoid them."

"These same pitfalls are the creation of your own free-will, and of your own free-will you must avoid them," said Eberstein decisively. "Only experience will teach the necessary lesson which has to be learned, and by making yourself receptive to the Eternal Ego you can always gain the guidance of the Great One, who works through that same Ego."

The young man sighed again, for this epigrammatic teaching was so difficult and—to him—so involved that he wondered why Eberstein did not speak plainly and have done with it. Walking to the window and looking out at the dark woodland a stone's-throw away, where the trees were being tormented by a blustering wind, he pondered over the problem, but could find no answer thereto. After a pause, Eberstein advanced and laid a kind hand on his shoulder, reading his thoughts and pitying his perplexity.

"Our teaching is meant to stimulate the mind," he said impressively. "Therefore hints are given rather than full explanations, and the pupil has to use his brains to expand those hints into the necessary knowledge. In this way he progresses, as what he gains by this system of instruction is thoroughly learned, which would not be the case if his path were made easier."

"I think Christ taught in the way you mention," mused Montrose. "I remember how many of His sayings puzzled me—and for the matter of that still do."

Eberstein nodded. "Regarding earthly things He spoke plainly, as in the case of giving tribute to Cæsar, because people could understand. But as they were unable to comprehend heavenly things the Blessed One could only instruct them in parables, and give hints. By doing this last He roused those He spoke to into puzzling out the meaning."

"Give me an example."

"The Four Gospels are filled with examples. To take one instance. When the people asked: 'Who is this Son of Man?' Jesus replied, 'Yet a little while is the light with you!' If the people could have connected the saying about the Light of the World with this speech, they would have grasped the fact that He spoke of Himself. He was the Son of Man: He was the Light of the World. But," quoted Eberstein sadly from St. John's Gospel, "though He had done so many miracles before them, yet they believed not on Him."

Before Montrose could comment on this speech, Alice entered the room and flew like a homing bird to her nest in his arms. She looked weak and very pale, with dark circles under her eyes, and had a general appearance of debility. For the moment she did not notice the doctor, but could only weep on her lover's breast. Mindful that he was not to ask indiscreet questions, Douglas could only smooth her hair and whisper comfortable endearments. After a time, Alice responded to this gentle treatment.

"I am so glad you have come, Douglas," she faltered wearily. "Last night I had two hours of great suffering in this very room. I felt as though all light were withdrawn and just as if I had fallen into an Abyss of Darkness. Then I heard, or fancied I heard, my father calling for me and went into the library, where he was sitting almost in the dark. He said that he wanted to speak about you. But I saw Señor Narvaez lying on the floor, and refused to stay. I went to bed and slept for hours and hours. I have just got up."

"Why was Señor Narvaez lying on the floor?" asked Eberstein quietly, and more to set her at her ease than because he wished for a reply.

"Oh, doctor, how are you? I am so glad you have come. Don't think me rude not saying anything. I feel so upset. My father said that Señor Narvaez had fainted with the heat of the room. It was hot."

"How long were you in the library?" asked Douglas with anxiety.

"Only a few moments. I could not bear to stay where Señor Narvaez was."

Eberstein glanced significantly at Montrose to draw attention to the fact that Alice was quite unaware of the flight of time when undergoing her ordeal. Then he asked her to sit down and spoke gently as he took her two hands within his own. "You said that you were in darkness. That is not the case now."

"No, it isn't, doctor. The feeling of light came back when I went to bed, and I did not feel so miserable. I was glad to sleep. And yet," Alice looked at the two men in a bewildered manner, "the rest doesn't seem to have done me any good. I feel as if I had walked miles. Do you think that what I suffered from the darkness last night has exhausted me?"

"Yes," replied Eberstein quietly. "That was the hour of your Gethsemane. Now you are feeling better: the light is around you again: the life-forces are rebuilding your strength. Look into my eyes."

Instinctively obedient, Alice did so. Already through the doctor's hands she felt a warm current passing up her arms and into her body, but when she met his steady grey eyes the magnetism of the life-power he was giving her tingled throughout her entire frame. The brightness returned to her eyes, the colour of health flushed her cheeks: her nerves ceased to thrill with pain, and her muscles grew strong. In silent astonishment Montrose looked at the rapid transformation which was taking place under his eyes. From a colourless statue, the girl warmed into rosy life, and when Eberstein dropped her hands she sprang to her feet to stand in the shaft of sunlight which had broken through the heavy clouds of the autumnal day.

"Oh, I feel that I have been born again to a more splendid life," she cried in ecstasy, and looked as though she were transfigured, which certainly was the case. "Oh, thank you, doctor: thank you: thank you. How did you do it?"

"Yes. How did you do it?" asked Douglas, also intensely curious.

"I suppose you would call it a case of hypnotic suggestion," smiled Eberstein, putting his explanation in simple words which they could understand. "I have stimulated Alice's will to command the inflowing of the life-currents from the vital body into the physical, and have added a trifle of my own strength, which I can well spare."

"It is wonderful: wonderful," cried Alice, radiant with unusual life, and smiling like the goddess of spring.

"All things are wonderful, because all things are God. He manifests in the many. Thank Him, my child!"

Alice was silent for a moment and breathed an inward prayer of profound gratitude, which was echoed in the thoughts of her lover. Then she descended to earth and apologised for the absence of her father. "He went to see if Don Pablo was better, and will be back to luncheon. That was the message he sent up to my room."

"I quite understand," said Eberstein, nodding gravely. "Of course Don Pablo is an old man, and has not much strength."

"You could give it to him," said Alice, rejoicing in her glorious vitality.

"I could but cannot, because Don Pablo would refuse to accept help from me, and I could but will not, because he would turn such strength to an evil purpose."

Alice nodded and shivered. "He is not a good man. I hate him."

"You must pity him. He is not good, it is true, but that is because he is dominated by his lower self. For him as for all men God has nothing but everlasting love."

"But he is my enemy," remonstrated the girl, perplexed. "I feel that he is my enemy, doctor."

"What of that? Does not the Great Master tell us to love our enemies?"

"But that standard is impossible to reach," said Montrose quickly.

"If you act in your own strength it is. But all things are possible with God, and only in His strength do we conquer. Do not think of Narvaez as bad, for by doing so your angry thoughts add to the burden of evil he bears. Send thoughts of love and pity to refresh his struggling soul, which the animal forces are striving to overwhelm."

"I am sorry for him in one way," murmured Alice. "At least I think that I am sorry."

"You have every reason to be, but I don't think you truly are," said Eberstein dryly. "Because you read the letter of the commandment and do not comprehend the spirit. I cannot very well explain either to you or to Montrose, as your limitations are yet great. But I ask you both to pity the man and to hope that he may grow better."

"Oh, I shall do that," said Douglas readily. "There is great room for improvement, isn't there?"

"In Narvaez, as in you, and in Alice, and in Enistor. Who can afford to throw a stone at any one?"

Montrose flushed a trifle at the implied rebuke, but never dreamed of defending himself, as he looked upon the doctor as an oracle to be listened to and obeyed with all reverence. Eberstein smiled approvingly when he noted how the young man curbed both thought and word, then changed the subject by commenting on the impressive looks of the house and its commanding situation. Alice was gratified to hear Tremore praised, but hinted at the uncomfortable atmosphere of the place.

"I always feel as though I were battling against depression here, doctor. The rooms and furniture are both so sombre."

"Every house has its own psychic atmosphere, which comes from the sayings and doings of those who live in it," explained the visitor. "I cannot say that the influence of this beautiful place tends to calm the spirit."

Montrose agreed. "When I first came here I felt that it was a kind of battle-ground, full of tumult and war."

"And so it is. Invisible forces of good and evil strive here continuously as I can feel. You sense them also, Alice, as you are more or less clairvoyant."

"Yes, I know," admitted the girl, with a nervous glance round the room. "And the evil is stronger than the good, I fancy."

"At present that is the case. But we must change the conditions and make this house a centre of holy power to bless instead of curse."

"You will have to keep Narvaez out of the place then," observed Douglas abruptly. "And that will be difficult, as he is a friend of the Squire's."

"Quite so," said Eberstein calmly. "I came here to aid Mr. Enistor, as well as to help you and Alice. He is being wrongly guided by Narvaez."

As if the mention of his name had evoked his presence, the Squire made his appearance unexpectedly. He did not look pleased, as Don Pablo had refused to see him, for the first time during their acquaintanceship. Enistor therefore returned in a somewhat gloomy frame of mind, but smoothed his brow and assumed his company manners when he greeted the doctor. He knew well enough that his guest was "The Adversary" so often mentioned by Narvaez, but knew also how the Law of Love which Eberstein obeyed prevented hostile treatment. He therefore felt safe and indeed rather contemptuous, since he was unfettered by scruples himself, and did not care what means he employed against the aims of the doctor, whatever they might be. Yet the downfall of Narvaez on the previous night should have warned him against over-confidence, and would have done so had not the man been so besotted with intellectual pride. Eberstein knew of this Satanic attitude, but gave no sign of his knowledge beyond a pitying glance at Enistor's powerful face when they shook hands.

"You have a beautiful place here," he remarked lightly. "I was just admiring the position when you came in."

"It is well enough, but a trifle lonely," said the Squire rather ungraciously. "Still, I can amuse you by showing our family treasures, which are many. How do you feel, Alice?" he asked, turning abruptly to his daughter, and anxiously wondering if she was aware of the information she had given on the previous night. "I hope you are better."

"Oh, I am quite well now, father. Dr. Eberstein has done me good."

"I have an excellent bedside manner," interposed Eberstein quickly, as he did not wish Alice to explain too much. "And I have cheered up Miss Enistor."

"That is well. She had a fit of the blues last night, and would not listen to what I had to say to her in the library."

"Señor Narvaez was there and he always makes me uncomfortable," protested the girl in a troubled way.

"You are full of fancies, Alice," retorted Enistor in an acid tone. "And as Narvaez had fainted you might have remained to help me. However, it was just as well you retired to bed and slept for such a long time, as you were not quite yourself last night. Well," he added with an assumption of benevolence, "as Montrose was away from you, it was natural you should feel dismal. Ah, these young men, doctor: they steal the hearts of our children."

"And exhibit no shame in doing so," said Eberstein humorously. "Cupid was ever a robber, Mr. Enistor."

Then the gong thundered an invitation to luncheon, which proved to be a truly delightful meal. Alice, with her recovered strength, was filled with the joy of life, and Douglas, seeing her in such good spirits, was very merry in his turn. As to the doctor, he made himself so entertaining in talking of all that was going on in the great world that Enistor unbent considerably, and silently acknowledged that The Adversary was better company than Narvaez. By the end of the meal, both Squire and doctor were on the best of terms. Not for many a long day had such gaiety reigned at Tremore.

After luncheon Alice and Douglas stole away after the fashion of lovers who desire solitude to express their feelings freely. Enistor was left alone to entertain his guest, and conducted the doctor to the library, to show him certain black-letter folios which were of great antiquity and great value. Eberstein, charmed with the treasures of the library and with the spacious room, revealed himself to be no mean judge of books and furniture and ancient manuscripts. More than ever Enistor felt that this debonair gentleman was not to be feared and became uncommonly friendly with him.

"I wish you would come and stay here for a week, doctor," he said impulsively. "It is such a pleasure to meet any one so well read and well informed on all subjects as you are."

"You flatter me," responded the doctor cordially. "I should be delighted to accept your invitation, and may do at a later date. Meanwhile, I have business which detains me in Perchton for a short time. But you have the society of Señor Narvaez," he added, with a keen glance. "And I hear from Mr. Hardwick, whom I met yesterday, that he is most entertaining."

"Hardly the word to be used," said Enistor composedly, and wondering why the reference was made. "He is learned and serious."

"I don't see why learning need necessarily involve seriousness. Knowledge should make one happy, and happiness shows itself in gaiety."

Enistor, fidgeting with a parchment, frowned. "Do you think that knowledge should make one happy?"

"Why not, if the knowledge be rightly applied?"

"In what way?"

"To help others less learned."

"Why should it be?" demanded Enistor defiantly.

"Why should it not be?" countered the doctor swiftly. "What is the use of hiding one's light under a bushel?"

"That is a strange sentiment from you, doctor. It implies vanity, as if you wished others to see and envy your light. Well, I suppose that would be a source of gratification to any one."

"It is but a narrow mind that finds gratification in possessing what another person lacks. You will find the explanation of my real meaning in saying what surprises you in the text: 'Let your light so shine before men that they may see your good works and glorify your Father which is in heaven.' It is the Father who does the works, and the Father therefore should surely receive the praise."

"Who is the Father?"

"In the greater sense God, in the minor degree The Ego, which is a part of God. Through the minor power the greater power works, and to Him be the glory, Mr. Enistor. I daresay you know something of these things."

"I know a great deal," said the Squire in a proud tone, "but I do not interpret them as you do. If I do anything I take the praise to myself. It is I who do it, not this Father, big or little, you talk about."

Eberstein quoted solemnly: "Thou couldst have no power at all against Me, except it were given thee from above."

"That is from the Bible, I take it," said Enistor scornfully. "Well, you see, I don't believe in the Bible. It is a series of old documents filled with contradictions and mistakes and impossibilities."

"Ah, you think so because you read the letter and do not understand the spirit. If you were not so limited you would comprehend the true meaning of the contradictions and mistakes which puzzle you."

"They don't puzzle me," retorted the other resentfully. "Such rubbish is not worth puzzling about. And I am not limited in any way."

"Ah. Then your knowledge is as wide as that of—shall we say Narvaez?"

"No. But then he is an older man and has had more time to study. But I am learning swiftly."

"And the personality you know as Squire Enistor of Tremore is taking all that learning to use for its own ends."

"Why not, when such personality is myself?"

"The lower self: all the self you know," corrected Eberstein serenely.

"What other self is there?"

"The Greater Self: that spark of God, which is you—the Eternal You. Bring your learning to That, Enistor, and you will become One with the Great Father through Christ the Son by the influence of the Holy Ghost."

"Well, if I am that Greater Self, as you say, I work for myself, and therefore deserve praise for my work and the reward also."

"You work only for the limited self which you know. You are not aware of your Greater Self, because it is veiled from you. All you are doing at present is to thicken those veils instead of thinning them. Are you not aware that God is the One manifesting Himself in us, the Many? We are all striving to return to Him, the source of our Being. This being the case, through life after life we have to widen our limitations, so that instead of knowing ourselves as man—as you do—we come to know ourselves as gods, one with the Great God, yet individualised for His holy purpose. Why do you seek to limit your powers, to circumscribe your knowledge?"

"What rubbish you talk, doctor," cried the Squire, opening his eyes in genuine amazement. "Why, I am trying hard to increase my knowledge and gain power."

"Power for yourself," said Eberstein quickly, "and by so doing you are narrowing your circle of action. By giving, you widen out to the consciousness of the Deity: by taking, you build yourself a little hut in which you sit as a very shabby little god."

"But Narvaez has powers you do not dream of."

"I know more about Narvaez than you think, Mr. Enistor. He is doing in a much greater degree what you are striving to do in a smaller way under his misguided instruction. Was not the warning given last night in this very room enough to shake your faith in his powers?"

The Squire started back frowning. "You know what took place?"

"Of course I know, and you know that I know. Come, Enistor, let us talk freely, for I want to help you, and you need more help than you dream of. Narvaez calls me The Adversary, and so I am: not so much adverse to you and him, as to your doings. Your spirit is one with my spirit, as is that of Narvaez', and I wish to aid that other part of myself to fight against the animal self which is trying to overpower it. The spirit cannot be harmed overmuch truly; but the soul can be made a slave to the senses."

"Have you come here to measure your strength against mine?" demanded Enistor in a furious manner.

Eberstein smiled. "If I put forth my strength against Narvaez, much less against you, the result would surprise you. But I act under the Law of Love, which gives every man free-will, and does not allow domination."

"Narvaez was dominated last night," admitted the Squire reluctantly. "Did you strike him down?"

"No. A Great Power struck him down in very mercy, as he was going too far, and it is hoped that the warning may turn him from his evil ways. He is my brother as well as you are, Enistor, and I wish to help you both."

"I don't want your help, unless you can make me rich and powerful."

"I could make you both, and you would use what I gave you to damn yourself yet deeper. Narvaez is dragging you down to the abyss into which he is surely descending. In Atlantis he lured you into his nets by promising to gratify your desire for personal power over men; by giving you wealth to pander to your animal passions. Life after life, as in Chaldea, he has made you more and more his slave by working through your senses."

"I am not a slave!" cried Enistor indignantly.

"Indeed you are. To Narvaez and to your own evil passions. You, who are a god in the making, obey him. Like Judas Iscariot he is a son of perdition and wishes to make you one also, because your intellect is useful to him. Again and again, in many lives, you have been helped in order that you may break away from this bondage; but you will not, and until of your own free will you elect to break away, nothing can be done to save you."

"Where is the boasted power of Christ?" sneered Enistor contemptuously.

"Poor soul, why blaspheme? Christ stands at the door of your heart waiting until you open the door. He does not enter unless He is invited, so how can He use what you call His boasted power, unless you will accept His aid. Humble yourself, Enistor. Say as did the prodigal son: 'Father, I have sinned against Heaven, and in thy sight, and am no more worthy to be called thy son.' Then you will learn how great is His mercy: how sweet His compassion."

"I refuse: I refuse! I am myself: none shall rule me."

"Narvaez rules you, and will you bend to him rather than to the Holy One?"

"I make use of Narvaez!"

"He makes use of you rather. Oh, blind, blind! Already he is plotting and scheming to gain you riches in this life as he did in others, so that he may bind you the more securely to him."

"If that is the case why don't you thwart his schemes?" taunted Enistor.

"He has free-will, and must act according to his own judgment. Moreover, those he plots against are delivered into his hand by their own acts. One is, at all events. Alice escaped from his rule in Chaldea when he slew her by his black magic, and since then he has striven vainly to enchain her again. Montrose is at his mercy and at yours, because of the crime he committed in the Temple of the Star-Angel. He stabbed you and carried away a vestal, in spite of my warnings. For this reason Narvaez has power over him, and as, through love, the Karma of Alice is connected with the Karma of Montrose, she has to suffer in a vicarious way. But Narvaez cannot rule her."

"He can rule Montrose however," sneered the Squire.

"Not in the way you think. Ignorance has made Montrose helpless, as he sinned through blind passion. But he has not deliberately given himself over to the Dark Powers as you have."

"I have not given myself over."

"You have—believe me you have," insisted Eberstein. "And even now your evil master fears lest you should escape, as your soul is striving mightily. There are germs of good in you which I am trying to awaken. Now a great chance is being given to you to escape from the bondage of sin. See that you take it."

"What chance?"

"Montrose owes you a life: he is possessed of a fortune which you think you ought to have. Forgive him his sin against you, and admit that he has a right to keep the fortune. Then your chains will break."

"And if I refuse?"

"The greater will be your sufferings, both in this life and in others."

"You threaten, do you?"

"I plead and warn. But I see that you will not listen, therefore I talk in vain." Eberstein was silent for a moment, then added quietly, "But it may be that the Blessed One working through Montrose may save you yet. Great is the mercy of God and great is His patience."

Eberstein then left the room. Enistor gazed after him with a sneer. "Why, I believe he is afraid of me," he muttered, with inconceivable foolishness.

CHAPTER XVII
THE DISCIPLE OF HATE

Dr. Eberstein came and went like a gleam of sunshine. His mere presence comforted the lovers, since they felt that he would be a source of strength in time of trouble. Truly that time had not yet arrived, but the hint given of its proximity made those who were destined to suffer both uneasy and apprehensive. As the doctor refused to explain what was about to take place sooner or later, the suspense was extraordinarily trying, and only the profound faith of the lovers in their tried friend enabled them to endure. At present, things certainly went smoothly, since Narvaez had ceased to persecute and Enistor was apparently agreeable to the marriage. Nevertheless the young couple felt insecure and sensed clouds gathering swiftly in the summer sky. It was the ominous calm before the breaking of the storm, and the sole comfort lay in the fact that Eberstein remained at Perchton, able and willing on their behalf to deal with the problematic future.

As to Enistor, after his one interview with the doctor he scoffed at the idea of such a man endangering the success of his schemes. In common with the majority of people, the Squire considered a loving disposition to be a distinct sign of weakness, and Eberstein's tolerant arguments only strengthened this belief. Judging the disciple of love by his own limitations, Enistor assured himself that if the doctor really possessed power he would make use of it to gain what he wanted. The Squire was not very clear in his mind as to what Eberstein really did want, but nevertheless believed that to secure his ends he would long since have exhibited some capacity to enforce obedience on his enemies. But far from doing this, or even threatening, the doctor had merely talked ethically. Enistor scouted such chatter, since he could not, and indeed would not, believe that the power of love was stronger than, or even as strong as, the power of hate. The fact that Narvaez had been reduced to impotence when exercising his evil will should have warned the Squire that he had to deal with overwhelming forces, but he shut his eyes to such a plain revelation and persisted obstinately in believing that he was superior to the gigantic power of good. It was simply a case of "neither will they be persuaded though one rose from the dead," and Enistor declined to believe the evidence of his own eyes. There is nothing stops the progress of any one so much as intellectual pride, since it persistently distorts the truth into what it wishes to believe *is* the truth.

Don Pablo could have enlightened him, since he was not foolish enough to underestimate the forces with which he fought, even though in his insane pride he pitted himself against those very forces. But Don Pablo had shut himself in his cottage, and again and again refused to see his pupil. And Enistor could not force himself upon the seclusion of the sage, as he knew by experience that Narvaez, less considerate than Eberstein, would do him an injury if annoyed. So the Squire likewise had to wait as did Alice and her lover. The nerves of all three were strung up to breaking-point, and the atmosphere of Tremore became more than ever insistently oppressive.

To escape the pressure Alice went down to see Dame Trevel in the village, leaving Douglas to write sundry letters. Afterwards he was to join her on the moors, so that they might go for a lengthy walk before dinner. The old nurse was at home as usual, but Alice was surprised to find Hardwick with her. The artist looked like a wax image for paleness, and was seated in the pet chair of the hostess with the appearance of a man who had not long to live. The momentary improvement in his health when he had gone to Perchton had passed away, and Alice uttered an exclamation of dismay.

"Oh, Julian, how ill you look! You should be in bed."

"And that's what I tell him, my dear," said Mrs. Trevel, looking anxiously at the young man. "Bed for the likes of he, say I."

"I'm sick of bed," said Julian, in a pettish tone quite foreign to his usual speech. "It does me no good to lie like a log day after day. Thank God, it won't be long now before the end comes."

"Oh, Julian, don't talk in that way," cried Alice tearfully.

"My dear, I have done all I can, and the result is of the worst. The Perchton doctor can do no good, and even Montrose's friend says that I shall never get better. There is nothing organically wrong. I am just dying of sheer debility."

"But careful nursing——"

Mrs. Trevel shook her ancient head. "Nursing and doctors and medicine won't do the gentleman any good, Miss Alice. He's come to me for some herbal cure, but there's nothing I can give. Only the Almighty can renew his strength."

"The Almighty does not see fit to do so," said Julian moodily. "Don't cry, for heaven's sake, Alice. Tears are of no use. After all it is just as well you refused to marry me, as I should soon have left you a widow, and an unprovided-for widow at that. Until your father found me insensible on the moor no one knew my secret, not even my sister; and I always managed to keep up, even to racing you to Tremore, if you remember."

"Yes, I remember! I never dreamed you had anything the matter with you."

"Nor did any one else save a London doctor. But of late this debility has gained on me, and the end is very near. My dear, I was selfish to propose to you without telling the truth."

"Oh, don't say that, Julian. Can nothing be done?"

"Nothing! My heart may stop at any moment, as the Perchton doctor says. One comfort I have and that is an easy death awaits me." Hardwick began to laugh in a feeble manner. "I don't look like a man who is able to enjoy a legacy, do I, Alice?"

"A legacy? What do you mean?"

"Why, Don Pablo, who always objected to me because I loved you, has turned out to be an unexpected friend. He came yesterday to see me and explained that he had left all his money to me. If I could only live, Alice, I should be a very wealthy man."

"Why has Señor Narvaez done this?" asked the girl, puzzled.

"Lord knows," replied Julian indifferently. "He says he has taken a fancy to me, and that as you are to marry Montrose he and I are in the same boat, as your rejected lovers. He's not a bad old fellow after all."

Alice shivered. "I can never like Don Pablo."

"Oh, I don't know. He's eccentric rather than bad, and perhaps he really did love you. At all events, he has behaved most kindly towards me during my illness, sending grapes and wine and other delicacies. I used to dislike him and wanted to refuse them, but he came and behaved so sympathetically that I accepted what he offered. But his legacy," Julian shook his head, "I shall never live to enjoy that."

But Alice could not bring herself to believe that Narvaez was the good unselfish man Hardwick made him out to be. "I wonder what is behind all this amiable behaviour, Julian?" she asked, pondering.

"Wickedness, dearie!" cried Dame Trevel unexpectedly. "Don't you never think as the leopard can change them spots of his. That foreign gentleman is the devil, if ever there was one, with horns and hoofs, and as black as a coal from the pit. He's got some wicked design on you, Mr. Hardwick, as he has with that silly girl, Rose Penwin."

"Oh, there is nothing wrong about what he is doing for Rose," said Julian, with a faint smile. "He told me that she had great dramatic talent and should go on the stage. He is willing to help her."

"He is willing to make a fool of her," said Mrs. Trevel, knitting vigorously, "and that's a fact. Why can't he leave the girl alone to marry Job and do her best to be a good wife; not that she ever will be, the pretty fool. Your Don Babbler, or Pabbler, or whatever you call him, will get his neck twisted by my lad, if he don't mind his own business. All the village knows how he's come between Job and his promised missus."

"He means well: he means well!" said Hardwick, rising and looking like an old and feeble man in spite of his great stature; "but perhaps he would be wise to leave Rose alone. Alice, will you give me your arm to my lodgings? I see that Dame Trevel can do me no good."

"I would if I could, my dear gentleman, but you're past the power of man to mend, as any one can see."

"Don't say that," cried Alice hastily, and helping Julian to the door. "It will be best for him to come to Tremore and let me nurse him. As to Rose Penwin I shall see Don Pablo."

"You'll do no good, dearie, and it ain't for the likes of you to go after so wicked a man."

"I shall appeal to his kind heart, as Mr. Hardwick says he has one. I want Job and Rose to be happy, so I shall ask Don Pablo to leave her alone to live out her life in Polwellin."

"I think if you put it to him in the right way he will," murmured Julian.

"If he don't, murder will come of it," said Mrs. Trevel wisely, and then stood at her door to see the artist being helped down the narrow street by Alice in a most tender manner. "Poor gentleman," thought the old woman, "there's death in his face, and such a fine figure of a man too. Him dying, and Rose taking jewels from that foreign beast, and my lad with murder in his heart—oh, it's a weary world."

All Alice's persuasions could not gain Julian's consent to go to Tremore to be nursed. But the girl could not bear to think of him dying in lonely lodgings, so she determined to write a letter to Mrs. Barrast and get her to visit Cornwall. Julian laughed at the idea.

"My dear, Amy won't come. And if she did she would only worry me. Let me die in peace. I can leave this world quite happy, as you are to marry such a good fellow as Montrose is. Oh, here we are. How lucky my sitting-room is on the ground floor, Alice, along with my bedroom. I don't think I am strong enough to climb stairs."

"Julian, I can't bear to leave you like this."

"You can do no good by stopping beside me. I am not suffering any pain, remember; only fading out of life as it were. I don't know whether it is owing to the fall of the year, or over-exertion on my part, but it is surprising to think how swiftly I have broken up altogether."

"I never dreamed that you were so weak."

Julian laughed and nodded. "I kept my secret well by only seeing you and others when I was feeling stronger than usual. However, I can play my part no longer, and anyhow it matters little. Now I shall get to bed. Look in occasionally and get Montrose to call when he has time."

Alice, greatly distressed, but wholly unable to improve matters in any way, took a tearful leave of the sick man and climbed up the path leading across the moors to the hill of the Roman encampment. There, by the Druidical altar, she had arranged to meet Douglas, and as the pathway ran past Don Pablo's cottage she decided to see the man about his interference in Job Trevel's love-affairs. The fisherman was certainly growing dangerous, and much as the girl disliked Narvaez, she had no wish to see him strangled. Besides, if her foster-brother allowed his temper to get the better of him to this extent he would undoubtedly be hanged, and that would break Dame Trevel's heart.

More than ever Alice wondered why the Spaniard should wish to benefit Rose by giving her a chance of exhibiting her beauty on the stage, and should desire to make Julian a wealthy man. So far as she could understand, Narvaez was anything but a philanthropist, and, although he had succeeded in convincing Hardwick of his kindly nature and generous disposition, Miss Enistor had her doubts. It was borne in upon her that for his own mysterious ends Don Pablo was acting a comedy which might—and in the case of Job certainly would—turn into a tragedy. Regarding Julian's legacy Alice had no wish to interfere, but so far as Rose was concerned she thought it would be just as well to warn the Spaniard that he was playing with fire. With this determination she came in sight of Don Pablo's cottage about half an hour before the time appointed for the meeting with Douglas on the mount.

It was such a glorious day that there were quite a number of people on the moors, mostly women, who were gathering bracken and cutting peat. The blustering winds of previous days had died away, and rain had ceased to deluge the country, so that the vast spaces of many-coloured herbage spread largely and clearly under the grey-blue sky. There were no mists to veil the view or blur the outline of distant hills, and but for the keen nip in the air and the presence of frost in deep hollows where the pools were iced over, it might have been summer. Alice quite enjoyed the walk in the pale sunshine, and her cheeks grew more rosy and her eyes brighter while she advanced towards the trysting-place. When she came unexpectedly upon Don Pablo taking the air, some trifling distance from his cottage, Miss Enistor looked more charming than ever the old man had seen her. He was aware of her coming with that preternatural acuteness which distinguished him, and came forward with a gallant air of greeting which ill accorded with his withered looks. The man appeared to be older than ever, and—as Alice thought—more wicked.

"This is indeed a surprise," smirked the elderly lover, bowing; "are you on your way to see me?"

"I am on my way to see Mr. Montrose," replied Alice coldly, for the man revolted her now as always; "but I did intend to call in at your cottage."

"How kind of you. Permit me to lead you into my humble abode."

"No, thank you. I can talk to you here. It is about Rose Penwin."

"Indeed! She has been telling you how I wish to forward her fortunes."

"No. But Dame Trevel told me and I came to expostulate."

Narvaez grinned wickedly. "For doing a kind action. Surely not."

"I don't see where the kindness comes in, to launch a girl on the London stage and place her in the midst of temptation, when she could be a happy wife in Polwellin."

"You talk like a woman of fifty, my dear Alice. What do you know of temptation, or of life at all? As for Rose being the happy wife of a rude fisherman, that is impossible to one of her beauty and talents. As one old enough to be her great-grandfather surely I am permitted to help her to do something in the world."

"Polwellin is all the world Rose needs," said Alice resolutely; "until you interfered she was quite content to marry Job. Why did you meddle?"

"Ask yourself that question, my dear," retorted Narvaez, coolly adjusting his fur coat. "I was engaged to you——"

"Never! Never! Never!"

"And you threw me over," continued Don Pablo, just as if she had not spoken; "therefore I tried to comfort my heart by doing good. Marry me and I shall leave Rose to become that oaf's wife."

"I shall not marry you."

"So you say, but I think differently. The game is not yet played out."

"What game?" asked Alice, looking at his malicious face with distaste.

Narvaez chuckled wickedly. "You know, yet you don't know," he rejoined enigmatically. "When you are my wife this problem will be explained to you."

"I shall never be your wife."

"Indeed you shall and your lover's fortune shall be restored to your father, who ought to have it. There are wheels within wheels, my dear girl, and much is going on of which you are ignorant."

"I daresay," said Alice firmly, "you are capable of any wickedness. But it is impossible for you to harm me or Douglas. You forget that we have a friend in Dr. Eberstein."

The Spaniard's wrinkled face grew black, and he looked like a wicked little gnome bent upon mischief. "I defy Eberstein and his silly power," he said shrilly. "He can do much, but I can do more. No one can hurt me."

"Job can and Job will, Señor Narvaez. You don't know the tempers of our West Country men. Already he is dangerous, and if you do not leave Rose alone he will break your neck."

"My neck is not so easily broken," retorted Don Pablo tartly. "I am not so feeble as my appearance warrants. There are other ways than those of mere brute force by which I can defend myself. Eberstein—pouf!" he snapped his fingers in disdain. "Job Trevel—pouf!" he repeated the action; "but Montrose," he added with a sudden change of tone, and raising his voice so that some women working in a near depression of the ground heard him. "I am afraid of Montrose. He may kill me."

"You are talking rubbish," said Alice, startled by the meaning hate in his tones. "Douglas scarcely knows you."

"He will know me better soon. I see him coming along yonder. Doubtless to meet you and enjoy those kisses which should be mine." Don Pablo with surprising activity leaped to the girl's side. "Do you think that I shall surrender you to him?" His hot breath fanned her cheek. "Shall I permit a fool to triumph over me? No!" He gripped her wrist before she could swerve aside. "You are mine. You shall be my wife, my slave, my helper, my instrument. And this is the sign of your bondage."

"Douglas! Douglas!" Alice shrieked as the hateful Spaniard threw his arm round her waist and endeavoured to press his withered lips to her own.

"Mine! Mine!" cried Narvaez, and the girl felt faint with disgust as he clung to her like a loathsome snake. The next instant he was whirled away by a strong arm, and Douglas was sustaining Alice, while the women from their work of peat-cutting and some men with them ran up, crying loudly.

"You beastly little devil," shouted the young man furiously, "I shall break every bone in your body."

"You hear! you hear!" screamed Don Pablo, raising himself on his hands and knees with an effort; "he threatens me. He wants to kill me."

Narvaez was no favourite in Polwellin, but he was rich and had made friends with the mammon of unrighteousness in the village. Therefore the men and women murmured something about the shame of a young man striking so old a gentleman. They had not seen the entire episode, and even if they had would not have blamed the Spaniard overmuch, since it was popularly reported that the younger man had stolen the promised bride of the older one. "Lat um be," said one of the men, stretching out his arm to prevent Montrose again falling on Don Pablo, which he seemed inclined to do.

"Yes, let him be," panted Alice, clinging to her lover, "he is mad. I shall tell my father how he has insulted me."

"Insult you!" shrieked Narvaez, crawling up with the expression of a fiend. "I wonder you think any one can insult you."

Montrose broke away from Alice and, gripping Narvaez firmly, shook him like a terrier shaking a rat. "You wicked wretch, how dare you! I'll kill you if you insult Miss Enistor further."

"Lat um be," growled the same man who had spoken before; "um be bad fur sure, but um be old, my young sir."

"Pah!" Douglas flung the little gnome away and took Alice's arm within his own. "Let him keep out of my way then. If he crosses my path again I shall rid the world of his accursed presence."

"You hear! You hear!" shouted Don Pablo again. "He threatens to kill me. If anything happens to me, remember all of you what has been said."

"Aye, we'll remember. But why didn't you lat her as is to be his wife alone?"

"She was to be my wife and he robbed me of her," snarled Narvaez, arranging his disordered attire.

"Come away! come away," murmured Alice, with white lips and dragging Douglas aside, for the young man's fury was overpowering him again.

"Yes, I'll go. I am not master of myself while that little reptile is about—oh, you toad—you——" Words failed Montrose, and he walked hurriedly away with Alice, after shaking his fist at Narvaez.

"You threatened to kill me: I'll remember that," shouted the Spaniard after him. "You threatened in the presence of witnesses."

Montrose, walking swiftly home with Alice, paid no attention to the cry, but turned to the girl with a white face of suppressed anger and dilated nostrils. "Why didn't you let me twist his neck?" he growled.

"He's an old man," apologised Alice, shivering.

"An old beast. Is age to protect him from being punished? I shall tell your father, and Narvaez will never enter again into Tremore. He won't come near me again in a hurry, I'll warrant, after that shaking."

"He is dangerous! dangerous!" said the girl, trembling violently. "There is some meaning in what he did. You heard how he called on those men and women to witness that you had threatened him."

"I'll do more than threaten if he dares to as much as look at you again."

"Douglas, he is dangerous. Keep away from him."

"I don't want to have anything to do with him. He is old as you say, and I can't thrash the life out of him as I should like to. Come, Alice, you will be all right soon. You have done with Narvaez; he has cut his own throat."

"He is dangerous! He is dangerous!" and that was all the girl could say, or think, since a dim feeling that future evil would come out of present evil haunted her in a way she could not explain.

Had the two overheard what Narvaez was saying and seen what he was doing, Douglas also might have deemed the man dangerous. He gave money to the men and women who had witnessed the affair, and told them to remember the threats of Montrose. "I am an old man. I love Miss Enistor as a daughter," whimpered Don Pablo, "yet my life is in danger. I shall get the police to protect me. As it is, this young ruffian has almost killed me," and with a feeble gait he tottered into his cottage. There he smiled grimly when within four walls and rubbed his hands. "That is the first act of the drama: now for the second."

CHAPTER XVIII
THE NIGHT BEFORE

Enistor was furious when he was told how Narvaez had insulted his daughter, for although he had little love for the girl, yet his family pride rose up in arms against such behaviour. Don Pablo was useful to him, as he knew a great deal about super-physical laws, which the Squire desired to know also, and in which he was being instructed. All the same the Spaniard had proved to be a hard master, and moreover had talked much about the recovery of the fortune, but had done little towards enabling it to be regained. Then again, Narvaez had been struck down in the moment of triumph by a stronger force than any he possessed, and that made him out to be less powerful than he claimed he was. In one word, Enistor was beginning to consider Don Pablo to be something of a humbug.

Certainly there were the pains to which he could subject his pupil when he so chose. But that was, as Enistor knew, mere hypnotic suggestion and could be nullified by an opposing will. Narvaez hitherto had possessed the more dominating influence, but since his capabilities appeared to be shattered by the intervention of the higher powers, it might be that he could not inflict further hurt. The Squire wondered if he could make his dark master suffer by taking him unawares while his forces were weak, and determined to do so if he could, if only to be avenged for the series of petty insults to which he had long been subjected. Why Narvaez should behave in such a crude animal way to Alice, the girl's father could not think. But as he had over-stepped the mark, it gave Enistor an opportunity of becoming openly hostile. Enistor was selfish and unscrupulous, but there was that in him which resented the treatment to which Alice had been subjected. Perhaps the germs of good to which Eberstein had referred were sprouting with unexpected swiftness. But be it as it may, Enistor sought the moorland cottage breathing out fire and fury against his former friend.

Narvaez refused to see him, and when Enistor, sternly angry, sent word by the old housekeeper that he would break his way in and take the consequence, he still refused. However, he improved upon his former message by sending an intimation that he would receive the Squire on the following afternoon. With this Enistor was fain to be content, as by breaking in he would only cause a scandal, which for Alice's sake was not to be thought of. The master of Tremore was a very proud man, and could not bear to think that his family name should be made the subject of police-court gossip. But when he returned home, he believed more than ever that Narvaez was a fraud, as he had not even attempted to inflict the usual pains by suggestion. The man was getting so old that he was losing his nerve, and shortly would not be worth considering whether as friend or foe. Having therefore lost the magician's dark assistance, Enistor decided to try to recover the fortune in his own way.

Alice, shaken by Don Pablo's conduct, had retired early to bed and Montrose was seated in the library with his host over after-dinner coffee and tobacco. He was still seething with anger, but since the Squire had taken matters into his own hands, he could do nothing but look on. After a full discussion of the affair, Enistor insisted that it should be shelved.

"We have talked enough about it," he said in a peremptory tone. "I promise you that Narvaez shall not enter these doors again. To-morrow I shall explain my opinion to him, and then he can go hang for me. With regard to his desire to marry Alice— —"

"Surely after what has taken place, sir, you would never think of any possible marriage," cried Montrose, glowing with wrath, "let alone the fact that you have tacitly agreed to Alice becoming my wife."

"I certainly refuse to think further of Narvaez as my son-in-law," said the Squire stiffly, "in spite of his wealth. But as regards yourself the possibility of your making my daughter your wife rests with you entirely."

The young man laughed and rested his reddish-hued head against the back of the chair. "If it rests with me the matter is soon settled," he said, with a relieved expression in his eyes. He thought that the Squire was talking in a remarkably sensible way.

"That depends upon how you reply to the question I am about to ask," said Enistor dryly. "You inherit the fortune of my sister?"

"Yes!" Douglas sat up, aware that the conversation was becoming serious. "We have not spoken about this matter before, sir, but I would have you know, now that the ice is broken between us, that never in any way did I seek that fortune. It was a surprise to me when I heard the will read by Mr. Cane."

"So I understand from Mr. Cane himself. I absolve you from fortune-hunting, since you knew nothing of Lady Staunton's intentions. But do you think it was quite fair of her to leave the money away from her own family?"

"That is rather a difficult question to put to the man who has benefited, Mr. Enistor. And let me remind you that by marrying Alice I bring back the fortune to your family."

"I think not. Your wife benefits, but I don't."

"Both Alice and I are prepared to be your bankers," said Montrose uneasily.

"To give me what is rightfully my own," retorted the Squire, with a curling lip. "Thank you for nothing. No, that won't do. Until my sister met you it was always her intention to leave the money to me, to restore the position of our family in the county. I want the fortune you hold to myself, as I am a poor man. It is not for a base ambition that I seek the income, but for the sake of going into Parliament and helping to govern. I want power, I want a great sphere to work in. Without money I am condemned to stay in this cramped neighbourhood eating out my heart."

"I quite understand that with such ambitions you feel the need of money, Mr. Enistor, and with Alice's permission I am willing to give you any reasonable sum you desire to forward your aims."

Enistor did not appear to be overcome by this generous offer, or even thankful for the same. "I take nothing as a gift and I claim my rights."

"The whole fortune of your sister?"

"Certainly! She ought to have willed it to me."

"I understood from Alice that you were quite agreeable that Lady Staunton should do what she wished with her own," said Montrose slowly.

"I don't tell Alice everything, Montrose. I accepted my small legacy and said nothing about the matter, as there was nothing to be done until you came. Now," Enistor fixed his dominating gaze on Douglas, "I ask you to let me have the money by deed of gift. In return you shall marry Alice."

"And what are we to live on?"

"I shall allow you five hundred a year."

"In return for five thousand." Montrose laughed at the boldness of the demand. "No, sir. I cannot do what you ask."

"Then you are a fortune-hunter after all," said the Squire bitterly.

"I am not!" Douglas sprang to his feet with the hot blood making red his cheeks. "So far as I am personally concerned I don't care for money, although I don't deny that I am glad my days of poverty are over. But this money has been given to me in trust to help others. I cannot be false to my trust."

Enistor waved his hand disdainfully. "That is only a young man's talk. Why should you help others? Let them look after themselves."

"I think differently. Dr. Eberstein has taught me differently."

"Dr. Eberstein," said the other with a sneer, "is a visionary. If you are to be my son-in-law you must allow me to advise you."

"I have always acted on my own responsibility during life," said Montrose sharply, "and I shall continue to do so. Dr. Eberstein knows so much about things not of this world that I am always glad to hear what he has to say."

"And do what he tells you."

"Certainly, in things which have to do with my spiritual welfare. But as regards earthly affairs I take my own way. Still, I admit," ended the young man frankly, "that in this instance Eberstein advises me to keep the money."

"Naturally! He can do what he likes with you and the money will be useful to him and his ambitions."

The taunt was so puerile that it failed to disturb Montrose. "Eberstein has no ambition save to do good, and is rich enough to execute his plans without aid from me. He cannot do what he likes with me, as you think, although I am always willing to take his advice, which is of the best. I am not a child, Mr. Enistor, but one who has gained experience through bitter trials. I may add that Eberstein's teaching inculcates self-reliance and individual judgment, so that each man may learn to stand alone."

"He is a dreamer as you are. However I care nothing for him or his teaching in any way. You have heard my conditions. Surrender the fortune to me and you marry my daughter: otherwise you must leave my house and never see Alice again. I give you three days in which to make up your mind."

"I make it up now," said Montrose, resolute but calm. "The money I have, and the money I keep. With or without your consent Alice shall be my wife."

"As you please," replied the Squire, frigidly polite. "You have heard my determination, from which I shall not swerve. In three days we can talk about this subject again; meanwhile let things go on as usual." And the conversation terminated in what might be called an armed neutrality.

To remain in the house on such a footing was by no means palatable to a young hot-headed man as Douglas truly was. His first impulse was to leave Tremore and do battle with Enistor from a distance: his second to stay where he was and give Alice the safeguard of his presence. Should he depart it might be that Enistor could coerce the girl into obedience, thereby causing her unnecessary suffering. Montrose loved Alice too well to submit her to such sorrow, so he swallowed his pride and said nothing about the conversation. As he was sufficiently self-controlled to appear at his ease Alice had not the faintest idea of what had taken place. Perhaps if she had observed her father's sudden change towards her lover from geniality to chilly politeness she might have been enlightened. But the insolent conduct of Narvaez had made her nervously ill, and she was too languid to take much interest in any one or anything. So matters remained much as usual, although the visitor felt that the atmosphere of the big house was insistently menacing and sinister. Eberstein could have told him that the conditions heralded the breaking of a storm, but Eberstein, watchful and silent, stayed at Perchton, saying nothing, but thinking much.

Meanwhile Polwellin seethed with gossip. The first item had to do with the sudden illness of Hardwick, who was said to be dying. Every one regretted the news, as the artist was a favourite in the neighbourhood in which he had lived so long. The doctor from Perchton came to see the sick man, and Mr. Sparrow, always a help in time of trouble, visited the bedside. Hardwick was grateful to see them both, but was too weak to take much interest in either his body or his soul. He was simply fading out of life, and things of this world were losing their interest for the departing spirit.

The second item concerned the quarrel of Narvaez and Montrose, which had been reported by those who witnessed it, with many additions. It was freely stated that Montrose had threatened to murder the Spaniard for the insult offered to Miss Enistor, and the gossips said that if he did he would only be forestalling Job Trevel, who was equally bent upon "doing for the foreign gentleman." It puzzled the simple villagers to understand why Don Pablo should return to Miss Enistor, when he had left her to philander with Rose Penwin, and arrived at the conclusion that he was a bad lot. Nevertheless, because the stranger was rich and scattered his money freely, there were a few who spoke in his favour. But the majority were hostile, since the mere presence of Narvaez seemed to irritate those he was with into quarrelling, even though there was no cause to do so. Undoubtedly the man had an evil influence, and the inhabitants of Polwellin would not have been displeased to see this male Atê leave the place. Then Mr. Montrose could marry the Squire's daughter and Job could make Rose his wife, which would mean wedding festivities and plenty to eat and drink. In this way the gossips talked and the rumours grew, so that shortly the whole village was infected with uneasy fear as to what would happen. It seemed as though the influence of the dark house on the hill had descended upon Polwellin. Perhaps it had, and perhaps it had been guided in its descent by that man who dealt with supernatural things in the cottage which squatted like a toad amongst the heather.

To that same cottage Enistor repaired the next afternoon to keep his appointment. He found Narvaez, looking older and more withered than ever, crouching over the fire, moody, broken-up and peevish; altogether unlike his ordinary serene self. At the first glance the Squire decided that his master was quite helpless and sat down with a glow of pleasure to take the upper hand. It pleased him immensely to show Narvaez that he also had a will, that he also could bully, and that the former relationship was now reversed. All the latent cruelty in Enistor rose to the surface at the sight of his helpless tyrant. The late under-dog now intended to bite and worry as the top-dog had done.

"Well, sir," said Enistor shortly, "what have you to say for yourself?"

Narvaez whimpered and crouched still lower over the fire. "I am an old man," he moaned, "a very old man."

"An old scoundrel, you mean. How dare you insult my daughter yesterday?"

"Are you against me also? Do you want to see Montrose murder me?"

"It would serve you right if you did get murdered," snapped the Squire with contempt; "you are of no use in the world that I can see."

"You did not think so once," muttered Don Pablo humbly.

"No! That is true. Because I believed you to be a clever man. Now I know that you are a fraud laying claim to a power you never possessed."

"You have felt my power," snarled Narvaez savagely.

"I admit that I have. And why? Because you had a trained will which you could concentrate to compel me to feel what you wished. That is a thing of the past. The Great Power that laid you low the other night has broken your will, and you are no longer able to control me."

"That is true! that is true! I have had a shock, a great shock."

"So if I put forth my will," continued the Squire mercilessly, "I could make you endure the pains you inflicted on me when I disobeyed."

"And would you?"

"I have a mind to do so at this moment. You set the example. As you did to me so I wish to do to you."

"I daresay." Narvaez straightened himself a trifle, and some of his old fire sparkled in his dull eyes. "But I am not yet so feeble that I cannot defend myself if necessary. I cannot control you, certainly, as The Adversary has scattered and weakened my will, but I can prevent you from hurting me."

"Well, I shall let you off this time," said Enistor, sneering, yet wondering why he should show mercy after Don Pablo's teaching.

"Let me off! Let me off!" screamed the Spaniard fiercely. "Try, if you dare, to measure your powers against mine, shattered as I am. I can gather myself together again, remember; then you take care, you take care."

Enistor felt a qualm, wondering if Narvaez was so weak as he pretended to be. There was a look in the rekindled light of those steady eyes which made him doubtful of his ground. Bold as he was, he felt that it would be rash to advance, and therefore he retreated skilfully by changing the conversation immediately. "You are wrong to think that Eberstein struck you down the other night. It was a Higher Power."

"Who told you that?"

"Eberstein himself. It shows me how broken you are, Narvaez, when you don't know that the man has been trying to convert me to his way of thinking."

"Yes! Yes! I am brought very low: very low indeed," muttered Don Pablo with a groan; "but if Eberstein tried to convert you he hasn't succeeded very well, since it is only the remains of my power that prevent you from giving me pain."

"I don't agree with what Eberstein says," retorted the Squire tartly. "He talked the usual weak Christianity of benefiting one's neighbours instead of one's self."

"Why not take his advice?" asked Narvaez, looking up with his former keen glance. "Benefiting one's self has brought me to this. If you follow my teaching you also may come to these depths."

"That is a strange thing for you to advise, Narvaez."

"Very strange! But I should not advise if I dreamed for one moment that you were disposed to take the Right-hand Path. The Power of Self is too strong for you, Enistor. Age after age it has dominated you."

"So Eberstein told me! But this time I have broken your bonds."

"Have you indeed?" said Narvaez in a strange tone, staring into the fire. "Ah! that will please Eberstein. Of course I lose a pupil and he gains one."

"No! I stand alone!" said Enistor proudly.

The answer seemed to satisfy Don Pablo and he chuckled. "I hope you will be able to stand alone against Montrose, now that I cannot aid you. He has the fortune, remember, and he will keep it."

"I have given him three days to surrender it or lose Alice for ever. And the mention of her name," cried the Squire, lashing himself into a fury, "makes me wonder that I don't thrash you for daring to insult her."

"No! No!" cried Narvaez, and his voice broke. "I am such an old man. Besides I can still help you. Montrose has a secret which you can use against him."

"What is that secret?" Enistor's hand, which he had raised to strike, fell by his side.

"Montrose is already married."

"It's a lie!"

"Ask your young friend if it is a lie. You talk about my having insulted your daughter, Enistor: what about the insult of a married man coming to woo the girl in so shameless a fashion?"

The Squire frowned and was too astounded to speak for a few moments, during which Don Pablo eyed him curiously. When he did speak it was again to deny the truth of the amazing statement. "Beyond the fact that Montrose will not give up the money which should be mine I have nothing against him. He is a well-bred gentleman and——"

"Very well bred to pose as a bachelor," sneered Narvaez contemptuously.

"I don't believe it. The man is honest. You will have to prove what you say, Narvaez. Do you hear?"

"Since you are shouting so loudly I can safely say that I do. Prove what I say: oh, certainly. Send Montrose here to-night and I can give him absolute proof that my statement is correct."

"I shall come with him."

"No!" said Narvaez sharply. "If you come I shall refuse to give the proof in any way. Montrose will be convinced that I can prevent him from marrying your daughter, and to put things straight he may be willing to give up the money."

"Even then," cried Enistor furiously, "I can't allow him to marry Alice. He would be a bigamist."

"That is his affair and hers," said Don Pablo cynically. "What you want is the money."

"I do, but not at the price of seeing my daughter's life ruined."

"Pooh! What does her ruin or his matter to you? Are you bent upon following the feeble Christianity of Eberstein?"

"Feeble! He was too strong for you the other night."

"He was not!" Narvaez raised himself to his full height and seemed to recover a trifle of his former dominance. "I could have dealt with The Adversary alone, but the power he summoned to his aid overwhelmed me. However, this is not to the point." The man collapsed again into a weak condition. "Do what I tell you about sending Montrose here at eight o'clock this evening. I can prove that he is a married man. If you like I can get him, through threats to expose him to Alice, to give you the money."

"I shall deal with that," said Enistor angrily. "All you have to do is to prove your statement. He can come alone and when he returns he shall explain what you say. But I don't believe that he is married."

"I think Montrose will believe," chuckled Narvaez, and then waved his thin hand. "Go now, Enistor. I am tired."

"Don't order me about in that arrogant way," shouted the Squire, "you have not the power to do so. You will be tired enough when Montrose has done with you, I can tell you."

"Perhaps I will. He threatened to murder me, and to keep his secret he may do so. I don't care: this body is very old and weak. I shall be glad to get a new one."

"To work more evil. Remember how you were warned on that night when— —"

"Go away! Go away!" cried Don Pablo in a shrill voice of anger, and his eyes flamed viciously. "I know more about the warning than you do and I despise it. Do you hear? I despise it!" And as on the night when Alice's soul had been loosened from its bonds of flesh he shook his fists in the air.

Enistor did not argue any longer, but went away with a contemptuous shrug of his shoulders. He was more than ever convinced that Narvaez had little power left: all the same the wounded snake might strike in hopeless rage, so it was not wise to tempt the man too far. Besides, on his way back to Tremore, the Squire was filled with rage against Douglas for tricking him. To think that the young scoundrel was married and yet came down to make love to Alice. Eberstein must have known that Montrose was not free, and yet he also had kept silent. So much for the Christianity he professed. It was with a black face and an angry heart that Enistor returned home. He found that Alice and her lover had gone down to see Hardwick in Polwellin, therefore he nursed his wrath until they returned, and it lost nothing by the delay. Even then the Squire did not immediately attack the young man, since the girl was present. After dinner, as he decided, he would be able to bring Montrose to book for his monstrous behaviour.

Alice could scarcely eat and retired early from the table. Julian was at death's door, as she told her father, and she doubted if Mrs. Barrast—to whom she had written—would arrive in time to take a last farewell. With the Squire's permission she returned to the dying man accompanied by the housekeeper. Enistor did not object as he rather liked Hardwick, and was sorry to hear that he was passing out of life at so early an age. But he put the matter out of his mind when alone with Montrose.

"I saw Narvaez to-day," he said abruptly. "He tells me that you are already married, and swears that he can give proof."

Montrose sprang up almost too startled to speak. "Is he mad to say so?"

"Mad or not, he declares that such is the case. What have you to say?"

"Say? Why, such an accusation is not worth answering. I have never looked at a woman until I met Alice. As to being married," the young man paused with an angry, bewildered look, "the thing is preposterous," he cried indignantly.

"Preposterous or not, Narvaez declares that if you go up to him to-night at eight o'clock, he will give you proof."

"Oh, will he!" Montrose glanced at his watch. "It is twenty-five to eight now. I will go at once, and shall arrive at Don Pablo's cottage shortly after the hour he mentions. Then— —"

"Well, what then?" demanded the Squire grimly.

"I'll force the lie down his throat," raged Montrose, who was quite beside himself with anger, and, unable to speak further, he left the room hurriedly.

"Is he or Narvaez the liar?" Enistor asked himself, but could find no reply.

CHAPTER XIX
THE MORNING AFTER

After breakfast disastrous news came from two quarters, and concerned both Don Pablo and Julian Hardwick. While the Squire, his daughter and his guest were ending their meal, the housekeeper rushed into the room with an agitated face to announce evil. Like all her class she was delighted to be the bearer of bad tidings, and counted upon making a sensation, which she assuredly did. Enistor had scarcely raised his eyebrows at her unceremonious entry when she burst into voluble speech.

"Oh! sir: oh! miss, here's dreadful goings on. That poor young gentleman who painted pictures is dead and gone."

"I thought he would die," said Alice, with a sob. "He had no strength when I left him last night. Oh! poor Julian: poor Julian."

"But that ain't the worst, miss. Señor Narvaez is murdered!"

Enistor started to his feet and overturned his chair. He could not believe his ears. "Murdered! Don Pablo! Be careful what you say."

"I am careful, sir," cried the housekeeper resentfully. "He's as dead as a doornail, lying outside his cottage with a broken neck. Mrs. Boyce as looked after him came on the corpse this morning, and is now in the kitchen crying dreadful and exhausted, as she well may be, having rushed across the moor at her age to tell of the wicked crime."

"But is it a crime?" asked Alice, deadly pale and anxious.

"For sure, miss. Men don't break their own necks."

"Who killed him?" demanded Montrose sharply.

"No one knows, miss—I mean, sir. Mrs. Boyce said as Señor Narvaez had some one to see him last night, but who he was she don't rightly know."

Enistor's eyes rested on Montrose, who started and flushed. "When did Mrs. Boyce discover the body?"

"When she got up early to make the old gentleman's breakfast," said the voluble housekeeper. "He wasn't in his room, as usual, but she thought he might have gone out for a stroll, as he sometimes did. Then later, as he did not return, Mrs. Boyce went out to look and found him dead just outside the gate, looking as quiet as pussy. And please, sir, she wants to know what she's to do, having come as quick as ever she could to tell, so that it mayn't be thought to be her fault, which it ain't, she being one as wouldn't kill a fly."

"Tell Mrs. Boyce that I shall go over to the cottage and see what is to be done," said Enistor quickly, "and send one of the men down to the village for the policeman. We must communicate with the Perchton Inspector."

"And what about Mr. Hardwick as is dead and — —"

"You needn't trouble about that. Do what I say."

The housekeeper vanished reluctantly, as she dearly wished to remain and discuss the deaths. The moment the door was closed Enistor turned to Montrose with a frown. "What do you know of this?" he asked imperiously.

Alice started and spoke before her lover could open his mouth. "Douglas cannot possibly know anything," she cried indignantly. "What do you mean, father?"

"I mean that Montrose was the last person who saw Don Pablo alive."

"You can't be sure of that," said the young man, very pale but very quiet. "I certainly called on Don Pablo shortly after eight o'clock, to question him concerning the lie he told about me. But I left him some time before nine perfectly well. His death is as great a surprise to me as to you, Mr. Enistor."

"I hope the police will take that view," sneered the Squire. "You returned here after nine and went straight to bed, when you might have guessed that I was in the library waiting for your report."

"I was too upset to give any report," said Montrose shortly.

"Oh, I quite believe that."

"Douglas! father," cried Alice imploringly, as she could not yet understand the precise situation. "What does it all mean?"

"It means so far as I can judge that Montrose forced the lie down Narvaez' throat, as he said he would, and very thoroughly."

"Do you accuse me of killing the man?" said Montrose hoarsely.

"Yes!" said the Squire, looking at him with grim directness.

"Then I deny absolutely what you say," declared the other vehemently; "as I said before, I left Narvaez in his room shortly before nine o'clock, after he had confessed to me that what he mentioned to you was untrue."

"What did he mention to father?" questioned the girl, terrified at the furious looks of the two men. "I was with Julian until eleven, and when I returned home you had gone to bed, Douglas. I came to tell you about Julian, father, but you did not say that anything had happened."

"Nothing had happened then so far as I know," said Enistor quickly. "My dear, I saw Don Pablo yesterday and he told me that Montrose was already married."

"Married! Married!" Alice started back the picture of dismay.

"It is a lie!" cried Douglas fiercely, and passed round the table to take her in his arms. "I swear it is a lie, dear. When your father told me after dinner I went at once to Narvaez. He confessed calmly that he had spoken falsely so as to prejudice my chances of making you my wife. Had he been a younger man I should have thrashed the life out of him. As it was I told him my opinion and then left him quite unharmed. I swear that I never laid a finger on him, but returned here shortly after nine o'clock to go to bed. I was too indignant at what had been said to seek out your father and explain."

Enistor laughed coldly. "That is a very neat story. Do you believe it, Alice?"

The girl clung to her lover. "Believe it: of course I believe it. Douglas would not tell a lie."

"Not even to save his own neck?"

"My neck isn't in danger," said Montrose haughtily.

"I don't know so much about that. The other day you threatened to kill Narvaez for the insult he offered to Alice, and many people heard that threat, as you know. To demand explanation of a lie—I daresay it was a lie—you left this house breathing fire and fury against Narvaez. When you returned it was to retire to bed without a word of explanation. Now we hear that the man, whom you regarded as your enemy, is dead—murdered. The evidence in favour of your having killed Narvaez is very strong."

"Purely circumstantial evidence," said Montrose, but turned paler than ever when he realised his position.

"Innocent men have been hanged on circumstantial evidence before now," said Enistor coolly. "Although on the face of it I do not admit your innocence."

"Father, how can you think Douglas would murder any one!"

"Ah, I have not the belief in him that you have, Alice."

"Indeed that is true," said Montrose bitterly. "You have always been hostile to me, although for a time you masked your feelings. Now it seems that without a shadow of proof you believe me to be a murderer."

"A shadow of proof!" echoed the Squire tauntingly. "Upon my word, I think there is much more than a shadow of proof. You threatened Narvaez and — — "

"And so did Job Trevel," interrupted Alice defiantly. "It is probable that Job murdered Don Pablo."

"Probable, but scarcely possible," said her father coldly. "However, I shall send for the Perchton police and strict justice shall be done. Until the truth comes to light, Montrose must lie under suspicion. Leave him, Alice."

"Never! Never! Never!" cried the girl, with her arms round Montrose's neck. "He is innocent: wholly innocent."

Enistor stepped forward and wrenched his daughter from the young man. "Obey me, Alice, I command you," he cried imperiously. "So far you have had your own way, but now the time has come for me to have mine. Go to your room and stay there until I look into the matter. As to you," he faced Montrose, who was quiet and pale and as still as a statue, "I should order you out of my house but that justice must be done."

"You mean to have me arrested on a charge of murder?"

"I mean to explain the whole circumstance to the Perchton Inspector and let him deal with the matter," retorted Enistor haughtily. "Meantime, if you try to escape you will be taken in charge at my instance by the Polwellin policeman. You understand."

"I understand that you are bent upon my destruction, Mr. Enistor. But you need have no fear. Being perfectly innocent, I shall not attempt to escape."

"Oh, Douglas! Douglas!"

"You *will* disobey me. Enistor dragged back his daughter and forced her to the door. "Go to your room, I tell you."

Montrose clenched his hands on seeing the girl he loved so roughly handled, but he could do nothing against the authority of her father. With one last sorrowful look, Alice disappeared and Enistor followed, leaving the unfortunate young man alone with his misery. The wicked atmosphere of the house seemed to bear down upon him with such force that he could almost feel the physical pressure. But this probably was imagination, as he was not sufficiently clairvoyant either to see or hear or feel the unseen. But in this agonising moment when it seemed that he was being swept away by a flood of evil, his thoughts turned swiftly to Eberstein. In that man he hoped to find aid, but even as he dwelt on the doctor's assistance a line from one of the Psalms flashed insistently into his mind. "Vain is the help of man" was the phrase, and he became vividly aware by some sixth sense that salvation could only come from the Great Power of Love as manifested in the Lord of Compassion. So intolerable a sense of his peril seized him that, almost unconsciously, the cry for help issued from his lips.

"Oh, Christ!" he breathed audibly. "Lord help me, lest I perish."

It might have been that the intense agony of the moment opened his interior senses, for he became conscious that some glorious light, not of the world, was enfolding him in its radiance. It welled—so he believed—from the golden heart on his breast, as if the stored-up sacramental power was issuing forth to do battle with the dark influence. But be this as it may, Montrose became aware that the gloom was receding, that the evil was being baffled, and that he was growing stronger by virtue of some higher force to resist the terrors pressing in upon him. The radiance which clothed him as with a garment gradually died away, and he found himself standing in the common light of day; but the peaceful, holy, uplifting feeling remained. He knew his innocence, and he knew also with profound thankfulness that God would make that innocence apparent to others. The trouble prophesied by Eberstein had indeed arrived, and very terrible it was; but behind the clouds which environed him shone the sun of righteousness, and its glory would sooner or later dispel the gloom. Having arrived at this knowledge in some way which he was wholly unable to explain, Montrose left Tremore and descended to Polwellin.

Here he walked straight to the post-office and sent a wire to Eberstein asking him to come over at once. He would have gone to Perchton instead, but that he did not wish Enistor to put his threat into execution and have him arrested by the village policeman. As it was, he became an object of suspicion to the fishermen and their wives. The news of Narvaez' violent death had travelled swiftly from ear to ear, and Montrose was apparently looked upon as the criminal. The evidence of those who had heard his threats against the man was too clear to admit of doubt, and already accusations had been spread broadcast, judging from the horrified looks which met Montrose's gaze on all sides. He had been tried and condemned without loss of time, and in spite of the sustaining power he felt his heart sink with purely human fear. It was with a feeling of relief that he met the vicar face to face. From a more educated man he at least hoped to have justice.

"Mr. Montrose," said the vicar, who looked more solemn than ever and was certainly more stiff, "are you wise to walk through the village just now?"

"Why should I not?" asked the young man defiantly.

"Well, there are rumours: rumours," said Mr. Sparrow, removing his clerical hat to brush his bald head with a nervous hand. "Señor Narvaez is dead, as you know, and it is said that you are responsible."

"Why should I be?"

"He insulted Miss Enistor the other day in your presence and you threatened to kill him, I understand. Of course I am not a believer in your guilt," added the parson quickly, "as from what I have seen of you I do not think for a moment that you would shed the blood of a human being."

"Thank you," said Montrose simply, and extended his hand.

Sparrow took it with a flush on his parchment face. "It's all rubbish as I have said," he burst out with very human wrath. "And as you are staying at Tremore, undoubtedly you will be able to show that you did not see Señor Narvaez last night."

It was on the tip of Montrose's tongue to confess his visit, but something—perhaps common sense—prevented him from incriminating himself. Instead, a question sprang to his lips to which he was extremely anxious to get an answer. "What about Job Trevel?"

"There you are," said the vicar quickly. "A rough hot-tempered man like Job is much more likely to have done the deed, though God forbid I should accuse him or any one unjustly. Yet Job certainly hated Señor Narvaez on account of Rose Penwin, and uttered many threats against him. But when the news came of this murder, Mr. Montrose, I at once went to see Dame Trevel, remembering Job's enmity. She tells me that Job went out fishing last night early and has not returned. Therefore he cannot be guilty."

"Then who can have murdered Narvaez?"

"It is hard to say. Of course he lived in a lonely situation and had much wealth, if rumour is to be believed. We shall see when the police come from Perchton. They should be here soon. I believe that Mr. Enistor and our village constable have gone to the cottage to see the body. Meanwhile, Mr. Montrose, I advise you to return to Tremore and wait until we learn more. Señor Narvaez was no favourite, yet it is dangerous for you to walk about amongst my rough parishioners, as they seem to think that you are guilty."

Montrose was no coward, yet he did not see the necessity of courting danger when no benefit could be derived from such foolhardiness. He bowed his head and accepted the warning, thankful to think that Mr. Sparrow did not believe him to have committed the crime. "And Hardwick is dead," he said sadly.

"Yes! Yes! Yes! It is a world of trouble, Mr. Montrose. I have just seen the body, and the poor fellow looks asleep rather than dead. Strange that he should die on the very morning when this tragic event takes place. Polwellin is such a quiet place: nothing of moment ever happens here. Yet now we have two deaths: one from natural causes and one by violence. It never rains but it pours. I have much to do: much to do. Now go back to Tremore, my dear young friend, and rest assured that God will prove your innocence in His own good time. You have my sympathy and my wife's sympathy."

"You are a good man and she is a good woman, Mr. Sparrow," said Montrose, deeply moved. "I assure you I shall not forget how you are standing by me."

"Pooh! Pooh! Of course I stand by you, and so will Mr. Enistor. There is absolutely no ground for these rumours against you, save your unhappy threat. You should keep your temper, Mr. Montrose: you should keep your temper."

"Rather hard to do when a lady is insulted," said Douglas dryly.

"Of course: quite so. If it had been Mrs. Sparrow now, I should have forgotten my calling. Still we must fight the enemy of evil feelings even against those who strive to harm us. Good-day: good-day and hope for the best."

Montrose, climbing the hill to Tremore, would have smiled on any other occasion at Mr. Sparrow's fight between human failings and the divine command to turn the other cheek to the smiter. But he did not smile, as he was very grateful to the man for his advocacy, and thought highly of him for standing up so boldly against public opinion. Sparrow was limited in many ways, but he had a considerable fund of common sense, which he used to the best advantage. He followed his Master as best he knew how and was very close to Him in his present attitude, which was one few men would have assumed in the face of such hostility. Montrose determined that when his innocence was assured he would repay the vicar in one way or another. Meanwhile he had to deal strenuously with his very disagreeable situation.

After midday Enistor returned and requested an interview with his guest in the library. The young man appeared, looking haggard and anxious, which was very natural considering the dangerous position in which he stood. Also he was angry at not seeing Alice, for by Enistor's orders she was not allowed out of her bedroom, the housekeeper being on guard. Douglas insisted that he should be permitted to have a conversation with the girl.

"You have no right to keep us apart," said Montrose indignantly.

"Until you clear your character I have," said Enistor coldly.

"But you don't think that I am guilty: you can't think so. Why, even Mr. Sparrow, whom you say is narrow-minded, does not believe that I killed Narvaez."

"Mr. Sparrow does not know of your visit to the cottage last night. Nor does any one but myself and my daughter. The Perchton Inspector came with several policemen and has examined the cottage and the body, and Mrs. Boyce, who looked after things for Narvaez. She declares that someone called last night, but could not say who it was."

"Perhaps Job Trevel?"

"Job went out fishing last night early and has not returned. Rose was with her mother all day and all night. Neither of these two can be guilty. And from your open threats it is said that you struck the blow, or rather broke the man's neck."

"I am not strong enough to do that," said Montrose, looking at his hands.

"Rage can make any one strong," said Enistor coolly. "And as you had every reason to be in a rage, seeing that Narvaez told what I believe was a wicked lie, you may have handled him too roughly."

"I did not handle him at all. How dare you say so!"

"Don't dare me too far, Montrose, or you may suffer. As it is I have a proposition to make to you. Only Alice and I and you know of your visit to the cottage last night. Alice because she loves you will hold her tongue. I am willing to do so also, if you will make over the fortune by deed of gift to me straightaway. Narvaez' lawyer from Perchton came with the police, as it seems my dead friend has left his money to Hardwick for some reason. It is a vain gift, as Hardwick is also dead. However, that is not the point. What I mean is that this lawyer can make out the deed of gift to-day and you can sign it. Then I shall hold my tongue."

"And if I refuse?" asked Montrose, seeing himself placed perilously between the devil and the deep sea.

"I shall then tell how you visited Narvaez last night, and I need hardly inform you that such an action coupled with your previous threats will bring you within reasonable distance of the hangman's noose."

Montrose nodded and swallowed, as his mouth and throat were very dry. "I see my danger. All the same I decline to give you the money."

"Then you must take the consequence."

"I am ready to do so. And I give you the credit of not believing in my guilt or you would scarcely compound a felony."

"You don't know what I would do or what I would not do," said Enistor coolly, "as you know little of my character. But you are in my power to hang, and hanged you shall be unless you surrender the money. I don't think," ended the man with a sneer, "that your dear friend Eberstein can aid you in this dilemma. What do you think yourself?"

"I think nothing about it," rejoined Montrose decisively. "I have wired to Dr. Eberstein to come over, but— —"

"But he has not yet put in an appearance," interrupted the Squire, with a harsh laugh. "And he never will."

"I disagree. When he knows of my peril he will come."

"He knows of your peril without your telling him, if he is the wonderful man you have made him out to be. However, this is an unprofitable discussion. The question is, will you give me the money to save your neck?"

"No!" said Montrose obstinately.

"I shall give you until six o'clock to decide," replied the Squire calmly. "And then, if you still refuse, I shall inform the Inspector about your visit to Narvaez last night. That will mean your immediate arrest and subsequent punishment."

"It will mean the first undoubtedly, but I may escape the second. I trust in God to prove my innocence."

"The age of miracles is past," said Enistor with a shrug, and left the library to again interview the Inspector.

Montrose remained where he was wondering why Eberstein did not either come over to help him, or at least reply to his wire. Enistor's taunt was surely true, for the young man had sufficient knowledge of Eberstein's wonderful powers to be certain he was aware of all that had taken place. With his ability to procure super-physical knowledge, he probably knew who had murdered Narvaez, so he would surely come to the rescue. But an hour passed and the shadows began to deepen without any information. Montrose began to feel his spirits sink, and again tried to invoke the helpful power which had aided him before, but without success. He felt desperately angry against the Squire for behaving so wickedly, and resented the hate directed against him. "Hate only ceases by love," as Eberstein had said, but how could he love, or even tolerate, a man who was bent upon encompassing his destruction. Montrose asked himself this question several times without getting any reply, and was well nigh in despair, when an interruption came. This was none other than the unexpected appearance of Alice.

"Oh, my dear, my dear," she cried, hastening across the shadowy room to throw herself into his longing arms. "I have been broken-hearted over you, but I could not get out to see you. Father came some time ago and said that I could try to persuade you to give up the money."

"And what do you say?" Montrose asked her softly.

"Give it up: give it up. What does this miserable money matter?"

"I care nothing for the money as you well know. But Eberstein told me to keep it, and I obey him in this as I obey him in all things."

"But why hasn't he come to help you?" sobbed the girl, trembling.

"He will come: he will do something. I have every confidence in him. Remember how he prophesied this woe, and said that we had to learn to walk alone. I can't believe that one who has helped me so much will desert me in my hour of need. Depend upon it, Alice, all will be well. What have you got here?"

"It is the Bible," she offered him the book. "I have been trying to find comfort in it. But I can't: I can't. Everything seems to be against us."

"Eberstein said that it would be," replied her lover gloomily, "and he has proved himself a true prophet. However, we can only wait and let your father do what he wants to do. I refuse to buy my safety by giving up the money."

"But why not?"

"Because such a surrender would be tantamount to my admitting guilt. Since Job can prove an alibi I don't know who murdered Narvaez, but I know my own innocence, and am prepared to face the worst."

"Then—then—" faltered Alice with white lips, "there is the danger that you may be condemned. Oh, Douglas, if my father reveals your visit, the evidence is so strong against you. Why not hide until we can find out the truth?"

"Would you have me sneak away like a cur?" cried the young man in high anger. "No. I am innocent and therefore can meet my accusers with a calm mind."

"But the evidence is so strong," pleaded Alice again. "If we can only get time to learn the truth there will be some chance of proving that evidence false."

"How can we get time?"

"You must hide, and meanwhile I shall see Dr. Eberstein and search for the person who is guilty. Oh, if Julian were only alive," moaned Alice, clasping her hands, "he would help. But he is dead: dead, and we have no friends to help us in any way."

"We have God, and Eberstein who is a servant of God," said Montrose tenderly. "Dearest, I must have faith and so must you. Besides, even if I did hide I know of no place where I could be concealed."

"I do," said Alice eagerly, and thinking that this speech was a sign of yielding. "There is a cave in the cliffs some distance away from the jetty where the boats go out for the fishing. I could guide you there and you could take provisions and candles and something to drink. There you could wait until things grew quiet, and with Dr. Eberstein I could find out the truth."

"The cave would be discovered."

"No. I have thought of that. No one but I knows of the cave—at least I fancy so. I found it one day by chance. And no one would ever think of looking for you there. They would never think you had taken refuge in a cave."

"My dear, I can't admit guilt by running away."

"If you don't, my father will destroy you."

This was true enough, and undoubtedly Enistor would press on the charge as strongly as possible. Montrose wavered. "It might be reasonable to gain the delay," he muttered. "Oh, I wish Eberstein were here to advise."

As if in answer to his speech, one of the servants entered with a telegram, which proved to be from the doctor. Montrose opened it when the maid had left the room, and found the message rather cryptic: also unsigned, save by the initial "E." It ran: "Matthew x. 23, twelve words!"

"Look up the text, Alice," said the young man eagerly.

The girl, luckily having the Bible with her, rapidly skimmed over the leaves and took the book to the window to read the small print in the fast-failing light. "But when they persecute you in this city, flee ye into another," she read slowly, and would have continued the verse, but that her lover stopped her with a gesture.

"Those are the twelve words," he said, folding up the telegram. "The rest of the verse doesn't matter. So Eberstein wants me to fly. I wonder why," and he looked woefully disappointed.

"Take his advice," said Alice eagerly, and glad that such a powerful opinion backed her up. "You always obey him, you know."

"Yes. All the same I did not think he would tell me to sneak away. It seems to be cowardly: it seems like admitting guilt."

"I said in London that I believed in Dr. Eberstein and I say the same now, Douglas," was Alice's decided answer. "He knows more than we do about things, as he prophesied that we should have trouble. Do what he says."

Montrose frowned and bit his lip, for his faith in the doctor was being sorely tried. He never expected to get advice coinciding with that of Alice. And the idea of flight was opposed to his sense of manhood. All the same there was no sense in being heedlessly rash, and undoubtedly Eberstein must have some powerful reason to telegraph as he had done. Alice watched his changing face eagerly and inwardly prayed that he might yield. She saw no safety for the present but in flight. Finally with a sigh he took her face between his two hands and kissed her. "I shall go to your cave," he murmured, but winced at such resignation to what he regarded as an ignoble course.

The two put the plan into execution at once and stole away across the moor into the gathering night after certain preparations. In the space of an hour Alice regained her room, and was apparently innocent of what had taken place. But Douglas was safe in the unknown cave with a scanty store of food, and wine, and a few candles.

"Gone," said Enistor furiously. "Then he is guilty after all."

CHAPTER XX
THE UNEXPECTED

As Montrose had stated to Alice, his flight was looked upon as a tacit admission of guilt. Up to that moment Enistor had not been quite certain that Douglas was the culprit, as the young man had never given him the impression that he was one likely to proceed to such extremities. But this sudden disappearance could only mean that he had done so, therefore Enistor very naturally concluded that Montrose had been infuriated by Don Pablo's bitter tongue into revenging himself hastily. Probably he now regretted that haste, but whether he did so or not mattered little to the Squire. All that the master of Tremore knew was that his enemy was now at his mercy, and he intended to take full advantage of the opportunity. His first step was to inform the Perchton Inspector of that fatal visit to the cottage.

Then, very speedily, the hue and cry was out, and for miles round the police explored the country. There was no doubt in any one's mind as to the actual truth. The threats of Montrose, his presence at the cottage at the time when the crime had taken place, and now the unexpected disappearance— these things showed that Douglas and none other was the guilty person. The next day every one was searching far and wide for the criminal, and Enistor was so vindictive that he offered a reward he could ill afford for the capture of the unfortunate young man. This he did to gratify the hatred which had existed for many incarnations, and also because he believed that when Montrose found it was impossible to escape the gallows, he would make over his wrongfully inherited money to Alice. And once Alice was in possession of the income, her father felt convinced that he would be able to handle the same. It was a very plausible plan, and Enistor worked hard to carry it out.

As Alice had come and gone in the space of an hour, and her absence had not been noticed, save by the housekeeper, the Squire was far from suspecting that his daughter had organised the flight and selected the hiding-place. As to the housekeeper, she was quite on the side of the lovers, since she did not believe for one moment that a nice young gentleman like Montrose had so vilely murdered Don Pablo. Therefore she procured the food and wine and the candles which Montrose had taken with him, and also promised to hold her tongue in spite of all temptation. Alice trusted her, and she was right to do so, for the woman was perfectly staunch. Moreover the girl was glad to have some one to whom she could talk freely. During those dark days she saw little of her father, but remained in her bedroom praying constantly for the safety of her lover. It was a terrible ordeal for one so young and delicate and friendless, but Alice felt that she was being supported by the Master of Love, and that out of sorrow would come enduring joy.

Mrs. Sparrow came to see her, and the narrow-minded grey woman proved to be unusually sympathetic. Neither she nor her husband could bring themselves to believe that Douglas was guilty, in spite of all evidence to the contrary, and for this loyal support Alice was duly grateful. Of course the vicar's wife was excessively aggravating with her platitudes, which did not give much comfort. "All is for the best!" "We must not murmur at the rod!" "It is for your good that you suffer!"—these cut-and-dried phrases dropped incessantly from Mrs. Sparrow's prim lips, and wrought on Alice's nerves to such an extent that sometimes she could have screamed. But knowing that the grey woman meant well, and appreciating her defence of Montrose, the girl controlled her feelings, and accepted these exasperating condolences as genuine, which they assuredly were. But she longed for the presence of Dr. Eberstein and wondered why he did not put in an appearance. Yet he remained absent and silent, not even sending a letter to comfort her in trouble. Still Alice had such a belief in the man that she did not resent his apparent neglect. All the same, her faith was being sorely tried.

Job Trevel did not return. According to his mother he had gone away in his boat to the fishing-grounds at six o'clock on the evening of the murder. No one therefore could suspect that he had anything to do with the matter, but the Polwellin folk wondered at his absence. Rose could give no explanation, as the death of her patron caused her so much grief that she took to her bed. There was no chance now that she would go to London and appear on the stage, and beyond possessing some jewels and a few articles of costly clothing, she had benefited little by Don Pablo's sinister friendship. She would not even have his name mentioned, and now that the man was dead both Dame Trevel and Mrs. Penwin hoped that Rose would marry Job and settle down. The gaudy bubble blown by Narvaez had burst, and the disappointed beauty had to do the best she could. Therefore, she and the two old women looked forward to the return of Job as the best thing that could happen to put the crooked straight. And as the weather had been stormy, it was presumed that Job had been driven for shelter into some distant cove, whence he would come back in due time.

Polwellin was quite excited over the tragic events which had taken place, and the village was in a ferment over the possibility of this person and that gaining the reward offered by the Squire. But although every acre of the moorland was searched the fugitive could not be discovered. It was over forty-eight hours before the first clue was found, and that clue came from a quarter least expected. Also it was given to the man who most wanted to learn the whereabouts of Montrose, on the second day after the commission of the crime. Enistor was the man, and Mr. Sparrow was the person who put him into communication with the individual who afforded the desired information.

"The most wonderful thing has happened, Mr. Enistor," said the vicar, entering the library on the afternoon of the second day. "The age of miracles is not yet past, my dear friend."

Enistor scowled. He did not like to be called a dear friend by the parson, as he thought the man was an ass, and he was quite sure in his own mind that miracles were all rubbish. He told Mr. Sparrow as much. "This isn't Palestine to be gulled by such things, and we live in a scientific era."

"In a very godless era," said the vicar in a tone of reproof. "And I only hope that the wonderful thing that has happened will convert those who do not believe in an Almighty Being to a more reverent frame of mind."

This was a hit at the Squire, who was looked upon as an atheist by Mr. Sparrow. But Enistor did not take up the challenge. "What is your miracle?"

"Mr. Hardwick is alive."

"What?" the Squire could not but feel startled at the announcement.

"Ah, I thought you would be amazed," said Mr. Sparrow complacently. "Wonderful are the works of God and — —"

"Oh, hang your platitudes! You talk rubbish. Why, you told me yourself that Hardwick was dead."

"I did. I saw him lying dead on his bed, and mentioned to Mr. Montrose that he looked as though he were asleep. It might be a case of suspended animation," continued Mr. Sparrow, brushing his bald head thoughtfully, "something of a cataleptic nature it may be."

"Well? Well? Well? Go on."

"There is nothing further to say, Mr. Enistor. The presumed dead man revived this morning and is now as well as you or I. I was sent for immediately by the landlady and called to express my astonishment. I have telegraphed for the Perchton doctor who deposed to the death. He will be amazed to learn what has taken place. Wonderful! Wonderful! Wonderful!"

"It is no doubt a case of catalepsy as you say," growled the Squire, turning to his desk again. "A good thing for Hardwick that he wasn't buried alive. Now he can enjoy Narvaez' fortune and have a good time."

"I hope he will be a good man, seeing that he has been raised from the dead like Lazarus. Not that Mr. Hardwick was bad. Indeed I always thought that he had signs of grace about him. Well! Well! His resurrection gives me a text for next Sunday. I thought you would be pleased."

"I am not pleased and I am not sorry," retorted Enistor. "Hardwick is a nonentity and is nothing to me."

"I thought you were friends, Mr. Enistor. He asks to see you, saying that he is sure you will come down to him at once."

"He presumes too much. I have quite enough to do in searching for this scoundrel who murdered my dear friend."

"I don't believe he did," said Sparrow decidedly. "Mr. Montrose is not the man to shed blood."

"He didn't," said the Squire grimly, "he broke the man's neck. And if he did not murder Narvaez, who did? Not Job Trevel, who was the other person who uttered threats."

"It is a great mystery," sighed the vicar, putting on his hat.

"Like this confounded resurrection of Hardwick. Why the deuce couldn't he stay in the next world after taking the trouble to go there? He's not much use in this one so far as I can see."

"Question not the decrees of the Almighty," said Mr. Sparrow rebukingly. "But there: I am speaking to a deaf adder. May I see Miss Enistor to comfort her and offer up a prayer in her present sorrow?"

"Yes. She's moping in her room and behaving like a fool. Offer up what prayers you like: they won't do any good. It is all her folly in getting engaged to that young criminal that has brought things to this pass."

"Mr. Montrose is innocent," said Sparrow obstinately, "and in due time God will prove his innocence. I wish you a softer heart, Mr. Enistor, and good-day," and the worthy parson stalked out of the room to seek Alice and console her.

Enistor did not resume his work immediately. It had to do with the disappearance of Montrose, as he was writing to the Perchton Inspector. Before the entrance of Sparrow with his wonderful news, the work had seemed very important, but now Enistor felt inclined to lay it aside and seek the lodgings of the artist. Certainly it was wonderful that Hardwick should recover, after he had been lying dead—as the doctor insisted—for so long a time. Undoubtedly it was a case of catalepsy, and Enistor felt curious to see the man who had been so nearly buried alive. His sister was due the next day to see about the funeral, and Enistor laughed when he thought how the frivolous little woman would be surprised. Disappointed also it might be, as she, being the next of kin, would have enjoyed Narvaez' money had her brother really passed away. It was all very strange, and after a moment's hesitation the Squire put on his cap and walked down to Polwellin. He would see for himself what had taken place, and would question Hardwick concerning what he had seen during his trance. For trance it was the Squire felt sure, and the recovery—in his opinion—was a perfectly natural one.

There was quite a crowd round the lodging, and Hardwick's landlady was recounting her feelings when the dead man had come to life. She certainly looked as though she had sustained a shock, and seemed rather disappointed that there was to be no funeral. Enistor listened grimly to her incoherent explanations, then pushed his way into the house and sought the artist's sitting-room. He found Hardwick dressed in his usual clothes and presenting an unusually vigorous appearance. His face was more highly coloured, his eyes were full of fire, and he moved about with the swift grace of a panther, alert, vital, impetuously and wonderfully alive. Enistor stared in amazement at the sight. Never had he seen before so splendid and powerful a man, or one so charged with life-force.

"Dying seems to have done you good, Hardwick," he observed dryly.

"It looks like it," replied the other, and although he spoke in his usual mellow voice, the Squire pricked up his ears and looked at him inquiringly. The tone was more imperious than that ordinarily used by Hardwick, and had in it a dominant, crushing quality which startled the visitor.

The two men stared hard at one another. Hardwick took up his position on the hearth-rug, leaning easily against the mantelpiece, while Enistor took possession of a deep arm-chair near the window. The door was closed, as was the window, so they were quite alone; entirely free from observation and eavesdropping. The Squire felt that in spite of Hardwick's late cataleptic trance the artist was more alive than he was, since wave after wave of powerful animal vitality seemed to emanate from him and fill the little room. Then Enistor cried out with sudden terror.

He had reason to do so. Every nerve in his body was aching with agony, and every muscle was twisted with pain. Some force ran through his frame like fire, excruciating, insistent and terrible. He could not rise from the chair, he could not even move a finger, but lay where he was inert and helpless, with that devouring flame tormenting him to madness. And indeed Enistor wondered why he did not go mad with the frenzy of pain, while Hardwick smiled on him quietly and calmly and unwinkingly, like an avenging god. After that one cry the miserable man uttered no other. He felt that it would be useless to protest in any weak human way. He was in the grip of a tremendous force and as helpless as a fly in the claws of a spider.

"I don't think you will taunt me any more with the loss of my power," said Hardwick suavely. "I am a fraud, am I? my will has been shattered? Eh? How do you like that, my dear friend?" and again there came another surge of the biting fire, which caused the perspiration to break out on Enistor's forehead.

"Who—who—who are you?" stammered the Squire brokenly. He was beginning to have an inkling of the appalling truth, for he well knew that only one man—if man he were—could exercise such devilish power.

"I think you can tell me that."

"Narvaez!"

"Exactly!" The magician withdrew his intense gaze, and loosened his victim from the bonds of torment, then sat down quietly, smiling and bland. "I think you have had enough proof."

Enistor feebly moved his limbs and wiped his forehead with his pocket-handkerchief. His mouth was so dry that he could scarcely speak, and he thankfully poured out a glass of water from a carafe which was on the table. As he drank, a delicious sense of freedom from pain passed through him, and he knew that the man lounging in the chair was curing what he had hurt. "I have had enough proof," gasped Enistor, setting down the empty glass. "You are Don Pablo in Hardwick's body."

"Yes! I am very well satisfied with my new suit of clothes," said the other, looking at his limbs complacently. "Hardwick's retiring soul left its earthly vehicle in good order. The organs are all sound, the blood is of the best, and the whole mechanism only needed the extra vitality which I am able to supply."

"How can you get the vitality?" asked Enistor rather nervously, for the sight before him was enough to shake an ordinary man to the core of his being.

"Never mind. I know how to tap the source of life and use what I will. Hardwick could not do that, being ignorant, therefore he died from sheer lack of vitality. A lucky thing for me, as it gave me a chance of replacing my worn-out body with this very splendid instrument."

"Did you kill Hardwick?"

"No. There was no need to kill him. His Ego had been drawing the soul back for a long time, and knowing that he would soon die, I made my arrangements accordingly so as to enter the body."

"Then your lie to lure Montrose to the cottage— —"

"*Was* a lie—in your interest, said Narvaez-Hardwick coolly. "It was necessary that Montrose should be there so as to be inculpated in my death. Do you understand now why I insulted Alice so that Montrose might publicly quarrel with me?"

"Oh!" The Squire turned pale as he began to comprehend the infernal ingenuity with which the magician had wrought out his scheme. "Then Montrose is not the guilty man?"

"No more than you are. My insult to your daughter was a comedy to deceive the public as to Montrose's feelings towards me. My behaviour when you called to taunt me was part of the same comedy. I think I played my part excellently well, Enistor, or you would have been afraid to say what you did. I suppose you are now convinced that I still have my powers: if not— —" he leaned forward to fix the other man with his eye.

"No! No! No, I am quite convinced," and Enistor cowered in his chair. "You are Narvaez true enough."

"To you and to The Adversary whom no disguise can deceive. But the rest of the world will know me as Julian Hardwick. When Montrose is disposed of, my friend, I can then marry Alice as arranged. She was not averse to becoming Hardwick's wife, so there will be no difficulty over that. And I am still rich, as I made over all my fortune by will to Hardwick, and inherit my own money. I have sent for the lawyer, who will come and see me to-morrow to arrange about the transfer of the property when my late body is buried. And I think," ended Narvaez-Hardwick pensively, "that I shall follow the corpse of my benefactor to the grave. Grace my own funeral," he laughed, much amused.

"Where is Hardwick's soul?" stammered Enistor, who felt the hair of his head rising with the natural terror of the human for the superhuman.

"Purging its baser qualities on the Astral Plane," said the other carelessly. "He won't stay long there, as he was such a pious ass he will probably get his share of heaven before long. I am not interested in him. I have done him no harm in taking his body. It was useless to him and is useful to me. Oh!"

Narvaez-Hardwick rose and stretched himself. "It is splendid to have so magnificent a vehicle. In it I shall live years and years gaining wider and wider knowledge to extend my empire."

"But the Great Power that struck you down and warned you——"

"Hold your tongue," snarled the magician, with a look which transformed the kindly face of Hardwick into the semblance of a fiend. "Leave me to deal with powers higher or lower as the case may be. I have held my own for centuries against all. Are you about to become a pupil of The Adversary as I suggested when you taunted me in the cottage?"

"No. And yet The Adversary has greater power than you have."

"It's a lie," shouted Narvaez-Hardwick imperiously. "What struck me down was a much Mightier Power, which I don't choose to name. I told you that before. Hold to me, Enistor, and I can give you the kingdoms of the earth."

"At what price?" Enistor shivered at the look on the other's face.

"You know the price. You must give me Alice for my wife, and you must obey me in every way. I cannot instruct you unless you do. And now that Montrose is in your power and has to pay back the life he took from you in Chaldea, you can force him to give up the fortune."

"He refuses."

"He dare not refuse if he wants to save his neck."

"But is he guilty?"

"No." Narvaez-Hardwick laughed contemptuously. "You might have guessed that no pupil of The Adversary would be bold enough to commit murder. He is full of silly scruples. You know who killed me!"

"No, I don't."

"Then you are a fool," said the magician roundly. "Job Trevel is the man."

Enistor started from his chair. "Impossible! Job was away in his——"

"Job was at the cottage on the evening when I died," interrupted Narvaez-Hardwick grimly. "I sent for Rose Penwin to come and see me some time after eight, knowing that Job would follow. I contrived to let him know by impressing a message on his foolish brain. He really was going out in his boat, and at six was about to start when he felt compelled to come to the cottage. He saw Rose on the moor and followed her. By that time I had drawn Montrose to the cottage, so as to incriminate him, and you know the means I used. After I had confessed that I had told a lie about the marriage he went away, and I saw Rose, to talk nonsense and rouse Job's jealousy. I went with her to the gate and kissed her there. She didn't mind, as I was an old man and had promised she should go to London next week. Job was waiting for her at the gate, having seen her enter the cottage. Then he sprang on me and broke my neck. After that Rose ran away and Job returned to his boat."

"He has not come back yet," said Enistor, horror-struck at the callous way in which Narvaez-Hardwick detailed his wickedness.

"Nor will he. He fears lest the truth should come to light and he should be hanged for my murder. Rose knows, but for her own sake she will hold her tongue. So you see that Montrose cannot escape. He can offer no defence and must be hanged. Go to him and offer him his life on condition that he surrenders the fortune. Then hang him, or pardon him if you will. I don't care in the least. You are bound to me by stronger bonds when the money is gained, and as Julian Hardwick I shall marry Alice and train her as a clairvoyante. We shall go to Spain, where I have my home, as Narvaez, and which as Julian Hardwick I inherit. I think I have managed everything very cleverly."

"Yes," faltered Enistor, awed by the power and frightened by the unscrupulous cruelty of this strange being. "But Montrose has disappeared."

Narvaez-Hardwick frowned. "I know that, but I don't know where he is. I have searched and searched without success."

"But you have not yet been out of doors."

"You fool, have I no means of searching other than in the physical?" cried the man wrathfully. "I have been looking for him from the other side. It is as easy for me to use my astral body as this physical one. But The Adversary has placed a veil round him. I cannot see where he is. Still Alice knows; I am certain of that. She will want to see him: follow her, and then deal with the man as you will. I have placed him at your mercy. But I am bound to say that this would not have been the case had he not killed you in Chaldea, my friend. The Adversary would have interfered."

"He may interfere now," said Enistor, rising slowly.

"He cannot. Montrose owes you the life of which he robbed you. You can do what you like. Where he is I cannot tell, as he is protected so far. But his evil Karma is too powerful for this protection to continue. He must work out his fate. Follow Alice: she will lead you to him."

"I am sure Alice does not know, Narvaez."

"Call me Hardwick, you fool, else you will be considered a lunatic and will be shut up for one. Alice does know. This much I am aware of. She assisted him to fly: she knows where he is hidden. Now I think that is all I have to see you about. You can go."

Enistor's pride revolted at being ordered about like a dog. "I wish you would speak more civilly, Hardwick," he said, scowling.

"You spoke civilly to me when you thought I had lost my power, didn't you?" jeered the other. "Don't bend your brows at me, or I shall make you suffer. I have done much for you and expect repayment. Nothing for nothing is the rule of the Left-hand Path."

"I'd like to kill you."

"Oh, my dog is showing his teeth, is he? Take care! I have shown you what I can do. If you want to be shown further——"

"No! No!" Enistor winced at the thought of again enduring that cruel pain.

"Then obey me. Go away and watch Alice so that she may unknowingly lead you to Montrose's burrow. When he is found come to me again. Good-bye."

Enistor gnashed his teeth at the insults hurled at him, but being in the grip of a greater force than he had within himself, there was nothing for it but to yield. He departed with a gloomy face, to carry out his orders. Narvaez, in the splendid body of Hardwick, rejoiced with unholy glee.

"I am winning," he cried exultingly. "Winning all along the line."

CHAPTER XXI
THE CHOICE

Enistor returned to Tremore in a black silent rage, wishing heartily that he could find some one with whom to discuss the position in which he found himself. But there was no one, as the mere statement that Narvaez had taken possession of Hardwick's body would be scouted by the most credulous. There were some things which could not possibly be believed, and this was one of them. The present generation was too material to entertain, for a single moment, so wild an idea, and Enistor knew—as his master had warned him—that he ran a very good chance of being locked up as a lunatic, if he even hinted at the astounding truth. Thus the Squire's dabbling in unholy matters had isolated him from his fellow-creatures, and, at the moment, he felt the deprivation keenly. There was nothing he could do but shut himself up in his library and think over his position.

It was not a pleasant one. By his own acts in this and previous lives he had committed himself to bondage, and was treated like a slave who had no rights of his own. What a fool he had been to doubt Narvaez' power, since again and again he had received proofs of it. On the evil hill beside the Druidical altar he had seen with other than physical eyes the terrible elemental creatures which Don Pablo could evoke, and whom he controlled by his powerful will. Any doctor would have told him that it was a case of mere hallucination brought about by the hypnotic suggestion of certain weird ceremonies. But the Squire knew better. There were ways of entering the invisible world which interpenetrates the visible sphere, and Narvaez, by centuries of study and training, had learned how to open the door. He had flung it wide to his pupil, but it could not be closed again, as Enistor did not know the necessary conjuration. This in itself showed the man how impossible it was for his ignorance to cope with the knowledge of Don Pablo.

And now that the magician's black arts had secured a new body, the perfection of which assured him a valuable instrument for many years wherewith to rule on the physical plane, Enistor saw painfully clearly that he would be more of a slave to him than ever. He had to obey Narvaez, as he had ample proof of how the man could enforce his will by inflicting torments. For the first time, therefore, the Squire began to consider how he could escape from his thraldom, and ruefully confessed the truth of the significant text, "The way of the transgressor is hard!" Had Enistor been master instead of slave he would not have troubled about the saying, but being at the beck and call of a merciless tyrant, he wondered why he had been such a fool as to take the Left-hand Path. So far as he could see there was no chance of retracing his steps.

Yet he had one great hope. With his own eyes he had seen the powerful Lord of the Dark Face struck down in the moment of his wicked triumph, so there was no doubt that the Power of Good was infinitely greater than the Power of Evil. It was in Enistor's mind to seek out Eberstein and ask for his assistance. The doctor knew as much about the unseen as Narvaez, and perhaps more, since he was in communication with higher planes than the magician could reach. Undoubtedly, Eberstein, always bent upon doing good, would willingly give his aid, but the price demanded would be the renunciation of revenge. That price the Squire felt that he could not pay, especially now, when Montrose lay at his mercy. The death in Chaldea he might overlook, since it was more or less, to the conception of his physical brain, the figment of a vision. But the money which Montrose unjustly withheld could not be given up, as Enistor needed it desperately to forward his plans for success in the social and political worlds. Therefore he did not seek out Eberstein, as the price which the doctor would ask for giving aid was too great. When the Squire came to this conclusion he heard a faint regretful sigh, which startled him not a little. There was no one in the library and both door and windows were closed. Yet the sound was quite distinct, and Enistor ardently wished that he was sufficiently clairvoyant to see who was present. In a fanciful moment he wondered if his guardian angel had taken his departure, seeing that it was hopeless to induce him to turn from evil to good. But the idea was ridiculous, as the Squire could see no use in anything that did not benefit himself. He rose to his feet fully determined to find Montrose and give him his choice of life or death. If the young man surrendered the money he would be permitted to escape; if he declined, then an uncomfortable death awaited him at no very distant date. Enistor felt quite virtuous in offering the alternative, as he considered that he was giving Montrose a chance of salvation which the man would be foolish not to accept.

As to Narvaez, Enistor hoped that shortly the magician—physically at all events—would remove himself from his path. If Montrose would only act sensibly and escape to Australia or America, after giving up the fortune, then Alice could marry Don Pablo, and go with him to Spain. Thus Enistor would be left free from all domestic relations and with five thousand a year to act as his ambition urged him. And of course the girl would think she was marrying Julian, for whom she had a great regard; so, failing the fugitive becoming her husband, which on the face of it was impossible, Narvaez, in the body of Hardwick, would have little difficulty in gaining his ends. In this way everything would be very nicely arranged and he could dispense with the assistance of Eberstein. In his insane egotism, strengthened by the wicked teaching of Don Pablo, the Squire never gave a thought to the idea that he was deliberately ruining an innocent man. He was too imbued with the iron rule of the Left-hand Path to flinch at such villainy, and considered that the weaker must give way to the stronger. That was only fair and logical. The irony of this thought was that Enistor, as inferior to Don Pablo, did not wish to submit to him, although the strength of the latter compelled him to do so. Yet he was exercising towards Montrose the very tyranny he resented being exercised towards himself. But no amount of argument could have convinced Enistor that he was illogical.

At afternoon tea Alice made her appearance, looking anxious but determined, since her faith in Eberstein, and in the Great Master of Eberstein, braced her to face the worst serenely. Things were dreadfully tangled, the outlook was black, and, humanly speaking, it seemed that there was no possible chance of happiness for herself and her lover. But since the doctor had foretold not only the coming of calamity, but the passing of the same, if bravely endured, Alice was perfectly certain in her own mind that in some mysterious way God would answer her constant prayers for joy and peace. Thus, although she was pale, her eyes were bright and steady, and she behaved in a calm reasonable manner, as though everything went well with her. Enistor marvelled at her composure, and would have dearly loved to shake it by announcing that he knew she had contrived the flight of Montrose. But this he could not do lest he should place the girl on her guard. Therefore he said nothing, having arranged mentally to follow her when she stole out to seek the hiding-place. "There is no news of that young scoundrel," said Enistor, unable to withstand the gibe. "He has concealed himself very cleverly."

"Douglas is no scoundrel," said Alice steadily; "circumstances are against him, and he does well to hide, seeing how bitter you are against him."

"A lie set forth in bad English," sneered the Squire. "He is a scoundrel, as every murderer is, and I am not bitter against him. I only wish to see justice done."

"You care nothing for justice, father. All you wish is to use this accusation to force Douglas to give up Aunt Lucy's money."

"You are very impertinent, but you speak truly enough. My main desire is to get that money, and unless Montrose surrenders it he shall hang."

"You will have to catch him first," said the girl coldly, but said no more. For her father was behaving so wickedly in her opinion that she found it difficult to speak to him with any degree of civility.

Enistor peered at her from under his strongly marked eyebrows and scowled in a menacing manner. It occurred to him that she might have gone to see Montrose during the afternoon, in which event she would assuredly not seek him after dark, and therefore he would not be able to follow her to the hiding-place. "Where have you been these last few hours?" he asked acidly.

"I went to see Rose Penwin, who is ill," said Alice quietly.

Enistor, bearing in mind what Narvaez had stated, started violently. "What did she tell you?"

"Nothing! What is there she could tell?"

"One never knows what a silly girl like that will say," retorted the Squire, reassured that the secret of the murder was safe. "What else have you done?"

"I saw Dame Trevel and learned that Job had not yet returned. Then, as I was told how Julian had recovered from his cataleptic trance, I called on him!"

"You must have gone to his lodgings immediately after I left," said Enistor quickly. "Well, don't you think his recovery is wonderful?"

"Yes! Mr. Sparrow said the doctor was sure Julian was dead, so it is little less than a miracle that he is alive and well. But——" Alice hesitated, and looked highly perplexed.

"But what?"

"Julian is different from what he was."

"In a way I admit that, Alice. He has more strength. It is a wonderful recovery, and I expect the case will be reported in *The Lancet*."

"I don't mean that exactly," replied the girl reluctantly; "but somehow Julian is quite different. I liked him very much, as he was always so good and kind," she hesitated again, then ended abruptly: "I don't like him now."

"Rather whimsical, don't you think?" said her father tartly, and wondering if the girl's intuition had informed her of the marvellous truth.

"I suppose it is," said his daughter wearily; "but whatever may be the reason Julian's illness has changed him into something different. I used to be so happy when with him, but now I shudder in his presence. He has the same terrifying effect on me that Don Pablo used to have."

"You are talking nonsense," said the Squire roughly.

"I know I am. An illness could not change any one into other than he was. I can't help my impression all the same. Julian was good, now he is evil. I never wish to see him again."

"That is a pity," said the man slowly, "for now that Narvaez is dead and Montrose has proved himself to be unworthy of your hand, I wish you to marry Julian Hardwick."

Alice started to her feet. "Never! Never! Never!" she cried vehemently.

"You are capricious, my dear. You were willing enough to marry Julian rather than Don Pablo."

"Of two evils I chose the least."

"You shall choose the least still, if Julian is the least. I objected to you marrying him because he was poor. Now that he has inherited the money of Narvaez he is a good match for you."

"No!" Alice struck the table so violently that the cups rattled in the saucers. "Douglas is innocent and Douglas shall be my husband. Even when Julian was his own dear self I would not have married him after meeting Douglas; much less would I do so now, when he has changed into something horrid."

Enistor saw that she sensed the presence of Don Pablo's black soul in Hardwick's body, but as she could not explain and would not be believed if she did explain, he merely laughed at her vehemence. "You are a silly girl to talk in this way. First you like the man, then you don't, and talk of a change which only exists in your imagination. Are you going mad?"

"I may be," said Alice moodily. "I have had enough to send me mad. But you will understand this, father, that I love Douglas and intend to marry him."

This was her final determination, and before Enistor could argue further she left the room, fearing a breakdown. When alone she flung herself face downward on the bed and tried to compose her mind. It was necessary that she should do so, as late at night she intended to steal out with food for her lover. Her father—as she thought—would never suspect her, and she could leave the house when he and the servants were in bed. Already the housekeeper had made up a bundle, which lay in a convenient cupboard, and would have accompanied her as chaperon, but that her mistress declined such companionship. Montrose was nearer at hand than any one suspected, so it was just as well that as few people as possible should seek the hiding-place. Alice, nerved by love to walk the lonely moors in the chilly gloom, intended to go alone, and in holding to this resolve became more heroic than she ever thought she could be. But in her heart perfect love had cast out fear, and she would have faced an army to succour the man she intended to marry.

The dinner was quiet and the evening was quiet, as Enistor spoke little and Alice was not inclined for conversation. Indeed there was nothing to say, as father and daughter were silently hostile to one another. Owing to the Squire's want of paternal affection they never had been friendly, and now that he wished to ruin her life by handing over Montrose to the police, Alice felt that she hated her father. Eberstein would have told her that it was wrong to do so, even in the face of excellent reasons. But Eberstein was absent and silent, so in this dark hour the girl had to fight entirely unaided. As a matter of fact, she was being guided along the dreadful path skilfully, and her every movement was being watched, as her every thought was known to her guardian. But her clairvoyant power being in abeyance, she did not guess this, and so far as she was aware, only the strength of her love for Douglas enabled her to battle against the dark influences which tried hard to sap her strength.

When Enistor retired to his library, Alice excused herself on the plea of a bad headache and went to her room. There she sat in the faint light of a solitary candle sending loving thoughts to the lonely lover in the cave under the cliffs. Nine o'clock struck and then ten, but it was not until eleven that the house became dark and quiet. A stolen visit to the library assured her that her father had gone to rest, so, thinking that all was well, the girl put on a warm cloak with a hood and took the basket, to leave by a side door which the housekeeper had left unlatched. In ten minutes she was through the darkling wood and on the bare spaces of the moor. But she did not see that her father was following with the skill of a Redskin on the trail. Enistor had watched and waited pertinaciously, and had little difficulty in getting on the track.

It was a stormy, blowy night, with a mighty wind rushing inward from the sea, and Alice struggled against the blast incessantly on her way to the cliffs. Every now and then there was a lull and she could hear the clamour of the waves and the thunder of the waters hammering against the rocks. In the vast hollow of the sky, black clouds were hurtling across the firmament at tremendous speed, unveiling every now and then a haggard moon, full-orbed yet with waning fire. It was a Walpurgis night, when warlocks and witches should have been abroad, rather than this delicately nurtured girl, made heroic by love. Enistor, toiling after her at a distance, wondered at a strength of character which he had been far from thinking his daughter possessed, and laughed grimly to think that unknowingly she was placing her lover within reach of the gripping hands of justice. Amidst the clash and clang of the elemental forces the girl, on her mission of love, and the man, on his errand of vengeance, staggered across the waste land drenched by the fierce rain and buffeted by the roaring winds. Occasionally a zigzag flash cut through the inky clouds, but the subsequent thunder was almost lost in the furious crying of sea and wind. Great as was the hate of Enistor to enable him to face such forces, greater was the love which strengthened Alice to attempt such a task of high endeavour.

Alice led her father down to the very verge of the cliffs, and halted there a stone's-throw from the coastguard station. Lurking in the background, the Squire strained his eyes to see her, and did see her, a momentarily clear silhouette against the pale illumination of the horizon, where the moonlight struggled to assert itself. Then a big black cloud drove ponderously across the moon, and when it passed, Alice was no longer to be seen. In some way she had descended the cliffs, and a cold feeling of fear lest she should fall and be dashed to pieces gripped Enistor's heart, rather to his surprise. He had never thought that he possessed sufficient love for Alice to make him wince in this way. But the love was evidently latent in him, and sent the man pell-mell towards the lip of the land to stay the girl from her rash adventure.

Bending over to look into the seething hell of water below, which bubbled and boiled like a witches' cauldron, Enistor caught sight, in the fitful moonlight, of a tiny dark figure dropping down to some unknown destination. Alice was safe as yet in spite of the fury of wind and wave, and scrambled down a narrow track with the sure-footedness of a goat. Not for nothing had she adventured her life in hazardous ways during the past year, and now the nerve she had gained came in useful when her lover's neck was in danger. She did not think of her own at the moment, but Enistor's heart was in his mouth, as the saying is, as he lay on his stomach peering down at the daring girl. Then a turn of the path below concealed the clambering figure from his eyes, and he debated within himself as to the best course to adopt. He was surprised to think that Montrose was concealed so near to the coastguard station, and no great distance from Tremore itself. But in the very daring of selecting so dangerous a hiding-place lay its safety, as he soon came to comprehend. But what Alice with her youth and lightness could do Enistor did not dare to attempt. He decided to wait until she came up the cliff again, and then he could force her to reveal the exact spot where Montrose lay hidden. Rolling into the shelter of a venturesome gorse bush which grew near the verge, he kept his eyes partly on the light of the not far distant station and partly on the place where the girl had descended. In this way he hoped to seize his daughter and to guard against being surprised by the Navy men, although these latter would be useful at a pinch to arrest the fugitive, when Alice was forced to reveal the truth. So Enistor lay there and the rain beat upon him, the wind blew, and the thunder rolled overhead a challenge to the tumult of the waves below.

Meanwhile Alice, never suspecting that she had led her father to within a stone's-throw of her lover's lurking-place, swung still further downward from the point where Enistor had lost sight of her. Finally the path, which was a mere goat's track, excessively narrow and dangerous, terminated in a small jagged hole no very great distance up the cliff from the sands and rocks below. It was marked by bushes, and would have passed unnoticed even by an experienced climber. The girl had found it during a day in spring, never thinking that it would ever be required for the purpose for which it was now being used. Speedily thrusting herself into this rabbit-burrow, as it might be called, she scrambled on hands and knees along a narrow passage until she emerged into a fair-sized cave. There she saw Montrose ready to greet her with a candle in his hand, and this he soon put down to take her in his arms. "My darling! My darling! How brave you are!"

"Oh, my dear! My dear! My dearest!" She could only cling to him and kiss him and feel that she had reached the heaven of his embrace. "You are trembling!"

Montrose lighted another candle from the stock she had brought and made her sit down on a block of stone fallen from the roof. "No wonder I tremble when I think of you climbing down that terrible cliff. You must not do it again. Do you hear? I would rather give myself up than expose you to such a risk. You might fall and——"

Alice stopped his protestations with a kiss. "I shall not fall. Again and again I have gone down that path out of a spirit of sheer adventure. Shall I then not come when your life depends upon my coming?"

"There never was such a woman as you are," cried Douglas brokenly, "but oh, my darling heart, how can you love me when I lurk here so shamefully?"

"You are doing right. Dr. Eberstein said that you were to fly. When the truth comes to light you can reappear."

"Will it ever come to light?" questioned Montrose uneasily. "Everything is dead against me. I must stay here for ever."

"You will not stay here for ever!" said a quiet steady voice, and the lovers turned their heads with a start to see Eberstein standing some little distance away, calm, benevolent, and encouraging as he ever was.

Alice cried out with natural terror at the sudden appearance of a man whom they supposed to be miles away, and Montrose, thrilled with the deadly fear of the supernatural, could scarcely speak. "How—how—did—you—come here?" he gasped, holding Alice tightly to his breast.

"In a way you know not," replied Eberstein, smiling so kindly as to strengthen both. "My true physical body is asleep in the hotel at Perchton. This I use now is one created for the moment, so that I may be seen and heard to speak by you both."

But for that reassuring smile and their knowledge of Eberstein's goodwill the lovers would have been terrified out of their lives. "But you are—you are flesh and blood," stammered Alice nervously.

"In one way, yes: in another way, no. The knowledge of certain laws which has been entrusted to me enables me to materialise myself in this way." He advanced to place one hand on the girl's shoulder and the other on that of Montrose. "You can feel my touch, can you not?"

"We can feel, hear and see," said Douglas, and his inclination was to kneel before his Master who manifested such power. All fear had departed now both from himself and Alice. It was as if an angel had come to them.

"Kneel only to God," said Eberstein solemnly. "It is His great mercy that permits me to come to your aid. The moment is at hand which will decide your future—the future of you both. Before you, Montrose, will be placed good and evil: as you choose so shall it be."

"I shall choose the good," cried the young man impetuously.

"Be not over-confident, lest you fall," warned the Master gravely. "One whom you wronged in the past has you at his mercy."

"My father?" questioned Alice, with a gasp.

Eberstein bowed his head. "In Chaldea you killed him, Montrose, and therefore you owe him a life for a life. Humanly speaking you are in his power for the moment, and he can hand you over to the officers of law."

"But I am innocent of the crime!"

"Yes! And he knows that you are innocent. But the teaching of the son of perdition, whom you know as Narvaez, has warped his nature, and to gain the money he claims he will place you, if he can, in the shadow of the gallows."

"He does not know where I am! He is——"

"Peace!" The Master raised his arm slowly. "What will be, will be as love or hate, fear or trust triumphs in your breast. Ascend the cliff, alone!"

"Alone!" Alice uttered a shriek. "No! No! Let me go also."

"Ascend the cliff alone," repeated Eberstein calmly, "and you, my daughter, kneel here in prayer that good may triumph over evil. May the will of God be fulfilled, and may the love of Christ"—he made the sign of the cross—"be with you in the hour of need, with the saving grace of the Holy Ghost."

Where he had been there was but the gloom of the cave faintly illuminated by the candlelight. Motionless with awe the lovers clung to one another, and Montrose, looking upward when movement came to him, breathed a voiceless prayer. Then he bent to kiss Alice, who had sunk on her knees, and loosening his clasp moved slowly towards the entrance to the cave. She did not seek to stay him, but with folded hands looked at his retiring form—it might be for the last time. But as she looked the exaltation and awe of that solemn moment opened her interior senses, and she saw a triangle of white flame, which showered on her lover's head purple rays of ineffable beauty. These shaped themselves into a cross as he disappeared, and then drew inward to a star, radiant and glorious, which shone in the gloom as the symbol of hope and salvation. To that high splendour—to the Power beyond—to the Father and to the Son and to the Holy Ghost proceeding from the Father through the Son, did she pray fervently. Not that her earthly parent might be spared the commission of a crime, not that her lover might be saved, but that the holy purpose of God, unknown and inexplicable, might be fulfilled according to His will. To such a height of trust in the Love which saves had the ever-compassionate Mercy of The Christ raised this weak, faltering, bruised soul.

CHAPTER XXII
RIGHT IS MIGHT

Montrose was so accustomed to obey his Master that he never questioned the order to climb the cliff and leave Alice alone in the cave. Yet as he straightened himself behind the bush which masked the entrance he wondered why such instructions had been given. Neither he nor the girl knew that Enistor watched for their coming, so the young man could only conjecture that Eberstein wished him to surrender to those officers of the law who were hunting for him. This seemed strange in the face of the doctor's telegram advising him to fly; but for want of knowledge Montrose was not in a state of mind to reconcile the apparent contradiction. His sole idea was to do what he had been told to do, even though—as seemed to be the case—he was risking loss of liberty and life. And indeed, with regard to the last Montrose believed that he might lose it otherwise than on the gallows.

The narrow, tortuous path sloped upward abruptly, with the cliff soaring high above it and the cliff dropping steeply below to unfathomable depths. Fortunately the mighty wind, which roared inland from the sea, enabled him to cling the more surely to the rocky face of the precipice, and by slow degrees he crawled towards his goal overhead. In a less degree than Alice was the young man accustomed to such perilous wayfaring, and only by persistent will-power did he manage to control his nerves. What with the screaming of the tempest above and the bellowing of the waters below, he nearly lost his head. The tumult of sound, the stormy darkness only fitfully dispersed by gleams of moonlight, his dangerous position midway between heaven and earth—these things were enough to daunt the bravest man. But that he had been supported by unseen powers, Montrose would never have succeeded in scaling that tremendous cliff. Yet he did so, painfully crawling upward inch by inch, shaken like a leaf in the grip of the wind and stunned by the uproar of great waters. At length, after many hours—so it seemed to him who had lost count of time—he reached the summit and cast himself breathlessly on the wet herbage. Panting painfully, he sat up after a pause, and then the lightning flaring in the dark sky showed him a tall figure rushing towards him. And at the very moment of the onset the winds swept clear the face of the moon to reveal in her waning light that Enistor had found him at last.

"I have you now," shouted the Squire, stumbling towards his victim with eager haste. "You shall not escape."

Montrose had no thought of escape and could not have saved himself even had he been so inclined. He was wholly spent with that fearful climb and was unable to cry out, much less shape his breath into speech. Yet with the instinct of self-preservation—since he was dangerously near the verge of the precipice—he rolled blindly to one side as Enistor dashed heedlessly towards him. One moment he saw the big man reeling with extended hands to clutch and capture in the half-light; the next and his enemy had disappeared over the cliff, crying hoarsely as he realised that he had underestimated the distance. The cry was echoed by Montrose, who nearly lost what few senses remained to him in the horror of the moment. Then it flashed across his bewildered mind that Enistor was dead and that there was no chance of capture for the moment. Striving to regain his breath, to control his mind, to master his nerves, that effort was the insistent thought which governed his whole being. Utterly unmanned, he sobbed hysterically.

But the loss of self-control did not last long. By a powerful exercise of the will Montrose succeeded in gaining the mastery of his being and on hands and knees crawled towards the edge of the cliff. He did not expect to see Enistor, as in his impetuous rush the man must have hurled himself directly into the thundering waves which broke far below in white and furious foam. In the moonlight, which radiated strongly for the time being against the face of the sea-front, Montrose saw a dark body half-way down. The Squire had fallen straightly for some distance, then had cannoned off one rock to strike against another, and finally came to rest on a projecting spur, where the senseless body remained, hanging helplessly above the boiling of the witches' cauldron below. Clearly and distinctly Montrose saw the perilous position of his enemy: clearly and distinctly he knew that his enemy could be saved. It remained with him to allow Enistor to die terribly (since the man's first movement when he revived would precipitate him into the hell beneath) or to descend and effect a rescue. How could he do so without a rope and lacking assistance? The young man did not know, but what he did know, and the thought burnt into his brain, was that Enistor could be saved, or doomed. And the choice lay with him.

The temptation was almost overpowering. Only Enistor could depose to that fatal visit to the cottage, and if such a proof was wanting Montrose knew positively that he could not even be accused, much less arrested. He was aware of his innocence, yet Enistor, who hated him, could prove him to be guilty, and hand him over to an unmerited death. This the man would assuredly do, and Montrose winced to think how his name would be covered with ignominy and how greatly Alice would suffer. Why should he save one who designed his disgrace; who desired his death? He asked himself this question, and then asked it of God. No reply came either from himself or from the Unseen. He felt as though the guidance of the Higher Powers had been withdrawn, and that he was left to choose unbiased, uninstructed, completely free. Then he recollected how Eberstein had said that both good and evil would be placed before him, and how swiftly he had declared he would select the good. His memory recurred to the subsequent warning: "Be not over-confident lest you fall." This was the time of choice, the crucial moment, which decided all. If he saved Enistor he saved the only witness who could bring about his condemnation: if he did not rescue the man he would be free to marry Alice, to enjoy the money, and to lead a peaceful life. But could a peaceful life be built up upon a crime? for a crime it was to allow his enemy to perish. No! Come what might, arrest, trial, condemnation, and shameful death, it was impossible to hesitate longer. Enistor must be rescued and he must be the man to do the deed. In a frenzy of eagerness, and in deadly fear lest the evil should overpower the good, Montrose sprang to his feet and hurried impetuously towards the lights of the coastguard station. There was not a moment to be lost, so he literally fell against the door and clamoured for admittance.

"What's the row? What's the row?" asked a gruff voice, as the door opened violently and a coastguard appeared. "You, sir!" The man had seen him before and recognised him in a moment. "Have you come to give yourself up?"

"Do what you like about that," gasped Montrose, clinging to the door, a wild figure ragged and streaming with water, "only help me to save Enistor."

"The Squire! What's that about the Squire?" and another coastguard laid down his pipe to step hurriedly forward.

"He has fallen over the cliff."

"You threw him over!" cried both men simultaneously.

"No! No! I swear I did not. But what does it matter? You can arrest me afterwards if you choose. Just now I want to save Enistor. His body is hanging halfway down. Get me a rope, a lantern; come and assist. I must save him." And Montrose, feeling a new and powerful life move him to action, rushed into the darkness.

The startled coastguards followed, both to see what had happened and to arrest the fugitive for whom the whole country-side was searching. But discipline prevailed in spite of their natural bewilderment, and they came to the verge of the cliff when Montrose shouted, with lanterns and a stout rope. The young man was lying on his stomach pointing downward to where the body was plainly seen in the moonlight. The coastguards recoiled in dismay.

"Is that the Squire?" cried one. "Then he's dead for certain."

"No! Tie the rope round me. I shall descend," said Montrose feverishly.

"It's almost sure death, sir," declared the other man more respectfully, for if the fugitive intended to descend upon such an errand of mercy it was impossible that he could be guilty of the murder.

"Death or life, I'm going," retorted Montrose, and hastily bound the rope under his armpits, assisted by the two men, while he slung one of the lanterns round his neck. "Now! Pay out the rope!" and he let himself down gradually, clinging dexterously to the scanty herbage of the precipice.

Luckily the storm was dying away and the wind had rapidly swept the greater part of the heavens clear of vapours. In the starry space above the sealine the moon shone out more strongly than usual, so Montrose had ample light to negotiate his downward course. The coastguards peered over the edge of the cliff, and twisted the rope round a convenient rock, measuring it out gradually. But hardened men as they were, they shivered as every now and then the daring adventurer swung clear, to hang like a spider at the end of the slender line, while the cruel rocks and hungry waters waited below for their prey.

But the Power that had supported Montrose before supported him now, and he felt singularly clear-headed and strong. Slowly but surely he dropped down the face of the precipice and finally alighted gently on the projecting spur of rock. Very cautiously he looped a twist of the rope round Enistor's body, knotting it to himself, for the least mistake would have tumbled both from the insecure foothold. As it was the spur trembled and vibrated dangerously under the added weight of Montrose, even though he was greatly supported by the line. However he managed to bind the Squire's insensible body to himself, then gave the signal to be drawn up. The coastguards made sure that the rope was safely attached to the rock, and then, hoping that it would not give way under the strain, they began to haul up the two men. With one arm round Enistor, who was bound more or less tightly to him by the rope, Montrose assisted as best he could with the arm left free and with his feet. But it was a perilous journey, and the two men above, as well as Montrose, heaved sighs of relief when willing hands dragged rescuer and rescued into safety. Notwithstanding the immense strain to which he had been subjected, the young man still felt able to deal with the situation. "Have you any brandy?" he asked the nearest man, as the three of them looked down at the insensible body.

"Yes, sir," and a flask was handed over.

Montrose knelt and forced the clenched teeth apart to pour down the ardent spirit. The Squire still lived, for his heart was beating faintly, but his face was woefully scratched, his head was bruised, and the mackintosh he wore was ripped to shreds by the tearing and rending of the rocks and shrubs which he had struck during his fall. That he was alive was a miracle, and so the bluff coastguards thought as they held the lanterns for Montrose to do his office of mercy. They respected the young hero intensely for what he had done, as few men would have dared the perils of such a descent in the stormy gloom of the night. But they did not know how truly heroic Montrose had been in saving the life of one who could condemn him to a shameless death for a deed he had never committed. Montrose himself did not consider the action further, being wholly occupied in aiding Enistor to recover his senses. What he had done he had done. There was no more to be said.

"Better?" asked the young man softly, when Enistor feebly opened his eyes to stare into the pale face bending over him.

"What's the—the matter?" murmured the broken man faintly.

"You fell over the cliff. Hush, don't talk. Take some brandy: you will be all right soon."

"No! I think—I think—my back—broken," the voice died away in a drawl of exhaustion and the eyes closed. With a last effort they opened again, and Enistor asked a question. "Who saved me?"

"I did!"

"You!" The voice expressed astonishment, disbelief, hatred, scorn; a whole gamut of disordered passion, as some all-comprehending sixth sense told Montrose. Then the sick man relapsed into insensibility.

"Help me to carry him to Tremore one of you," said Montrose, rising and looking at the men, who were staring curiously at him in the mingled light of the moon and the lanterns. "The sooner a doctor sees him the better."

"I can take him along with my mate here, sir," said a coastguard gruffly; "if you go you will be arrested for the murder of that old foreign cove."

"As I am innocent I don't mind being arrested. And if you two hand me over to the police I understand that a certain reward— —"

"Don't speak like that, sir," broke in the other man hastily; "a gentleman what risked his life to save him as was hunting him down ain't no murderer."

"Thank you," said Montrose thankfully and simply. "All the same I am going to surrender. Meantime, we must take the Squire home."

The men stared and wondered, admiring Montrose more than ever, since he was risking his liberty as he had risked his life to save the man who was so bitter against him. One coastguard returned to the station, but Montrose and the other carried the body of Enistor on a hurdle—taken from a near sheepfold—to Tremore. They took a long time to cover the distance across the dark misty moorland, and as they approached the great house Montrose little by little felt the artificial strength which had sustained him so far ebbing away. He wondered why it was leaving him: he wondered what would happen when the police took him: he wondered if Alice was still in the cave: and finally broke down altogether on the threshold of the dark house. When the coastguard rang the bell and roused the servants he handed over two insensible men to be taken indoors. Like a blood horse Montrose had kept up the pace until he reached the goal, and then had fallen into as unconscious a state as that of the man whom he had saved. But as his senses left him he glimpsed a glorious radiance round about him: he saw the smiling, approving face of his Master, and knew that a hand was raised in benediction. And soundlessly the words of a Beatitude came to him as soft and refreshing as summer rain. "Blessed are the merciful: for they shall obtain mercy!" After that gracious saying he knew no more.

Then Montrose lost count of time. From the moment when he sank in the darkness before the door of Tremore until the hour he woke in his own bed time had no existence. A screened lamp illuminated the room, the blinds were drawn, the door was closed, and a fire was burning in the grate. He was clasping a tender hand, and his eyes opened to see the face of Alice bending over him with that motherly look which all women give to men in time of sickness. It was certainly night, Montrose thought dreamily, and he probably had been carried to his bedroom a few minutes since. But how had Alice come so swiftly from the cave? Was this another miracle in this life of miracles?

"Did you come after us?" he asked weakly.

The girl uttered a cry as his lips moved and thankful tears fell on his pale face. "Douglas! do you know me?"

"Alice! Yes, I know. Alice! I am all right." He strove to rise, but fell back.

"You are weak still," said the girl, arranging his pillow, "don't attempt too much, dearest. Take this," and a strengthening drink was held to his lips.

"But I must see what is happening," muttered Montrose impatiently, his brain becoming gradually clearer. "Your father lies insensible at the door with that coastguard in charge."

"Father is in bed and the coastguard is gone, Douglas. It was last night you came here."

"Last night! Impossible! It is night still."

"My dear one, you have slept for twenty-four hours. The doctor said it was the best thing that could happen after the strain you have undergone. You will soon grow strong. I am your nurse and have been watching you for hours and hours. Now," Alice rose and moved towards the fire, "you shall have some soup."

"I do feel tremendously hungry," admitted the patient; "and your father?"

"Hush!" Alice's face grew sad. "You must not talk. Shortly you shall know all that has taken place. Drink the soup and then try to sleep."

Montrose wilfully argued and objected, but the girl was firm. Finally he finished the bowl of broth and closed his eyes again. When he was quite asleep Alice left the housekeeper to watch beside him through the night and retired to her own room for a much-needed rest. Anxious as she was about many matters both with regard to her lover and her father, weariness, mental and physical, demanded its due and she slept soundly until ten o'clock the next morning. Her first waking thought was for her father, and after she had learned his present condition she sought the sick-room of her lover. But Montrose was no longer sick. He was up and dressed, with a healthy colour in his cheeks and very bright eyes, ready for his breakfast and anxious to learn what had taken place during his insensible condition. Even the thought that he might be arrested on that very day did not daunt him. Knowing his innocence, and aware that he had conquered selfish fear to the extent of saving the life of the sole witness who could condemn him, he felt convinced that in some way—he did not know how—things would be made smooth. Therefore he went down to the dining-room with Alice and, after making a good meal, he accompanied her to her very own sitting-room to hear explanations.

"Your father is in danger of death, you say?" he asked, when they were seated.

"Yes, Douglas. The fall hurt his spine and the doctor does not think that he will recover. However, he is sensible enough and can talk."

"What does he say?" asked Montrose nervously.

"Scarcely a word. And that is why I am so anxious to hear from you all that took place after you left the cave. Both the coastguards told me much; but you can tell me more. In the first place, where did you meet my father?"

"In the first place," said Montrose, asking a counter-question, "am I to be arrested for murdering Narvaez?"

"No! While you have been asleep wonderful discoveries have been made and your character has been entirely cleared. It was Job Trevel who broke Don Pablo's neck."

"Job? But his mother said that he went out fishing some hours before the death!" said the young man, startled and puzzled by the revelation.

"So his mother truly thought. Job did go down to take his boat out, but jealousy of Rose brought him back to Polwellin. He suspected that she intended to see Don Pablo, and when he found she had gone out he followed her to the cottage on chance. Rose was there after you left and Don Pablo came out with her to the gate. Then Job, crazy with anger, sprang on him and—you know the rest."

"I don't know how Job escaped, or why Rose held her tongue when I was in danger of arrest for what I did not do!"

"Rose ran home terribly afraid lest she should be accused of having had something to do with the murder, and took to her bed intending to be silent out of selfish fear. Job returned to his boat and went away. He has not yet returned, and I don't think he ever will."

"But how was this found out?"

"The doctor who attended Rose became suspicious of something she said when half delirious. He told the Perchton Inspector, who saw Rose and forced her to reveal the truth. Now the police are hunting for Job, and you are entirely exonerated, although you will no doubt be called upon to state the hour when you left Don Pablo."

"Thank God for his mercies," said Montrose devoutly. "It is a most amazing thing, Alice. And to think that last night I nearly decided to let your father die, since he alone would witness against me."

"I expect that was the test that Dr. Eberstein spoke of, Douglas. I don't know how my father came to be on the spot unless he followed me by stealth when I came to see you at the cave."

Montrose nodded. "No doubt your father suspected you and followed as you say, dear. The moment I reached the top of the cliff, he rushed at me, but making a mistake about the distance in the gloom, he hurled himself over the precipice. I saw that his body was lying half way down, and it was in my mind to leave him there. Oh! what a struggle I had," cried the young man passionately, "only Christ's love could have nerved me to save the man."

"Yes! Yes!" Alice fondled his hand. "The descent was very dangerous."

"It is not that I was thinking about. That was nothing. But my doubts, my hesitation: my desire to save my own life at the cost of his. I wonder my hair has not turned grey. And to think that all the time things were coming to a point which would proclaim my innocence. Had I let your father die I should have committed a purposeless crime. But thanks be to Christ the All-Loving and All-Powerful, I did as I would be done by, and gave my enemy his life. What a moment of anguish it was: what a bitter, bitter moment," and the young man wiped the perspiration from his brow.

Alice drew his head down on her breast and murmured over him as a mother murmurs over a child. And Montrose really was a child at the moment as what he had passed through shook him still to the core of his being. "It's all right now, dear; it's all right now," she urged gently. "You have conquered your greatest enemy."

"Your father?"

"No, dear, yourself. And perhaps my father also. He does not seem to be so bitter against you as he was. Twice he smiled when your name was mentioned."

"Then he has recovered?"

"He will never recover," said the girl sadly. "The doctor says that his spine is injured."

"Poor man!" cried Douglas generously, "can I not see him?"

"Not at present. The doctor says he is to be kept quiet just now." Alice burst into distressful tears. "Heaven only knows that I have little reason to love my father; but it is heart-rending to see him lying there, broken down and helpless, with no future save a painful death."

This time it was her lover's turn to soothe and console. Drawing the sobbing girl closer to his heart, he said what he could. "Death is the gate of Life, we are told, dear."

Alice made no reply. The phrase did not tend to disperse her grief, which was rather that of pity than of love, although the two are so much akin that the one can scarcely be distinguished from the other. Montrose wisely said no more, thinking truly that silence was more comforting than words, and they both remained silent for some minutes. A knock at the door parted them, and Alice dried her tears to receive a card from the incoming servant. At once her sad face lighted up with pleasure and hope.

"Oh, Douglas, Dr. Eberstein has come," she exclaimed joyfully. "Bring the gentleman here at once, at once!" And when the servant had departed the girl turned to her lover with an air of relief. "The doctor will put everything right. I feel certain of that."

"So do I," replied Douglas confidently. "He may even cure your father."

Eberstein was shown in at this moment, and when the door was closed, he walked over to Montrose with a glad smile to place his two hands on the young man's shoulders. "You have conquered, my son. As a true follower of the Blessed One you have forgiven your enemy in the face of overwhelming temptation to act otherwise."

"Then Mr. Enistor truly was my enemy?" asked Montrose hurriedly.

"Life after life he has been your enemy. Remember the vision which you saw in London, and the wounded man who came between you and the girl you love."

"Enistor!"

Eberstein bowed his head. "He was then a priest of the Star-Angel, Mars, in Chaldea. Alice was a vestal and you a noble who loved her. I warned you then not to pluck the fruit before it was ripe, but you would, and in carrying away the girl you murdered Enistor. This is the sin which has parted you and Alice for many ages. Now the debt is paid; for the life you destroyed you have given a life in saving your enemy. The shadow has vanished, and now," Eberstein placed the hand of Alice in that of Montrose, "now you are one once more. In union lies strength, therefore let the sorrows you have passed through bind you truly together for service to God."

"How wonderful! How wonderful!" gasped Alice, holding tightly to her lover as if she feared to lose him again. "Will there be no more trouble?"

"The troubles which all undergo when dwelling in the flesh. But these, in many cases, you will be able to avert, since you have much light and more will be given. But the dark Karma of Chaldea has been dispersed for ever. Thank God, my children, that you have been so wonderfully guided through the mists of error into the clear day of truth."

"We do thank Him," said Douglas reverently, "and you for so guiding us."

"I am but the instrument used for God's high purpose," said Eberstein, with a solemn look, "and I thank Him that I have been so honoured. Now you both must do as you have been done by, and aid in the salvation of Korah Enistor."

"My father! How can we do that?" inquired Alice anxiously.

"We must wait for the arrival of that Son of Perdition who wishes to keep that most unhappy soul in bondage. Then will Love and Hate battle for the prize. The result depends upon that soul's choice."

"But Narvaez is dead," said Montrose, puzzled.

"Narvaez is more alive than ever in the body of Julian Hardwick."

"Oh!" Alice recognised the truth of this astounding statement at once. "I knew Julian was different: that he was evil instead of good."

"You sensed Narvaez' black soul in Hardwick's body," said Eberstein simply. "Be strong, be ready; for the hour of strife is at hand."

"Let us pray!" cried Alice fervently, and the two did pray with full hearts, while the Master strengthened the selfless petition.

CHAPTER XXIII
THE ETERNAL STRIFE

For three days Enistor lingered on, fighting inch by inch for his life with obstinate courage. The doctor told him that there was no hope, but he declined to believe in such croakings. With all his pride and all his will he resisted the coming dissolution of his body, and therefore lived much longer than would have been the case had he been of a less resolute nature. Night and day Alice and the housekeeper nursed him by turns, and he seemed grateful for their attentions, although he said very little to either. Montrose wished to see the dying man and assure him of forgiveness, but Enistor declined an interview. Narvaez-Hardwick also called with feigned expressions of regret, but was forced to depart without seeing the man his wickedness had brought so low. As to Dr. Eberstein, he took lodgings in the village, so as to be at hand at the last moment, and waited patiently for a summons to the bedside.

"It will come," he assured Montrose. "It will surely come, since the last act of this terrible drama has to be played by all who have taken part in it, with the exception of Hardwick, who has done his share and passed over. But you and Alice and Narvaez and I have to face Enistor."

"For what purpose?"

The doctor answered rather irrelevantly. "The extension of Enistor's life beyond what is natural, considering his injuries, is not permitted without a good reason. The poor creature is taking part in a tremendous struggle between the little good he has in him, and the enormous quantity of evil which, through ignorance, he has accumulated in this and other lives. I am trying constantly to increase that good, while Narvaez is putting forth all his wicked power to strengthen the evil."

"Who will win, you or Narvaez?" asked Montrose abruptly.

"Only God knows the issue of the conflict, my son, since Enistor, having free-will, can choose either the good or the bad, the Left-hand Path or the Right-hand Path. You were given the same choice in another way, but with you the Power of Love prevailed. Whether it will prevail with this miserable man depends upon himself."

"But cannot you tell, Master? You know so much."

"I know much, but I do not know all. God alone is omniscient. Did not one of your poets say: 'We mortal millions live alone'? That is a great truth greatly put. Each soul must find God for itself through Christ by the power of the Holy Ghost. It can be helped and instructed by those who, like myself, are humble servants of the Most High, but the soul alone can choose whether to rise or fall. I tell you, Montrose, much as Enistor suffers physically, he is infinitely more tormented mentally. Night and day, and day and night, the strife continues between evil and good, in which Narvaez and I take part. Only Enistor can elect which side will win."

"Can I not help?" asked the young man, distressed at the terrible plight of his whilom enemy.

"You have helped—helped greatly. Enistor is constantly trying to understand why you saved him, when he could have, and would have, condemned you to a shameful and unmerited death. It is well nigh impossible for him to grasp such self-abnegation, but the positive fact that you acted as you did is the spar to which he clings, and which prevents him from sinking in the troubled waters of evil desires which Narvaez is bringing up against him."

"Why don't you smash Narvaez?"

"That would be against the law of justice. Narvaez has his rights, as every one else has. If he chooses to abuse those rights he will bring destruction on himself, as he is surely doing. Hate only ceases by love, so all that I can do is to offer Narvaez the assistance which he refuses to take. With my greater powers, poured through me for selfless ends by the God of All, I could use force and render him harmless. But such force would mean employment of the power of Hate. The influence is always the same in its essence, but becomes good or evil as we employ it."

"Still, if you ended Don Pablo's wickedness, Enistor would be saved."

"I cannot tell. But he cannot be saved at the cost of injustice to Narvaez, my son. By his own acts in this life and others he has placed himself in the power of Narvaez, and must abide by his choice."

"Still he may want to escape?"

"If so, and I truly hope that such will be the case, he has only to open his heart to the incoming of Christ, and the Mighty Power of the Blessed One will sweep away Narvaez like a straw. Love is stronger than evil, and must prevail when election is made to use it. Now go, my son, for even now the Son of Perdition is putting forth his strength to overwhelm the soul, and I must withstand him. Pray constantly, my child, and tell Alice to pray; for the fight is desperately bitter."

Without a word Montrose departed, leaving Eberstein to wrestle with the Powers of Darkness. Seeking Alice, he brought her to the altar of the parish church, and there they remained kneeling for many hours. It was well that they fled for refuge to the tabernacle of God, for within all was light, and the Dark Powers halted at the door, helpless, fierce and furious, and—baffled.

During those days of the struggle Montrose's worldly position had been made secure. The confession of Rose, who had seen Narvaez murdered, proved beyond all doubt that Job Trevel was the culprit. That man never returned now or thereafter, and it could only be conjectured that he had been lost at sea in the storm which took place when the crime was committed. But Montrose was fully exonerated, and in their rough way the villagers of Polwellin apologised for their wrongful suspicions. He more than regained the place he had lost in their affections, for the coastguards had told everywhere how the Squire had been rescued and at what a cost. That Enistor should have been saved at all was a matter of regret to his tenants, who detested him for his many acts of oppression. Throughout the village there was not heard one pitying word for the man now at the point of death, so doubtless this feeling of ill-will also tormented Enistor in his then sensitive state. But as the man had sown, so the man had to reap, and by his own acts he was condemned to a punishment which went far to excuse his wickedness.

In reply to Alice's telegram Mrs. Barrast came down to see the last of her brother and was desperately annoyed to find—as she thought—that he had completely recovered. Of course for his own ends Narvaez-Hardwick played the part of a grateful brother, and to get rid of the little woman he gave her a handsome cheque out of the property he had acquired. That the same had merely been transferred from Narvaez to Narvaez was a fact not known to Mrs. Barrast, who quite believed—and very naturally—that Julian had been cured in some miraculous way of his illness by the Perchton doctor. What that gentleman himself thought no one ever knew, as he held his tongue very wisely, through sheer inability to explain matters. But his practice benefited greatly, and he made full use of his enhanced reputation. Mrs. Barrast thanked him for the wonder he had wrought, said that she would mention his skill to her friends and send them to Perchton for treatment. Then she went across the Channel with Frederick to spend the handsome cheque in Paris and did not trouble any further about her brother. Which was just what the individual masquerading in that brother's body desired. Hardwick's sister was such a trifling little butterfly that it was not worth while breaking her on a wheel. Even if, out of sheer malicious amusement, the magician had wished to do so, he had no time. All his energies were taken up in fighting the strong power of Eberstein for the soul of his escaping slave. The adversaries came to grips on the night of the fourth day after Montrose had wiped out his sin by the rescue of his enemy.

After dinner on that evening, Alice and her lover were waiting in the library, feeling sorrowful and depressed. The young man was seated in an arm-chair before the fire and Alice, on the hearth-rug, inclined her dark head against his knees. Having watched throughout the previous night by the bedside, she had slept all day, and now was giving her whole attention to Douglas before returning to her new vigil in the sick-room. Neither of the two was speaking, as the shadow of evil lay thicker and blacker than ever on the house, and there was a feeling still more terrible in the air. Montrose felt little of such things, cased as he was in less sensitive flesh; but Alice was alive to battling forces, invisible and menacing, which thrilled her soul with agony and helpless grief.

"Death is here," she said at length, without removing her gaze from the burning logs, and Montrose knew enough of her clairvoyant powers not to exclaim at the weird remark.

"Do you think he will die to-night?" he asked, looking nervously round the brilliantly lighted room.

"I think so. Something dreadful is coming nearer and nearer. Very cold, very powerful, yet very merciful."

Montrose shuddered and recalled a play by Maeterlinck which he had read some years back. The atmosphere of the library was exactly that suggested by "L'Intruse," and he felt, as did the characters in that wonderful piece of writing, that the being with the scythe was about to enter the door. When a sharp knock came, his shaken nerves extorted a start and a cry. But it was only the housekeeper who came to announce that she wanted Alice to take up the watch by Enistor's bedside and also to tell both the young people that two gentlemen had arrived simultaneously at Tremore.

"Mr. Hardwick and Dr. Eberstein," said the housekeeper.

"Tell them to come in," replied Alice quietly, in marked contrast to her lover, who started to his feet much perturbed.

"Why do they come together?" he asked uneasily. "They have never met before to my knowledge."

"It is the beginning of the end, Douglas!"

"They then bring death with them?"

"Señor Narvaez brings death and Dr. Eberstein brings life," said Alice, still in the unemotional tone which she had used throughout. "But not in a physical way, you understand. Hush! Here they are."

The two men entered quietly: Narvaez, splendid and strong in the beauty of his stolen body, and Eberstein, elderly, grey-haired, and weary-looking. But Alice, looking through the masks of flesh, saw that they lied. Eberstein was the ever-young, glorious soul, radiant with immortal life, and Narvaez but a black evil shadow, distorted and venomous. Outwardly the magician resembled Milton's fallen archangel, magnificently sinful, while the doctor, like his Great Master the Man of Sorrows, seemed to bear the burden of other people's sins. Here indeed were the representatives of the eternal strife, the types of Heaven and Hell, bearing the cross and the wine-cup. And the world-battle on a smaller scale was about to be fought out between them. As Alice greeted the one and the other, the housekeeper turned at the door to speak.

"The Squire knows that Dr. Eberstein and Mr. Hardwick have come, miss, as I told him. He would like to see them along with you and Mr. Montrose. But I don't think it is wise, miss."

"You can go," said the girl quietly, and the housekeeper departed, grumbling at the risk of visitors to the sick man. "Shall we see my father now?"

She addressed Eberstein, who bowed, for the situation was too tense for the use of many words. But Narvaez spoke with an insolent smile. "I hope Mr. Enistor will not be the worse for my coming."

"I think he will be very much the worse, Don Pablo."

"I am your dear friend, Julian Hardwick," sneered the magician.

"I know better."

"Clever girl. But you do not know all," he taunted.

"Enough to be aware that you are an evil man, exercising more than human power. Also Dr. Eberstein has recalled to my recollection what I saw during the trance. I know who you are, Señor Narvaez, and what you are. With me you cannot masquerade as an angel of light."

"I leave that rôle to our friend here," scoffed the other with a shrug.

Eberstein did not take the slightest notice. With Narvaez he was very watchful, but intensely quiet: always on his guard, but never offering the fuel of words to kindle useless argument. And time being precious at the moment, he softly intimated to Alice that it would be as well to seek the bedroom immediately. Without objection the girl led the way, and shortly the whole party were in the presence of the Squire.

Enistor lay in bed, propped up with many pillows. Other than a shaded lamp on a small table beside him, there was no illumination save the crimson glimmer of the fire, so that the room was filled with a kind of artificial twilight, sinister and eerie. It was a large apartment furnished in that heavy cumbersome style prevalent during the first half of the last century, eminently comfortable but markedly inartistic. The green rep curtains of the bed were looped back to show the white suffering face and sunken eyes of the sick man, on whom the gaze of the quartette was centred. The silence was intense; as the rain had ceased, the wind had died away, and only the heavy breathing of those present, or the fall of a burning coal, broke the stillness. This calm before the storm suggested itself to Alice as much more terrible than the storm itself could possibly be. It seemed as though the whole of creation waited anxiously to hear what choice the dying man would make between evil and good. The words came slowly from him, as he fixed his weary eyes on Montrose with wondering inquiry.

"Why did you save my life?" he asked.

"I was sorry for you."

"Sorry for one who intended to have you hanged for a crime you did not commit. Impossible!"

"That I saved you showed it was not impossible. I had a struggle: oh, yes, I had a great struggle. Not knowing that my character would be cleared, I nearly decided to let you perish lest you should condemn me. But I could not: I could not."

"Why?" demanded Enistor insistently. "Why? Why?"

Montrose pressed his hands tightly together to control his emotions. "How can I explain? Something higher than my ordinary self acted for me."

"The Christ, Who is building Himself up within you, spoke," said Eberstein gravely.

"Weakness spoke," struck in the magician. "The weakness of a coward who was afraid to remove an obstacle from his path."

"Montrose did remove an obstacle," said the doctor, addressing Narvaez-Hardwick for the first time. "One which was blocking his upward path."

"His murder of me in Chaldea?" questioned Enistor, after a pause.

"Yes! He owed you a life. Only by giving back in another way what he had robbed you of could he learn his lesson and cleanse his soul."

"Where is the life that has been given?" sneered Narvaez-Hardwick. "There is Enistor dying. A valuable gift indeed."

"Montrose did not know that Enistor was fatally injured by his fall. So far as he was aware he gave back what he had taken and at the risk of losing his present life unjustly. The sheet is clean."

"Sophistry! Sophistry! You are trying to make black white."

"Not so. Man is judged by his intention in whatever he does. Thought precedes both words and acts, so if the first be right the two last cannot be wrong."

"We are here to listen to a sermon, it appears," said the other man mockingly. "You are woefully dull."

Eberstein ignored the spiteful speech to advance towards the bed. "Enistor, you are about to pass away from the physical plane to reap as you have sown, and painful will be the harvesting of your sheaves."

"Tares he should call them," mocked Narvaez-Hardwick contemptuously.

"Not all tares. Always the germs of good have been in your victim."

"A victim! I?" cried the Squire, pride and indignation lighting up his faded eyes, to the delight of his dark master, who approved of the sinister quality.

"Yes," said Eberstein steadily. "Age after age, life after life, you have been the victim, the slave, the tool of this man, who is stronger than you are. By taking his gifts, you have submitted yourself to his will. Break your chain, Enistor: now, at this very moment, assert your freedom as a son of God, owing allegiance only to that Power of Love which is co-extensive with creation."

"And by so doing you render yourself the servant of all," said Narvaez-Hardwick vehemently. "Whatever you gain you must use for the benefit of others and not for yourself. Think of it."

"Yes," came the quiet voice of the White Master. "Think of it, and think of how the powers you gain through evil are used for the benefit of your dark tyrant. He does not even give you gratitude."

"I give more than gratitude: my gifts are more substantial. Virtue is not its own reward in my service. Service indeed. And who has done service? I ask you, Enistor. Did I not scheme to place this young fool in your power, and did I not do so? You failed to use the golden moment properly and crush him, or you would by now have been wealthy, by regaining your lost property, and he would have been waiting his trial in prison. Have I not rendered you a great service? Do I not deserve gratitude in return?"

"Gratitude for ruining me," said Enistor, wincing at the fiery glances cast upon him. "You ask too much. You have plotted and planned, it is true, but your schemes have been brought to naught."

"By you," said Narvaez-Hardwick scornfully, "since you failed to grasp the prize I placed within your reach."

"It was Douglas who conquered," said Alice suddenly. "He chose the good instead of the evil, and hate was overcome by love. Father," she moved forward swiftly to kneel beside the bed, "you have no bitterness against Douglas now: you cannot have since he has saved your life."

"For the moment," scoffed the magician, "a pretty saving truly."

"I have had a terrible time since regaining my senses," said the Squire feebly. "All my old life has been broken up, and I am beginning to see things in a new light. Love is stronger than Hate, I admit that, since Montrose acted so unselfishly as he did. Douglas," he held out a trembling hand, which the young man gladly took, "I thank you for what you have done, and I ask you to forgive me."

"Willingly! Willingly," said Montrose, with fervour. "If we had only understood one another better, you would not now be dying."

"There is no question of dying," cried Narvaez-Hardwick, furious to see how his empire was slipping from his grasp. "Don't hearken to this weak babble, Enistor. Listen, I can cure you: I can make you as well as ever you were."

The girl and her lover started up with incredulous looks and Enistor gasped in amazement. "Can he do this?" he demanded, looking at Eberstein.

"Yes," assented the other calmly. "His knowledge is great, even though it is wrongly used."

"Wrongly used to cure the sick? Ha! What of your Master who saved the lives of those past human aid?"

"He saved through the power of love, and left those He saved free. You would use that same power after your own evil fashion, changing its good into bad, so that you can bind Enistor the more closely to you as a slave."

"Slave! Slave! What parrot repetition. Always slave: victim: tool! Lies, I tell you, Enistor, lies. You are my friend. If I did make you suffer, it was to test your strength, so that you might become strong enough to handle those great powers which I use. I can make you omnipotent as I am myself."

"Omnipotent," echoed the Squire doubtfully. "How can that be when you were struck down in your moment of triumph?"

"I was taken by surprise," said Narvaez-Hardwick sullenly. "Had I been on my guard I could have held my own."

"I think not," observed the doctor gently; then addressing Enistor directly, with marked emphasis: "My son, creation is sustained by love, and where love is not, destruction must needs come. By pandering to self, this man has acquired a small empire, which he has cut off from the great one of God. His force is only that little which he has gained and which he is strong enough to hold. But my force," Eberstein stood up very straightly, "is the force of the whole, which is necessarily greater than the force of the part acquired by Narvaez. Through me, as through all who strive to work selflessly, the mighty power of love is poured, for the benefit of those who need aid. Only this can give you power, and will you consent to be a slave in the petty kingdom of this man, which will be destroyed when his measure is full?"

"It will never be destroyed," cried the magician, hatefully proud. "For centuries I have endured alone, defying all."

"You seek isolation, and isolation you shall have," said Eberstein sadly. "Life after life you are building thicker and thicker the prison-house which shuts you in from the source of all life. Oh, my Brother, have we not pleaded with you again and again to repent, and turn to Him who alone sustains the worlds, and you will not, in your mad pride of self. Rapidly and surely you are descending into the Abyss, and would drag this man with you. But so great is the Love of Christ, who died for you and for all, that He will forgive you even at the eleventh hour, as He forgives this poor mortal."

"I haven't asked for forgiveness!" growled Enistor savagely.

"No. Don't be so weak," said Narvaez-Hardwick eagerly. "Eberstein talks rubbish. If you turn to his foolish ways will he save your life?"

"No," said the doctor with decision. "Enistor must pass on to exhaust the evil that he has made by suffering. But in that necessary suffering he will be supported and aided by Him who suffered Himself."

"There," the magician turned triumphantly towards Enistor, "you see that he can only promise pain. A nice bribe for you to turn into a silly saint, isn't it, my friend? Now I"—the man's voice became dangerously persuasive and bland—"I can make you whole again by curing your hurt and renewing your vital powers. You have heard Eberstein admit that I can do so. Then, since you have stood the tests of inflicted pain, which were necessary, I can now instruct you in the higher magic, which will give you power over men. Also I can make you rich. Let this money of your sister's remain with Montrose and let him marry your daughter and pass out of your life. You and I, my dear friend, will go to Spain, and there you shall share in my greatness. Together we shall sway this generation, making and unmaking men and nations."

"Don't listen to him: don't listen to him," implored Alice, putting her arms round her father's neck. "Remember how cruel he has been to you: remember how he was struck down by God: remember how his schemes have failed. He is a liar, like his Father the Devil."

"There is no devil but what man makes for himself," sneered Narvaez-Hardwick. "But we will let that pass. You have heard, Enistor. Eberstein offers you death in this world and pain in the next— —"

"Through which you will pass to a wider and more glorious life, when the past has been expiated," said the doctor swiftly.

"While I," went on the magician, paying no heed to the interruption, "can give you a long physical life with power and wealth, and ease and knowledge. Also in the next world I have my empire and you shall share it when we pass over this time, to return more powerful when we next incarnate. Choose! Choose!"

"Aye, choose," said Eberstein solemnly. "The Path of Pleasure, which leads to destruction, or the Path of Pain, which ends in the radiant light of the Godhead. The narrow way: the broad way: the Way of the Cross, or the Way of the Wine-cup in which the serpent of self lurks."

On one side of the bed stood the Dark Master, on the other stood the White Master, and between, prone with anguish, lay the body which contained the soul for which the opposing forces of good and evil struggled. Alice clung to her father and Montrose knelt prayerfully by the bed. The room was charged with battling powers, but in that dread moment of choice the influence of both stood aloof from the soul, which had to make its choice by what knowledge it had garnered painfully through many incarnations. Enistor felt suddenly feeble, felt that he was in a dense gloom, pricked here and there with wan lights, which represented all the good he had gained: and great indeed was the blackness of evil. Of himself he could do nothing, yet he knew intuitively that behind the gloom was a glorious and radiant Power of Love, which would dispel the evil when called upon. Narvaez offered him the kingdoms of the world, which rise and fall and pass away as a burning scroll: Eberstein offered him the glories of eternal good, which endure for ever and ever. He had in many lives tested the lower: now was the time to reach out to the higher. Yet so strong was the temptation of the flesh that the man paused, hesitated, faltered and held his peace. Alice sensed the conflict, and strove to surrender her gain of good to him who had treated her so cruelly.

"If it is permitted, let what I can give go to help my father," she cried, and then the miracle happened.

Enistor felt an inrush of light, not very strong yet wholly pure, and it was sufficient to turn the scale in spite of the strong insistence of the evil darkness. Yet not in such strength could he conquer. Something greater was needed, but the aid of Alice gave him power to call upon the greater might. "Hear us, oh! Christ: graciously hear us, oh! Lord Christ," he cried, in the suddenly remembered words of the Litany, and in broken tones.

Narvaez retreated suddenly with a snarl of baffled rage, driven back by a glorious power, which flooded the being of his escaping victim with ineffable light. As by magic the darkness vanished, and the radiant tenderness of Perfect Love descended upon the weary soul. Enistor's face grew young and bright. With an expression of joyful awe, he stretched out imploring hands of surrender and remorse. What he beheld Eberstein saw, as his head was reverently bent, and Narvaez saw also, for he fell back slowly towards the door; driven into his self-created darkness by the overwhelming glory of the Cross. Alice, clinging to Montrose, murmured incoherently: "Do you see Him: do you see Him? There. With His hand on my father's head."

The Lord of the Dark Face had vanished: the Lord of Compassion had come in power. Like a child who is weary the dying man fell dead on the pillows, his soul passing onward so gently that the two young people scarcely realised that all was over. A moment later, and the Presence was gone. The supernal light, visible to all save Douglas, faded away, and Eberstein stepped forward silently to close the tired eyes.

"May God lead him to a place of refreshment, light and peace," he said in solemn tones, and over the body he traced the holy emblem of salvation.

"Amen," murmured the two who knelt by the bedside.

And away into the night fled the Son of Perdition, baffled, broken and beaten, despoiled of his slave, who was lost to him for ever. And his was the eternal torment of self, which flies though no man pursueth.

CHAPTER XXIV
DAWN

For six months after the death of her father Alice travelled abroad, with Mrs. Sparrow as her chaperon and companion. The strain to which she had been subjected demanded removal from surroundings so intimately connected with the ordeal, and meanwhile Tremore could be safely left in charge of the housekeeper. It was with some reluctance that Montrose agreed to the Continental tour, which had been suggested by Eberstein, as it parted him for half a year from the girl he loved. But the doctor pointed out that absence would make Alice more self-reliant, since she would have to deal single-handed with her sorrow, unaided by her lover's sympathy and companionship. Each human being, he declared, must learn to become a centre of power, depending on God alone for help, since only in this way can such a one develop the necessary strength to act as a useful servant of Christ. It was a drastic training for the young people, at which they winced; but when Eberstein fully convinced them that the flesh must be dominated by the spirit at all costs, they agreed to the separation. It was a final test of their obedience, and a great one.

Alice selected Mrs. Sparrow to accompany her, for two reasons. First, she was sorry for the childish woman, who led so dull a life, and wished to brighten her grey existence. Secondly, the girl was immensely grateful to both the vicar and his wife for their championship of Montrose in the face of strong evidence as to his guilt, and desired to give some tangible proof of her feelings. Indeed she asked Mr. Sparrow to come abroad also, but met with a refusal, since he could not see his way to leave his parish for so lengthy a period. However, Douglas induced the good man to pay him a few visits in London during his wife's absence, and these gave great pleasure to Mr. Sparrow, besides which they helped to widen his views. Therefore he was delighted to think that his better half should chaperon Miss Enistor, and took unselfish pleasure in the preparations for the great event.

As to Mrs. Sparrow, to journey abroad, and see with her own eyes very many things she had only read about, was like a glimpse of paradise, or a drink of water to a thirsty man. She left behind her a colourless life of scraping and screwing, of cutting and contriving, to enjoy comfortable days of ample means and constant novelty. France, Switzerland, Italy, Germany: Mrs. Sparrow saw them all, and wrote daily letters to her husband concerning her experiences. Her being blossomed like a rose in the sunlight of prosperity, and she regained in a great measure the youth which had been crushed out of her by sordid cares. Alice enjoyed the naive delight of her rejuvenated companion as much as she did the sights which brought forth such an expression of pleasure, and in this way, amongst others, was aided to forget her late trials. The tour was a complete success, and when the two returned to England during the early blossoming of spring, they were bubbling over with the joy of life. And the end of the journey terminated in lovers meeting, which was fit and proper, according to the dictum of Shakespeare.

The sorely tried pair were married quietly in London. Mr. Sparrow came up to perform the ceremony, Mrs. Sparrow acted as the one and only bridesmaid, while Dr. Eberstein gave the bride away. Then came a pleasant wedding breakfast and the departure of Mr. and Mrs. Douglas Montrose to Eastbourne for a delightful honeymoon. Mrs. Barrast was annoyed that she had not been asked to the great event, since the wooing had taken place in her house, but she soon got over her pique, and sent a present to the happy pair, together with a letter in which she complained that Julian, exiled in Spain, took not the slightest notice of her. Douglas laughed over the characteristic selfishness of the butterfly, and wondered openly what she would say if she really knew the weird truth. Alice replied that she would never believe it, which was extremely probable, considering Mrs. Barrast's limitations.

"And I only hope that Don Pablo will leave her alone," continued Mrs. Montrose. "He is just the kind of man who would play her some malicious trick."

"I don't think he would be permitted to do that," rejoined Douglas thoughtfully. "Narvaez is a kind of super-human criminal, and will be kept within bounds by the Great Powers which control the world. Mrs. Barrast is a frivolous little woman, who does no harm, even if she does no good, so she will be protected until she is strong enough to endure suffering."

"It seems rather cruel that if one gains strength and improves one's character, one should only grow better to invite sorrow."

"We cannot become gods in any other way, dear. The burden is always fitted to the bearer, and what is demanded from the strong is not asked from the weak. 'Whom God loveth, He chasteneth,' you know."

"I could never understand that text," objected Alice, raising her eyebrows.

"Eberstein explained it to me," replied her husband. "Through ignorance one accumulates bad Karma, life after life, which is gradually paid off in such a way as not to bear too hardly on those who have to suffer. And until that Karma, which is of our own making, is paid off, we are unprofitable servants working—so to speak—only for ourselves, since it is to get rid of the burdens which inconvenience us that we labour. But when any one vows himself or herself to the service of Christ and desires to work, as the Master did, for humanity at large, the evil Karma must be got rid of very speedily, so as to leave freedom for the work."

"Well?" asked Alice, when he paused, and still not seeing clearly.

"Cannot you understand? The quicker the Karma is paid off, the sooner will the servant of Christ be free to do what he or she wants in the service of the Master. Thus an appeal is made by the soul to God for such freedom, and it is answered by the payment of the evil being concentrated in three or four lives, whereas, ordinarily speaking, it would be spread over a hundred. Therefore at the soul's request, trouble after trouble descends without intermission, and the greater speed means the greater pain. Thus do we see many people of blameless lives suffering terribly and, humanly speaking, unjustly. But the chastening is only the love of God drawing them swiftly to Himself by allowing them—at their own request, mind you—to pay off the evil of past ignorance at one sweep—so to speak—instead of by instalments."

"I see. But Mrs. Barrast?"

"She is in the A B C class. Only easy payments are demanded from her."

"What about ourselves? Are we free?"

"In a great measure I think we are—for this incarnation at least, since we have been so bitterly tried. But of course I cannot tell if we have discharged all the evil debts of the past. I don't much care. What is gained is well worth the pain."

Alice shivered. "The pain is very great."

"So is the gain. If one works for super-human things, one must be content to suffer more than the ordinary person. But don't distress yourself over such things, dear heart," added her husband, taking her in his arms. "We have passed through the clouds and now stand in the sunshine, so what we have to do is to help others as we were helped."

"I have helped Mrs. Sparrow, and you have helped her husband," said Alice thankfully. "She is quite a different woman, so gay and bright and hopeful."

"And Sparrow is as happy as the day is long. As the living is in your gift, Alice, I have arranged to add to the income, so that the two may enjoy more of the good things of this life. And when we live at Tremore we can do much good in the parish."

"Yes! Yes!" Mrs. Montrose's face lighted up. "I am quite anxious to get back and begin some good work. But"—her face clouded—"it will not be pleasant to live in Tremore: it is such a gloomy house, and the atmosphere— ugh!" she shuddered at the memory.

Montrose laughed in an encouraging manner. "As you gave me permission to do what I liked with the house during your absence, I have made very great improvements," he said significantly; "also Dr. Eberstein is there at present."

"Why?" Alice was curious.

"Wait and see. I don't fancy you will find Tremore such a disappointing residence as you think it will be."

Try as Alice might, she could get no further satisfaction on this point, and consequently became desperately anxious to return and see what had taken place. Montrose resisted her desire to go back until he received a telegram from the doctor, and then agreed that they should start for Cornwall on the next day. During the journey from Eastbourne to London, and the journey from Paddington to Perchton, they talked hopefully about the future and made many agreeable plans, mainly concerned with asking less fortunate people to share the happiness and wealth which they enjoyed. For unlike ordinary mortals this bride and bridegroom looked to finding happiness in clothing the naked and feeding the hungry, in teaching the ignorant and comforting the desolate. Only the man who has had toothache can fully sympathise with the man who has it, and in a like manner what Douglas and Alice had suffered made them intensely anxious to save others if possible from the purgatory of pain. It was an astonishingly unselfish attitude for a happy pair returning from their honeymoon to adopt, since such people are usually wrapped up entirely in themselves. But then they had been fortunate enough to have the friendship of Eberstein and the enmity of Narvaez to bring them to such a pitch of noble resolve.

At Perchton, the bride and bridegroom were received by the vicar and his wife, a very different couple from what they had been some months previously. There was no greyness about the bright-faced woman: no stolid endurance of a dismal life about the genial man. Mr. Sparrow was cheery and helpful: Mrs. Sparrow smiled on one and all, beautifully dressed, and looking years younger.

They had learned to be optimistic, instead of giving themselves over to religious pessimism, and were able to enjoy the gracious beauty of the world without the rebuke of a morbid conscience. Sparrow preached more about the Loving Father of the New Testament, and dwelt less on the jealous and angry God of the Jewish theology. Alice and her husband had begun their work well, for they had humanised two people by helpful kindness, and had their reward when they saw the beaming looks of the couple.

"And Dr. Eberstein is at Tremore," said the vicar, when the motor-car was whirling across the long, white moorland road. "You will be pleased to see him, Mrs. Montrose."

"Of course, Mr. Sparrow. Dr. Eberstein is the best friend my husband and I ever had, or ever could have."

"I agree," said Mrs. Sparrow brightly. "He is a most delightful man."

"I think so myself, and I approve of him," remarked the vicar thoughtfully, "although his views are scarcely orthodox. He believes in the strange doctrine of Reincarnation; although I am bound to say he did not attempt to convert me to his way of thinking."

"Did you attempt to convert him?" asked Montrose, with twinkling eyes.

"Well, I did," confessed Mr. Sparrow, "as it seemed a pity such a man should be in error, and credit a pagan belief which has come down to us from the dark ages. But he merely smiled and declined to argue. It is a great pity," repeated the vicar regretfully, "as he does much good and possesses a really fine nature. However, we must not lose heart. He may yet change his views."

"I scarcely think he will," said Montrose dryly. "And as he is a servant of Christ as you are, what does it matter?"

"There is much to be said on that point," retorted Mr. Sparrow sententiously. "For you know that Christ said nothing about Reincarnation and——"

"Edgar," interrupted Mrs. Sparrow quickly, "this is not the time to talk of such things. Later, dear, later. Meanwhile, I am sure that Alice is anxious to know all that has taken place in Polwellin since she went away."

"Nothing has taken place, Jane. Things remain as they were. Though I am glad to say," ended the vicar hopefully, "that the parishioners pay greater attention to my sermons than they did."

"Because you preach more cheerfully, dear," said his wife, and then addressed herself to Alice: "Dame Trevel is quite reconciled to the loss of her son."

"Has he not returned?" asked the girl quickly.

"No. And the police cannot find him. He has vanished altogether, and as there was a storm on the night he murdered Don Pablo, it is thought that he has been drowned."

"It is very probable," struck in the vicar. "Job went away without his mates—urged to flight by a guilty conscience no doubt—and so could not handle the heavy boat by himself. I am sure he has been drowned. It is just as well—if you do not think me harsh in saying so—for he would only have survived to be hanged, and that would have broken his mother's heart."

"It is already broken," said Mrs. Sparrow, with an expression of pain. "But I can't say the same for Rose Penwin," she added energetically. "That misguided girl has gone to London with the idea of appearing on the stage."

"Well, she is beautiful and clever. She may succeed as an actress."

"But the temptations, Montrose! They are many. I consider Señor Narvaez did wrong in putting such ideas into her head. Rose has been trained in my Sunday school, and may resist temptation, but I dread the worst."

"I hope for the best. Let us not be hard on her, Edgar. We are none of us perfect, you know, dear."

"You are," the vicar patted his wife's hand, and by so doing added the beauty of a fond smile to her face. "And I am sure Montrose thinks that his wife is."

"That goes without saying," replied the newly made bridegroom, in high good humour. "Here is Polwellin at last."

The villagers received the couple with loudly expressed joy, having an eye to the future. Enistor had been a tyrant, and so desperately poor that he had extorted the last penny of rent from those who could ill afford it. But the new Squire and his wife were young, and rich, and soft-hearted, so the tenants hoped for glorious times of peace and plenty. And the hope was duly fulfilled, for the relationship between Polwellin and Tremore became much more friendly than it had been in the old bad days. Douglas, as the vicar's right hand, laboured as the Moses to his Aaron in dealing with the temporal prosperity of the parish, while Alice acted as Lady Bountiful for ever and a day. Therefore, having such true premonitions of a joyful future, it was no wonder that the bluff fishermen and their tall womenfolk welcomed their benefactors with loud cheers and smiling faces, as they called down profuse blessings on their young heads.

At the foot of the hill rising to Tremore, Montrose and his wife sent on the car with their luggage, and alighted to visit the grave of Enistor, which

Alice wished to do before re-entering her old home. The vicar and Mrs. Sparrow took their departure, and the girl with her husband turned aside to the grey windy God's acre wherein so many generations of the family were laid to rest. Here, over the last Squire's remains, rose a broken column of white marble, emblematic of his abruptly ended life. On its base was inscribed the name "Korah Enistor," with the date of birth and the time of death, together with the significant text from the Psalms: "Thou also shalt light my candle: the Lord my God shall make my darkness to be light!" None but Alice and her husband and Eberstein understood the full meaning of the hopeful saying, therefore much comment was made on its mystery. But aware that through God's mercy her father had set his feet on the way of the Cross, which leads to Eternal Light, the girl was able to pray for the dead without tears. Douglas also removed his hat and offered up a petition for his former enemy, after which he led his wife from the churchyard towards the great house on the hill.

"Welcome! Welcome! thrice welcome," said Dr. Eberstein, who waited for them with outstretched hands at the door. "Now indeed, made one by the sacrament of marriage, do you step forward into the full sunshine of peace and joy, to work for the Great Master by helping His children."

Alice and her husband each clasped a hand, but could say nothing, as their hearts were too full to speak. But the servants, headed by the smiling housekeeper, demanded attention, so the young couple controlled their feelings and graciously thanked one and all for their kindly greeting. Then the domestics retired to a festival of eating and drinking in the kitchen, while Eberstein conducted Douglas and Alice through many rooms which had been rendered brighter and lighter by modern improvements. There was still the dark oak panelling, the grave family portraits, the low ceilings and old-fashioned furniture. But everything had been renovated in the best possible taste, and the effect of the whole was less gloomy than it had been. But something more than furbishing up rooms and furniture had been done to make the house feel so cheerful and bright. What it was Alice could not say, and looked round with a puzzled air. The doctor enjoyed her perplexity, and when he finally led the pair into the library, guided the girl to one of the low casements. "Do you see any change in the ground?" he asked, smiling.

Alice, who had not taken notice of her surroundings when entering the house, looked out wonderingly. The dark wood had a more cheerful appearance, as many of the trees were budding with spring green, fresh and delicate, while the ever-leafy branches of cedars and stone-pines and yews sparkled with the refreshment of a light shower, so that they also hinted at renewed youth. But the greatest marvel of all was that the space of beaten ground immediately surrounding the house was covered with an emerald carpet of turf, and the golden crocus, the pale snowdrop, and many violets were to be seen here, there, and everywhere like gleams of faint many-coloured fire. Out of doors a new life seemed to burgeon and bloom, while within there was a fresh living atmosphere, charged with creative power and fertile with the promise of glorious doings, noble, unselfish, holy. Quite unable to explain this mystic change from death to life, which made Tremore a centre of joy and abiding tranquillity, Alice turned to inquire mutely how the miracle had come about. Apparently Douglas knew, for Douglas smiled; but he waited for the master to enlighten his wife.

"I have cleansed the house," said Eberstein gravely. "All those forces of hate and destruction, which created so evil an atmosphere, have been broken up and dispersed. They had their source in the selfish thoughts of your father, strongly accentuated by Don Pablo's wicked teaching. Now that the Squire is dead and Narvaez has departed for ever, the shadow has lifted. By the performance of a powerful ceremony I have exorcised the dark elementals. And now— —" he touched Alice lightly between the eyes, bidding her use the clairvoyant sense he had thus awakened.

The room was filled with a luminous rosy light, alive with scintillation of diamond brilliancy. And her sight, piercing the walls, beheld the whole house bathed in this celestial radiance, although towards the back, where the servants congregated, the clearness was somewhat dimmed by their ignorant thoughts of self. Life was everywhere, pulsating in great waves, welling up gloriously from the heart of the world, so that, within and without, Tremore was alive with the splendour of unhampered force. Alice could now understand how the beaten ground round the house, formerly rendered barren by hate, was now covered with verdure and many-hued with flowers. Love was in the mansion, love was in the garden, love was in the woodland, and that mighty power had caused the desert to blossom like a rose. The light sang, softly, musical with the murmur of innumerable bees, and the girl felt as though she were in the heart of an opalescent sphere which vibrated with harmony. When her eyes looked again on physical things, the doctor was speaking.

"See that you do not disturb the harmony by any thought or word or deed of self. Here you have a centre of holy power, to which those tormented by the warring forces of the world can come to find peace and heavenly refreshment. Such in the days of old were the shrines, whither pilgrims travelled for the healing of their souls. You and your husband are the guardians of this place, and here many weary men and women will come for solace. See that you send them not empty away. A great trust is reposed in you, my children; a great work is given you to do. Thank therefore the Christ who has chosen you for this service of love."

After this solemn admonition, Eberstein became his usual quiet genial self, and passed a very pleasant evening with the young couple. After dinner he discoursed to them at length, giving many wise counsels, and instructing them how to deal with the future. When they retired to rest he told them to rise at sunrise and meet him in the garden, since it was his intention to leave Tremore before breakfast. Knowing that he had much work to do, Douglas and Alice never thought of pressing him to stay, although they greatly regretted that he could not give them more of his company. They said little to one another, for all that had taken place awed them considerably. But when the east was radiant with the promise of another day, and awaking birds twittered amongst the darkling trees, they came out on to the dewy lawn, to find their guest ready to depart. He was dressed for travelling, his portmanteau was already on a motor, which panted far away at the gate of the avenue, and in the silence of the dawn he came forward to bid them farewell.

Taking each by the hand, Eberstein led them to a small hill towards the back of the house, where the sun could be seen rising over the undulating line of the moorlands. An arc of fire was just showing above the horizon, and a splendour of light was changing the rosy hues of the eastern sky into a golden haze. Silently prayerful, the three stood looking at this aerial magnificence. It was the doctor who spoke first.

"See there the promise of your future," he said quietly. "The darkness of the night has fled away before the glory of the celestial orb. So have the black clouds amidst which you walked of late been dispersed by the Sun of Righteousness, which has risen with healing on His wings. You know what work you are appointed to do?"

"Yes," said Montrose gravely. "Six months in the year Alice and I must live in London, seeking out the lame, the halt, and the blind; both the spiritually sick and the physically crippled. We must give to them money, attention, sympathy, love and instruction, looking on every man as a brother and on every woman as a sister, irrespective of race or creed."

"Just so," said Eberstein, nodding, "because all are one, and you are in others as others are in you, all being in the Father, through the Son by the power of the Holy Spirit. And then?" he turned to Alice.

"For six months in the year Douglas and I must live here," she said, equally gravely, "and here we must bring those who need rest and help. We must not pauperise them by indiscriminate charity, but must teach each to become a centre of power, to develop his or her latent faculties. Finally, we must never think of self, but let the Power of Good flow through us unhindered by selfish desire."

"Just so," said Eberstein again, and smiled approvingly. "Remember that to be channels of the Divine power you must surrender all. A single thought of self and the channel is choked. Freely the power is given to you, so freely must you give it to others, and in passing through you on its beneficent mission it will cleanse you both body and soul, strengthening each so that you may be strong, wholesome servants of The Christ. You have learned your lesson well, my children, so it only remains for me to go."

"We shall see you again, I hope?" asked Douglas anxiously.

"Oh, yes," responded the doctor cheerfully. "Every year I shall come and stay with you, for there is much instruction in higher things to be given. By following the Master and living as nearly as possible His gracious life, you will refine your physical bodies to such a degree that in time you will be able to link up with the desire body and the mental body—consciously, that is. Already every night you both work and help in the next world, although you cannot yet remember what you do. But when the time is ripe you will remember, and consciously pass from this world to the other. Afterwards you will pass consciously from the desire world to the mental sphere, and so you will work constantly on three planes as the servants of Him who died on the Cross. Think then, my children, how glorious is your future."

The faces of both brightened, but Douglas spoke rather mournfully. "There is much to do in the physical world alone," he protested. "Look at the unrest that prevails everywhere."

"Be of good courage, my son. This unrest you fear shows how rapidly humanity is progressing. This is the era of individualisation, when each has to think for himself. Is it then any wonder that opposing wills clash, when all are so ignorant? But Chaos must precede Cosmos, and the human race is in a very hot furnace being shaped towards the ends intended by the God of All. The inner teaching is being given out freely to the West and to the East, to the North and to the South, therefore is a new spirit being infused into all religions for the enlightenment of mankind."

"Into *all* religions? questioned Alice dubiously.

"Yes! All the great religions are true in their essence, for all worship the One True God in Trinity, or in Duality, or in Unity. What men quarrel over and what they reprobate are only those external things which have been added by the ignorance of man. But the time is at hand when such errors will be dispelled, and then all religions will be unified by the Blessed One. To this nation and that God has spoken in different ways: soon He will speak to all with one mighty voice, and all men will learn that they are the sons of one great Father. Notwithstanding the turmoil of the present, be of good cheer, I say, for 'All things work together for good,' as St. Paul has set forth."

In the glory of the sun, now wholly above the horizon, Alice and her husband walked down the avenue to where the motor-car throbbed as if impatient to start. There was a clean, fresh look about the world, as if it had been newly made, and although husband and wife were a trifle sad at the departure of Eberstein, yet their hearts were singing with joy, and they were filled with gratitude to God for what He had done for them.

"Farewell, and may the Master bless you," said Eberstein, from the body of the car. "When I come again let me find that you have worked in the vineyard as true labourers. And so— —" he traced the sign of the cross in the air, and Alice saw it visibly outlined in dazzling light as the motor sped swiftly down the hill, through Polwellin and towards Perchton over the purple moors.

"Dear!" Douglas took his wife in his arms, "do not cry."

"These are joyful tears, I think," said Alice, smiling. "God is so good."

"Let us try to show ourselves worthy of His goodness," replied the young man, with an answering smile. "Come, dear, our work awaits us."

And in the glory of the spring morning, under the budding green of the trees, and across the soft grass of the lawn, they passed into their dear home, no longer the house of hate, but the Mansion Beautiful, wherein great works were to be done by them in their day and generation.